Rough Start

Chaunce Stanton

Chaunce Stanton Author Services

Copyright © 2022 by Chaunce Stanton

All rights reserved.

No portion of this book may be reproduced in any form without written permission from the publisher or author, except as permitted by U.S. copyright law.

For usage permission, please contact the author at **info@chaunce.biz**.

DEDICATED TO MINNESOTANS AND THE WEIRDOS WHO LOVE THEM.

Special thanks to my pal Al, the inspiration for the Norwegian Pontoon Mafia and my chief technical consultant.

You get trapped by stories. Though I've got this reputation for being out of control, it's not true. It just happens to be a more interesting story than the truth.

Terry Gilliam, Actor/Creator/Director born in Minnesota

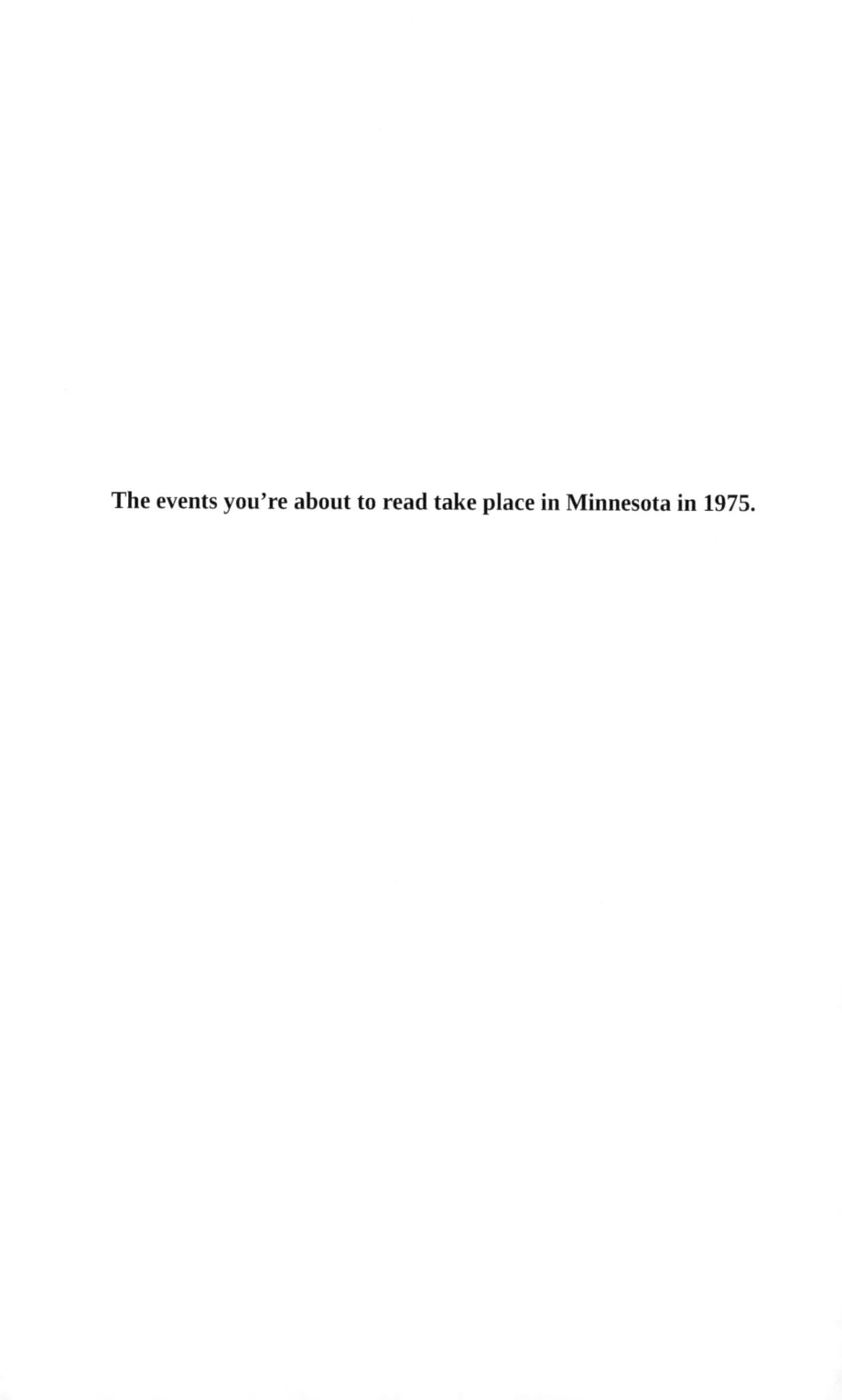

The events you're about to read take place in Minnesota in 1975.

Chapter 1

Hats Off To Thee

LIFE ON A LAKE is pretty darn good. At only forty-eight, Nat Lachmann had a lot of lake life left in him.

He wandered out of the main house toward Little Paw Lake to look at the stars. Avi had said those stars, so bright, were souls. Each of them was the glowing embodiment of an ascended master or some crap like that. The lake was calm. He walked right into the cold water barefooted. The sand and mushy weeds oozed through his splayed toes.

Was that sitar music floating from the sky, or was he just having a far-out hallucination? It was a hypnotic, twangy version of "The Minnesota Rouser." He covered his ears to muffle the music, then he took his hands away. Nope, the music was still there, and it came from the treehouse.

"Right on, Garv." Nat chuckled. Garvey was a pretty interesting dude. Maybe a little paranoid, but he always blew people's minds with his sitar. It might not have been the first sitar Minnesota had ever heard, but it was the loudest, and it was definitely the first sitar in Fornborg. More than a few neighbors on Little Paw Lake complained about Garvey's "Indian banjo" keeping them awake at night.

Garvey had offered to teach Nat to play as rent payment, but Nat let him and Avi and the rest of the freewheeling hippies, yippies, and beatniks stay rent free because he cared about them. Why Avi shacked up in a treehouse with Garvey, who was definitely older than her, was none of Nat's business. She probably had unresolved father issues, but hey, who was he to judge? He was an unresolved father himself. So those two would live in the treehouse until winter, then they'd move into the main house or a cabin so they wouldn't freeze to death. Maybe then, at ground level, Nat would accept Garvey's offer for sitar lessons, but until then, there was no way Nat would climb up and down that rickety ladder. Cripes, at his age, one fall and he'd break a hip.

It already was getting harder to keep up with the young folks sprawled over the braided rugs in his living room. His legs didn't bend as well when it was time to sit cross-legged on the floor. They sought refuge, Triscuits, and a place to crash where 'The Man' wouldn't hassle them. Nat looked after them. They were like his children.

Not his real children, though. His two real children were total bummers.

He breathed in deep and held it like Avi had taught him. Then he laughed as he exhaled, thinking about his parents and how they would roll over in their graves, their precious resort property overrun by hippies. "Well, mom and pops, it's not a resort anymore," he told the night sky. They'd roll over in their graves again, what with his hair touching his shoulders and him beating the bongo drums where his family once listened to Gene Autry's Melody Ranch on the radio. Nat was happy that their resort had found a wonderful new life as a sanctuary, an escape from the rat race.

His parents hadn't been bad people–far from it. They were just super squares. Nat was done being square. He felt like a teenager again, hanging out with his friends, away from prying eyes, away from the petty judgment of small-town Fornborg, Minnesota.

His fingers, the lake, the tips of Norway spruce, all glowed in the starlight. It made Nat think of a catchy song Garvey had played earlier. "You're right, Garv. Everything *is* beautiful, in its own way."

He noticed something laying on the dock, and it glowed. What was it? He plodded out of the water, his feet sucked in by the sandy bottom. He shivered as the air hit his dripping-wet legs.

Nat blinked and rolled his eyes around in their sockets like a maniac to clear his vision. Was that a big, glowing spider on the dock? That couldn't be right. It wasn't big, glowing spider season yet.

"Are you seeing this too, Garv?" Nat called again, but the little window in the treehouse had a better view of the tree trunk than the lake. "It's still there. Wowwee..."

Like Avi said, in a universe of universes, anything was possible. So it was just possible that a hand-sized glowing spider was on his dock at Little Paw Lake. Wouldn't it be wild if the spider, like, wanted to communicate with him? Avi always said that all things are sentient, the rocks, the trees, the giant glowing spiders.

Man. That spider wanted to tell him something. *Take me to your leader* or something square like that. Well, there weren't any leaders at Nat's place, man! Lesson one, Mr. Spider: Love is the answer.

Nat stepped toward it, unafraid of cosmic connections, even of the arachnid kind. As he got closer to it, he realized it wasn't a spider after all, and he burst out laughing. Wait until everyone heard about this. It was just some crazy banana peel sitting in the middle of the dock. A banana peel! Some prankster put a banana peel there so Nat's feet would go shooting out from under him, like in a cartoon, and BAM! He'd land on his keister, and then Garvey or someone would drop a cartoon piano on him.

"Nice try, Garvey," Nat called up to the treehouse from cupped hands, but the sitar-version of the "Minnesota Rouser" continued unabated. The fight song reached the ending cheer, and Nat bent down to pick up the banana peel. He shouted along with the music, "Minnesota! Minnesota! Minnesota!"

Maybe they could hear him all the way across the lake. Good. Let the squares dig his joyful sounds.

The peel wouldn't budge on the first attempt. He tugged harder.

"Yaaayyy, Gophers!"

The still night roared to life in an explosion that shattered Nat Lachmann's body as easily as it snapped the planks on the dock beneath him.

Chapter 2

The Joys of City Life

EDIE FISKER WAS HOLDING on, but just barely. The pan of bacon-wrapped Spam bites burned her fingers through the hot pad. It was her second attempt, and if she dropped the pan, there wasn't any more Spam or bacon until Sam's next paycheck. It was too late to turn back now. She swung the broiling pan from stove to counter faster than Billie Jean King whooping on Bobby Riggs in the Battle of the Sexes. The crispy bites jumped in the air when the pan hit the counter, freeing Edie to wave her burned hand and curse.

Why had the hot pad not stopped the heat from burning her? Maybe because it was wet. It smelled fruity, and those purple stains were new. Edie tried not to think too many angry thoughts about a certain eleven-year-old boy who must have used the hot pad as a rag when that same eleven-year-old boy spilled his grape soda. This also explained the sticky floor leading to the living room that had made her slippers make an adhesive sound as she worked in the kitchen all morning.

Between Arne and his father, Edie was constantly cleaning up other people's messes. Yes, Arne was her son, the one who spilled sodas and wiped things with hot pads. He also had developed a reputation in the neighborhood as a troublemaker. She half-expected to see little junior-sized wanted posters at the post office with Arne's goofy grin and big ears on them.

So her son wasn't perfect—who was? Definitely not her husband, Sam. Dealing with the two of them wore her down some days. Or caused bodily harm, like burned fingers.

"Remember what the book says," she reminded herself through gritted teeth as she ran water over her fingers. She needed to give her son and husband room to grow. That was her job: to make a pleasant home so Arne and Sam could become the men they were meant to be. At least, that was where her head was for the moment, thanks to a best-selling book she'd checked out from the library: *A Woman's Place is in All the Rooms*.

You could learn a lot with a library card, like boys will be boys. Boys will spill grape soda. Boys will help burn mommy's fingers, but that was okay because, like the book said, boys will be boys. Edie took a deep breath as she tossed the grape-stained hot pad into the laundry basket, unsure if it was even machine-washable.

"Look on the bright side," she told herself and counted her blessings, like book suggested. It was a lovely day in May. It was quiet in the apartment because Arne was off playing Lord-knows-where, and Sam was at work. The fragrance of crabapple blossoms wafted through the only operable window in the attic apartment. The landlord had nailed the other windows shut, either to keep burglars out or to keep renters from throwing themselves on the front lawn below in despair.

Nature's perfume (the only kind she could afford at the moment) filled her senses, causing her to forget her son's penchant for finding trouble and the Fisker family's overall financial uncertainty. In this blissful intoxication, she sang along with a Carpenters' song ("Only Yesterday") while dipping dishes into the glistening foam bubbles of Dawn soap. Her eyes glistened with the tragic beauty of it all: pain, loneliness, sadness—but then hope, love, and a tomorrow.

Her voice moved dreamily along with the voice of Karen Carpenter. They were one, perhaps not in quality, but at least in emotional intensity. Singing, Edie knew, was all about heart.

Hard pounding erupted below her fee, followed by the sound of Mr. Jaworski, the downstairs neighbor, dialing his rotary phone and then yelling in a one-sided conversation. Edie turned off the radio, feeling a flush of embarrassment. That old man had a way of catching her off guard with his unneighborly interference, and he never relented. He despised the Fisker family and would sneer through his front window at them whenever they walked past. He was a dragon guarding a perfectly good set of stairs inside the duplex, forcing them to trudge up the fire escape stairs attached to the house, a permanent disfiguring iron scaffolding that left their hands and, sometimes, their clothes, stained with rust. There he would stand, gripping the faded curtains as if they were the only thing restraining him from busting through the living room window and attacking them like a vicious parade float.

In the six months they'd rented the small, converted attic in "Nordeast" (the name locals used for the neighborhood just across the river from downtown Minneapolis), Edie Fisker had gone from actively trying to be nice to Mr. Jaworski to dreading his scowling, hate-filled looks. The last straw had been when she made him a casserole and Mr. Jaworski dumped it on the walkway, shattering the blue cornflower Corningware casserole dish, leaving her with only three in the set.

In any other situation, Sam Fisker simply would have confronted the man and told him to dry up, but there wasn't much they could do: Mr. Jaworski, bitter and mean, was the landlord's father. That put them in a bind, unless the Fiskers wanted to move again for a fourth time in two years.

Her new strategy was simply to ignore him, which sounded good in theory, but Mr. Jaworski did not ignore them. He pounded on the ceiling whenever they had a family conversation, watched television, splashed too much in the bath tub, or sneezed. He would swear at them in a mix of Polish and English. It was tough on Edie, because she wanted to be nice to everyone. Being nice was what normal, well-adjusted people did, and being normal meant everyone should like her and her husband and son.

The Fiskers lived as quietly as was possible for a young family with an eleven-year-old boy who became excitable at the mere mention of bionics. Sam and Arne even had taken to peeing while sitting down to muffle the splashing sounds in the toilet bowl. What more could they do?

No, they didn't have to be nice to the landlord's father, but they had to put up with him. They could afford the rent (for now), so long as Sam held down a job, which wasn't a sure thing. His employment tended to be "reasonal" rather than seasonal, meaning he would work a job for a few months until it ended for any number of reasons—none of which were Sam's fault, according to Sam.

She poked at the Spam bites with a fork, assessing whether they could be salvaged when a handsome but streetwise patrol officer came padding up the fire escape, saying that a 'certain downstairs tenant' had demanded that Edie Fisker be arrested for disturbing the peace. The twinkle in his eye signaled to her he knew that the 'certain downstairs tenant' was a meddling nuisance.

"I wasn't even singing that loud," she said, pouring the policeman a cup of coffee before slicing a thick piece of apple bread that may or may not have received too much baking soda.

"I hate to say this, but according to our anonymous concerned citizen, the complaint had more to do with the quality of the singing as opposed to the volume."

He obviously wasn't taking the complaint seriously, not with that twinkle in his eye, the slight smile on his lips. Still, it was embarrassing.

"Well, that's just dandy," Edie blushed. She'd always thought of herself as a decent singer. She could sing as well as she cooked. "He wouldn't like it if Judy Garland herself lived right above him."

"No one would like that, ma'am. Especially at the end. What with the pills and the booze."

"She was born up north, in Grand Rapids, dontcha know," Edie chattered, showing off her knowledge based on an article she'd read in *People*. "Her real name was Frances Gumm."

"Is that so? I heard she died on the sh—" he winced, correcting himself. "In the restroom. Mind if I smoke?"

Edie said she didn't mind, even though she did, mostly because she was definitely trying very hard to quit smoking herself. He lit up, and she watched the smoke coiling from the cigarette like it was the last flight out of Vichy Morocco. He introduced himself as Sergeant Ralph Borden, born and raised in Minneapolis, but south. They talked about the Nordeast neighborhood and how it was changing, not necessarily for the better.

As she watched Sergeant Borden smoke, Edie barely even thought about the secret pack of Dignity cigarettes she kept in the back of the cupboard behind the graham cracker box for emergencies. Sam didn't smoke, and he didn't want her to smoke. Smoking had killed his father. Well, to be precise: a case full of Winstons had fallen off his delivery truck and crushed him.

"Would you mind, ma'am?" He gestured at her with a quick-rolling hand motion.

"Mind?"

"Singing a little something. Just for the report."

"Well, I don't know," she stammered. If any time was the right time for an emergency Dignity cigarette, certainly a command performance for the Minneapolis Police Department counted. She opened the cabinet and scrounged around behind a can of fruit cocktail until her fingers found her emergency cache. "This is very upsetting, to be arrested just for singing."

"You're not under arrest, ma'am. Not yet, anyway. How about a little tune?"

"I'm just so nervous."

"If you've got nothing to hide, then there's no cause for concern," Sergeant Borden said, lighting her Dignity with a match. "I'd hate to think that old man is right. Just prove him wrong for me, and I won't even bother putting this visit down on paper."

Edie didn't want the old man to be right, either. She took her first delicious deep drag of the day. She exhaled, squinted into the ensuing cloud of silver-gray smoke tendrils.

"If you think it will help. Let's see…" Faces of celebrity songsters flashed through her mind: Freddy Fender, Paul Anka, B. J. Thomas, John Denver, Gordon Lightfoot…She'd heard each of them that very morning on the radio, but not a single song came to mind. "Isn't that always the way? When you're put on the spot, answers just fly out of your head."

"You better not go on that *Name That Tune* show, then."

She laughed. "No, I guess I better not."

Sensing her trouble, he suggested she just sing the song she sang before. "You know, whatever song triggered the gentleman's complaint and brought me here."

The way he said it made her think of herself as a mythical siren, drawing men to their deaths on rocky coasts with the alluring power of her ship-smashing voice. Yes, she remembered enough of "Only Yesterday" to prove that she sang just fine, and he could jot that down in his little police report. She cleared her throat and sniffed to clear her nasal passages. That's probably what all the professional performers did, only they did it backstage while still in curlers.

She sang for him, softly at first, but then louder as her confidence improved. She reached the chorus, and he winced and put up his hand for her to stop.

"Well, look," he said. "You're trying, I'll give you that. You seem like a nice lady, so I won't write this one up. But, maybe in the future, remember you do have neighbors."

Embarrassment painted her face. She *was* a siren, after all: a police siren.

Sergeant Borden stayed only long enough to finish his cigarette and his coffee, but he left the apple bread she'd made after only a single exploratory nibble. After he left, she brought the saucers and cups to the sink. The beautiful dish-soap bubbles were gone, as was the morning's fresh smell of crabapple blossoms. Only the smell of Dignity cigarettes still lingered. She let the saucer drop, still littered with crumbs, and it clattered against the chipped enamel sink, as loud as you like, which prompted a new barrage of pounding from the floor below.

Edie stuck out her tongue and stamped her foot.

Arne Fisker shimmied as far out on the branch as he could, his lips still stained purple from the can of soda he'd snuck before leaving the apartment. Grape was his favorite kind, and he wished he had a can of it right now. He worked up quite a thirst climbing up there. Below him, the Mississippi River flowed strong. Further downstream, he could see the island in the middle, where the herons hatched their chicks and flew off for the season. Heck, he could see the IDS building from his perch about thirty feet off the ground.

After tying a bowline knot, he pulled the remaining length of rope through the loop, just like his dad showed him. That way, when he tied on the tire at the bottom, the knot would cinch against the branch nice and snug. The rope he'd found in the train yard on his way to the river, lying near the neck of one of the switching tracks. There were several tires scattered along the river, so he had his choice of those.

He wondered if the water was deep enough for him to dive from there. That would be pretty cool—more cool than just swinging on a rope tire. The river sure looked deep enough—at least in pockets—but he also saw plenty of rocks and logs. It might be worth a try. He wasn't afraid, was he? Nah, he wasn't afraid, but he wasn't stupid, either. He'd swing on tire as far as he could and *then* dive into one of those deep pockets between the rocks. That was smarter.

He climbed down, investigated a discarded Atlas Weatherguard snow tire that didn't seem too bad to him. It had the right combination of sturdiness and hole-to-tire ratio he was looking for. Stuff like old tires were was part of why he liked coming down to the river. You never knew what kind of cool junk you could find. As he rolled the tire up the embankment toward where his rope dangled, he heard the rustling of branches and saw two boys, about his age, looking down at him. They held sticks like machine guns.

"You've got big ears," the first boy said.

It was true, Arne did have big ears. It was the first thing people noticed about him, so he noticed all sorts of things about them right back. Mean things. The meaner, the better.

"Yeah? You've got a butt where your head's supposed to be. So what?" He was used to the insults. It didn't matter to him.

The boys partly slid, partly galloped down the slope, picking their way through young trees and rusted barrels.

"They're big like Dumbo ears." The second boy got in on the action. "Can you fly with those things?"

"You think I can do anything about my ears?" His mom used to tell Arne his ears got stretched out because God tried to keep him from leaving heaven. "Besides, *Dumbo* is a movie is for babies."

"You could cut them off. And look. He's got buck teeth. You can do something about that, can't you? You can at least get your teeth fixed, can't you?"

"I'll fix your teeth," Arne muttered, letting his tire roll down to the river as he stood to face them both, his fists raised.

"You want to fight us?"

"Yeah. Let's light this turd." He charged them. The two boys hadn't expected him to come after them, two against one. That's because they weren't winners like Arne Fisker. They scrambled up the hill, with Arne gaining on them. He was smaller than they were, but he was wiry, and he was a go-getter.

It was just like his dad always told him: the only thing that can stop you is you.

The phone rang in the Fisker apartment, triggering another round of Mr. Jaworski's angry pounding. Edie's jaw tightened, hollering, "Oh, go pound yourself. Even prisoners get one phone call." She'd honestly had more than enough of that man.

"It's me," a woman said.

"Hi, Mom."

"I hope I'm not interrupting your afternoon nap or anything."

"What do you want, Mom?"

Edie could feel a headache coming on, but her thoughts brightened when she remembered the secret cigarettes. She stretched the yellow curly phone cord nearly straight as she struggled to reach the corner shelf. Yes, a smooth and bold Dignity cigarette would be just the thing to help her through a conversation with her mother.

"Don't be so touchy. I just know how tired you get having to live with that man."

"That man is my husband," Edie shot back. On her tippy toes, Edie slid the ancient box of graham crackers out of the way. Her fingers found the lavender pack of cigarettes. She tucked one in the corner of her mouth; her head tilted to cradle the phone against her cheek.

"Listen, I'm kind of busy. I'm just getting supper started."

At least Edie didn't have to hide the matches. Those they had in abundance because many businesses offered free matchbooks with their advertising on the cover. She found a pack from the Cafe di Napoli, an Italian restaurant on Hennepin where she loved to eat spaghetti bolognese—when they could afford to go to restaurants, that is.

"Oh? Are you using any recipes from the book I sent you?"

"No, I'm sort of winging it."

"Wouldn't you feel more confident in the kitchen if you followed the recipe directions?"

'Yes' was the answer her mother wanted to hear, but Edie wasn't in the mood for yes. She wasn't in the mood for following directions, either. Her supper game plan—and dessert—was all set. She searched for a can of pineapple on their canned food shelf. It should be there unless Arne or Sam ate out of the can like hobos.

"What do you want, Mom? It's long distance, after all."

Edie enjoyed throwing this back at her mother, who usually was the first to point it out, regardless of who had called whom. As it was only five in the afternoon, her mother's call from Phoenix cost more than thirty cents a minute.

"How's my grandson? Is he all grown up yet? Did he get my Christmas presents?"

Edie laughed quietly to herself. Her mother knew perfectly well that Arne had received her presents. They'd talked on the phone on Christmas Day, New Year's Day, and practically every week thereafter.

"For all I know," her mother continued, "he's joined one of those street gangs that steal car antennas."

"At least that would give him a project. Oh, Arne is definitely eleven, I'll just say that."

"And is 'he' still working?"

'He' meant Sam. It was a loaded question. Sam's employment had been erratic. They both knew it, but still…

"Yes, mom, he's still working. You know he tries."

"Maybe he should try a little harder. Or maybe…"

"Don't even say it, Mom."

But her mother didn't need to say anything. The script of their conversations filled the silent cracks, and Edie could hear her mother's voice repeat what she'd said too often.

…you could leave him.

Still no sign of the canned pineapple.

"Mom, can you use fruit cocktail instead of pineapple for glorified rice?"

"I wouldn't think so."

"I mean, it's not against the law or anything?"

"Well, it would be a crime against nature. I don't know what you're making with fruit cocktail, but it wouldn't be glorified rice."

"Well, I saw it in a recipe..."

"But not from the recipe book I sent you."

"No, it was in a magazine."

"Smut," her mother concluded. "Most magazines today are just pure smut. Women's lib and now fruit cocktail?"

"Never mind. Listen, I really should get supper ready before Sam gets home."

"Will he ever settle down, do you suppose?"

She was like a dog with a bone.

"Yeah, I really think he'll do well at this job. He just told me this morning how much he likes it there. The other guys are nice. He doesn't mind the work."

"What type of work is it? This time."

"He's working on small engines and boat motors."

"It can't pay much. Are you going hungry? Do you need me to send you money?"

The thought of a little extra money definitely tempted Edie, but she was stubborn: half Norwegian (her mother's side) and half German (her father's side). Her mother dangled money from strings—thick strings. They were snares, and Edie wasn't about to fall for them.

"No, thanks, Mom. We don't need your money." She took a drag on the cigarette, too loudly, apparently.

"Are you smoking again?"

"No, I'm not smoking." She reflexively moved the cigarette away from the phone as if to hide it from her mother. Edie smoked only when she felt stressed. She needed to get another pack soon.

Edie couldn't figure out where the money came from. She had worked only the odd job, waitressing and cashiering, and Edie's father hadn't left them anything. When he died, he just cost more money. About the time Edie was itching to run off with Sam, her mother stopped fretting about money and started offering wads of cash wrapped in strings, claiming it was pension money from her father, an apprentice cement worker when he died young from *that*.

"But even if I am smoking a cigarette, so what? It's my choice. I'm an adult."

Edie's mom let out a humph.

"Adult? You should have thought of that before you hitched your wagon to that man. You were just a child."

The script was dog-eared by now: She'd made a mistake. She'd married too young. She'd married the wrong man. Sometimes, though, the script stuck in her head, and maybe that was the point.

"I was seventeen. How old were you when you had me?"

"That's not the point. Times were different then."

Just for that, Edie made the rash decision to open the can of fruit cocktail.

"Well, times are different now too."

The truth was Edie's mom just didn't like being the world's youngest grandmother. At only forty-six, Dolores Schmidt (née Lachmann) still wanted to convey the illusion that she was more Jane Russell (va-va-voom) than Jane Wyman (dustpan and broom).

"It's not your fault, entirely. Older men just seem to home in on younger women. It's like shooting ducks in a barrel for them."

"Because ducks are stupid, I suppose?"

"They're the ones in the barrel, aren't they?"

"Well, I'm not a duck, and Sam is only a year older than I am."

"I don't want to fight."

"Could have fooled me," Edie sputtered.

"Listen, Edie, I've got news."

Edie heard footsteps coming up the fire escape stairs.

"I think Sam's home. Can you call back tomorrow? I've gotta go."

"Okay, but Edie?"

"Yes?"

"You're not really going to put fruit cocktail in the glorified rice, are you?"

"No, Mom. I have to go. Bye."

A sense of alarm rang through her as she hung up the phone. She had forgotten something. Crap. The cigarette. Sam would smell it. Chaining the door shut, Edie tossed the cigarette out the window. She snatched up the sports section of the morning newspaper and lit it on fire to make decoy smoke.

Three hard knocks shook the door to their apartment. Had Mr. Jaworski called the police on her again?

"Just a minute." She fanned the flaming newspaper around the kitchen, making the air nice and smoky. She tossed the paper out the window before it burned her hand. She opened the door to reveal a man with close-cropped red hair and a neck the size of her thigh, pinching Arne by his big earlobe.

"What's on fire?" he growled.

"Just a little cooking fire. Nothing to worry about." She flipped on the exhaust fan above the stove. "Why are you hurting my son? Let go."

"This lop-eared rabbit beat up my boy and another boy." The man yanked Arne forward by his ear before letting go. Arne clapped a hand to his head and rushed to his mom's side.

"Arne? Is that true?"

"They started it."

"He can't just go around bullying other boys like that." The man was angry, and Edie wondered if she would have the guts to smack him with a rolling pin if it came to that. Crap. She remembered Sam had broken the rolling pin at Christmas smashing walnuts because Arne had destroyed the heirloom nutcracker. "My son is a pitcher for the pony league, and this little monster hurt his throwing arm. Who's going to fix that?"

"Look, I'm sorry that your boy's hurt, but there are usually two sides to a story, aren't there?"

"Oh, you're one of them moral relativists, are you? Well, in this case, there are three sides to the story, and two of them say this boy attacked the other two without provocation."

"Arne?"

"It's not true,"

"Arne, I want you to apologize to this man for what you did."

"Oh, he doesn't need to apologize to me. A little twerp like this? Why, he wouldn't bother me one bit if I were his age because I wouldn't stand for it, and we wouldn't be having this conversation." He looked around the kitchen from the doorway, leaning forward. "Are you sure nothing's burning?"

"I'm sure. I'm sorry, did you just threaten to travel back in time to beat up my son?"

"If that's what it takes, then yeah, I guess I did."

"So between stopping baby Hitler and beating up an innocent eleven-year-old American boy, you're going with the American boy."

"Hitler didn't hurt my son's throwing arm, lady."

"Okay," Edie shooed the man out of the doorway. "I think we're done here. I'll have my husband deal with this when he gets home."

"You mean Sam?" The red-haired rhino snorted. "The only thing he'll deal with is a pack of playing cards. Just beat the kid for me so he learns his lesson. Otherwise next time, I'll do it for you."

"Goodbye." She pushed the door shut fast enough that the man had to step out of the way.

Several minutes of interrogation revealed a few facts: there was an altercation; it wasn't Arne's fault; he was just minding his own business by the river; you should have seen him pound on those dopes.

"You were down at the river? After I specifically told you not to go there? Arne, there are hobos and child killers at the river."

Arne shrugged. "It's better than playing in traffic, I guess." He learned that phrase from his father. His nose wrinkled, and he sniffed, following the scent to the open window.

"Mom, that jerk was right. Something is on fire."

Edie remembered the burning newspaper she'd thrown out the window. Sure enough, a small black circle grew in the smoldering brown grass below. She rushed to the sink and filled a pot of water. She raced back to the window and dumped it out, hoping to douse the slow-moving conflagration. Her pot tipped forward, and the water spilled out, falling almost in slow motion. Too late, she noticed the men below, the red-haired man stomping out the fire with his work boots and Mr. Jaworski hollering in Polish like *he* was on fire. The men looked up at her, and Mr. Jaworski received a face full of refreshing Minneapolis tap water.

The fire was out, but the two men still burned with anger.

"Sorry!" She grimaced and ducked inside, wincing at the curse words she heard from the both of them. She kept her eyes shut, her mouth locked tight. She was unsure if she was about to laugh or cry, but something was about to spill out.

When Sam burst through the door, he smelled of beer, but she smelled of burning lawn and Dignity cigarettes, so it all worked out.

"Honey, I'm home."

He drew Edie to him and gave her a deep kiss, and she was sure he would taste the cigarette on her breath. She should have popped a Certs in her mouth, but he didn't seem to notice. She pulled away.

"How was work today?"

"That? Oh, fine."

"Well, you're not going to believe what your son did." She told Sam about the fight and the red-haired man and the fire—a story from which she was careful to omit the true cause.

"You didn't scorch any of the good parts, did you?" He playfully spun her around. "Good news. Your rear end isn't engulfed in flames."

"This is serious. That man was angry."

"Okay. I'll take care of it. Where's Arne?"

"He's out playing."

"In this neighborhood?"

"What do you mean, 'this neighborhood'? This is where you wanted to move."

"Whoa. Easy. Let's not start that. In fact..." He pressed hard against her. "Let's go to the bedroom and start something else."

"Easy, pardner," she pulled away. "I've got to finish supper."

"What are we having?"

"I found this terrific recipe. It's *Occhi di Pernice* in Aspic." She didn't mention that the Italian name for the tiny circle pasta meant "eye of the possum."

His face contorted.

"You mean like SpaghettiOs in Jell-O?"

"Just go sit down until dinner's ready."

"I can see the can of SpaghettiOs right there." He pawed at her again. "Come on, baby, let's go make love. And then we'll just eat the SpaghettiOs all on their own. Let's not get Jell-O involved again, okay?"

She tried to explain that a chef in New York had developed it especially to appeal to kids, but she couldn't get the words out. He was kissing her, and she wasn't fighting back.

Chapter 3

Sugar, Sugar

IT WAS TUESDAY AT Irwin's Marine and Small Engine Repair on Hennepin Avenue. That meant it was Jimmer's turn to pick the radio station. Naturally, he swung the dial away from the "beautiful music" station that Voodoo Andy picked on Mondays. Sam got to pick Wednesdays, and they flipped for Thursdays and Fridays. The three of them were the mechanics (aka "grease monkeys") who worked for Teddy Irwin.

Sam worked with the enthusiasm of a badger when it came to tearing engines apart, but when it was time to reassemble them, well, by then, he'd lost interest—and often lost the little parts that were meant to go back together. Overall, he didn't like his job; in fact, he had a tough time thinking of any job he would like—and this was a subject he thought of often as he scoured the floor for tiny machine screws. *It's for Edie and Arne*, he reminded himself. It was all for them, so he took it one day at a time, sweet Jesus.

Sweet Jesus.

He'd been listening too much to Voodoo Andy's beautiful music, after all. He'd heard the Marilyn Sellars version of that song one too many times over the past few weeks, thanks to Voodoo Andy. (Jimmer and Sam called Andy 'Voodoo Andy' only because he was from Haiti, home of the mysterious magical practice of voodoo. In reality, Voodoo Andy was a devout Jehovah's Witness, and apparently, that church frowned on the practice of voodoo. But Voodoo Andy sounded better than Jehovah's Witness Andy.)

Jimmer O'Keith, who was about Sam's age, had just gotten discharged from the Army. He said that if you could fix helicopters sprayed full of 7.62-millimeter rounds by angry Viet-Cong guerrillas waving AK-47s, then you could fix anything. Sometimes he tricked Sam into having too many beers after work.

The shop was just down the block from the Jewish synagogue in south Minneapolis—the one that looked like the Jefferson Memorial. Many of the shop's customers were members there, as was Teddy Irwin himself. He mostly stayed out of their hair and ran the interference with the dumb-ass customers who dropped off their lawnmowers, snowblowers, garden tillers, and outboard boat motors. This was a double-edged sword: good because the customers were a pain in the butt to deal with; bad because Teddy would promise them the moon. More than one irate customer had wandered into the work bays to belittle the mechanics and yell about having to postpone their fishing trips on account of no-good, lazy grease monkeys.

Sam had pointed out to Teddy that just about every project took about twice as long as Teddy promised. Sam shared the wisdom of his father: *Don't write checks your ass can't cash.* Teddy's response to that nugget had been clear enough: the door wasn't broken, and Sam could leave anytime he wanted.

Teddy Irwin really hated Tuesdays because he especially didn't like Jimmer's taste in contemporary music. During the catchy chorus of "Sweet Home Alabama," he came out of his office with the wild expression of a man who just had gasoline injected in his veins.

"What is this noise? Is anyone here actually from Alabama?" Their silent stares were the only answer he needed. He switched off the radio. "Could you even point out Alabama on a map? God forbid. We don't need any more of that hippie rock music in here, understand? This is a place of business, not Woodstock. We've got a big client coming in today."

"Client," Sam snorted. "Fancy."

"This guy could buy your fanny and have it shipped to Timbuktu first-class, Sam."

My fanny is not for sale, Sam thought.

"But I'll tell you what is fancy: it's his Mercury 1250 Super BP outboard motor."

Jimmer whistled, and Voodoo Andy raised his eyebrows, but Sam remained indifferent.

"What? Maybe you don't think a Merc 1250 is fancy enough for you, Samuel?"

Sam shrugged, wiping his hands with an oily rag. "I've seen better."

"So when he gets here," Teddy ignored him. "I want you all on your best behavior. No cursing, and no hippie music."

"No problem, boss," Voodoo Andy answered. To his two co-coworkers, he added, "Looks like we'll be listening to Andy's beautiful music today."

Just as the crew unpacked their wax-papered sandwiches from home and poured coffee from their thermoses, a shiny red Caprice convertible pulled up, blocking both bay doors.

Teddy Irwin snapped at the men that lunch break was over and to look sharp as he rushed out to greet the driver, who slid out of the driver's side like a can of cranberry sauce. He was pretty stocky for a guy who was almost six feet tall. His thick, dark hair coiled over his forehead. He wore a sporty red windbreaker and a pair of tight white tennis shorts. A forest of black leg hair rippled in the warm breeze all the way down to his white cotton socks and blue Adidas tennis shoes.

Jimmer nudged Sam. "That dude made a fortune in catalog sales."

"I think he's very rich," Voodoo Andy added.

"What gave it away for you?" Jimmer quipped. "Was it the new car, gold necklace, or the fancy outboard motor?"

"It's the way he carries himself. He stands rich."

Jimmer and Sam thought that sounded funny, even if it were true, and they laughed. Teddy shot them a warning glance over his shoulder.

"You three come up here and meet Mr. Randall."

The phantom black Mercury 1250 Super BP outboard, carefully strapped in a utility cart pulled behind the convertible, shone in the sun. They soon forgot about that marvel of modern engineering, though, after they noticed the young woman in the passenger seat shaking her blonde hair loose from a ponytail. The thin straps of her sundress angled off her shoulders, in danger of being tugged down.

"I'd like to work on *that*," Jimmer muttered.

"She is a child of God," Voodoo Andy warned, but he was looking at her too.

"With a body like that?" Jimmer's expression screwed into doubt. "God must have a dirty mind."

"Hey, you," Russell Randall pointed at Jimmer. "Put your eyes back in your head."

"I'm sorry, Russell, please." Teddy tried to block his workers from his client's view. "These men are animals, but very talented in the shop. It's so hard to find good help."

"Tell me about it. I've got a thirty-thousand-dollar deal on hold because of *schmucks* like this."

Sam Fisker wasn't familiar with the word *schmuck*, but judging by the contempt in Russell Randall's voice, *schmuck* wasn't a compliment. Sam didn't like being insulted. Not in any language. He was about to fire something back when Russell Randall narrowed his dark eyes on Sam.

"You. Grab me a cup of coffee. I take it black."

Sensing a certain lack of enthusiasm in Sam's response, Teddy Irwin intervened.

"Today, Samuel. You can pour for Mr. Randall from my personal coffee maker."

"Fancy," Sam mumbled as he padded off to get coffee from the forbidden coffee maker that sat next to Teddy's desk.

"And you," Sam heard Russell Randall command one of the other two mechanics. "Why don't you make yourself useful and get my, uh, niece, a Coke."

Sam poured coffee into a Styrofoam cup, noting the little coffee station that Teddy kept for himself and his most precious clients like Russell Randall. A glass sugar shaker with a chrome screw-on lid stood sentinel next to a stack of powdered dairy creamer packets and a cup full of plastic stir tubes.

"Ooh la la," Sam muttered. "Must be nice to be the boss."

Randall had said he took his coffee black, hadn't he? Heck, a little sugar never killed anyone, except maybe diabetics. Sam poured sugar into the cup. He didn't even stir it; he just let it settle to the bottom. That would be a nice surprise for good ol' Russell Randall. Come to think of it, didn't Sam deserve a little sugar too? Of course, he did. He slipped the sugar shaker into a deep pocket in his coveralls.

After handing over the coffee and Coke, Jimmer and Sam hoisted the Mercury out of the trailer while Voodoo Andy guided the rotor over the slatted cart walls.

"Not a scratch," Russell barked. "I suppose these *yutzes* need to go home and go to bed after all this standing around."

"Don't worry, these *yutzes* aren't going anywhere."

We'll see who's not going anywhere, Sam thought.

"Now, finally, can I tell you what I need for my baby?" Russell asked Teddy. "Or are we just going to watch these *momzers* as they *fercockt* my Mercury?"

"Sure, sure, Russell. What do you need?"

"It's got a rough start." He took a sip of his coffee, eyed it suspiciously, and dumped it on the ground. He shot a hard look at Sam, suspecting deliberate sugary sabotage. The smile never left his face, however, and he called to his, uh, niece. "Come here, princess."

She hopped to his side, and he pulled her close by the waist.

"Can you believe I found this one at a photoshoot for an eyeglass catalog?"

She giggled, and Voodoo Andy whispered, "I don't think that's his niece."

Jimmer, straining as they frog-marched the outboard to a work stand, snorted and said, "I don't think she's a princess, either."

"And I don't think she needs eyeglasses," Sam added. He couldn't imagine it, running around on Edie like that. Not in a Chevy. And definitely not in a convertible for the world to see. This guy was shameless.

"I want a complete overhaul," Russell bellowed. "Make it run smooth. Daddy likes it smooth, doesn't he, princess?"

The woman kissed Russell's cheek and giggled some more.

"Hey, Jimmer," Sam nudged his coworker. "Let's you and me work together on this Mercury."

"Nah, brother, it's all you. I got my own worries with the Lawn Boy over there. The compression dropped, so I gotta figure that out."

Sam didn't even bother asking Voodoo Andy for help because Voodoo Andy knew as much about fixing boat motors as he knew about rock music. As Sam set up his workstation, Teddy and Russell Randall hovered next to him, engaged in their own conversation about a steakhouse they both liked.

"I mean, they really put the 'exceptionale' in 'Charlie's Cafe Exceptionale.'"

"A better sirloin I've never had," Teddy agreed. Sam had heard of Charlie's over on seventh street, but he wouldn't be taking Edie there anytime soon unless they started giving away free food.

"Now, do you pay these jerks to stand around like statues, or is it museum day?"

"Well, Samuel?" Teddy tried to sound tough, which he wasn't. "Get to work. I'm not paying you to play with yourself."

The two men stood way too close to Sam. He could hear them breathing when they weren't talking.

"You got it, boss." Sam grabbed an oozing grease gun and let the nozzle waggle too near the men's legs.

"Hey." Russell took a fast step back. "These shoes cost more than the dental work you're gonna need if you splatter that on me."

"Sorry," Sam said. "Need a little elbow room, I guess."

He saw Jimmer snickering in the next bay, and he smiled too. The smile faded as he heard Teddy Irwin promise Russell Randall that the motor would be ready first thing in the morning.

"Good as new," Teddy assured him.

"Smooth starting, that's all I want. Is that so much to ask?" Russell directed the question specifically to Sam, but it wasn't like he waited for an answer before bobbing back into the convertible and driving off with his young catalog model. The question hung in the work bay, oily and rhetorical, but Sam had an answer for him, just the same.

It took hours, but Sam had the Mercury buttoned up before six-thirty. He could barely see straight, having lost a half-hour looking for the brass nut from the carburetor mounting stud under the rubber floor mat. He'd called Edie before five to tell her he was running late and not to hold supper for him. Not a big sacrifice, really, considering she was a terrible cook. She'd said she was getting worried because Arne hadn't come home yet. Sam told her not to worry: he was probably having the time of his life playing cops and robbers with some kids.

Before he left work for the night, Sam stopped by Teddy's makeshift office, wedged between greasy banker's boxes in what used to be a parts-washing bay. Teddy's work shirt was clean. The red-stitched *Teddy Irwin* in scripted letters was meant to look as if Teddy had handwritten his name on his own chest.

Sam didn't have a name on his coveralls, and his coveralls looked like a carnival spin-art splatter of grease and oil.

Teddy made notes with one hand while holding a sandwich with the other.

"Must be good to be the boss," Sam said as a way of greeting. "Nothing but clean hands and counting the money."

Without lifting his head, Teddy peered at Sam from the top of his thick army-issued glasses.

"I should be so lucky." He pushed a ledger away from him. "Did you take good care of Mr. Randall's rough start?"

"Oh, sure. Yeah, no problem."

"That's good. He's a big spender with lots of friends."

He knew what Teddy meant: *lots of rich, arrogant friends.* Sam shuddered at the thought of even more people like Russell Randall.

The rich got the nice boats and the pretty girls while Sam got grease under his fingernails every day and left the shop with the smell of fifty-to-one gas/oil mix permanently burned in his nostrils.

As he passed Teddy's coffee station, Sam returned the sugar shaker to its place next to the stir tubes and powdered dairy creamer.

The sugar shaker was empty.

Chapter 4

Poor Uncle Nat

POTATO SALAD LOAF. THAT'S what the recipe called it, but Edie was not excited about the name. She'd figure out something better to call it so it wouldn't scare off Arne and Sam. Glazed potato salad, maybe?

She peeled a potato under cold, running water, just as the recipe suggested, because sometimes even the old techniques still worked well. An old-fashioned potato peeler, in the right hands, is sophisticated technology that can be a real time-saver for today's modern housewife, compared to using a paring knife, according to the article in *Family Circle*.

The phone rang, the pounding started, and Edie growled. She dropped her sophisticated potato peeler technology and turned off the faucet. It was her mother.

"Hi, Mom. Can you call back tomorrow, or next week, even? I've got to peel a crapload of potatoes."

"No, I really can't. I've got to tell you something. It's important."

"Can it wait?"

"Your Uncle Nat is dead."

Weird Uncle Nat, Edie thought, but she kept that to herself.

"Did he kill himself?"

"What do you mean by that?" Her mother sputtered on the other end of the line. "He would never."

"I don't know. I just figured he went a little nuts after Gloria took the kids, and maybe it all just caught up with him."

"That was years ago, and for the record, he threw her out."

It was tough to know exactly what to say. She didn't know her uncle very well. The last time she saw him, she was just a little girl trying to avoid being thrown in the lake by her two cousins, Jeffy and Lana.

"Well, I'm sorry he's gone."

"He had some kind of boating accident, and it was absolutely not 'that'."

"That? You mean suicide?"

"Stop saying it."

For a liberated 1970s grandmother, Dolores Schmidt still had a lot of hang-ups, and talking about suicide was one of them. Maybe because Edie's father, Robert Schmidt, had driven into a tree at eighty miles an hour, which could have been an accident, except he'd left a note that Edie wasn't supposed to know about.

"When was the last time you spoke to him?"

"It's been years. Listen, his funeral is on Saturday in Fornborg. I need you to go up there."

"Up to Fornborg? We couldn't. That's a two- or three-hour drive."

"I can send you money, you know, for gas and incidentals."

Incidentals. That made it sound like Edie was a private investigator taking a case, like on the *Rockford Files*.

"It's not just money. Sam's got work on Friday, and..."

"Nat was your uncle, Edie. Family"

"Well, he was your brother. Are you hopping a flight to Fornborg?"

"It's not a good time for me."

"Why should I go if you're not going?"

"Couldn't you, for once, just do what I ask?"

"That's not really an answer. Just tell me why you won't go."

There was a pause. Her mother had left Fornborg before Edie was born. Why her mother left the little Minnesota town, Edie didn't know. That was another verboten topic akin to suicide and self-pleasure.

Finally, her mother answered, "Are *you* hosting the Canasta Club on Fridays?"

Edie sighed. She was going to lose this one, she could tell.

"I'll talk to Sam. It's just short notice."

"Yes, isn't it just too bad your poor Uncle Nat couldn't have sent you an invitation before he got blown up?"

"That's not what I meant, Mom, and you know it." Then her mother's last statement kicked in. "Wait. Did you say blown up?"

"Yes, some kind of boating accident. It's such a shame, too, because he planned to reconcile with the kids."

"Where'd you hear that? I thought you said you hadn't spoken to Uncle Nat for a while."

"That's true," she said quickly.

"Well, if it's been years since you last spoke, why would you think he was going to make up with Jeffy and Lana?"

"Oh, just things the attorney told me, I suppose."

A thought tickled Edie's mind.

"Does the attorney think the death is suspicious?"

Her mother's response was swift.

"I don't know what attorneys think."

Another non-answer. Nothing was suspicious. Nothing was wrong. Everything was a coincidence, an accident, and shouldn't be discussed. Edie just wanted to get off the phone and get back to making the potato salad. You can't have potato salad loaf without the potato salad.

"Look, I'll talk to Sam about the funeral and everything, but this call is costing you a fortune, so let's talk again tomorrow night."

She didn't wait for her mother to protest or to inject any type of insinuation, well-intentioned or otherwise, before she hung up.

Edie met with the usual culinary resistance at supper. Arne said the potato salad loaf looked like yellow Play-Doh.

"It probably tastes like Play-Doh, too," he added for good measure. "Right, Dad?"

"I'm sure your mother tried very hard on this...what's it called, sweetheart?"

"Glazed potato salad."

Arne pushed his plate to the center of the table, knocking over a bottle of ketchup.

"Fun fact about Play-Doh," Sam told Arne. "Did you know it wasn't made as a toy for kids like you to play with? It was used to clean coal dust from wallpaper."

"You're joshing me, Dad."

"Honest. I wouldn't lie about Play-Doh, kiddo."

"Arne, please just try it." Edie nudged Arne's plate in front of him.

"No way." Arne crossed his arms and scowled at it. "I want a hamburger."

She cast a desperate, pleading glance at Sam. "Sam, could you step in here and maybe encourage Arne to eat a little?"

"We can't force-feed the boy." Sam shook his head helplessly. "When he gets hungry enough, he'll eat it. Won't ya, Arne?" Sam ruffled Arne's hair.

"Not this cowpoke," Arne stated, which made both Sam and Arne laugh like hyenas in heat. It did not make Edie laugh.

"Fine," Edie stood and grabbed the pan of potato loaf. Arne and Sam watched in surprise as she threw it in the garbage, pan and all.

"Whoa, whoa, whoa," Sam blurted. "You can't just throw out good food."

"So you're admitting you liked it."

"I liked it fine," Sam replied. "With ketchup." Sam liked ketchup. She could steam a lobster, and he would dip it in ketchup.

"I give up," Edie lamented. She leaned against the counter, weary from her own potato loaf tantrum. "My Uncle Nat died, and we're going to the funeral on Friday."

"Your weird Uncle Nat?" Sam went to Edie and placed a comforting hand on her shoulder. "Did he off himself?"

"I wondered the same thing," Edie said. "But my mom said it was just an accident."

"That's exactly what people would say, to cover up the other thing."

"I know."

"I mean, his wife left him. His kids don't like him. Sounds like he ran his parents' resort into the ground."

"Well, we're going up there."

"Up there to...what's it called?"

"Fornborg," Edie tried to sound as matter-of-fact as possible. Her mind was made up. "It's only a few hours away."

"Yeah, and then a few hours back, and two or three more hours consoling strangers and eating weird food in a church basement."

"He was my uncle," Edie stated.

"He was your weird uncle," Sam amended. "Besides, you hadn't seen him since, what? Twenty years ago?"

"Up and back, I promise." She scrounged a can of tuna fish. Arne would eat boring ol' tuna salad sandwiches, so she stirred in mayonnaise, mustard, and pickle relish. Then she smeared it on a slice of Wonder Bread and folded it in half, just the way he liked it. This was the sixth time in two weeks she'd given in, but at least this time wasn't a hamburger.

"Is your mother going?" Sam asked.

"No, she is not."

"Okay," He sighed, long and loud, resigned to defeat. "At least there's that. I'll ask Teddy if I take Friday off." He wrapped his arms around her waist from behind. "If you're nice to me."

She didn't know if he was turned on because of getting a day off from work or because of the tuna salad, but she wiped her hands and pushed him away.

"You're still breathing," she said. "That's nice enough."

Edie waited until Sam and Arne were settled in front of the television before retrieving the loaf pan from the garbage.

The next day, Sam was working up the nerve to ask Teddy for Friday off. He wiped his hand on a rag as he rehearsed his speech.

"Teddy, as you know, I'm a family man..."

So what? Teddy would say. *And I'm not?* Then he would tell Sam how he'd raised six kids in a house with a dirt floor in North Minneapolis, started from nothing, and built the business from nothing.

Sam didn't have a good comeback ready for that. Mostly he knew Teddy would not like being down a mechanic on such short notice. They were booked with Spring tune-ups.

"Courage to the brave," Sam recited. It was a little charm he'd heard in a cowboy movie when he was a kid that always kind of stuck with him. He took a deep breath and started heading to Teddy's office when he heard Teddy slam down the office phone. All three grease monkeys look up and then at one another from their respective work areas.

Teddy glared at Sam over a stack of dog-eared and heavily stained repair manuals and stood, moving toward the coffee station.

"*Drek*," he cursed, returning to his desk. He yelled for Sam.

This couldn't be good. Sam hesitated, keeping his work boots firmly planted on the oil-splattered concrete floor of his work bay, pretending to be very interested in his torque gun.

"Get your *tuches* in here."

Reluctantly, Sam wandered past the coffee station and stood across the desk from a seething Teddy Irwin.

"I just got off the phone with Mr. Randall. You may recall he brought that Mercury 1250 in for an overhaul."

"That was a beauty." Sam nodded. "It was a hundred and twenty-five horse, if I recall."

"Yeah, you recall correctly." Teddy raised his hand to reveal the empty sugar shaker. "Too bad you didn't recall that sugar in the gas tank would foul the engine. My friend and best customer got stranded in the middle of Lake Minnetonka, thanks to you."

"There are worse places to get stranded."

"Lake Minnetonka," Teddy continued. "During a meeting with some very important men."

"A meeting? On a lake? Come on. They were probably drinking beer and fondling their, uh, nieces."

Teddy's rage exploded. "What they were doing is not the problem, you moron. Your antics just cost me three hundred bucks."

Sam shrugged like he didn't care, but he shifted his weight. He didn't like what would come next.

"But maybe you've got your reasons. Maybe you're upset that the war is over or that Nixon is gone. Maybe you don't like having a nice job. Maybe riding around on the motorcycles like those two *yutzes* in the *Easy Rider* is for you. Here." Teddy pulled a wad of cash from his pants pocket and counted out sixty dollars. "This is your final check."

Sam grabbed his thermos and lunchbox, as Teddy watched him carefully, and he packed the few tools that belonged to him, as well as one or two sockets that weren't his but were within reach.

On the upside, Sam got paid for a full day of work even though he'd only put in three-and-a-half hours, but he knew that wouldn't mean much to Edie. If it were just the two of them, him and Edie, losing a job wouldn't matter so much, but there was Arne to consider. But, dang it! It had felt so right at the time.

"See ya around," Jimmer told him.

"I'll pray for you," Voodoo Andy said, clapping his shoulder.

"Well, fellas," Sam began. He saluted Jimmer and Voodoo Andy feeling a little surge of emotion building. He was going to miss those guys, but he sure as heck wouldn't start bawling like a baby. "Jimmer can have my Wednesdays for the radio pick."

"Yes!" Jimmer was thrilled, but Voodoo Andy was not.

Sam left them to sort out things as he left Teddy Irwin's shop for the last time. He opened the rear gate of the station wagon and set his toolbox inside. Should he call Edie from a payphone and tell her? Or just be a man about it and tell her about it in person after he downed a few beers? Leaning against the car, he unscrewed his thermos, poured the last sip of lukewarm coffee into the lid, watching the busy small engine shop, where the two worker bees in oily jumpsuits disassembled and reassembled engines.

I used to be like you, he thought smugly. *But now I am a free man.*

Free, that is, until he went home and broke the news to Edie.

By the fourth beer at the local watering hole, Sam knew he didn't have to tell Edie a darn thing about his job. He was his own man. Why, he could walk into any shop in the Twin Cities and find work tomorrow, and by golly, he just might do that, too. Then he'd tell her he found a different job, a better job. But later, not right away.

"Look on the bright side," he told himself. "At least I didn't have to ask anyone for Friday off."

In a brilliant flash, he realized he could just blame the whole thing on her uncle's funeral.

I had to choose, right there and then, Edie. When Teddy said it was either show up for work on Friday or attend an important family event, well, what kind of man would I be to let you down? I told him to shove that job.

The fifth beer knocked some sense into him. She would see right through that jive. Better not to tell her anything for now.

Chapter 5

Hobo Helper

ARNE WASN'T SUPPOSED TO play by the river because, according to his mom, he could drown, get snatched, get lost, fall down a well, eat a poisonous berry, and catch rabies from a squirrel bite, all in the same day. But what did she know? The river was exciting. You never knew what you were going to see, like that tree—an entire tree, leaves and all—wedged between rocks in the middle of the river. Maybe a beaver was building a dam. How neat would that be? A beaver dam right in the city. You wouldn't see something like that hiding in your kitchen, finding new ways to poison your family with supper.

Flotsam (a broken Styrofoam cooler, a beer can, various branches) collected in the tree's branches. Arne squinted to see if there was anything worth swimming out to bring back. The snap of twigs startled him. An old man stood about ten feet away, which was far enough that Arne wasn't worried. Arne could outrun most everyone, except maybe a racehorse. His threadbare blue flannel shirt and patched denim dungarees suggested he wasn't on the Sears Catalog mailing list. A canvas sack writhed at his feet.

"Whatchya lookin' at?" The man asked.

"That tree." Arne pointed, but now he really was looking at the man's canvas sack.

"I seen better." The man scanned the ground. He gave an excited shout when he found a cache of discarded cigarette butts. Tearing the filters off, one by one, he pressed the remaining tobacco—paper and all—into the bowl of a short pipe. "My name's Byron," he said as he lit his pipe. "I just rolled back into town. Easy come, easy go, like. You got a name?"

"Arne."

"Arnie?"

"No, just Arne."

"What kind of name is that?"

"First name."

The canvas bag squirmed again, and the man, Byron, kicked it with his scuffed-up boot. He could have been a lumberjack, the way he dressed, but he was much thinner. Arne supposed a lumberjack carried a good amount of extra meat on his bones from all the ax work. Arne's palette of lumberjack imagery was limited to Paul Bunyan, so, to be fair, real-life lumberjacks would have a hard time filling those giant boots. Byron's nose was long and narrow, poking out of a tangle of shaggy gray beard crusted with meals past.

"Are you hungry, Arne?"

Arne was more curious than hungry. Whatever was moving around in the sack was likely for dinner, and he wanted to see it.

"I guess."

"Well, come on over this way." Byron waved him along. "I bet we can find some of my colleagues just waiting for a little lunch unless they were called away on important business."

"Like what kind of business?"

"Well, like hiding from railroad bulls or picking seam squirrels off one another."

Arne didn't know what any of that meant, but it did sound like they were busy people, for gentlemen of leisure.

"We'll just go real quiet up here so as not to attract attention. You'd be surprised how many people don't appreciate the life of leisure."

Of course Arne knew better than to wander off with a shabby stranger on the banks of the Mississippi River. It was one of those things that his mother had hounded him about, right up there with *Don't play with matches* and *Stay off the railroad tracks*. But what did she know? Arne was always playing with matches—sometimes right on the railroad tracks. He bet she'd never done anything fun in her life, so, to her, everything seemed dangerous.

"Mister, are you a hobo?"

Byron tittered, revealing a remnant of teeth. "I guess so. Although, me and the boys prefer to be called *gentlemen of leisure.*"

His mom would not like this at all. But according to her, what you really had to watch out for was bums. Then it was child-snatching maniacs. Then you had to watch out for drugged-out hippies. And *then* it was hobos. So, in the scheme of things, wandering off with a hobo was a pretty safe bet. Hobos were the tire swings of derelicts.

As they followed a narrow, stony track along the slope, Arne asked Byron all the important questions about the hobo life, like what he did when it turned cold or when nature called (you know, number two). Byron answered each question honestly and with a fresh assortment of curse words Arne never heard before. They finally reached a ridge where five other "gentlemen of leisure" sat on rickety stools and broken concrete blocks around a fire pit.

"Wow," Arne whispered. He'd never seen a gang of hobos before.

Byron held the sack in the air, and it leaped from side to side all on its own.

"I got lunch, boys."

"Hey! It's Byron!"

"Just got in from Winona."

One man pointed at Arne with grimy fingers emerging from fingerless gloves.

"What's with the little lamb, Byron?"

"Yeah. Get a load of them ears."

The men rose, their eyes focused on Arne's head.

"Gents, this here is Arne. He's our guest."

"Well, that's a relief," another man growled. His nose was so bent to one side it looked like it was pinned that way. "When you said you brought lunch, I thought you meant the kid."

"I got better than him." Byron laughed. The bag rattled, and everyone backed away from Byron and his writhing sack.

"What'd ya got there? Some kind of snake?"

"Yup. It's a timber rattler," Byron explained. "They sun themselves on the river bluffs down there, and enterprising fellas like me bag 'em up for good eating."

"You...eat...rattlesnake?" Arne gulped. He knew people ate some weird stuff, like whatever his mom cooked, but rattlesnake was a new one to him.

"You betchya. Tastes just like chicken marinated in butter."

"He's right." A one-eared man nodded. "Darn fine eating, as long as you don't get bit first."

"Yup," Byron agreed heartily. "Avoid getting bit, throw it in some noodles, and it's like Hobo Helper."

Now Arne didn't know much about eating exotic animals, but speaking as an eleven-year-old boy who'd watched more than one episode of *Mutual of Omaha's Wild Kingdom*, he knew rattlesnakes didn't belong in the cast-iron frying pan that a hobo was greasing up for the fire. Arne knew that rattlesnakes, like most wild animals, belonged in shoe boxes or terrariums in Arne's bedroom. He wanted that snake for himself.

As soon as Byron set down the canvas bag, Arne snatched it up and bounded up the slope. He didn't look back even as the men yelled at him to stop. His body had a mind of its own, pumping energy to his legs for running. The sack was heavier than it looked, and it writhed, making the climb tricky, but he was careful to keep the snake well away from him.

Man, were those hobos angry. He learned even more words he wouldn't be able to say around his parents. But there was no way they were going to catch Arne, especially the one with the crutch. Heedless of the thorny brush as he ran, Arne knew he was getting ripped up pretty good, but a torn shirt and a few scratches were worth it: a rattlesnake.

When you get a sack with a rattlesnake in it, the first thing you're going to want to do is get a good look at it. That's exactly what Arne did once he had put enough distance between himself and the hobos. He crossed all the tracks in the railroad switching yard and found a secluded spot in a drainage ditch. He unknotted the neck of the sack, and spun it around so it was wide enough for him to look in. What he saw astounded him so much he nearly lost his cool and ran away. Peering back at him was a large, tan, triangle head with little black eyes. The thick coiled body was banded brown and gray. The snake seemed pretty angry, like it might spring at him, so Arne spun the bag closed again.

Getting a snake is an important responsibility for a boy, especially a venomous snake. He was pretty sure his dad would be the parent to approach about this first. Maybe they could just keep it as a secret from his mom, like the time Arne caught his dad spitting dinner into his napkin to throw away. Arne started doing that too. With a pet snake, they could feed it whatever nonsense Arne's mom dreamed up in the kitchen. That was the feeding part all figured out, but where would it live? He didn't have a cage or a terrarium, and it was definitely too big for a shoebox.

Where he would stow the timber rattler was a mystery until he saw the family station wagon parked in front of the duplex. That meant his dad was back from work. That also meant Arne was late for dinner. But at least now he knew where he could keep his snake—for one night, at least—until he thought of someplace better. He opened the rear door on the passenger side and set the sack carefully on the floor of the family wagon.

"Good night, Rover," Arne whispered. "I'll see you tomorrow."

Rover waved goodbye with the rattle in his tail.

Chapter 6

Taco Hot Dish Night (Yuck)

SAM TRIED TO READ the paper, but the snippy chatter between Arne and Edie and the tinny laughter from the television was too distracting. He let the paper cover his chest as he reclined in the second-hand Lazy Boy, his big bare feet blocking the actor's faces on the television. Arne had only just gotten home, and already he was getting the third degree because his clothes were dirty or something. Whatever was bugging her, at least it kept her from asking Sam too many questions about his day at work.

Correction: his *last* day at work.

"Were you down by the river again?" she interrogated the poor kid while she poured hydrogen peroxide on his bloody knees. "You go wash up. Then get back in here for supper, pronto."

Arne went padding off to the bathroom, which allowed Sam to set Edie straight. The boy was getting harangued by his mother again for the simple crime of being a boy.

"Lighten up, Edie." Sam swung himself out of the chair in one fluid motion. "It's normal for a boy like Arne to run around and get into trouble."

"A boy *like* Arne? I'm talking about Arne, not a boy *like* him. He's running around the Mississippi River and all those industrial sites like a wild animal. I get dirty looks from all the other moms in the neighborhood, and one kid even called me 'Missus Bully.' The boy needs structure and discipline, Sam. Set an example."

"Sounds like he needs a drill sergeant, not a father." Sam crossed his arms. The conversation had moved pointedly in his direction. The blame for Arne's wildness was veering towards him. He tried to fend it off with the pity deflection. "I had a drill sergeant for a father, Edie.

Don't think that solves all the problems. It's about applying the right amount of discipline."

"Oh, is that right? And would any discipline qualify as the right amount?"

Sam let that comment go. "I get it. I'm not a drill sergeant. But good gravy, boys will be boys."

"You lived in a town of...What? Two thousand people?"

"Well, eighteen hundred, but—"

"We're talking about a million people in Minneapolis and a big river, Sam. And he crosses train tracks and busy streets too."

Sam whistled an exhale. "You've got to stop watching so much television. The whole world's not out to get us, ya know?"

To be fair, Sam liked television as much as the next guy. There's no way they would stop watching it. He especially liked *All in the Family*, the way Archie Bunker just said whatever was on his mind. The boy loved that *Six Million Dollar Man* show, and Sam watched it with him. Sometimes Sam caught himself wishing he had superhuman anything: grip, eyesight, hearing, whatever. With his luck, the government probably would give him superhuman smell. *'What's that?' Bionic Sam scents the air with his six-million-dollar sniffer. 'Dead raccoon. I'd say it's about a mile off.'*

Hardly worth having his own television show, he supposed.

Arne returned to the table, wiping his hands, still dirty, on the front of his pants.

Edie closed her eyes and pressed her fingers into her temple.

Pulling his chair out from the wobbly dining table, which they bought at an estate sale in Columbia Heights for three dollars, Sam sat down with a big, forced smile on his face. "Can we just sit down and eat...whatever this is?"

Edie scowled at him.

Arne pointed at the plate she'd worked on for the past hour and a half.

"Yeah, what is that? Hobo helper?"

Sam cracked up at that. "Where did you get that line? Oh, that is a zinger."

"For your information, this is a taco hotdish." Edie sounded hurt. He didn't mean to hurt her feelings, but holy cripes! Who made up this crap?

"Olé," Sam said, trying to lighten the mood.

"I found the recipe in *Woman's Day*, and I'll have you know Barbara Streisand is just crazy for it."

"You can send ol' Barbara Streisand my serving, Mom."

"And there's glorified rice for dessert, smart guy."

She pointed to the serving dish she'd already laid out on their round dining table.

Sam's jaw dropped. "For cripes sake, Edie. Is that fruit cocktail in there?"

The pounding under their feet and Mr. Jaworski's muffled cursing made them freeze momentarily. He actually made them wonder if they were too loud; but no, they were only normal-loud, a typical American family about to partake in the great experiment of Edie's cooking.

"Every time he does that," Edie hissed, "I just jump out of my skin."

"I know what you mean," Sam agreed. "I forget all about him, and then he starts knocking. Hey." Sam's face brightened. "Do you think he's trying to say he loves us?" Sam started singing "Knock Three Times" by Tony Orlando and Dawn. It was one of the last songs he heard on the radio before he got fired.

Arne joined his dad in the song while Edie solemnly served taco hotdish as if it were the eucharist. Then Arne told Sam about a big tree he'd seen making a dam in the river and how he'd seen a snake.

"I'm pretty sure it was a rattler," Arne added, sniffing at his plate with a hint of disdain for the square of taco hotdish she'd insisted he sample. Sam told him that rattlers didn't live in Minneapolis, that they lived in the river bluffs in the southeast along the Wisconsin border, because Wisconsin is infested with all sorts of vermin, like Packers.

Arne seemed like he was about to argue the point but stopped short, instead turning his attention to Edie with big, pleading eyes. "Mom, can I have a hamburger instead?"

"This dish has hamburger in it—and tomatoes and corn chips," she answered sternly as she pushed his plate towards him. "You like all those things, mister."

"Yeah, but I wouldn't want them all mushed together in a chocolate cake, either," he retorted.

"The boy is smart," Sam said, taking a bite. "Just like his father." Unlike Arne, Sam tried Edie's recipe experiments. Sometimes they turned out okay, but it was like playing Russian roulette. You never knew which recipe was going to do you in. After swallowing his first bite, his expression became serious.

"Edie, let me ask you something. Tacos are pretty good on their own, right? So why cram them all together and overcook them? It's a little complicated for my taste."

"Yeah, Mom. It's too complicated." Arne pushed away his plate and let his fork clatter on the table. "I want a hamburger."

Edie was winding up to lose her temper with them both, but footsteps on the stairs and knocking on the door prevented her from sharing her thoughts on the complexity of taco hotdish.

A raggedy-looking man began yelling at them before the door was fully open. Sam rose, flared out his chest as he tried to make sense of what the man was saying. Something about Arne stealing food from hobos, and now this man lost another tooth trying to catch the boy, and how everyone in the neighborhood knew which kid he was looking for on account of he was *the* biggest troublemaker in Nordeast. Well, this level of commotion was too much for Mr. Jaworski downstairs, who lent his energies by pounding and hollering until the entire apartment was louder than General Mills.

"Here," Sam said, thinking as quickly as he could under the circumstances. "Eat this." He thrust the pan of taco hotdish into the man's arms and gave him a nudge out of the apartment. He returned to the table across from Arne, his eyebrows raised as Mr. Jaworski's yelling and pounding eventually faded away. Edie stared at Sam with her mouth hanging open.

"What?" Sam shrugged. "The poor guy looked hungry."

Edie turned her focus on Arne, her arms folded, head cocked to one side.

"Well?"

"Well, what?" Arne responded too quickly, pushing his helping of taco hotdish from one side of his plate to the other.

"Did you steal from hobos?"

"And what was that he said about a snake?" Sam asked.

"Hobos and snakes?" Arne chuckled dismissively. "That's crazy. He was stinky drunk or something."

"Drunk or not," putting his elbows on the table, Sam rested his chin on his fists and said calmly, "I know you did something, kiddo. We will find out."

Edie gurgled in frustration. "Even the hobos hate us. You know what really bothers me? All these angry people make a beeline right over here. That's the second one this week. Arne can't really be the biggest troublemaker in the neighborhood, is he?"

Arne smirked, and Edie caught sight of it.

"Oh, no, mister. That is *not* a good thing. You just wipe that smile off your face, and finish what's on your plate. Then you're going straight to bed."

"Don't make me eat that," Arne whined. "I didn't do anything!"

Chapter 7

Who Wants a Big Boy Burger?

FRIDAY MORNING CAME, AND Sam lost the coin toss to 'encourage' Arne to get out of bed.

"Come on, sleepyhead." Sam compressed the boy's chest so that he bounced up and down on the mattress.

"I don't want to go." Arne was getting too old for his powder-blue Aquaman pajamas, but Edie insisted he wear them because of their flame-resistant material. *You never know with him*, she'd said.

"Aw, that's just the grumps talking. You don't want to miss an exciting road trip into the big woods and lake country, do ya?"

Arne grumbled something unintelligible and was in danger of drifting off.

Sam threw back the bedcovers.

"Come on. You might see a bear. Or maybe a pack of wolves."

Arne folded the pillow over his head, and Sam tickled him until the boy released the pillow, pulling him flailing and laughing from his little bed.

"We want to leave early enough to allow for detours or flat tires or what have you. Always plan ahead, that's what a man does."

❧ ⋅ ❖ ⋅ ☙

Planning ahead always sounded like a good idea, especially if you knew what you were planning for. Sam had checked the weather, and they knew it was going to be unseasonably warm over the weekend, so that was good to know. Pack some shorts and extra-strength antiperspirant. But there were certain unforeseen circumstances that even the best-prepared person couldn't anticipate. A plague of locusts, for example. Or an asteroid.

Or, in the Fisker family's situation, the strange rattling noise that began as soon as they nosed the station wagon on the highway.

"What the heck is that?" Sam turned down the radio, unsure of what he was hearing. "It sounds like a blown radiator hose." He checked his temperature gauge and then focused on the hood to see if any steam was rolling off the engine. Nope, everything looked normal. "Hmmm... I'd like to check it out before we get too far from civilization. It's almost lunchtime, anyway. What do you say we just stop at the Big Boy?"

That question usually elicited excited agreement from Arne, but Sam could see the boy sitting stiffly in the back seat, his face tense.

"What's the matter? Aren't you hungry for a Big Boy burger?"

Arne nodded his head tersely, his gaze dropping low.

Sam shot Edie a puzzled look. "Maybe he's not feeling well. We should stay home, hunh?" Arne loved going to the Big Boy ever since he was little—not as much as he loved going to the Jolly Troll Smörgåsbord with its weird robot trolls that slowly raised and lowered their robot limbs, but the Jolly Troll was in Golden Valley, and that was out of the way.

"Oh, we're going even if that boy has rubella."

The rattling sound came and went again, urgent, then quiet.

"That doesn't sound like an engine problem," Edie added. "It sounds like it's coming from inside, doesn't it?"

Sam laughed and patted her knee.

"You let ol' Sam worry about the mechanical things, sweetheart. I'll check it out when we pull in."

Within ten minutes, they pulled into the parking lot, and Sam announced, "There he is, Arne."

The 'he' was the Big Boy statue: a cherubic man-boy in red-and-white checked bibs, proudly holding aloft a hamburger platter above his pompadour hair pile. In case anyone had forgotten who he was, 'Big Boy' was imprinted on the shirt peeking out over his bibs.

"Hey, did you see that, Arne? I think he winked at us!" No dice. For all the visual excitement that a Big Boy statue afforded, Arne remained quiet.

It was only eleven-thirty, so they had their pick of parking. Sam headed right to the front of the building, directly toward the Big Boy statue. As he braked, he heard the rattling again and felt something coil around his leg—something alive and snaky. Fear pumped adrenaline into his system, causing him to jerk various parts of his body: his right foot hit the accelerator, and his arms spun the steering wheel in a hard right to avoid the rapid approach of a Big Boy statue. Sam heard screaming: his own, mingled with Edie's and Arne's screams. His foot found the brake just in time, sending the station wagon to a screeching halt just before sideswiping the Big Boy.

"What happened?" Edie was frantic.

Sam didn't answer right away. The snake had uncoiled from his leg, and he didn't feel any bite wounds, but the dang thing was still down there somewhere.

"Are you okay, Arne?"

Arne nodded, but he looked terrified.

"Well?" Edie yelled at Sam. "Why did you almost kill us with the Big Boy statue?"

"I don't want to alarm anyone," Sam said as calmly and quietly as he could, considering his heart was thumping in his chest. "...but there's a snake in the car. That's where the rattling came from."

"Oh, come on." Edie scoffed, but a renewed round of rattling made her go deathly pale.

"Edie, I want you to—slowly, now—open your door. You, too, Arne. Open your doors and ease out of the car."

Edie and Arne thankfully didn't give him any backtalk. They moved like people pantomiming in a pretend wind as they slid from their seat and onto the walk in front of the restaurant, which the station wagon now blocked.

Sam turned off the car. The seat leather made a sucking sound when Sam set first one foot, then the other, carefully on the ground. Then he exited the car in a flash and slammed the driver's door.

"Is everyone okay?" Edie announced she hated, hated, hated snakes, which meant she was okay, at least. Arne still said nothing.

"Calm down, everyone." Sam knew what a man's job was during times of crisis: crowd control. Soviets about to launch a nuclear attack? Hippies taking over the license bureau while you're taking your driving test? Rattlesnake loose in your car? The man must show his primitive strength and restore order. "It's more afraid of us than we are of it."

"Bull crap!" Edie retorted.

They stared at the station wagon as if it had just goosed them. Then the questions began, the primary one being, *How the heck did a rattlesnake end up in the car*? Then it dawned on Sam that there just might be a connection between the hobo's enraged claims from the night before and Arne's nervous silence today.

"Start talking, mister," Sam demanded, but Arne held his tongue.

"Arne," Edie warned. "If you don't tell us what's going on, I swear I will break an arm off that Big Boy statue and paddle your butt with it."

Soon enough, Arne started bawling as he spilled the beans about stealing a rattlesnake from a hobo gang.

"It's a timber rattler," Arne added defensively. "And they're poisonous, and I earned him fair and square."

"Are you hearing this?" Sam asked.

"Yeah," Edie blinked. This was one of those moments when parents just look at one another to make sure they weren't hallucinating or trapped in a nightmare. "What are we going to do?"

Sam cupped his hands to the back window. The rattler's tail poked out from under the back seat.

"Arne," Sam barked. "I'm going to grab my toolbox from the back, and when I say so, I want you to open the back door and then run to your mother as fast as you can. Got it?"

Arne nodded. Sam grabbed his toolbox, and after Arne threw open the door, Sam fell to work, unbolting the back seat from the station wagon.

"Now the other side," he told Arne, and they repeated the same routine so that the seat was free, but the rattling was as loud as ever.

"Crap."

"Samuel. Language."

"Sorry. Cripes." He wrestled with the back seat alone until a clueless Good Samaritan approached them. You could tell he was a Good Samaritan because of the dopey smile on his face and the *Good Samaritan* bumper sticker on his car.

"Having some seat trouble?"

"Uh, yeah," Sam answered, the sweat beginning to bead on his forehead. Now he knew what those bomb squad guys felt like when they were defusing a 'mysterious package.' Of course, he was just trying to defuse the back seat, but it presented the same stress level.

"Maybe I can give you a hand. What's that rattling sound?"

"I dunno," Sam played dumb. It came natural to him. "Leaky radiator hose, maybe?"

Together, the two men freed the seat from the station wagon and hoisted it on the roof rack, where it tipped back, revealing a four-foot-long timber rattlesnake glaring out at them. As everyone knows, no good deed goes unpunished, and by way of 'thanks' for the unsolicited help, the snake shot forward at the stranger, perhaps hoping to give him a hug. The Good Samaritan leaped back. "Looks like your radiator hose is hungry."

Sam waved to the man as he ran into the restaurant. "Thanks for the help!" Then to Edie and Arne, he added, "There's still good people around, ya know?" He ran a tie-down strap around the seat and through both back windows. "There. That's not going anywhere."

"What about the snake?"

"Oh, he'll be fine. We'll just let him air out."

"I don't want a fresh snake," Edie countered. "I want no snake."

"Sure, I understand, but he'll just get scared of blowing around on the highway, and he'll probably go flying off."

"And what if it doesn't? What if it slithers back in the car and kills us?"

"We'll keep the windows closed on the way up, just to make sure." Sam rubbed his hands together. "Hey. Who wants a Big Boy burger?"

Sam and Arne did. Edie grudgingly ordered a tuna melt with avocado and a side of pineapple cottage cheese.

With the back seat still strapped to the top of the car, they continued their trip. The car was swelteringly hot with the windows closed as a snake-proofing precaution.

When they pulled over for a bathroom break in Saint Cloud, Edie ran from the car as if it were going to explode. She slammed the car door behind her.

"Don't let that snake sneak in," she hollered, as if Sam had any influence over the snake's choices. He checked the seat. "Ope!" Sam backed away quickly. The snake, still coiled, looked angrier than ever, with no sign of flying off like they'd hoped.

"Is he still there, Dad?"

"Yup, he's still there." Sam tried not to act scared. "That is one tenacious snake."

"His name's Rover," Arne explained.

"I wish we could send Rover right over, if you know what I mean," Sam said, but Edie wasn't having nearly as much fun as Arne and Sam. He tried to lighten her mood by pointing out the bright side. "At least the rattling stopped."

Then it was back on the road. The long, sweaty road. He tuned the radio station away from the static-filled beautiful music station and found Bachman-Turner Overdrive on an FM station out of Fargo.

"There!" He announced. "That'll help us take care of business the rest of the way to Fornborg, Minnesota."

Chapter 8

Welcome to Fornborg

IT WAS HOT IN the car and miserable. Hot enough that Edie pursed her lips when she breathed in air. That seemed to help cool it down.

"Can't we open the windows just a little?" Arne begged.

"Yeah, how about it?" Sam agreed. "After how poorly we treated that snake, I'd say the odds are slim he'd want to come slithering back in here when we're cruising along at sixty miles per hour."

Edie was adamant. "No," she repeated for about the hundredth time. At least Arne had the entire back of the station wagon to himself to stretch out now that the back seat was out. It's true the poor boy wasn't enjoying the drive 'Up North' half as much they'd promised him he would, but when you want to get a kid in the car so you can make it to a funeral, you say just about anything.

Farm fields gave way to forests and the occasional pothole lake. They saw more and more pine trees, and Sam suggested they come back around Christmas with an ax, which Arne thought was a pretty good idea. They headed north at Sauk Centre, with Arne claiming that they spelled both 'sock' and 'center' wrong.

"No, they're just different words," Edie grumbled.

"Oh yeah? What do they mean?"

"Well, c-e-n-t-r-e is just a fancy way of spelling center."

"So spelling words wrong is fancy?"

She gave up trying to reason with him. Besides, she wasn't ready to tackle an explanation for the 'Sauk' part of the city's name. Maybe it was French? Maybe it was a typo on the city sign?

"And the Sauk River. Do they call it that because it smells like a sock?"

"You got that right, kiddo," Sam said.

Trying to distract him, Edie pointed to a different sign that said the city's claim to fame was the boyhood home of Sinclair Lewis.

"Isn't that neat?" She tried to sound enthusiastic, but Arne blew a raspberry.

"Who is *that*?"

Dang it, Edie thought. She knew the name: he was famous. But for what? She asked Sam if he knew.

"Yeah, fun fact about Sinclair Lewis. He invented the gasoline pump, and that's why they named all those Sinclair stations after him."

"Is that true, Mom?"

Arne was wise enough to not believe everything his father said, so she and Arne had that in common. But in this case, a little made-up history was fine. Anything to take their minds off the heat. Another thing kids love to do to take their minds off long, hot car rides is was singing. Unfortunately, Arne remembered this as they left Sauk Centre, boyhood home of the guy who invented gas pumps. He launched into a throaty rendition of the ninety-nine bottles of beer song, which included actual belching, thanks to Sam teaching the disgusting trip to their son.

"How much further?" Edie whined, fanning herself with a bingo card.

"Another half-hour." He patted her leg but withdrew his hand. "Eww. You're all sweaty."

She shot him a false smile. "Thanks."

Time passed slowly and it felt like they were crawling towards Fornburg.

"Take one down, pass it around. Three bottles of beer on the wall!"

"Oh, look, Arne," Edie said with a burst of relief, pointing frantically to the sign announcing Fornborg. "We're here."

She had never been more relieved to arrive somewhere, even if it was under unfortunate circumstances. And under a snake. Literally.

Past the welcome sign and its barricade of towering aspens and craggy oak trees, the view of downtown was partially obscured by Fornborg's most notable landmark: a giant Viking longboat.

"Holy crap!" Arne pressed his face to the window.

"Language, mister." Edie scolded him, but he had every right to be impressed. She'd forgotten it until now, but as a child, she, too, had been awed by the longboat. Her Uncle Nat had let her and her cousins climb around on it, even though the signs clearly stated KEEP OFF.

"Wow." Sam admired it too. "That's gotta be, what? Eighty feet long?"

Edie was bad at guessing those sorts of things and told him so.

"Must be as long as three semi-trailers," he concluded, although she had no idea why men always wanted to put a number on everything—even on women. (He'd once told her that Raquel Welch was a 'ten', but that he thought Edie was a solid eight. At least he didn't measure her in quantities of semi-trailers.)

Flashes of childhood memory came back to her: how Uncle Nat said Fornborg wore a permanent smile because the main street rounded to accommodate the bowing shore of Big Jack Pine Lake; the churches poked the giant, rolling sky with their little crosses atop steeples; the old storefronts on Gull Drive (the main street), with their tall windows reflecting golden lake light on hot summer days. She even remembered the old hand-painted sign on the front of the Cozy Corner Diner, the diner's name floating on the steam rising from a big hamburger.

"I don't know about you," Sam said as he pulled in front of the diner, "but I sure could go for a piece of pie."

"We should find a place to stay first. I don't want to be seen in public all..."

"Sweaty?" Arne suggested.

"No." Edie shook her head. "I don't like that word. Mussed," she concluded. "Besides, we want to make sure we get a room. What if everything fills up?"

"We won't be long," Sam assured her. "I'm not going to eat a whole pie. Just a quick piece." He looked over his shoulder at Arne. "What do you say, kiddo? Pie?"

"Yeah!"

"No fair," Edie mumbled. "His vote would always be for pie."

"Maybe we can ask about places to stay. No one knows the area better than the locals."

Sam reminded them to exit the car as calmly and as rapidly as possible because of the snake.

"Once you're out, just run like heck to the front door of the diner."

In the diner, a waitress named Marie greeted them from behind the counter.

"Sit where you like," she said, but there was only one open booth. Where they liked to sit was where no one else was already sitting, so the choice was clear. Men—fishermen, judging by their clothes and the way they smelled—filled the other tables and seats at the counter. That made Edie a little more comfortable: as sweaty and uncomfortable as she felt, she wasn't the worst of the bunch.

They slid into the open booth. In ten seconds flat, Edie had to slap Arne's hands away from the rack of jelly and from playing mumblety-peg with a fork and pouring sugar in a pile on the table. Reprimanded and bored, Arne read aloud each and every one of the ads on the paper placemat. He waved it in front of her, pointing to the box with the address for Lulu's Cafe.

"Look! They spelled coffee wrong." He was at that age where he was convinced he'd win a Congressional Medal of Honor for spotting mistakes that adults made.

"No, that's *cafe*, and that's exactly how *cafe* is spelled," Edie assured him. "It's just a fancy word for coffee."

"Like *Sauk Centre*? So all words that are spelled wrong *are* fancy?" His finger jabbed at another example. "And what about this? The Fornborg Movie Theatre? Is that a fancy way of spelling theater?"

Edie had to admit, *theatre* was another fancy way of saying something in American English. Sometimes she regretted he had learned to read.

On the upside, Arne did find them a lodging option from the placemat. One of the ads he read aloud was for the Lakeview Lodge. *Clean, Cheap, and a Pleasant Stay.*

"Sounds good to me," Sam said. After a slice each of pecan pie with a scoop of vanilla ice cream on top, Sam guzzled what was left of his coffee. They ducked into the car. A quick glance at the roof of the station wagon revealed that the itinerant snake was still tucked safely in the seat springs with no plans of disembarking.

"That snake must be Norwegian," Sam quipped. "Never gives up."

Edie wasn't a big believer in the virtues of being Norwegian based on her experiences with her one-hundred-percent husband and mother.

"Maybe it's just dumb."

Chapter 9

Magic Fingers

THEY FOUND A ROOM in Fornborg in the late afternoon at the Lakeview Lodge motel. Sam, a little punch drunk after their road adventure, was giddy.

"Happy to be alive," Sam answered when the clerk asked him how he was doing. Sam figured that kind of response would spark up a conversation, something along the lines of *Really? Boy, that sounds like a good story. Tell me more.*

But the clerk, who must have been about sixty, sixty-five, just pointed to a register and told him to put his real name and license plate number.

"Your *real* name," the clerk emphasized. His name tag said 'Dale.' Dale probably owned the place and probably regretted it every day he woke up, thanks to annoying strangers like Sam.

"Lakeview Lodge," Sam mused as he signed in. "Kind of a funny name for a motel that isn't on a lake and isn't a lodge, isn't it?"

"Kind of funny to have a perfectly good car seat strapped to the roof of your car, isn't it?"

Sam smiled. This was his chance to tell Dale all about their harrowing encounter with the snake, but the sign behind Dale clearly laid out a ten dollar extra charge for pets.

"Ice machine to the right," Dale said. "Keep the noise down after nine, and don't bust anything. You break it, you buy it."

He handed Sam a key connected to a puce octagonal keychain with 237 in bold black numbers.

"You're in room 105."

"But the key says 237."

Dale leaned one direction and jerked a thumb at the key wall behind him. All the keys said 237.

"Got a good deal on 'em," Dale explained. "Hotel auction in Colorado."

Room 105 was as sparse as Dale's conversation. The red and green floor tiles were disorienting, the gray block walls cold and austere, but it had all the modern comforts: black-and-white television, a toilet, and a Magic Fingers bed.

"Wow." Arne ran his hands over the Magic Fingers box. "What is this thing?"

"Don't touch anything, Arne," Edie warned.

"It makes the bed shake. Like a body rub. Fifteen minutes of vibration for a quarter."

"Let me try. Can I have a quarter?"

"Oh, no." Sam put his foot down. "A quarter to just get shaken? I'll shake you for free."

"Oh, come on, Dad. Just one quarter?"

"Nope. Sorry, kiddo. We're not throwing away any more money on this trip. That machine is just a quarter sucker."

Arne laughed.

"Dad called it a quarter sucker."

"Hey, Arne." Sam may not know all the latest parenting techniques that Edie read about in her women's magazines, but he knew that sometimes, as a responsible parent, you had to trick your kids, like a magician, to divert their attention. "Did you see they've got a little swimming pool out there?"

"Really?" Arne popped the button on his pants and scooched them down to his ankles before tearing into the nearest suitcase. Edie pulled him back when he started burrowing like a groundhog looking for a winter home.

"But I need my swim shorts," he complained.

"Wait. I'll help you. I'll help you. Slow down." Edie went to the other suitcase and carefully took out the blue and red swimming trunks she'd folded. It rested atop Arne's only formal suit, but Arne was only interested in the swim trunks. He sloughed off his little pair of jeans like, well, like a snake shedding its skin, put on his shorts, and tore out of the motel room.

Sam pointed to Arne's powder-blue suit in the suitcase.

"You really going to try to squeeze him into that?"

"We're going to a funeral," Edie pointed out. "He can't look like he's going to camp. He is going to wear it."

Sam nodded, dubious that Arne would even fit in that tiny suit, but she usually knew what she was doing, except when it came to cooking. He locked the door handle and attached the security chain. As Edie busied herself with unpacking, he reached behind her, pretending to pull a shiny quarter from her ear.

"Magic Fingers?" he asked, raising his eyebrows.

Afterward, Edie unpacked her case, the first item being an old *Minneapolis Tribune* newspaper. She'd read in *Good Housekeeping* that when you were staying in a motel, you didn't want to let your clothes touch anything, including dresser drawers. She spread the front page in the top drawer and the sports section in the middle drawer. The room's little coin-operated black-and-white television picked up two stations and, fortunately, one of them was CBS, so she could watch *Tattletales* while she contemplated mortality. She also contemplated Bert Convy: that thick hair, those dark eyes. Plus, he knew all the answers.

Arne pounded on the door, and Edie undid the chain. He came bursting in, sopping wet, with a pair of goggles pushed up on his forehead.

"I found a dime in the pool!" He jumped on top of Sam, who was still sprawled out on the bed. "All I need is another dime and a nickel, right, Dad?"

"You're making me cold, buddy." Sam set Arne on the tile floor. "Well, you better get back out there to find the rest."

"But then I can try the Magic Fingers, right?" Arne read the words along the coin slot. "Uh oh."

"What's wrong?"

"It says it only takes quarters. Can I trade two dimes and a nickel with you?"

"Sure, kiddo."

Arne left, leaving puddles of footprints behind him.

"Did you give him swimming goggles?" Edie asked.

"No." Sam shook his head. "I figured you packed them."

Someone knocked on the door. Dale from the front desk stood on the threshold, looking grim.

"Your boy the big-eared one?"

Edie sighed. "What'd he do?"

"Seems he borrowed some swim mask or other and won't give them back."

"We'll take care of it," Edie assured him and shut the door. "Actually, can you deal with Arne? I have to call my mom and let her know we made it. Get out there and spend some time with that boy."

"As if a three-hour car ride wasn't long enough?"

"Parents don't get coffee breaks, Sam." She'd read that in an article about parenting being a thankless, full-time job that ended only when you did. "And don't let him rub his eyes or else he'll catch pink eye from those goggles." Sam didn't hop to like she wanted, so she shook his leg playfully, making his whole body wriggle.

"Ooh, someone's got the Magic Fingers." He clawed at her, but she jumped back.

"Quarters only."

Apparently, Arne wasn't the only troublemaker in the family. This time, Dale knocked on their room door to warn Sam about throwing objects in the pool, especially heavy metal objects, when there were swimmers in there.

"Well, Dale, I don't know why you put the horseshoe pit so close to the pool. For cripes sake, I was just getting warmed up."

Dale sighed and shuffled off.

"Poor guy," Sam remarked. "Nothing better to do than harass paying guests for having a good time. And after we paid fifteen bucks for this dump."

Arne laughed; Edie did not. She held up the dress she'd brought with for the funeral.

"This doesn't look wrinkled, does it?"

"Mom, what are you gonna say?"

"What do you mean?"

"When it's your turn at the funeral." Arne tugged at the dress hem, and she pulled it away from him. "What are you going to say?"

Arne had the idea that funerals were a time when friends and family members all got to say their piece, good and bad, about the deceased. Edie explained funerals didn't really work like that.

"Only a couple people will probably speak. Funerals are more of a chance to be consoled by the minister."

Arne thought quietly for a moment.

"What was he like?"

"Uncle Nat? Oh, I don't know. He was kind, I guess."

"Kind of what?"

"No, not *kind of,* just kind. Like nice. Generous."

"Oh," Arne contemplated. "Like, if I asked for a quarter, and he gave me one?"

"Yes," Edie agreed.

"But you're not getting any quarters from us." Sam interjected. He held the ice bucket. "I'll be back in a couple minutes."

The only thing Edie could remember about Uncle Nat was the way he'd put on a feather boa to play tea party with her and her cousin Lana on the dock. He'd worn that feather boa even as Edie and her mother drove off later that day. Who knows? Maybe he never had taken it off.

They watched *Sanford and Son*, laughing at the way Redd Foxx kept having fake heart attacks.

"Is your uncle in Heaven?" Arne asked.

"For a boy who steals from people and shoves poisonous snakes in cars, you're feeling pretty philosophical today, aren't you?"

"I guess so," Arne stated. "Mom?"

"Yes, Arne."

"If you touch a dead guy, do you turn into a zombie?"

Edie chuckled. "Now, there's the boy I know."

Just then, the motel room door burst open. Sam had returned with a bucket of ice and a paper bag that probably hid a pint of schnapps.

"Son of a biscuit!"

"Sam. Language."

"I'm sorry, but some son of a biscuit stole our car seat. Right off the roof."

Arne's eyes grew wide, and he took a deep, heaving breath.

"Is my snake gone?"

"Yes, your snake is gone, along with a seventy-dollar bench seat."

"Who would do that?"

"Beats me, but I hope they get bitten over and over again so they get so many holes in 'em they drown in their own bathtub."

"Samuel! Don't say that kind of thing in front of him!"

"Fine. Then I hope whoever stole our car seat enjoys the comfort of solid American engineering and comes back for the rest of the car. That better?"

Edie shook her head. "I guess we know where Arne gets his sassy mouth."

Chapter 10

We're Not Lake Lutherans

NO ONE WANTS TO attend an open-casket funeral except eleven-year-old boys.

Arne was asking all about funerals, what to expect, what happened to the dead body—all the gory details.

"Can we touch the body?"

He wasn't grasping the more spiritual side of the event and how important it was to mourn the loss of someone he had never met.

"And you are *not* going to a funeral wearing swim trunks. Come here."

Naturally, Arne didn't like her tone, and she had to chase him around the motel room, giggling as he avoided her reach. It was a fun little game they played. Well, fun for Arne. She eventually cornered him and forced him into his powder-blue two-piece suit. She'd found it on the discount rack at Sears last year when it still fit him. Even if the sleeves and pant legs were too short, at least it wasn't swim trunks.

Edie breathed a sigh of relief now that the struggle with Arne was over.

"God, would you look at him? All dressed up?" Sam, wearing only a tank top and a pair of boxers, held Edie's waist as they admired their son as he jumped up and down on the Magic Fingers bed in his suit.

"Hard to believe he came from our love, isn't it?"

"Yeah," Sam nuzzled her cheek. "Kind of looks like he's packed in there so tight, his ears are squeezing out of his head."

Arne, who plainly heard his dad's comment, grabbed the nearest item on the bed and smacked Sam across the torso. Only it wasn't a pillow. Arne hit Sam with an empty suitcase. Instead of a playful father-son pillow fight, a melee ensued. The nightstand was smashed, the curtains, torn from the hooks, lay in a heap on the floor. Other motor lodgers peered out their windows to watch a big-eared boy in last year's suit trying to outrun a very angry man as they ran around the parking lot of the Lakeview Lodge.

Miraculously, Edie convinced the motel's manager not to call the cops, that they would pay for damages—with what money, she wasn't sure yet. Could they pawn a boy's suit?

After calming everyone down, Edie talked both her boys into a temporary truce. Yes, she knew Arne needed to be punished, but his sentence could wait until after the funeral. By then, they could tack on a whole bunch of other crimes.

"Besides," she added to Sam, "You kind of had it coming, teasing him like that."

"It's just a fact. He's got big ears. It's not like he doesn't hear it all the time, just like if he were very tall or fat or if he had polka dots. People are going to notice."

"Well, I'd rather they notice his ears than notice a grown man trying to club his own son to death with a newspaper in the parking lot of a motel."

Sam shrugged. "You say tomato. Hey, you look nice. Got a date or something?"

"Shut up." She shoved him away, laughing, but she couldn't help but be pleased that he'd finally noticed she wasn't wearing jeans and a tee-shirt or shorts. Thanks to the versatility afforded by most items in the Sears Fall Catalog, it was the same dress she wore to any special occasion: a jacquard weave double-knit with a beet-red-and-white pattern.

"Shouldn't you be wearing black, though?"

"I can't afford black," she responded. That felt like her mother creeping out of her. She regretted it. Maybe she would make it up to him on the Magic Fingers later.

To avoid getting his little suit even more creased or torn, Arne rode to the church on Edie's lap in the passenger seat.

"I'm sorry, but there's popcorn and sticky root beer barrels and God-knows-what-else from under the car seat, so I can't have you rolling around the back of the car and get all filthy."

He wriggled, he fussed, but she held him tight. He was a wiry little fighter: she could see why boys even bigger than him might end up on the losing end when Arne got angry. She could make this work for a two-minute drive to a church, but there was no way she could hold him for three hours on the way home to Minneapolis. By then, he could roll around in dirt, or maybe they'd find the bench seat and get the station wagon back to normal.

"Are you sad about your uncle?" Arne asked. Maybe it was a trick to get her to relax her grip. Well, she wasn't letting him squirm away.

"To be honest, Arne, I didn't know him that well, but he is family. Family is important, so in that sense, yes, I'm sad that someone in our family..." She paused, waiting for the right word to come to her.

"Croaked?" Arne suggested.

"Passed," Edie corrected.

"Like gas?" Arne giggled.

"You're adorable, aren't you, funny guy?" She tickled one of his armpits, immediately regretting it as he tried to twist away, banging her bare shin. She reprimanded him, her good humor turning sour quickly as the pain shot through her leg.

"Don't you dare tear my dress, mister."

"Then don't tickle me."

They struck another truce as they took in the sights along Highway 6 that led from the motel to downtown Fornborg. Arne asked about the types of trees lining the lakes they passed.

"Tamaracks, maybe," Sam answered. "Or hemlock."

"You don't know anything about trees," Edie scolded.

"I'll tell you what I do know," Sam began. "Guy at the motel said that Fornborg is the only town in Minnesota to have more lakes than Lutheran churches."

"Wow!" Arne said. "Is that true?"

"Well, how many lakes have you seen since we've been here?"

"Five? No, six?"

"And how many Lutheran churches have you seen?"

"None."

"There ya go."

Edie held out hope that children turned out smarter than their parents.

They arrived at the Fornborg Glorious Truth Lutheran Church with only a few minutes to spare before the funeral service would begin. Sam pulled in on the street as the church lot was full. A shiny olive-green '68 Grand Prix parked behind them immediately drew Arne and Sam's attention. They both guessed at engine sizes, with Sam convinced it was a four-twenty-eight under the hood, and Arne agreed that sounded about right.

A man wearing a Hawaiian shirt and flip-flop sandals leaned against a service truck a few spaces away. His unbuttoned shirt revealed chest hair as curly as the brown hair on his head. Where you might expect to see a shark-tooth necklace or puka shells, he wore dog tags. The truck he leaned against had built-in toolboxes and metal racks welded to the bed. Lettering on the side door revealed it belonged to a plumber—*Aloha Plumbing*—and Edie figured the man in the Hawaiian shirt watching them was Mr. Aloha, the plumber himself.

Edie stood alone on the curb as the final stragglers climbed the stairs to the church entrance. She wriggled her hips and tugged down the skirt that had ridden up on her in the car.

Mr. Aloha watched Edie wriggle with calm interest as he filed his nails. She smiled at him, but he didn't smile back. He just looked at her like she was a fire hydrant in a twenty-one-dollar dress.

"Hey, you two," she called to Sam and Arne. "Come on. We're late."

She steered Arne clear of dog doo on the church lawn.

"Watch where you step," she warned.

Together the three Fiskers made their way up the stairs, past the sign announcing tomorrow's sermon would be JESUS WAS A COUNTRY BOY TOO, to be preached by Reverend E. Horseldoff.

As Sam reached for the door handle, a chunky man in a thin gray suit and a wide blue tie glided out of the church door, blocking their way. He squinted past them, his gaze falling on the plumber in the Hawaiian shirt outside. The plumber's head swiveled sharply, giving the 'no' signal.

"I'm sorry," he said, his voice reedy and wheedling. "This is a private event. A very solemn event, in fact."

"Yeah?" Sam said. "So?"

"It's not open to the public like a library or an adult theater."

"Listen here," Sam said, puffing out his chest. Edie touched his arm warningly.

"We're here for Nat Lachmann's funeral," she said calmly. "He was my uncle."

"Oh." He took her hand, holding it like a small sandwich in both of his. "I'm so sorry for your loss." He made the okay sign to the plumber before shaking Sam's hand in the sandwich style. He also tried to shake hands with Arne, but Arne hid behind his mother's skirt.

"Look at the ears on that young fella," the man said.

Sam nudged Edie.

"See?"

"I apologize for keeping you. I thought you might be some of those Lake Lutherans."

"What's a Lake Lutheran?"

"Oh, they're people who come here for the summer to fish and waterski and stuff, and then they wander into church when they get hungry."

"Sounds like bears."

"Yeah, I suppose. If bears waterskied."

"Well, rest assured," Edie interjected. "We're not Lake Lutherans."

"Of course, you're not," he replied, patronizing her in a tone that would have been even more complete if he'd patted her on the head. "By the way, I'm Jacob Dugrave of Dugrave-Hull funerary services. It was my honor to prepare your dear uncle for viewing."

"Oh," Sam sparked. Edie knew he was going to say something dumb, and it was too late to stop him. "So you're one of them corpse mechanics."

Arne reappeared from behind Edie, now curious to see the man who touched dead people for a living.

"Well, most people might consider my work more artistry than mechanical in nature. You should have seen him when he turned up here. What a mess. Couldn't believe they were moving ahead with an open casket service. But I said to myself, *Dugrave, you have been at this for twenty years. If you can't make the top half of a man look presentable, then you might as well throw in the towel.* Mind you, that explosion didn't leave me much to work with. Let's just say I had to rob Peter to pay Paul, in a sense."

Edie cut him off, finding the topic too gruesome for Arne. She put her hands over her son's big ears.

"Thank you, Mr. Dugrave, but we should probably get inside."

"Of course, of course." He held the door open for them, and they passed inside. "Enjoy." He called after them as they became awash in organ music. A photographer with a boxy commercial camera posed an older married couple in front of the casket. He waved for them to squeeze together. Edie had never seen that, but then again, she hadn't been to that many funerals.

"Which side do we sit on?" Sam whispered.

"It doesn't matter," Edie whispered back. "You're thinking of weddings. Let's just sit in the back."

Edie didn't recognize anyone. And how would she? She hadn't been to Fornborg in many years, and the only people she'd met were his now ex-wife and two children. They'd be in their thirties now. She remembered that her cousins, Jeffy and Lana, had red hair, so unless they had gone gray, they might be in the crowd. She looked but didn't see any red-haired people.

The minister rose and adjusted the microphone in the pulpit, and the organ music paused.

"I know we had some latecomers," he looked right at them in the back. The way he said *latecomers* sounded a lot like *Lake Lutherans*. "So, we'll wait to until everyone has a chance to get their photographs taken at the front. Remember, you can order keepsake prints from Roger Molstad of Molstad Photography after the service. All proceeds will go to the church annex fund, minus Mr. Molstad's processing costs, of course." He continued to look at them expectantly, finally urging them forward with an impatient wave.

"I guess we better go up," Edie said.

Sam looked at her, unsure. "Is this what people normally do?"

"I guess so," Edie whispered. Her smile was very tense. "People are looking at us."

They shuffled out of the pew and walked to the front, where the entire congregation watched them in silent consternation as if they were Lake Lutherans or something. Arne unabashedly peered into the casket, his hands on the lacquered trim. Edie scooted him away before he had time to make inappropriate comments. She didn't look at her uncle carefully except to notice he seemed rather flat. They then turned to face the camera, Sam and Edie standing next to Arne in front.

"Smile," Mr. Molstad commanded them, even though he himself wasn't smiling. A flashbulb went off and then another, and they tottered back to their pew under the collective scorn of regular Lutherans.

The minister rose and led them in an opening prayer, during which Edie prayed for God to forgive Arne and Sam for anything they might do to embarrass her during the funeral. A low hiss of whispered conversation interrupted her chat with the Lord. The disturbance came from Sam and a woman seated next to him, a beautiful blonde about Edie's age. She wore a black two-piece skirt set purchased specifically for funerals. Her hair was pulled back from her smooth face by a black scarf, revealing a little upturned nose and high cheekbones. To Edie, she seemed like a European actress playing the role of someone attending a funeral in Fornborg, Minnesota.

Edie heard her ask how they knew the deceased, no doubt trying to determine if they were Lake Lutherans. Sam explained to her that the woman next to him was the man's niece.

That's what he said: *the woman next to me.* Not 'my wife.' Not 'the mother of my child.' Not 'my partner through thick and thin, 'til death do us part, amen.' No, 'the woman next to me.'

Sam was thick even on the best of days, but his drop-dead gorgeous pew mate had him behaving like more of an idiot than usual. To be fair, the woman was beautiful enough to make most men behave as foolishly as Sam, but she was way out of his league. Besides, the man next to her, probably her husband, was very handsome. Late twenties, maybe thirty, with a sweep of thick white-blonde hair combed to one side. His light-colored mustache, neatly trimmed, matched his hair. Sort of Robert Redford-y, but more rugged. He seemed amused with Sam's awkward attention, like how Sam explained how he'd driven "the woman next to him" up from Minneapolis.

Edie was about to pinch her husband's hand to return him to an attitude of prayer when something the woman said made her lean in, curious.

"I can't believe his own son wouldn't turn up," the knock-out whispered. She smelled like Cristalle by Chanel, a perfume that Edie had sniffed once at the Dayton's makeup counter in downtown Minneapolis. It was citrusy, like lemon and bergamot, with an almost foresty undertone. And it was expensive: Edie had almost fainted when the woman working the makeup counter had told her the price.

"Is that right?" Sam acted like he was interested in the family dynamic. He wasn't. He barely paid attention to his own little family unless it was holding the plate of mashed potatoes for him.

"Of course, you probably know how both of his children hadn't spoken to him for years."

"Yes, that's right. He must have been a real ass—" Sam was about to swear in church, and Edie knew it, but he caught himself. "...difficult person to live with."

This wasn't true. Nat's ex-wife, Gloria, got caught in an affair and ran off with the kids when they were still small. That happened the winter after Edie had last seen him. Thanks to ample photographic evidence provided by a private investigator, Uncle Nat didn't have to pay alimony.

"I can't imagine he was *too* difficult," the woman said. "Although we barely knew Mr. Lachmann and had only a neighborly acquaintance with him," she said, but Edie wondered why her eyes were damp with tears. "We live to the north of his, uh, commune."

"Commune?"

"Well, that's what it's turned into," the Robert Redford-y husband chimed in. "It's like Woodstock over there."

Arne's attention picked up at this revelation, and Edie had to calm him down, telling him it wasn't the Woodstock from the Snoopy cartoons. He poked at her, begging for a mint. She gave in, rummaging through her little tan purse that had seen better days. Her husband and the blonde bombshell may not have any sense of decorum, but at least she could block her son's talking hole for a few minutes with a Certs.

The prayer ended, and the congregation rose to sing "Nearer My God To Thee," rendering conversation impossible as there seemed to be a competition as to which key the hymn should be sung in. Edie sang louder than usual, just to help drown out further conversation. As the hymn came to a close, Edie yanked Sam's hand, forcing him to bend his ear to her mouth.

"Please don't talk during the service."

Sam whispered back. "Did you hear that? Your uncle turned the resort into a hippie commune, according to Vicki."

"Vicki?"

"Yeah, with an 'i'."

Edie had missed more of the conversation than she realized. How long had that first prayer been?

Arne was swinging his feet, the bottoms of his shoes catching against the pew in front of him. He dragged them down the polished wood, making a disturbing squeaking with the rubber soles. She slapped Arne's legs and told him to sit still, with one part irritation for the noise he made and one part mortification that her son was wearing his red, blue, and white gym shoes. The toe tip of the left one said HOME, and the toe tip of the other said RUN, but at least they fit.

The minister nodded to a young woman in the far corner of the first row, half-hidden by a green felt banner with a gold cross overrun with bunches of purple grapes. She rose, her long raven hair spilling over her azure calico-patterned peasant dress. She turned to the congregation, smiling sadly, and spoke in a quiet voice.

"Hi, I'm Avi. Some of you know me..." she began, but the minister urged her to step into the pulpit where she could speak into the microphone.

The woman was barefoot. One of those earth children you read about in *Time* or saw lampooned on sit-coms. Wasn't the hippie movement over after Nixon blew away?

"Hi, I'm Avi," the young woman began again. "Some you know me from when you've chased me out of your stores."

Several heads bobbed in recognition.

"Papa Lock. That's what we called the man you knew as Nathaniel Lachmann."

Her voice was calm, and she looked out at the congregation without fear. Edie would have been shaky and tentative, stumbling and clearing her throat. She hated speaking in front of people and always had since the time she misspelled *sexagenarian* in the fifth-grade spelling bee.

"To us, those of us who shared his life, he was like a father. A brother. He was family."

Edie practically spat. Family is family, and friends are friends. You like your friends. With family, you don't have to like them (or love them, even), but you can't escape them, like mud after a rain.

From the pew crowded by the purple banner, a long-haired man in a sleeveless olive-green vest and a red kerchief for a headband hollered, "Right on!"

"He opened his life to us, and we are better people for his generosity and his wisdom. He left us here on the physical plane too soon, and yet he remains a part of us even as he has become one with the cosmic plane."

Shouldn't the minister put an end to this? Where was the mention of Jesus and Heaven? The word cosmic certainly couldn't appear in the Lutheran dictionary.

The hippie woman ended her eulogy by placing her hand over her heart and wishing them all Love and Light, whatever that meant.

The young man in the sleeveless vest clapped, triggering silent, shocked outrage from the real Lutherans.

As quickly as he could, the minister regained the pulpit and led another prayer. Edie shot a warning glance at Sam just as he turned his head toward Vicki with an 'i' to renew their conversation. She was about to pinch him again when the entrance door to the sanctuary thudded open with a kick. Mr. Dugrave, the mortician, who had continued to stand guard, reeled backwards from the force.

A red-haired man wearing a tight-fitting collared silk shirt and flared canvas pants paused for a moment, surveying the crowd of mourners. A familiar form writhed in the air, desperately trying to escape.

It was their snake.

"Take this, Dad!" The man charged down the aisle with all the ferocity of a cavalry charge.

"That must be my cousin, Jeffy," Edie hissed, shocked at the sight of a long snake tail dangling in the air very close to the heads of Lutherans in their pews.

Sam nodded, satisfied. "At least now we know who stole the middle seat from the station wagon."

"Hey! That's *my* snake!" Arne jumped out of his seat at the end of the pew and ran after the man, barely escaping Edie's reaching fingertips. Sam jumped up, too, pushing past Edie's bare knees with brute force as he chased after the two of them. The man hurled the snake in the coffin, and with a thud, it struck Uncle Nat's body, such as it was, barely stitched together, like a baseball made by Soviet prisoners in a gulag.

Quick as he could, Sam gripped Arne's shoulder to hold him back, and then he slammed the coffin lid. An outburst of appalled chatter erupted. Men rose halfway from their seats in case the minister gave the order for them to attack.

"It's okay," Sam announced. "It's okay, everybody. Just don't open that lid again."

Maybe overcome by the weight of what he had done, cousin Jeffy tried to shoulder past Sam and open the lid, but Sam wrestled him away; they tumbled into the first row of pews, scattering an enclave of well-dressed men who looked like the cover models for *Chamber of Commerce Monthly*.

"That's my dad!" The distressed man flailed his arms, tears now replacing anger in his eyes. "I want to see him again!"

"Too bad," Sam replied, finally gripping Jeffy in a tight bearhug around the midsection. "You shouldn't have brought a poisonous rattlesnake in here, then."

Jeffy's eyes bulged, and his cheeks were red from the lack of oxygen.

"We. Don't. Have. Rattle. Snakes. This. Far. North," he managed to gasp.

"You do when they're driven here from further south."

Then Arne tried to lift the coffin lid, but by this time, the minister had decided he'd better try to establish order and get the ceremony on track. He held Arne back by the ears while Sam waited for Jeffy to submit or pass out.

"So, you're cousin Jeffy?" Sam asked him casually.

Cousin Jeffy went limp, either from lack of oxygen or a hint of recognition.

"Oh. So you're Edie's husband?"

"Yeah. You stole our car seat," Sam said, renewing the pressure of the bearhug.

"I didn't know it was yours. Is that Edie back there?" Cousin Jeffy waved at Edie even as Sam lifted him up and down like a sack of potatoes. "Hi, Edie!" He waved limply as Sam spun him in mid-air. "Thanks for coming, everybody!"

Meanwhile, Arne broke free of the minister's hold by kicking him in the shin, causing the man to invoke the Lord's name out of a religious context, which further stunned the congregation. Arne and his home run gym shoes ran down the aisle, and Edie saw he must have stepped in dog crap on the way in. There was a trail of stains leading out the door.

"Where's our car seat, Jeffy?" Sam demanded.

Edie put her hands over her face to block out the chaos. She wondered: Is it wrong to wish you were the dead one at a funeral?

Chapter 11

No Offense

YOU HEAR PEOPLE SAY, *I could have died from embarrassment.*

To say that Edie had been embarrassed was an understatement. There is a specific word for extreme embarrassment experienced at funerals: mortified. She was mortified. Her brain short-circuited. It was like her spirit had left her body and floated far, far away. The clamor of her immediate environment faded, and she was standing on a dock—her uncle's dock—and she was her nine-year-old self again. Uncle Nat sat cross-legged in front of her, pretending to pour tea. He wore the pink feather boa, just like she remembered. The lake: well, she couldn't see across it. It was too misty. Everything was misty, then even her uncle disappeared in the pearly white light. His voice came to her one last time, drifting from far away.

Gophers, he said.

Then Edie was back in her body, hunched over in the pew. Vicki with an 'i', the beautiful blonde, came to Edie's rescue, hustling her out of the sanctuary and into the fresh air, murmuring encouraging words the entire way: *There you go. Just a little further. Watch out for the dog doo.*

Edie regained her footing and pulled away from Vicki.

"Thank you. I'm better now." Only she wasn't. She was craving a cigarette, and if she'd seen a discarded butt laying on the ground, she would have smoked it, and if a groundskeeper or a hobo would have tried to get in her way, well, she would have resorted to violence to get it.

"I thought we were going to lose you in there," Vicki said. "I'm Vicki Svensson." She held out her hand and Edie took it.

"Edie Fisker."

"Well, Edie Fisker, I have to tell you, that was the most exciting funeral I've ever attended."

Edie covered her eyes as the images of what just happened flooded back into her consciousness. She wept.

"Oh, it's alright." Vicki embraced her. She smelled nice. "It wasn't so bad. I was just teasing."

"Which funeral were you at?"

"Okay, it was pretty bad," Vicki allowed.

Edie wondered if her secret emergency cigarette was still in the bottom of her purse. She could really use a little Dignity right now. Edie stopped rummaging through her purse when she realized that Arne and Sam were still in the church. So much more could go wrong. Her eyes widened.

"Oh, my God. I've got to get back in there and stop them."

"Don't worry." Vicki stopped her from bolting off. "My husband and some of the other men stepped in. My Toby works for the Department of Natural Resources." She said it as if the State of Minnesota trained DNR employees in special weapons and tactics. "They've got it under control." Vicki brushed a loose strand of Edie's chestnut hair away from her face, gazing intently at her ear. "Was that your son in there?"

"Based on what just happened, I shouldn't admit it. But, yes." Edie released a deep sigh of relief as she found her cigarette wrapped in a tissue. She lit it with a match, watching Vicki's nose crinkle in disdain as the smoke curled from the tip.

"He certainly has big ears."

Edie scowled, took a deep, meditative drag. Now wasn't the time to heap insults on injuries.

"We're hoping he grows into them."

"It's just so interesting. Neither you nor Sam have abnormal ears."

She called him *Sam* like they already were old friends. And she'd already had a good look at Sam's ears when they flirted during the funeral.

"It must skip a generation, like manners," Edie said pointedly, shrugging off Vicki's hand from her shoulder.

"Oh, I'm sorry. I wasn't thinking. Of course, you'd be sensitive about it. The poor boy must have such a difficult time with the other children. Kids can be so cruel."

"Yeah, kids." Edie's eyes smoldered with anger.

Vicki laughed. "You see what I did there?"

"Yeah, I saw."

"No, I mean, now you're angry with me, right? You probably want to sock me in the nose."

"Now that you mention it..."

"But now you're not embarrassed about the funeral. You see? We transferred your emotions from the chaos in the church onto me. Like a scapegoat. I was just the conduit who gave you a channel for emotional release."

"Oh, God. Are you a shrink on top of being gorgeous?"

"Heavens, no. I've got a subscription to *Ms.* magazine."

It was Edie's luck to be stuck in a small town in northern Minnesota, surrounded by hippies, radical feminists, and dog poo.

"I've learned so many useful psychological tips in there. But I take my recipes from *Woman's Day*."

The ice melted from Edie's heart.

"Me too." She broke down, sobbing about the taco hotdish debacle and how her life was turning into one long funeral.

People began trickling out of the church, the minister first. He set up shop on the top step so he could shake hands with everyone as they passed by.

"Looks like the ref must have called it," Vicki quipped. "Are you ready to see people? Or should we go to your car and freshen your makeup?"

Edie, who wasn't wearing any makeup, decided that meant she wasn't ready to see people. Vicki's husband waved to them, and Vicki called back, "I'll just be a few minutes with Missus..."

"Fisker," Edie finished.

"Mrs. Fisker." To Edie, she said, "That's my Toby."

"He's good-looking, too. You both should be in the movies."

"That's very kind, although, to be honest, I don't particularly go for how the movies portray modern women. We're either sex objects or heartless career women who also are sex objects."

"Amen," Edie agreed. She asked Vicki about the man in the Hawaiian shirt.

"What is he doing here? And why is he wearing open-toed shoes before Memorial Day?"

"That's the town plumber. I suppose he's here on behalf of the local men's club. We call them the Norwegian Pontoon Mafia because they're crooked and try to run everything on the chain of lakes." Vicki let a hiss escape as she looked at John Kvalstad and his shaggy hair and saggy shorts. "Those Norwegians are so stubborn and so dumb."

"I'm half Norwegian," Edie warned.

"Oh, no offense."

"And Sam is full-blooded."

"Oh, I'm so sorry," she said before adding hurriedly, "You really can't tell."

But whether Vicki was sorry about the Norwegian blood coursing through the Fisker veins or whether she was sorry she had disparaged Norwegians, in general, wasn't clear.

"What's your other half?"

"German."

"Well, that's good," Vicki said enthusiastically. "Not that it matters, really. We're all humans, right?"

Edie said she couldn't argue with that, Martin Luther King and all.

"And we can at least be thankful we're not Polish," Vicki concluded, which made Edie wonder if Vicki might have skipped the articles in *Ms.* magazine that addressed racial bigotry.

A man in a light blue suit walked toward them and called out to them.

"Are you Mrs. Edie Fisker?"

"Yes." Edie hesitated, searching Vicki's face for guidance.

"That's Phillip Logner," Vicki explained. "He's a lawyer. Be careful what you say to him. He's one of them."

Edie didn't know who *them* were. Lawyers? Men in powder-blue suits with white socks and black shoes? Men with comb-overs and red whiskey noses? In the meantime, Vicki had returned inside the church.

The man with the Hawaiian shirt and dog tags whistled to attract the lawyer's attention, and the lawyer veered from his course to confer with him. They both looked over to where Edie and Vicki stood, making Edie supremely aware she was slouching, just like her mother always said she did. She straightened herself: after all, she had a Dignity.

"They run this town," Vicki muttered. "It's an outrage."

"Those two men run the town? A lawyer and a plumber?"

Vicki nodded her head.

"Norwegians." Her lips twisted around the word like she chewed a curse.

The two men broke off their conversation, and Phillip Logner gripped the other man's shoulder. Edie just barely heard him say, "Not to worry. I'll take care of it."

"I've got to go," Vicki hissed before returning swiftly to the church.

The lawyer came up to Edie with his hand extended like a man running for political office.

"Are you Mrs. Edie Fisker, niece of Nathan Lachmann?"

"Yes, that's me," she answered, wondering if she should have her own attorney present for this sort of thing. She shook hands with him.

"I'm Phillip Logner. First of all, my condolences for your loss. Mr. Lachmann certainly was one of a kind."

"Thank you," Edie replied. It's just something people said, *my condolences,* and then you said *thank you,* and you didn't say the truth, that you hardly knew the man and hadn't spoken to him since a time when you were still afraid of the monster in your closet.

"I'm overseeing the execution of your uncle's will and the disposition of his estate. Your mother mentioned you would be here to represent the family."

"She did, did she? When did you last speak with her, out of curiosity?"

"Oh, beginning of the week, I suppose."

That sounded about right. Her mother had known all about the reading of the will, and that's why she wanted Edie to turn up in Fornborg. Not to represent the family like she'd claimed on the phone. Uncle Nat probably left her boxes of books or bowling trophies or other heavy objects that needed to be delivered, and it would be up to Edie to haul them back to Minneapolis and figure out how to ship them to Phoenix.

"And that is just so convenient that you're here in Fornborg in person," Mr. Logner continued. "Otherwise, I would have needed to track down your address and gone through certified mail. Why, the entire process could have been delayed for weeks. But now that you're here, might you have some time after the service for the reading of Mr. Lachmann's will?"

She said she'd have to check with her husband, and Mr. Logner gave her his card with the address on the front.

"Can't miss it. It's right under the water tower. The reading will be at three this afternoon."

Seeing Sam and Arne each still in one piece was a relief. Sam shook cousin Jeffy's hand at the base of the stairs.

"No hard feelings, I hope."

"None." He clapped Sam's shoulders. "I was way out of line, what with the snake and all."

"A little." Sam laughed. "It was a funeral for your dad, after all."

"Couldn't have happened to a nicer guy," Jeffy said.

"Sam," Edie called. "Ask him about getting back the car seat."

Chapter 12

Last Will and Pestilence

A QUARTER TO THREE o'clock, an older woman led Edie and Sam into Mr. Logner's cramped office. The chain around her neck, attached to her eyeglasses, clattered as she walked. She directed them to sit wherever they liked, except for the comfortable swivel chair behind the desk.

"That's where Mr. Logner sits," she explained.

This left them their choice of metal folding chairs crammed in a row. Sam's knees pressed hard against the back of the desk.

Happily, they'd convinced Arne that if he stayed at the hotel (and didn't break anything and didn't go wandering off and didn't take swimming accessories that didn't belong to him again), then they'd let him have a try on the Magic Fingers later—twice.

"Do you really think he'll stay put?" Edie asked.

"At this point, I don't care if he gets shanghaied by pirates."

Mr. Logner appeared from a side door that swung inwards, opening only wide enough to allow him to enter sideways. A stack of banker's boxes full of legal documents blocked it from opening fully.

"First to arrive. Good." He sidled past them, sucking in his gut so as not to knock them over with it. "We'll just wait for the others to arrive before we get started."

Edie had assumed she and Sam would be the only attendees, but her assumption evaporated when cousin Jeffy entered with a stocky red-haired woman, possibly Edie's cousin, Lana, only older and much *sturdier* than the younger version Edie remembered. She wore a man's work shirt, the kind you might see at a mechanic's shop like where Sam worked, only the sleeves on her shirt had been cut off.

A look of surprise crossed all their faces. Jeffy masked the awkwardness by introducing Sam to Lana. Edie would never have guessed that these were the same two cousins she had splashed around with in Little Paw Lake. The intervening years were like mismatched socks: unkind.

Lana said to Edie, "I haven't seen you since you were about ten."

"Well, you've certainly filled out since then." Edie couldn't believe she said it out loud. She could claim possession by her mother's sharp-tongued ghost, but her mother wasn't dead. Yet. Maybe Edie was just turning into a w-i-t-c-h. She tried to bury her faux pas with more inane small talk. "Were you at the funeral? I didn't see you."

Lana shook her head. "I wouldn't get caught dead anywhere near that man."

There apparently was a lot more going on between Uncle Nat and his children than she realized, but pursuing the topic while waiting for the will to be read just didn't feel appropriate. Mr. Logner's secretary announced another arrival.

"Mrs. Svensson phoned from the corner. She's on her way up."

Edie and her cousins looked at each other questioningly, none of them knowing any Mrs. Svensson.

"That's fine," Mr. Logner told her. "We're still waiting for one more, anyway."

One more? They hardly had room enough for the four of them on the folding chairs as it was.

A light tap came on the door, and it pushed open to reveal the young raven-haired young woman who spoke at the funeral before all hell broke loose.

"Ah, Miss Starshine. Please, come in."

She was still barefoot, and whether it was the sight of her naked feet or just her overall hippie-ish appearance, the four other attendees stiffened noticeably. It was one thing to see hippies on the television; it was quite another to have to share the small amount of oxygen remaining in the room.

"Hello, all." She smiled at them, fully aware of their discomfort but choosing to ignore it. Edie remembered her first name was Avi: Avi Starshine. That wasn't a real name unless she's a Cherokee princess or something. She settled in right next to Edie, who drew her elbows tight to her body as if she were in a room full of lepers smeared with a plague virus.

Had she and the other commune members brainwashed poor Uncle Nat into squandering his fortune? You heard about hippie cults. Like the Manson family or the Symbionese Liberation Army. They could make people do crazy things.

A flurry of pleasant chatter in the outer room suggested that the mysterious Mrs. Svensson had arrived, but when she walked through the door, Edie couldn't help but gasp. Mrs. Svensson was Vicki with an 'i'.

"Hi, Vicki." Sam waved at her like an idiot. Edie backhanded him across the chest.

Holding a large manila envelope in both hands, Mr. Logner leaned in toward the people sardined together in front of him. Canceled postage stamps, worn corners, grape jelly, and/or bloodstains suggested the envelope had gone through the mail.

"Mr. Lachmann provided me with each of your names, except for Mr. Fisker, whose name I do not have listed." He smiled at Sam for an uncomfortably long time. Sam smiled back, shifting uncomfortably in his seat.

"I guess I could leave," he offered, but Edie's grip kept him from rising from his folding chair.

"Just the same," Edie batted her eyes, pretending to be dumb, "I'd like my husband to stay, so he can explain all the big words to me."

"Would anyone else care to object to Mr. Fisker's presence?"

Mr. Logner looked hopefully at Vicki, Jeffy, and Lana, but they registered no complaint. He pointedly did not look at Avi Starshine.

"Fine. We'll continue with the reading of Mr. Lachmann's will, which I received only after his unfortunate accident." He flipped the envelope to show them it was still sealed. He opened his top desk drawer and removed a bronze letter opener. The globed handle was painted with the old red, blue, and white of the Norwegian flag. He lifted the envelope flap and removed a half dozen typed pages, dropping the envelope into the wastebasket. He peered down his nose at the paper in front of him, squinting and then tipping the pages to read them.

"There's the usual language here. Sound mind, and all of that."

"Ha!" Jeffy countered.

"Now, first, we have a summary of Mr. Lachmann's assets: there is a house on six acres of land with approximately thirteen hundred linear feet of lakeshore on Little Paw Lake. The property includes four cabins and was previously operated as a commercial resort by Mr. Lachmann's parents, both of whom are deceased. The property includes all furnishings, other than items belonging to current, ahem, *guests*. One 1969 Ford F100 Ranger truck, complete with title. One 1958 thirty-five horsepower Evinrude Lark outboard." Here Mr. Logner lowered the paper and looked pointedly at Edie. "That's a boat motor, ladies."

Edie's face flushed red. Why did men always assume that women were idiots? And follow-up question: how far away she was from a pack of Dignity cigarettes?

"One United States Series E treasury bond in the amount of two hundred dollars," Mr. Logner continued, "one decorative glass tube vase, whatever that is."

Here, Avi Starshine chuckled, causing Mr. Logner to cast a stern glance at her.

"That's a bong, man," she said, and the lawyer shrugged, not knowing what either a decorative glass tube vase or a bong was.

"And finally, cash on hand totaling sixteen dollars and thirty-seven cents. Before we move ahead to the discussion of distribution, are there any questions? No? Mrs. Fisker?"

Edie slouched again, shaking her head. "No, I'm ready."

"To Miss Avi Starshine." Logner peered over his spectacles at Avi, adding, "No fixed address. Mr. Lachmann hereby bequeaths one Ford truck and one decorative glass tube vase."

Avi laughed but covered her mouth as tears welled up in her eyes. "I dig it, Papa Lock," she said, addressing the ceiling. "Blessings, man."

"To Mr. Lachmann's children, Jeffrey Tobias Lachmann and Lana Tabitha Lachmann, goes the entire amount of cash, to be divided equally among them."

Cousin Jeffy bolted upright, sending his metal chair skittering against the wall behind him.

"What the heck?"

"Please sit down, Mr. Lachmann. Or leave."

He sat down, turning to his sister, who glowered at the lawyer as if he were personally responsible.

"Is that all he left us? Sixteen bucks?"

"And thirty-seven cents," the lawyer added.

"Is he giving us the resort?" Jeffy pounded the tops of his legs. "Just tell us."

His sister Lana backhanded him across the chest with the elegance of a railroad crossing arm, easily knocking the air out of him. "It's

Dad's will, not a Sears catalog. You don't get to order what you want here."

Mr. Logner raised two fingers in a gesture that urged patience.

"To Mrs. Edie Marie Fisker, née Schmidt, Mr. Lachmann bequeathed the real estate property, all furnishings therein, and the boat and motor."

"Son of a..." Jeffy jumped up again, and that was enough for Sam. He twisted Jeffy into a headlock once again, and the two men wrestled, jostling against the women on either side of them. Lana gripped Edie's arm.

"I need to talk to you after this," she said in her husky voice. Edie nodded as Mr. Logner continued, raising his voice to be heard over the melee.

"And finally, to Mrs. Vicki Svensson goes the two-hundred-dollar savings bond. This concludes the reading of Mr. Lachmann's last will and testament."

After kicking her cousin Jeffy in the shin so he'd stop fighting, Edie looked quizzically at Vicki Svensson. Vicki's sculpted lips opened and closed like a fish contemplating a spinnerbait. She turned to face Edie.

"I had no idea," she concluded. "Honestly."

Soon Logner's office turned into a parade of three confused people, two angry ones, and one smiling, contented barefoot hippie, all ushered out by Mr. Logner himself. He closed the door behind them and turned to his secretary. His benign expression changed quickly to distress.

"Get me Bud Langskip on the phone right away."

❦❧ — ◆ — ☙❧

Once outside, Cousin Lana shooed her brother away with some very salty language, the kind you'd expect to hear from a longshoreman. Edie told Sam to give her a few minutes as Lana led her around the corner of the building and lit a cigarette. She offered Edie one from the pack of Kents.

"I'm trying to quit," Edie admitted. Lana was about to return the pack to her shirt pocket when Edie added quickly, "So I can only have one. Thanks."

Kents were fine, but they weren't Dignity, that's for sure. She might get a headache after just one of them, but her nerves were steadying.

"Look, I don't want any trouble, Edie."

Edie, who initially hadn't been expecting any trouble, now was expecting trouble.

"But?" Edie encouraged.

"But you need to do what's right."

"Which is?"

"The only thing that makes sense. Sell that dump and split the money with Jeffy and me."

"You know, that's kind of what I was thinking," Edie replied. She told her cousin how all of this came out of the blue, and she just didn't feel right getting in the way.

"I'm glad you feel that way. I didn't want any problems about this." Lana stubbed out her cigarette under a heavy leather boot. "Me? I don't care about the money, but it's only fair after how that man broke up the family and ruined my childhood."

Lana delivered a thumbnail sketch of her life after her parents split up. How her mom had to work two jobs to make ends meet. How she'd married a man twice her age just to regain stability for Lana and Jeffy. How their new stepfather made them work at the quarry to make ends meet.

"It was hard," Lana said. "But I'm glad it happened in the long run. I learned a lot. Now I'll probably inherit the business when the new old man kicks off because, as you can tell, Jeffy is pretty worthless at everything."

Edie wondered why Lana hadn't mentioned her mother's affairs. Maybe she didn't know. Maybe Gloria had controlled the story so well that her kids thought she was a saint. Well, Edie wasn't about to tarnish that halo.

"I suppose everything works out in the end, doesn't it?" Edie said optimistically. She didn't really believe that, but it was the sort of thing people were supposed to say when you didn't know what else to say.

"Yeah," Lana grunted. "We all die alone."

⋘ ⋅ ◆ ⋅ ⋙

They climbed back in the car, Edie asked Sam, "What's a bong?"

It had puzzled her. She could guess it looked like a glass vase, but apparently, it wasn't quite a vase at all.

"I'll tell you when you're older," Sam laughed. "Do you need me to explain any of the other big words?" He chuckled, pleased with the outcome.

"Why would he leave me the property? Why not his own children? I hadn't seen the man for years."

"Maybe because Jeffy is a knucklehead." Sam craned his head, peering at the blank area behind them. "Speaking of which, we've got to get our seat back from that maniac. Hey, let's pick up the kiddo and head out to see this resort of ours."

"It's mine."

Sam, who had just started pulling out of the parking spot, hit the brakes. The car squeaked to a sudden stop.

"What's that now?"

"The property is mine. You weren't even invited to the reading, remember?"

"Well, I mean, we're married," Sam said slowly. "What's mine is yours and the other way round."

Her mother's voice came to mind, like a chill breeze, *You could always leave him.*

"Not this time. This time I get a say. We've got our life in the city. You've got a job you like. Let's not screw that up."

Sam grew sullen, which he did whenever he didn't get his way. He'd passed on that little genetic trait to Arne. Must be the Norwegian in them, as Sam was full-blooded—another little fact he failed to mention prior to their getting married. She might have thought twice about yoking up with him if she'd known. Shouldn't there be some kind of marriage disclosure law? Or even one last check by the minister at the altar: *And Samuel Knut Fisker, have you now, or have you ever been, a member of the Norwegian-Americans?*

Ah, but what use would it have been? She'd been in love, or whatever passed for love when you're seventeen. He'd charmed her socks off and a whole lot more. She would have married him even if he'd shown up at the wedding wearing nothing but the Norwegian flag. Besides, Edie was half Norwegian, it's true; but at least Nature had enough good sense to give Edie a half ration of German blood through her father to help counteract the *Norwegianitis* that crippled common sense on her mother's side and in her husband.

Sam once chased a squirrel down Theodore Wirth Parkway because he wanted his peanut back.

They drove in silence back toward the Lakeview Lodge.

"I suppose it wouldn't hurt to just look at the…" Edie almost said *commune*, but the word hurt her mouth, and she corrected it to *resort*.

"That's the spirit." Just like that, Sam was his usual charming self.

They were only a few blocks away when Sam cranked the steering wheel hard to the right, taking a sharp turn down an alley between Lulu's Cafe and the Fornborg post office. The movement sent Edie sliding into Sam's shoulder.

"What the hell are you doing?"

He alternated his view from the rearview mirror to the narrow path ahead of him.

"Sorry about that. We're being tailed."

She looked back to see a white service truck nose into the alley and brake hard, backing out slowly. She recognized the truck as belonging to that strange man in the Hawaiian shirt who'd parked in front of the funeral.

"You think we're being followed by a plumber?"

"Well, not anymore, thanks to me and James Rockford."

The Rockford Files was one of Sam's favorite television shows. Nine o'clock on Friday nights, he turned the channel to NBC, right in the middle of *Six Million Dollar Man*. "Sorry, Arne," he'd say. "Time for my driving lesson." Now anytime he jerked the steering wheel in an alarming manner, he chalked it up to that fictional private investigator.

"Looks like we lost him."

"Great, maybe you can outrun the postman or the milk truck next."

Still, it definitely *was* the same service truck. She recognized the palm tree logo on the side. Aloha Plumbing. There couldn't be many of those in northern Minnesota. Why would a Hawaiian-themed plumbing company tail them or stand guard at her uncle's funeral—or, for that matter, have a private conversation with the lawyer who was about to divvy up her uncle's estate?

As they pulled into the parking lot of the motel, any prospect of visiting the resort that day fled their thoughts. Two fire trucks, billowing smoke, and their son's earlobe being gripped tightly by a seething hotel manager awaited them like the front-page news photo of some horrible tragedy.

"Let's just keep driving," Edie suggested. "What do you say?"

"I guess we better see what this is all about," Sam replied. "But be ready to run like hell, just in case."

That was some good Norwegian thinking right there.

The sheriff's deputy served as a translator between the motel manager, fire chief, and the Fiskers.

"That your boy?" The deputy pointed to Arne who wriggled like a fly on a spider web.

"Depends on what he did," Sam answered. "Can you get that man to let go of my son before I pop him one?"

"Some ears on him," the deputy said. "Big enough to match his mouth." Apparently, carrying a gun the size of the one in *Death Wish* gave a person a license to be rude, but the deputy convinced the manager to remand custody of Arne's big ears to his parents. Arne beelined to his mother, his face red from crying and having a meltdown. She hugged her to him, even though he was sooty and smelled like Smokey the Bear's worst nightmare.

"From what I gather, you left this boy alone in a motel room for quite some time."

"It was only an hour or so," Edie said sharply. Was he accusing them of being bad parents?

"It seems the boy had no coins, and he figured out how to hot-wire the Magic Fingers vibrating bed, but the wires sparked and caught the room on fire."

"And now you owe me for the damages to that room!" Dale, the motel manager, yelled, being held back by the deputy's meaty hand. "Cash only. I'm not taking a check from you city people."

Sam assured him they'd make things right, but that was the kind of thing he always said to end difficult conversations. The deputy took their information and confirmed Sam's identity with his driver's license. The manager agreed not to press charges, so long as they paid for the destroyed furnishings, including the Magic Fingers and a thorough renovation.

"You can't just paint over smoke damage, you know," Dale grumbled.

"Absolutely," Sam nodded along. The truth was they were about out of cash—not just on their persons, but in their checking account too. They wouldn't have enough money to fill the wagon for the ride home. If Edie looked in her purse right then, she wouldn't have more than a few nickels and absolutely no Dignities.

"You outta whoop that boy," the manager added indignantly. "Whoop him with the buckle end of a belt."

Sam winced. Edie knew he was thinking of his own father, who had done that very thing to his own children.

"Absolutely," Sam repeated, gritting his teeth. "Whoop him, sure."

"And it goes without saying you're not allowed back to the Lakeview Lodge for eternity."

"Well, we wouldn't want to stay in a firetrap like this anyway." Sam puffed out his chest. He'd reached his limit for the day. "What?

Is this place made out of wooden matches and kindling?" To Edie, he added, "For cripes sake, a little fire in a dumpy motel room, and they make a federal case out of it. You'd think he tried to assassinate the president or something."

The deputy set a hand on the gun poking out of his holster. "He didn't try, did he?"

"Of course not! I don't think he even knows who the president is."

"More importantly," Edie interjected, "he's an eleven-year-old boy who doesn't assassinate people."

The deputy shrugged. "I hear that a lot."

The fire department had graciously hauled out all their belongings from the smoldering room and heaped them on the curb. Even more graciously, they had laid out all of Edie's under-delicates on top, exposed to the fresh air and view of the other motor lodge guests. She balled them up and shoved them in the suitcase, relieved to find Arne's little blue suit intact: sooty, but otherwise unharmed. A small blessing.

"Well, folks." Sam turned to Arne and Edie, sounding as cheerful as he could. "Looks like we're car camping tonight."

Chapter 13

On the Hook

OF THE MEN IN northern Minnesota, only a small percentage owned a Hawaiian shirt. John Kvalstad owned sixteen of them. Each one had a different tropical pattern and told a different story. They kept John's heart warm all year long. Wintering in Hawaii kept his heart warm too. Wearing his favorite shirt, the red one with the white palm trees, he pulled into Bud Langskip's driveway. He got out of the Aloha Plumbing truck and straightened the shirt so it hung evenly from his shoulders. Bud didn't like how John dressed but, even worse, Bud didn't like bad news.

Today, John was the bearer of bad news.

He knocked on the front door, which was solid oak and thick enough that he doubted the sound of his knuckles would reach anyone inside, so he used the doorbell. A young girl, about ten, answered. Bud's granddaughter. She eyed him suspiciously with her brown eyes. Curly brown ringlets flowed to her shoulders, springing from a cap that matched her traditional blue dress, which was overlaid with a white apron.

Have to be nice, John reminded himself.

"Hi Jemme," John smiled. "That sure is a pretty dress."

"It's called a *bunad*, dummy."

"That's right." John tried to maintain his aloha spirit. "Well, sweetie, I'm here to see your grandfather. Is he home?"

"And whom shall I say is calling?"

Whom. Boy, she really didn't like him. The feeling was mutual, but he kept smiling.

"Oh, you know who I am." He lowered his sunglasses. "It's me. Wahoo John."

"Granddad, that weird man from Hawaii is here for you."

She grimaced and shut the door.

John heard a muffled response, and the front door clicked open again.

"He's in his office," she said, letting him find his own way through the main room with its high ceilings and timbered rafters. The view of the lake was incredible, thanks to a series of thick-paned windows that comprised almost the entire western wall. The rough-hewn walls on either side boasted trophy fish mounted by a master taxidermist, interspersed between ancient swords, helmets, spears, and shields. John drank it all in. A museum would love to get its hands on that collection.

John moved slowly toward the corridor, dreading Bud's response to bad news. As the owner of Langskip Lures and the chieftain of the Sons of Gunnar, Bud expected everything—and everyone—to run smoothly. He rapped lightly before opening the door.

"Aloha, Chief" John said.

"What'd you learn?" Bud snapped without looking up at John.

"I learned that my truck doesn't take corners as well as a '71 Ford Country Squire station wagon." John decided too late that a light-hearted approach wouldn't work with Bud Langskip. Just the facts was a better approach. "I lost them just before the motel."

"John, they were driving a family car. With the family in it."

"I know, and it's my fault. I think they spotted me."

"Maybe it was that shirt," Bud sniped.

"Well, they didn't see *me*, but they must have recognized my truck."

Bud sighed. "Okay. What else can you tell me? They go out to the resort?"

"I don't think so." John shook his head. "Not yet anyway. Looked like they had their hands full with some kind of accident at the motor lodge."

"Good, that's something." Bud pushed away a stack of papers from in front of him and peered into John's face. "When they go there, I want you with them. Keep a close eye. Maybe be a little more discrete. Put on a normal shirt."

"Sure, Chief," John lied. He was never wearing a 'normal' shirt again. Five years in the Marines had been enough normal for him. From now on, John Kvalstad only wore shirts he loved.

Bud spun in his chair to face the lake. He flicked his wrist like he was casting a line into the water.

"You know why I love fishing, John?"

John knew better than to guess answers to Bud's questions. He'd learned over time that some of them were what college professors called *rhetorical*, which meant they didn't have answers. Sometimes the answers were self-evident. Sometimes the question-asker was just a jerk. John kept quiet.

"I love fishing because it makes me rich." He lifted a shiny spoon plug, unpainted, with two treble hooks dangling on either end. "This little doo-dad costs about a dime to make and another dime to advertise. You know how much I sell it for?"

Yes, John knew that too, because he'd heard this story before. But he still wouldn't answer.

"A buck twenty-five. Now, I'm not saying I'm a genius..."

"No, of course you're not," John agreed, shifting his weight from one flip-flop to the other.

"My father figured it all out, and I just picked up the ball and kept running with it. And soon, my boy, Lester, will take the ball from me and keep running."

Running and running and running. John wondered what the Langskip family was running toward, some imaginary goalpost in the mists of the future? He almost chuckled out loud at the thought of one of these bullheaded Langskips running headfirst into an actual goalpost, knocked unconscious at the finish line.

"So I guess I know a little bit about business, wouldn't you agree, John?"

"For sure, Mr. Langskip." John nodded, sensing it was time to kiss a little heinie. "Langskip Lures is a household name among fishermen, even in national fishing tournaments."

"So when I say I'm disappointed that Nat Lachmann didn't leave the resort property to the Sons of Gunnar, you know I'm not just blowing hot air, right? I mean, I am really disappointed. I'm talking about a deep, crushing hurt in my heart, like when the Vikings lost to the Dolphins in the Superbowl last year."

John heard the name *Tarkenton* spat out like a curse word after that game.

"Now Logner tells me that Nat's will threw us a curveball. And he would fix the documents for us. He could do it. Easiest thing in the world. Everyone knows that lying is all lawyers are good for, anyway, but apparently, his professional ethics are more important to him than loyalty to the club." Bud snapped a perfectly good pencil in two and tossed it in the waste can next to his desk. "I won't forget that."

"He's been a good man otherwise," John offered. He didn't like when Bud started thinking poorly of other members. Bud could get some strong ideas in his mind that translated into strong actions.

"Be that as it may," Bud continued, "we've just got to move forward from here. The fact is, we've got to deal with these people from the Cities..."

"The Fiskers."

"Right, the Fiskers. They're a wildcard. I don't want to play with wildcards. I only play straight cards. Nothing wild."

But he's okay with cheating with straight cards, John thought bitterly.

"I need your help, John." Bud rang a bell, and one of the other club members appeared with a manilla folder. The man was a knuckle-dragger called Rollo. He never said much, but when he did, it was usually too late. He worked for Bud, along with Petie Gjerstad, as a combination bodyguard and butler. Rollo handed John the folder and then left, closing the office door behind him.

"I'm promoting you to *forkvinne*," Bud explained, a little smile on his lips.

Being *forkvinne* was like being a project manager for the Sons of Gunnar. It meant John got a budget and could tap other members of the club for support. It meant Bud trusted him—even if he didn't like John's Hawaiian shirts. It gave John clout. It also put pressure on him to do the project well or be snapped in two like a pencil.

"Wow, I really appreciate it. Thanks, Chief."

"You know my boy Lester screwed up his shot as *forkvinne*. With your professional experience in the trades, you know how to get things done. You can set a good example for him and the others. Show them what determination and focus can do."

"Sure, just what exactly do you need me to do?"

"All the details are in the file. Basically, just do what you do best: plumbing. Get that resort unstuck. Get it back in play for the Sons of Gunnar."

John blinked. He wasn't sure that plumbing was, in fact, the thing he did best. He was a pretty strong waterskier too, and he was a generous lover. He'd even won some trophies (for the waterskiing), but no trophies for plumbing.

Sensing his hesitation, Bud raised his voice.

"You hear me, John? Remove the wildcard from the equation. Get me that resort."

It was a tall order, and John didn't know where to start.

"I will try, Mr. Langskip."

"Try is good but done is better. I want weekly reports, more if something important comes up. Otherwise, I don't want to see you here except at club meetings."

"Makes sense, Chief."

"And I don't suppose you'd get a haircut and dress in clothes befitting a Minnesotan? A man's style is his personality on display, and you look like a god-forsaken luau."

"No can do, Chief," John laughed.

"I thought I'd try." Bud's demeanor lightened. He fancied himself a man of the people, regardless of whether the people agreed. After playing tough guy, he always tried to make a soft landing, as if whatever hard feelings he'd created could be erased by a pat on the back as he shoved you out of his office.

"I've got my reasons, Chief." John wasn't about to elaborate on them with Bud, however. "I should remind you I leave for Hawaii again in October."

"You better get on the stick, then. Let's call this *Operation Last Resort*."

Bud Langskip spun around in his chair once again, fetched the shiny lure from his desk, and tossed it. John reflexively cupped his hands to catch it without getting the hooks caught in the soft flesh of his fingers. "Keep that as a reminder of this conversation. Either we're the baiters, or we're on the hook."

John backed out of the office, eyeing the lure like it was a time bomb of hooks.

And aloha to you, he added silently as he tucked the project folder under his shirt.

John paused one last time in the spacious living room to take one last look at the lake from inside. How was it possible that a lake could look so much better from inside a house than standing on the shore? He guessed it was something about the way it was framed by those big windows, how the trees on the shore swayed in a breeze unfelt in Bud Langskip's luxury lake home.

"You need to leave now," came the girl's voice, Jemme. She looked down at him from the lofted second floor. "I need to practice my song."

"Sure thing," John agreed. "Aloha."

"You mean *farvel*," she spat back. *Farvel* meant goodbye in Norwegian. And *rakkerunge* meant brat. Jemme was in the Little Shields, learning the Norwegian language and culture, and she was a holy terror.

"Yeah, *farvel*, kiddo."

John pulled the heavy front door shut behind him, closing himself off from the high life. As he stepped on the cobblestone path leading to his truck, a burgundy MG convertible, top down, pulled in the gravel drive with Lester Langskip at the wheel. It definitely wasn't the car you'd expect to see a family man driving around, but Lester Langskip drove what he wanted. His wife had her own car and a maid, so there was your women's liberation. The MG was his summer car. He had a Pontiac LeMans for winter driving. Kept in the heat better, so the whole liberated family could stay warm on the way to eat steak and walleye at the fancy Hawk Point Bistro.

"Hey, Wahoo." Lester waggled his fingers like a hula dancer. People called John 'Wahoo' because they were too lazy to say the extra syllable in Oahu, which is the island John preferred to spend his winters instead of freezing his tail off in Fornborg.

Lester was good-looking and well put together, with a sports coat slung over his shoulder. He looked a lot like Bud, only he was twenty-five years younger and fifty pounds lighter. As heir to the fishing lure throne, he could afford to look good and drive nice cars. He was the next in line to run that ball into the future.

"What are you doing here?"

"Just discussing a little plumbing problem." John kept it ambiguous. If Lester didn't know about his father's plans, it wasn't John's place to spill the beans.

"Did you see my little girl in there?"

"Yes, I did." John tried to muster the appropriate amount of enthusiasm for the bratty girl. "She really will be a star in the Little Shields."

Lester looked at the house to make sure no one was watching them. He walked closer to John, eyeing his bare, hairy legs and baggy shorts suspiciously. John didn't like Lester—or Bud, either—but when you're rich, you don't need people to like you. You need people to do what they're told, and John had taken an oath to the Sons of Gunnar.

"Hey, you were in the military, right?

"Marines, Ninth Engineer Battalion, First Division.

Lester nodded and stared at the ground thoughtfully.

"You blew up stuff, didn't you?"

"Sometimes." John shrugged. "If it was in the way, shot back, or we were just bored."

"Yeah, I was a supply officer attached to Fort Carson. My ticket to 'Nam almost came up, but luck of the draw, I guess."

"I guess." Luck and maybe some campaign contributions to the right congressman from Lester's dad.

"Did you hear about Saigon?"

"Yeah, I heard." Everyone had heard. It was like asking, *Did you hear Kennedy got shot?* Lester might have money in his wallet, but he sure lacked small-talk skills. The fall of Saigon had been on the news a few weeks back, the dramatic footage of helicopters pulling people off the roof of the American embassy. The Viet Cong were closing in, and there was going to be hell to pay for whoever they left behind.

"Did you know anyone there?"

Staring hard at Lester, John wondered if he was serious.

"I don't think so. Everyone I knew was dead already or toured out."

"It makes you wonder, doesn't it?" John shook his head solemnly. "What it was all about?"

"Yeah, I guess. But I don't like to think about my time in the military any more than I have to."

"I understand that. Still, some nights I have these dreams. You ever get the dreams, Wahoo?"

"Yeah, sometimes. But then I wake up, and I put on my favorite shirt. I drink some tomato juice and take a deep breath. Life is pretty good."

Lester shook his head and laughed. He clapped John on the back.

"You always were fubar, Wahoo. That's why I like you. Someday, when I'm chieftain, I'm going to make you my right-hand *forkvinne*. What do you think about that?"

"Yeah, that'll be great," John nodded, thinking, *Well, this is awkward.* He didn't want to rub it in Lester's face that Bud had already picked him as a *forkvinne*. Only last year, Lester had really messed up when he was *forkvinne* on a project they'd called *Operation Chain Link.* He was supposed to convince certain key property owners to sell or otherwise find ways to oust them so the club could connect two more lakes to the chain. Lester nearly got himself blasted by an angry old woman who lived in a rust bucket trailer home.

"Well, I better go see what ol' screwball is up to," Lester said as he slid on his sports coat. A guy like Lester, it was hard to tell if he was a baiter or on the hook.

John tossed the manilla folder on the passenger seat of the truck. He headed over to the Loonie Bin to wash the taste of the entire Langskip family from his mouth by downing a couple cold ones.

Chapter 14

Unhappy Campers

THE FISKERS PULLED INTO Hilmir State Park just after sunset, like thieves, with their headlights off. Nestled east of Fornborg between three lakes on the Rabbit Chain, the park's tall pines and spruce were now a wall of massive black shadows. An owl asked, *who cooks for you*?

"Looks like they're already closed for the day," Edie noted.

"Yup, that's good," Sam replied. "No need to pay an entrance fee."

Sam got out and unhooked the thick chain that blocked the drive past the entrance booth. Edie gave a nervous glance at the sliding window where, only an hour before, a ranger would lean out to collect money for overnight camping permits.

"Are you sure this is a good idea?" she asked when Sam returned to the car. Guilt gnawed at her like an ever-present little mouse in the cupboard.

"Yeah, we want to stay off roads and parking lots. Besides, we pay state taxes, so this is our land."

Arne stuck his head over the front seat and began bellowing "This Land is Your Land," but Edie clapped her hand over his mouth.

She didn't want to alarm Arne, so she tried to disguise her anxiety in a quiet, girl-like voice when she asked Sam if there might be bears in the area.

"Maybe," he answered.

"Cool," Arne said, but his voice was muffled because Edie had forgotten to take her hand away. Why was his face always sticky?

"We'll lock the doors, just in case," Sam assured her, and then in his best Yogi Bear voice, he added, "No pick-a-nick baskets, please."

Sam turned on the running lights before they headed down a narrow gravel drive to a rustic campsite right on a lake. They kept the windows rolled up tight and not for poisonous rattlers this time: it was to keep out the squadrons of mosquitos that flitted against the windows, humming their ceaseless tune late into the sweltering night. They parked next to a picnic table made of round, rough-cut logs, but that table, the fire pit, and the beautiful lake would all go unused, thanks to Nature's perfect pest: *mosquitosaurus rex*.

You often hear about the dark night of the soul. Well, it couldn't get much worse than being crammed into the family wagon like they were locked in a tin can, sweating, and with the smell of smoke from the burning motel room still filling the air from their sooty suitcases.

"Look on the bright side," Sam offered. "At least we don't have to spring for another night in a motel."

Edie and Arne took turns fanning one another with a folded program from Uncle Nat's funeral, but it only pushed around more hot, smoky air, and they eventually tried to lie as perfectly still as possible.

"Mom?"

"Yes, Arne?"

"Are we going to die?"

"Maybe."

"Mom?"

"Yes, Arne?"

"Can toads and frogs mate?"

Edie thought for a moment. "Yes, they can," she answered seriously. "They make little trogs."

Maybe it was the heat or the stress of a long, eventful day, but the Fiskers laughed at her half-baked joke. Sam broke into song, growling "Wild Thing" as he tickled his son, and Edie joined in the tickling too. Not the singing, though. The visit from the Minneapolis police still made her feel self-conscious. Eventually, they fell asleep side by side in the back of the wagon with the white light of the moon shining on them through the trees.

⇽⇾ — ◆ — ⇽⇾

Pounding on the window startled them. Edie instantly thought of Mr. Jaworski pounding on the ceiling.

"No, *you* be quiet," she muttered groggily. Arne shouted and flailed in panic, smacking the side of Edie's head. It was still night, and the sudden burst from a flashlight made them all squint, backing away from it like the Frankenstein monster away from fire.

"What are you folks doing out here?" A man's voice asked, muffled by the glass.

Sam opened the side door and crawl out.

"We're just having a little snooze. Would you mind turning off the light?"

The flashlight beam cut out, leaving only a yellow-white haze in Edie's field of vision. She blinked until her eyes adjusted to the darkness, and she and Arne climbed out of the car behind Sam. The air was cool and moist, a welcome relief from family car sauna time.

"Well, it's you!" The man holding the flashlight was Vicki Svensson's handsome blond husband, the DNR officer, looking very fit in his tan uniform and brown shorts, with a patch on his chest in the shape of a badge. "I'm Toby Svensson. Vicki's husband. We sort of met at the funeral."

"Yeah, that's right." Sam offered his hand, and they shook like they were old war buddies. "Say, how's that wife of yours?"

"She's fine, I guess. She did a little grocery shopping after the funeral and whipped up some chopped chicken liver paté. That woman is going to make me fat someday."

Chopped chicken liver paté. Yes, Edie remembered seeing that recipe in last month's issue of *Today's Sophisticated Woman*. She'd wanted to try it, but she knew better. Sam and Arne would say it looked like brown snot and wouldn't touch it.

"Well, it was interesting to see her again after the funeral," Edie added. "I hope we didn't scare her too much."

"Oh? Did you run into her at the store?"

Edie realized that Toby Svensson, who hadn't been at the reading of Uncle Nat's will, may not have known that his wife had been there. Maybe even perfect people had secrets. She shifted the conversation to the cool night air, and weather in general, before Sam could blunder in and say something indiscrete.

"The thing is, and I hate to do this," Toby said, "you're parked on state lands without a permit with the intent of overnight camping. I'm afraid I'll have to write you a ticket."

"You're kidding me." The statement triggered Sam's outrage. "How much is that gonna run us?"

"It's only a ten-dollar fine," Toby said, pulling a ticket book from his shirt pocket. "But it's fifty if you don't pay it in sixty days." He tilted the ticket to get the best moonlight as he filled in the ticket with a short pencil.

"I don't believe this." Sam stamped his foot, the same way Arne stamped his foot, upset with life's unfair oppressions.

"You must not have seen the signs." Toby tore the ticket free and handed it to Sam. "All ten of them."

They had seen the signs. They'd laughed at those signs as they drove past.

What are they gonna do? Sam had said like a Johnny scofflaw. *Give us a ticket?*

❖❖ — ◆ — ❖❖

They pulled along the gas pumps at Stig's Gas and Repair station in downtown Fornborg. They needed gas, anyway, so they would be paying customers just as soon as the station opened at seven. Sam shoved the gas pump nozzle for pump two into the neck of the station wagon's fuel tank. The pumps were inoperable until the station opened, but he didn't want to be accused by the sheriff or the DNR or the Girl Scouts—or anyone else—of trespassing on private gas station property. If they happened to catch some sleep while they waited, well, so be it.

"Just three more hours," Sam noted, bleary-eyed. He lowered himself between Edie and Arne in the back. Without the back seat, they at least had more room to spread out, if you didn't mind getting poked by exposed bolts.

Arne, wide awake, shoved his head out the window, which was now mercifully cracked as the mosquitoes weren't bad in town.

"Hey, Dad?"

"Yeah, kiddo?"

"Did Sinclair Lewis invent these gas pumps too?"

Sam and Edie laughed sleepily.

"Yup, he sure did," Sam mumbled, drifting to sleep with the familiar smell of gas and oil in his nostrils.

Pump two turned out to be a full-service pump, and when the pumps turned on, the young attendant kindly filled up the car for them. He even cleaned their windshield, careful not to wake them until it was time to pay him fifteen dollars and thirty-nine cents, which, he noted, didn't include a tip. He wore a blue polyester jumpsuit with a tire pressure gauge sticking out of the breast pocket just above where his name was stitched: *Lance*.

"I didn't want full serve, Lance," Sam complained, wiping his face with both hands.

"Unless you can go back in time and undo the full service I gave you, there's really nothing I can do about it, mister."

"We're not the Rockefellers, you know," Sam growled as he counted out sixteen dollars and collapsed in the driver's seat.

"We've got enough for breakfast and coffee at the diner if we split an order of pancakes," Sam told them. "On the bright side, the bears didn't eat us."

Edie would pawn her wedding ring if it meant they could get a pot of coffee.

They sat in a booth at the Cozy Corner Diner with three large menus sticky with maple syrup. The wainscoting, with its scuffed, bone-white paint, rose above child height and with good reason: the walls were laden with old rusty junk, like garden tools, a washtub, and a dusty old pickaxe that had tetanus written all over it. It looked like someone had stapled the contents of their shed to the walls. The only cozy-looking piece of decor was a framed Norman Rockwell print of the soda jerk sniffing the girl's corsage after the prom that hung behind the cash register, along with a picture of Hubert Humphrey that said, *Don't Blame Me. I Voted for the Happy Warrior.*

Sam and Edie took deep sips of coffee while they waited for an order of hotcakes, three sausage patties, and a glass of orange juice for Arne. (Edie wasn't about to let her boy become malnourished, no matter what happened.) She noticed white powder on Arne's lips and cheek and saw the empty packets of non-dairy creamer.

"Arne. Those are for coffee."

"But I *want* coffee."

"Well, you can't have any. It'll stunt your growth," she answered, and she knew what Sam was thinking: *If only it would stunt his ears.*

The waitress, Marla, brought them the food and refilled the dingy white coffee mugs. She eyed Arne suspiciously and removed the wire rack that held the red ketchup dispenser, the yellow mustard dispenser, the salt and pepper, the sugar, and the jelly packets.

"Let me just give you a little more room," she said, trying to sound helpful, but she wasn't helpful. She was protecting the restaurant's condiment assets. Here they were, out of cash, two hundred miles from home, and their son was pilfering powdered non-dairy creamer like a raccoon.

Sam stopped her and removed the glass sugar shaker from the rack.

"Might need this," Sam said, which was weird because they didn't take sugar in their coffee.

They split the cakes three ways and used an abundance of syrup. Marla seemed relieved that they actually paid the check when it came instead of running off and leaving her the sticky pile of plates, but she frowned when she didn't see a tip.

"Do we have enough gas to make it home?" Edie asked when they returned to the car.

Sam closed his eyes hard, doing math. "Let's see. Eleven miles to the gallon in a seventeen-gallon tank...It'll get us close."

"I suppose you could call the shop first thing in the morning and get a lift from one of the guys. Mr. Irwin wouldn't want you to show up too late for work, so maybe if we could at least get close to the Cities..."

Sam seemed surprised at the suggestion and hurried to change topics.

"While we're here in town, why don't we at least look at your uncle's place. We could take a drive out to the property. You know, just to, uh, honor your uncle's memory."

"Oh, poo," Edie retorted. Her puffy eyes burned from lack of sleep. "You don't give a crap about honoring him or anyone. All you want is to see what the place is worth."

"Whoa, whoa, whoa." Sam looked hurt. "We're talking about family here. Now, true, I didn't know the man, and yes, you hadn't been in contact with him for twenty years, and yes, his only sister didn't even bother to show up for his funeral."

Arne's head appeared between them. He had a piece of sausage stuck to his ear lobe. How? She had no idea.

"Let's go see the property!" Arne shouted, hyped up on powdered creamer and vitamin C.

Edie scowled, and the front of her head ached. She was too tired to argue.

"Fine," she relented. "But just a quick look, and then we head for home."

The Rabbit Chain of Lakes forced roads to bend in the most unexpected places, and the Donnelly County public works department wasn't exactly fanatical in putting out warning signs on sharp curves. Arne loved it, screaming like it was an exciting carnival ride. Edie *didn't* love it, also screaming like it was an exciting carnival ride.

Sam found the gravel county road that led them to Little Paw Lake. Two wrong driveways later and they wound up at the right place.

"This is it," Edie announced. She recognized the house, hulking and dark, and the four little cabins that dotted the shoreline. "Okay, we can head back now."

"No way, Mom!" Arne kicked the back of her seat. "Let's check it out!"

"The kid's right," Sam agreed, pulling into the dirt driveway. "Pretty good size house."

"I guess," Edie answered unenthusiastically. She did not want to add any fuel to Sam's overactive imagination.

"We'll just take a quick walk around the place, okay?" Sam opened the door, drawing in a deep breath of air. "Ah, this is the stuff." Arne copied his dad. "What do you say, kiddo? Would you like to live at a place like this?"

"Sam, knock it off," Edie called through the passenger window. "We're not keeping it. It's a lake resort, not a puppy."

Sam put up his hands and tried to look innocent. "No one said we were. We're just looking around."

"Dad, can we get a puppy?"

Both Fisker parents answered with a unanimous 'no.' At least they could agree on puppies.

"Come on, Fiskers," Sam said. "Let's check out that lake." He led Arne around the corner, and Edie grudgingly got out and followed behind them. The house was built into the slope so that the basement level walked out in the back from a sliding glass door. Sam and Arne were already side stepping down the hill leading to the water, but Edie found the timber stairs wedged into the earth and used them like a normal person.

Arne ran down the beach, picking up rocks and skimming them across the water.

"Don't drown, Arne," Edie called, but he ignored her as he threw tree branches in the lake.

"Holy crap!" Sam yelled.

"Samuel, language!"

"I'll put a dime in the swear jar, but look at the dock."

The dock lie in two jagged sections. Edie realized with a chill that had been where she and her uncle had their tea party the last time she'd seen him. Now it was blackened and broken. Probably had bloodstains from her uncle, not to mention the embedded guts of countless fish filleted right on the dock.

"That whole thing needs to be replaced," Sam noted. "Might as well get a longer one so it can have more boats moored during the busy months."

"That's not for us to worry about," Edie interrupted him. "I'm selling this place."

Sam said nothing in reply, but she could hear the wheels turning in his head. She continued on before those wheels cranked out some harebrained idea. She looked down the beach. No sign of Arne.

"Right now, we just need to find Arne and get going. Where'd he get off to?"

"Oh, he's probably playing in the woods over there or something."

"Or in the lake? Do you think he went into the water and drowned? I specifically told him not to drown."

"Relax. He knows how to swim. I think."

"I'm not really worried about that. It's just that he'll come back all wet and filthy and get the car wet and maybe even catch chiggers."

"Don't panic. He's fine."

"Oh, I think a healthy dose of panic is warranted in this case."

Edie waited as if expecting Sam to run off and search for Arne, but he didn't budge.

"He'll get hungry eventually and come back," Sam said calmly. "Those pancakes will wear off pretty quick."

Edie huffed. "Fine. I'll go look for him over in the woods. Looks like there's a path. He might have gotten lost. You look here, no stone unturned. Please, Sam, make sure…" She lowered her voice. "…make sure none of these hippies has snatched him."

"Sounds good. He'll be fine," Sam insisted without any factual basis for the claim.

"Meet right back here," she insisted. "And then we're leaving."

"Sure, sure," Sam said, distracted by the main house. He was sizing it up, she could tell, to see if they should move in.

"I'm serious, Sam. We're not staying here. We find Arne, and then we leave."

"Um hmm," Sam intoned absently.

"Sam."

"Yes, right back here." She glared at him. He pretended to be motivated, calling out for Arne as he wandered around the back of the house with no particular urgency.

◆◆◆ ◆ ◆ ◆ ◆◆◆

Edie had disappeared into the woods looking for Arne, but Sam wasn't worried. It gave him time to survey the estate. Why, the very sound of it made him feel wealthy. *Survey the estate, ye mighty, and despair.* It was an old poem or something.

Cripes, he was already getting classier too. He doubled back to the front of the house, a giddy feeling filled his stomach, and he just had the feeling this was it.

An olive-green '68 Grand Prix pulled in the drive and braked hard, sending gravel spraying awfully close to the family wagon. It was a real boat of a car, long in the front, long in the back. The car door opened, and cousin Jeffy emerged wearing a tight-fitting collared shirt and flared canvas pants. He caught Sam lusting after the car.

"That you, Sam?" He lowered his sunglasses. His mustache was more brown than red. Didn't match his hair or long sideburns. "It's Edie's cousin, Jeff."

"Oh, I remember you, Jeffy." Sam nodded at the car. "What do you got under the hood? A four hundred?"

"A four twenty-eight."

Sam whistled.

"I'm glad I caught you," Jeffy said, tucking his sunglasses in his chest pocket. "Well, glad isn't the right word. I'm just hoping you'll talk some sense into that wife of yours."

"Edie? What do you mean?"

"Before my dad died…"

Weird Uncle Nat, Sam thought.

"He wasn't with one hundred percent of his faculties, if you know what I mean. Just look at the riff-raff he was hanging out with. So he told Aunt Dolores he was leaving her the resort if anything happened to him, and she insisted he change the will so the resort went to cousin Edie."

"What!" Sam was flabbergasted. "Really? Edie didn't say…I didn't know that."

"Yeah. And me and Lana never got a thing from that crazy bastard except a half-dose of Norwegian blood. He was a horrible rat bastard when you get right down to it."

That's because he didn't like you. Sam could have said it out loud because even cousin Jeff and his sister must have known that weird Uncle Nat couldn't stand them long before he made his final will and testament. Instead, Sam said, "That's too bad."

"Yeah, it is," Jeff said tersely. "So I want you to help us out. Talk some sense into Edie. Get her to give us the resort."

"Look, this is the first I've heard about it. Let me ask Edie what's going on."

"And if you help me out here, I'll give you 5 percent of whatever we sell it for."

"You're gonna sell it?"

"Hell, yeah. Only a fool would try to run a resort in this economy. Whatever you make goes into repairs and taxes."

"So, you sell it, and we'd get 5 percent of what? Like, how much do you think it would sell for?"

"You tell me," Jeffy lifted a hand like one of those models on *The Price is Right* game show. "Four cabins and the main house with three bedrooms on a six-acre lake lot with a quarter-mile of sandy beach connected to a chain of lakes."

"Sounds like a million dollars."

Jeff laughed. "More like two hundred grand. So you'd get somewhere around ten grand for helping us out, free and clear."

"And you're just going to sell the place if you get a hold of it? Why not take a chance and run it?"

Cousin Jeffy shook his head, disappointed that other people just didn't get it.

"My old man ran that place for twenty years before he gave up and let it get overrun with hippies. He never turned a profit on it. When he was running it, he was married to that place and never had time for us or our mom. That's why she left."

Sam knew that wasn't quite true. Cousin Jeffy's mom had left because weird Uncle Ned caught her skinny-dipping with the Warroad varsity football team—and they hadn't even been staying at the resort. But Sam would keep that fact to himself. People get very touchy about their mothers and football.

"Like I said, I'll talk to Edie," Sam offered his hand, and the two men shook.

That was no lie. He would talk to Edie—just not about what Cousin Jeffy had suggested. Sell this great big golden goose? That would be insane. The place was a gold mine full of potential with the right vision and an enterprising young couple to nurse it back to life.

Jeffy excused himself, saying he had to look around the house for 'personal effects.' Sam didn't feel it would be right to stop him, but he also didn't like it. He was feeling territorial about the place, and Jeffy seemed like the kind of guy who might just do something spiteful, like pour cement in the drains or use up all the ice and not refill the trays. As itchy as it made him, Sam watched helplessly as Jeffy disappeared inside. Soon, angry words erupted inside between Jeffy and a woman. Jeffy appeared a few minutes later, lugging a cardboard box under his arm with trophies, framed photos, and a glass bong (probably the *decorative glass vase* mentioned in the will). Avi Starshine padded behind him, barefooted. She begged him to leave the bong, as the will instructed.

"I don't know who you are or why a pretty little piece like you would go for an old man unless you were gold-digging."

"Gold digging? For a bong with sentimental value and a shitty old truck? Oh, I really hit the jackpot."

"Yeah, well, my dad was always full of nasty surprises."

"Your father was a kind and gentle man." Avi's fists clenched. It must take a certain kind of Jeffy to make a hippy fist. "He only had good things to say about you, but I guess he was wrong about that."

"So you want my dad's water bong?" Jeffy said as he pulled it from the box. "Fine. Here." He hurled it at the pickup truck, and it shattered, leaving a spiderweb of cracks in the windshield.

"That was hand blown by Froggo, you jerk!" Avi growled through gritted teeth. If she had been a peace-loving hippie a few minutes before, she was now vying for the fly-weight champion title. Avi windmilled punches at him. She looked angrier than a moose caught in a clothesline.

Jeffy told her to do some pretty awful things, and she suggested certain activities she thought Jeffy should consider, and the whole scene was angry, ugly, and loud. As the two of them yelled their lungs out, Sam wandered over to the big Grand Prix, buffed with a gloss coat, wondering just how big cousin Jeffy's fuel tank was. He could have been juggling babies, and those two wouldn't have noticed his presence, they were so furious with one another. It just so happened Sam still had the sugar shaker from the diner, and he slipped it out of his pocket and stepped over to Jeffy's car.

Finally, Jeffy backed away from the confrontation, having lost the ability to combine all the four-letter words he knew into any further unique combinations. He set the box of personal possessions on the passenger seat of the car through the open window, gave a terse nod to Sam, and drove off.

Sam told Avi it was too bad about the bong. "I don't know if this will do you much good, but you could give it a try." Sam handed her the sugar dispenser. It was now empty.

Chapter 15

Natural Talent

ARNE ROUNDED A BEND on the lakeshore so he was out of sight of his worrywart parents. Out in the middle of Little Paw Lake was an island full of trees and just dying to be explored. It was the kind of island with buried treasure or an old, haunted cabin or an abandoned gold mine. He knew a lot about islands thanks to the television shows he watched. It was a little bigger than his thumb from where he stood on the shore. That was an old Boy Scout trick: you held up your thumb and then did some other stuff to figure out sizes and distances. He couldn't remember the other stuff, but he remembered the thumb part.

It didn't seem that far across the lake. Arne could probably swim to it, explore, dig up some cool artifacts, or catch a bear or something, and be back before his parents knew he'd gone anywhere. Even in the pool at the motel, he'd touched the bottom and nearly made it the entire length of the pool holding his breath underwater. He was a pretty good swimmer. He had found that dime on the bottom of the pool, after all.

He kicked off his shoes and slipped off his shirt before wading into the water. The bottom was sandy, and the water was warm in the sun. He walked out as far as he could, hoping it was shallow enough to walk all the way to the island, but about twenty feet from the shore, he had to start swimming. There was a drop-off beneath him. He could feel it because the water was colder. He stuck his head underwater, but he couldn't see the bottom anymore. It was just blackness beneath him. Like crossing a shaky rope bridge when you're swimming in deep water to an island, it's best not to look down.

Slowly Arne swam his way further and further from shore, but the island didn't seem to get any closer. He saw a fishing boat bobbing in a bay, but he heard another boat skimming across the wake, the motor growing louder. He could see the boat's prow aiming right at him.

What if they didn't see him? They might run him over.

Maybe he had to dive underwater. He swam faster, gulping a mix of air and lake water. His breaths came in coughs. He was nearly in the middle of the lake. No one could see him and, even if he could get enough air in his lungs to yell, the whine of the fast-approaching boat motor was too loud for anyone to hear him.

He waved his arms like a football referee signaling a timeout. It must have worked. The boat slowed and veered, coming up alongside him. Arne panted, now reverting to doggy paddling like a baby just to keep from sinking in the wake generated by the boat as it towered overhead. Painted in glittering gold script, the boat's name read *Catalog King*. An attractive young blonde woman peered over the side. At first, she looked like one of those naked ladies because the only parts of her that Arne could see were naked. As she turned to yell something to the boat driver, he noticed her pink bikini, the top tied around her back, the matching bottom circling her hips, and he realized she was only a half-naked lady.

A man's head appeared next to the bathing beauty. He was older than she was, older than Arne's dad, even. The man reached out a big blocky hand for Arne to grasp.

"Well, what do we have here? Some kind of lake monster? Looks like a boy with Flopsy and Mopsy ears on the side of his head. Kid, you want to keep drowning, or can I take you to shore?" He grabbed Arne and hauled him onto the boat.

Arne huddled against the gunwale, catching his breath. The young woman offered him a towel. Arne felt relieved. For a second, he thought he could have actually died, and that wasn't something he was used to.

"You want a soda, kid?" The man lifted the lid on the cooler and rummaged between cubes of ice and cans of High Life. "I got grape, and I got cherry. Unless you want a beer."

"Grape is my favorite," Arne said, stretching out his hand. His mother's voice floated into his consciousness. *What do you say?* "Please," he added quickly.

"Oh, a health nut, this one. Slow down! Don't drink it too fast," the man warned. "I don't want you to get the bends."

Arne noticed a pair of skis like he'd worn at the Trollhaugen ski resort, only these were wider, and there was a rubber collar where you slipped your feet in instead of using boots.

"Are those waterskis?"

"The kid's a genius. Not much of a swimmer, but a genius. What? You never saw waterskis before? Do you live under a rock?"

"I've seen people waterski before, like on television and stuff. I just never saw the skis up close before." He told the man about how he'd been downhill skiing a few times, but the man ignored him and tossed him a lumpy orange life vest.

"Put that on, Einstein. Then get back in the water."

"You're going to leave me here in the middle of the lake?"

"Like I said, this kid's a genius. No, Einstein. You're going to try waterskiing. You tell me you've been skiing before. You're sitting next to a pair of waterskis. You're alive. So what better way to celebrate but to try waterskiing? Besides, this one..." he nodded to the young woman, "she just wants to lay around in the sun. Perfectly good skin she wants to bake. Let's put those skis to use."

A big grin spread on Arne's face. He dove in, plugging his nose. This time he floated easily with the help of the life jacket. The man adjusted the foot brackets to make them smaller. Then he slid both skis in the water, one at a time, and Arne flipped over in the water like a barrel his first few attempts to put them on, but he finally managed one, then the other.

"Good, now don't let them slip off." The man tossed the tow rope, the one with the wood handle, to Arne. "And keep your legs together, or you just might split in two. A problem like that, you don't want."

"Maybe he should have a lifejacket for each one of those ears," the young woman giggled. She waved at him.

"It's going to be a rough start pulling you up," the man explained. "Just hang on and push your weight down into the skis. Understand?"

Arne nodded. He hoped the boat pulled him out of the water and into the air. He'd had dreams like that, where he was flying. His heart pumped, and he shivered a little. He was cold now, but he didn't care.

"Okay, we're going for it." He shifted a lever, and the boat motor churned a roiling pile of water behind the boat as it lurched forward.

On the first try, Arne did just like the man said: he pushed his weight down into the skis, and he was up on the skis, sending water spraying behind him. He felt a little wobbly, but he was up. The man and his companion looked impressed. Arne's body filled with joy in the sun and spray, and he gave a triumphant yell, hoping the entire lake would hear him and look out to see him.

The man pumped his fist in the air, and the woman applauded him, yelling something Arne couldn't hear over the roar of the shiny red outboard.

The boat pulled him right past the resort, and Arne could see his dad talking to a young woman he didn't recognize. Arne shouted for him, but he was too far away. The boat turned, following the shoreline where it jutted into the lake like a pointing finger, and Arne leaned into the turn so that his body barely hovered over the water. He went over the wake with a sudden jolt, and for a moment, he was airborne. Flying, almost. The skis landed hard and forward, jolting him back to reality, but he did not fall.

Arne figured if that was all there was to waterskiing, using your body weight and pressure, he could probably do other neat stuff. He pulled the handle to his waist and twisted his hips, and the tips of his skis turned like windshield wipers until he was perpendicular to the boat but still gliding along. Then he turned back to face forward. The man and woman gaped at him, and the man immediately sent the throttle handle down to cut the engine, and Arne's first waterskiing session ended as he sank to his waist in Little Paw Lake.

The boat circled around to him, and the man looked at him suspiciously.

"I thought you said you didn't know how to waterski."

"I don't. Well, I didn't."

"How did you do all those tricks out there if this is your first time, smart guy?"

"I don't know. It just felt right."

"Well, let's get you back to shore. You need a talent agent or something, kid."

Arne wrestled with the skis to get them off, and the first one shot off, nosing toward the boat like a torpedo.

"Watch it, Einstein. Don't scratch that motor. My baby's been through a lot."

The man's baby, Arne realized, was the outboard motor. Arne could see why the man would be concerned. The shiny red Mercury looked expensive.

Chapter 16

Coffee and Smörgåstårta

EDIE DIDN'T KNOW WHERE Arne had gone off to any more than she knew how to do a backbend kick over in fourth-grade gymnastics class. Arne could have gone anywhere by now. If it were up to Edie, she would have followed the lovely little path leading from her uncle's property through the oak trees and gooseberry bushes and blackberry canes. It looked like a lovely, peaceful foray into nature.

Arne was as likely to be in the woods as anywhere, she reasoned, so she took the path, calling for Arne every so often. It was cooler in the shade, and dark, which made her slightly uneasy. Squirrels skittered through leaf litter while an unseen bird screeched somewhere overhead.

Was it a blue jay? Or did they have some kind of remnant carnivorous dinosaur-bird in the north woods? And those squirrels: was that foam around their little mouths? She hadn't been in actual woods since she and Sam had gone hiking years ago. Mostly, she was used to sidewalks and grocery aisles for her rambles.

She hastened her pace. Maybe it hadn't been a good idea to take the path after all. What if hippies or hobos lurked behind the trees, waiting to ravish her? What if the timber rattler was loose in the trees?

She should have sent Sam.

Oh, a cigarette sure sounded good. It wouldn't be much protection against hippies or snakes, but it would at least calm her nerves.

"Arne?" she called feebly, not wanting to alert the entire population of rabid squirrels as to her location. Besides, if she couldn't hear Arne, he wasn't nearby. The boy wasn't exactly what you'd call stealthy. He made his presence known.

The path ended (thankfully), and the landscape changed from untamed woods to cultivated lake-home lawn, with hostas, deer-nibbled fruit trees, and mowed grass.

In other words: civilization.

Edie mouthed a silent *thank God* when an A-frame chalet came into view with its wide deck overlooking the lake. On the deck, she saw Vicki Svensson, now out of her funeral attire and radiant in a bright yellow sundress and a matching sunhat and gardening gloves. Seated at a potting bench, she transplanted plants into pots. She could have been on the cover of *Better Homes and Gardens*.

"Hi. Vicki." Edie announced herself. "I'm looking for my boy, Arne." She lifted her hand to waist height. "He's eleven and about this tall. He's wearing a red shirt and blue shorts."

"Oh, I remember him from the funeral. The one with the ears, right?" Vicki replied. "No, I haven't seen him, but there are plenty of places a boy his age might be around here. There's the old trapper's shack and the bear cave and the marsh…"

"Thanks, that's very helpful."

"Oh, I'm sorry. I don't mean to worry you. What I meant was, he's probably off exploring somewhere. You know how boys are. Come on up. Let's have some coffee, and then I can help you look for him." Vicki pointed to the staircase, and Edie climbed. The view from the Svensson's deck was incredible. She had a clear view of Little Paw Lake and the island, thanks to manicured trees.

"Boys are such a challenge, aren't they?" Vicki shook her head. She said it like she would know from having her own children. Edie had a hard time believing that. There weren't enough broken and abandoned toys lying around. No swing set. No basketball net on the garage. No terrified terrier being chased around the yard.

"How many kids do you have?" Edie asked.

"We don't have any," she murmured. "I lost one. A girl."

That made Edie's heart melt.

"Me too," Edie admitted. She hadn't told anyone else before, except her mother, and that had been a mistake. "It was another boy. Just before Arne."

Vicki removed her gloves and set them on the bench. "It's hard, isn't it? She'd be two now. Every day I wonder what she would have been like."

"To be honest, at two she'd be a holy terror. Arne was a terrible two, but he never grew out of it."

They both laughed until the laughter ran out.

"Would you like to try some smörgåstårta with the coffee?" Vicki offered. "I just made it."

"Sure," Edie answered hesitantly, but followed Vicki through the sliding glass door. Smorga-something. Maybe she'd misheard? "What is that? Smorga..."

"Smörgåstårta," Vicki explained. "It's an old Swedish recipe. You know, we *are* the Svenssons, after all. Swedish to the bone, both Toby and me."

"Ah, Swedish," Edie said for no particular reason. Her mind raced to the list of things she knew about Swedes and/or Sweden. The only thing that came to mind was a joke she'd heard at the butcher shop.

"I know a joke about a Swede," Edie began. "It seems that Sven and Ole were at the lumberyard..."

Vicki looked appalled. "I'm going to stop you right there, Edie. I just can't sit back and allow those types of jokes to be told. They're so racist."

Edie blinked. "But it's got both Swedes and Norwegians in it."

"But is one or both of the men, this Sven and Ole you mentioned, portrayed as a racial caricature? Perhaps the humor comes at their expense? Makes them seem stupid?"

Edie's mind jumped to the punchline: *No. De veelbarrow is de von vit two handles!*

"I guess so," she concluded. "Sorry. Please, tell me more about the...what was it? Smores and something?"

"Smörgåstårta," Vicki sat up straighter, her guard up a little against Edie. "It's a layered sandwich cake filled with little shrimp and eggs, mayonnaise, cream cheese, lemon juice, and fish roe. Some versions call for fresh tomatoes and cucumbers too, but it's too early in the season for those, so I use canned corn and Vlasic pickles. Call me crazy."

To say that Vicki's kitchen was spacious and contemporary was like saying Liberace was slightly homosexual. The color scheme, butter yellow and gloss white, appeared on cabinets, the tiled backsplash, the matching hand towels, and the crocheted throw rug. Dazzling stainless steel appliances rested on butcher block countertops. There was even a built-in wine rack, and it was full of wine bottles, the kind with actual corks. The last time Edie and Sam had drunk wine, it had been from a screw-off bottle of Thunderbird fortified wine because Sam thought it sounded like its powerful automotive namesake. They drank the entire bottle while fooling around in his old roadster after school.

A rack full of copper cookware hung over a lemon-yellow bookshelf, and it was actually full of books.

"Are those cookbooks?"

Vicki tittered in a practiced manner. "Guilty. I collect them. I just love trying new recipes, don't you?"

"I do," Edie agreed. She didn't have cookbooks, but she accumulated quite the collection of clipped-out recipes from her favorite magazines. (Hopefully the librarian wouldn't notice the damaged pages.) She taped them into a spiral-bound notebook.

"Well, Toby doesn't seem to mind. He keeps accusing me of trying to make him fat, but no matter how much that man eats, he never puts on an ounce."

Vicki opened the door of the harvest-gold refrigerator and removed a platter with what appeared to be a cream-cheese frosted fortress of food, speckled with corn kernels and ringed with pickle spears. She cut a slice, and it looked like a cake made from leftovers. Edie's culinary imagination ran wild. Vicki handed her a tiny silver fork, but Edie wasn't sure how to attack her piece, so she waited to see how Vicki did it, slicing off a sliver of the corner for a dainty bite. Edie followed suit.

The dish would have been completely impractical at the Fisker household, where hamburgers and potato chips were the coin of the realm. After taking her first bite, Edie couldn't imagine life getting any better in a perfect yellow kitchen, eating fancy Swedish food and watching little boats bob on the lake.

"Now tell me about your uncle," Vicki said. "When was the last time you spoke with him?"

"Years and years ago. I was just a girl." Edie smeared smörgåstårta on her cheek and quickly dabbed it with her shirt sleeve.

"We do have napkins." Vicki nudged a wooden rack containing folded yellow cloth napkins toward her.

"Of course." Edie dabbed her face with one. She was used to living with two animals whose mission in life was to stain everything in their immediate environment.

"You must have been so pleased that he remembered you in his will."

"Yes…" Edie offered tentatively. "I guess it was nice of him, considering that I hardly knew him."

"Well, you and I are going to have such a good time cooking up interesting dishes, aren't we?"

"What do you mean?" Edie smiled politely, not comprehending what Vicki was talking about.

"When you move in, of course. Oh, it will be such a relief to have normal people next door. Not that your uncle wasn't normal," Vicki hastened to add. "He was very normal. He just lived in very unusual circumstances. I hope I didn't offend you."

"No, no offense," Edie cleared her throat and sat up straight, realizing she was slouching just like her mother always said she did. She hated when her mother was right. "We're not going to move here, though. We'll most likely just sell it. We've got our life in the city, what with Sam's job and our apartment. The shopping is good too."

When we can afford it was the phrase she left unspoken.

"Oh, that is too bad. I think we could be such good friends. I hope you'll reconsider."

"That's a big change, and there's Arne to consider. He'll be starting fifth grade in the fall…"

Starting fifth grade over, she corrected herself mentally. Arne hadn't done too well this past year, and the school thought it would be wise to hold him back so he could mature a little, *like a cheese wheel* the principal had said.

"Kids adapt," Vicki offered. "Lots of space for a boy to play in the fresh air around here."

That's what worries me, Edie thought. The more space Arne had, the more problems he could make.

"It all just came out of the blue, you know, how Uncle Nat left us the property. I mean, he never even laid eyes on Arne or Sam, but we did send him Christmas cards, come to think of it. Do you think it was the Christmas cards that won him over?"

Vicki laughed, her face lighting up.

"Oh, Nat wasn't much for Christmas. At least not these past few years. Mostly, he celebrated what he called the winter solstice, the big pagan." Regaining her composure, Vicki added. "Sorry, no offense. I shouldn't go around calling your recently deceased loved ones pagans."

"No offense taken, especially since you knew him much better than I did. Tell me more about him."

Vicki blinked rapidly. "Like I said, I didn't really know Mr. Lachmann. We kept a neighborly distance."

There was that phrase again, Edie noted. *Neighborly distance.*

"Sometimes he would come over to apologize to Toby for the noise because sometimes the hip—the guests, I mean, would be up all hours of the night, drumming and singing and such."

Edie chuckled, the sudden thought of Mr. Jaworski, the downstairs neighbor in Northeast, having to contend with a wild band of hippies.

"Not that we minded much," Vicki hastened to add, interpreting Edie's laughter as disapproval. "We supported the peace movement, especially after Toby got home from overseas."

"Was he in Vietnam?"

Vicki nodded. Edie took another bite, more carefully this time. A sweet and tangy combination of flavors just smacked of sophistication, or whatever the Swedish word would be for *classy*.

"He came back different," Vicky admitted, and Edie had to refocus her attention from mentally reverse-engineering the smörgåstårta recipe. "How about Sam? Was he in the military?"

"No, he wasn't." Edie didn't elaborate about the great pains Sam had taken to avoid military service, including showing up drunk for his physical examination and claiming he heard the voice of Lawrence Welk commanding him to mazurka. The military might have straightened him out if he survived the war. Three of their friends from high school died over there, but Edie decided it would be in poor taste to mention that.

"You must have been so happy when Toby came home," Edie said instead.

"Mmm-hm," Vicki agreed after taking a large bite of her smörgåstårta. A pickle spear tickled her upper lip and looked in danger of getting stuck in her nostril. It left a little dab of cream cheese on the tip of her perfect nose, and Edie smiled. Vicki smiled too, but only out of politeness. She didn't realize she had smörgåstårta smeared on her face. Edie might mention it after a while, but in the meantime, it helped her petty jealousy toward Vicki evaporate. Yes, Vicki was gorgeous, so of course, a man like Sam would drool over her. And, yes, she also had a perfect kitchen and a handsome husband. But Vicki Svensson substituted ingredients with what she had on hand, just like Edie did, and she had cream cheese on her nose.

The two women continued to smile at one another as they ate, content to bask in the moment, while Edie carefully dabbed a napkin to her mouth after each bite.

"Is your husband home?" She asked finally.

"Toby headed off to work after the funeral. They're spinning turtles today."

Even though Edie worried about Arne's safety, the turtle statement stopped her dead.

"I'm sorry. Spinning turtles, did you say?"

"Well, you know how turtles get during mating season," Vicki said, apparently certain that simply everyone must be familiar with the love lives of turtles. "They wander hither and yon, and now with boating season underway, an alarming number of the poor things get run over. So each year, the DNR collects thousands of turtles and puts them in this contraption that spins them round and round, like those art-o-whirl thingies at the fair."

"Don't the turtles get dizzy?" Edie imagined dozens of horny turtles, all excited on the spinning ride at first, but after the first couple of minutes, feeling nauseous and throwing up cotton candy and hot dogs. At least that's how it was with Arne, who was now floating in the water in the middle of the lake as the boat circled back around.

"That's the point. The turtles get dizzy and disoriented, so when Toby and the others release them back in the wild, those poor little creatures just don't want to wander off. Oh, he's always doing something exciting in nature. He loves it. What did you say your husband does?"

"Oh, this and that. You know, what with the economy and all." Edie had learned you could blame the economy for just about everything: crime, the price of tuna, and recurring job loss. "He's pretty handy. Right now, he works as a mechanic."

Edie wanted to switch topics from that of husbands, especially when the difference between Sam and Toby was as stark as the difference between her rented shoebox of a kitchen and Vicki's perfectly appointed gallery of the culinary arts.

"Can I ask you something?" Edie began, hesitating. "Kind of...personal?"

For some untold reason, Edie felt especially nervous about broaching a very delicate topic, one that had been bothering her for days after speaking with her mother on the phone.

Vicki set down the little silver fork on her platter and looked earnest. "Of course."

"Do you ever make glorified rice?"

"Yes, sometimes. Not until after Labor Day, of course."

"Have you ever substituted fruit cocktail for the pineapple?"

A look of horror washed over Vicki's face.

"Never. I don't even know what that would be. Who would do that?"

"I know, right?" Edie laughed awkwardly, regretting her decision to open up to new people. Hadn't her mother raised her better than that? "Certainly not me. It was just...a recipe I saw. I would never..."

"I should hope not. Fruit cocktail, of all things." Vicki hummed with laughter, the cream cheese still stuck to her nose. "Maybe for those people who drink wine out of screw-top bottles."

Like good old Thunderbird, Edie thought in a flash, burning with shame.

"You've got a little something on your face," Edie said firmly, hoping it didn't sound too terse. She was wound up pretty tight just then. Vicki quickly rushed her finger, draped in napkinry, to various points around her mouth, and Edie provided non-specific guidance as to the location of the cream cheese, much like a game she and Arne played.

"Warmer," Edie said encouragingly. "Warmer. Hot. You got it."

Vicki, peering past Edie out the window facing the lake, broke the awkwardness of the moment.

"Isn't that your son out there?"

Edie looked, and her mouth dropped.

"Yes, it is."

She couldn't believe it. Her son was on the lake: literally on the lake, speeding along on waterskis having the time of his life.

"I thought so. Even from here, I could recognize those ears." Vicki touched Edie's shoulder. "No offense."

"None taken. Vicki, who is that man driving the boat?"

"I don't know. Probably some drunk fisherman from the Cities. No offense."

"None taken," she replied again, but she wondered if some amount of offense was called for. "I don't know that man, either," Edie added nervously. Why would a stranger be dragging her son behind a boat with a rope in such deep water? She decided she'd better try to wave them in and announced to Vicki she should get going. But before she could leave, Vicki told her to wait.

"I found this charming recipe for marble fudge brownies in last month's issue of *Better Homes and Gardens*. Have you made it yet?"

Edie admitted she hadn't. Her neighborhood library only had issues up until September of 1973. Apparently, dentists around the

Twin Cities were stealing the latest issues from libraries for their waiting rooms.

Vicki piled a half-dozen brownies into a burnt orange Tupperware *servalier* container (with the built-in Instant Seal technology, of course).

"You give these a try, and if you like them, I'll copy the recipe for you when you return the container."

Crap, Edie thought. *Now I have to return this container before we leave town.* Why don't people understand that unwanted food gifts are not generosity? They're emotional blackmail.

Vicki walked Edie to the front door just in time to see the Aloha Plumbing truck back out of the Svensson driveway.

"Oh, dear," Vicki said, watching the truck.

Edie thought it funny how different life in the country must be compared city life. If someone turning into your driveway by mistake was cause for alarm, how would Vicki deal with prowlers, renegade Girl Scouts, and a downstairs neighbor who beat the ceiling with his cane?

"It's a long driveway," Vicki explained. "We just don't get random people turning around here, especially someone who knows the area so well."

"He's the guy in the Hawaiian get-up who was outside the funeral, right?"

"Yeah, that's him. It's just that.."

"Go ahead, you can say it. You seem worried."

"Well, it's just that John Kvalstad—he's the plumber—he's a member of the Sons of Gunnar.

"Is that the local men's club?"

"Yes."

"Okay, so why does that bother you?"

"They're bad news," Vicki revealed hurriedly. "They're radical Norwegians, and I can't think of anything more dangerous than that. No offense."

"I'm only half Norwegian," Edie reminded her before they completed their long, elaborate Minnesotan goodbyes.

Chapter 17

Magic Brownies

AVI STARSHINE, BAREFOOT AND with the bells on the hem of her peasant shirt tinkling, offered to show Sam around the property.

"Are you sure you don't want to wait for your wife?"

"Oh, yeah, that's fine." He waved off the suggestion. "Knowing her, she's probably off clothes shopping or something." He didn't know why he said that, but it was the first thing that came to mind. He felt nervous around this pretty young hippie, almost as nervous as he'd been around that Vicki with an 'i'.

The place was crawling with pretty ladies. Jimmer would love it up here. Sam would have to invite him up once they opened for business. Might even give him a slight discount.

"I'm so glad the place is going to someone in Papa Lock's family. I mean, other than his spiritual family."

"What the heck is a spiritual family?" Sam laughed involuntarily. The phrase sounded churchy and weird, especially from a young, barefooted woman who had nearly gotten into a fistfight over drug paraphernalia.

"A spiritual family, you know, the people you connect with at the heart level," she explained. "You see them for who they are, as their true spirit forms. Eventually, one by one, as we recognize this in all the people around us, we know that everyone in the whole world is part of our spiritual family."

"Could you imagine the fights?" Sam quipped. This was like that Coca-Cola commercial where the weirdos wanted to teach the world to sing in perfect harmony. Seeing she was serious, he amended this with a more appropriate comment. "Wow, that's, uh, heavy."

It was Avi's turn to laugh. "You really aren't comfortable with any of that, are you?"

Sam shrugged, hoping the humble gesture endeared him to her. "I'm just a simple Norwegian. Most mornings, I'm lucky to find both my shoes."

She stepped close to him, put her hand on his arm.

"Any chance you'd let us stay on? Just for a while, until we line up new digs."

"How many of you are there?" Specifically, he wondered how many more young, attractive women might be lying around. He could hear Jimmer's voice, *The more, the merrier.* Followed swiftly by Voodoo Andy's voice, complete with that Haitian accent, *They are children of God.*

"Well, there were fourteen of us."

"Holy crap!"

"Is that a lot?"

"It's like a baker's coven of hippies."

She laughed with ease. Probably stoned on the wacky weed, he realized. Objects may appear funnier than they actually are.

"But everyone else split," she explained. "They knew it wouldn't be the same without Papa Lock. Now it's just me and Garvey left."

"Garvey? Is that your cat or something?"

"No, man. Garvey's my old man."

"Your dad?"

"No, my spiritual husband. He lives in the treehouse."

"Treehouse? What is he, twelve?"

"Better. He's a musician."

Of the scant knowledge Sam had stored on the topic of music, none of it returned a connection with treehouses. Seeing the confusion on his face, Avi tugged at his arm.

"You gotta meet him," she urged. "He's got something to tell ya. Looks like the treehouse is a good place to start the tour."

They walked toward the lake, Sam's gaze resting on the expanse of lakeshore, the cabins, the house. Oh, the house! Two stories above a walk-out basement. It must be two thousand square feet, easy. Those cabins: they could rent them for fifteen, twenty bucks a weekend.

Avi led him to a tree which, according to her, was *the* tree. Sam peered up. He could barely see the floor planks from the ground. The treehouse was thirty feet up a sixty-foot basswood tree. Old barn boards nailed directly to the craggy trunk formed a ladder that disappeared into the tree's upper branches.

"So this Garvey of yours lives up there?"

Avi nodded. "Just through the summer."

"You up there, Garvey?" Sam called through cupped hands.

"Oh, he's up there," Avi stated.

The strains of "Rhinestone Cowboy" drifted from on high from an instrument Sam couldn't place.

"What is that?"

"That's Garvey playing his sitar. Groovy, huh?"

"Yeah, real groovy." She was a few years late to the hippie party as flower-power had pretty much petered out, replaced by store-bought granola, jaded disillusionment, and Dacron polyester.

"You live up there with him?"

"Sometimes."

"And the other times?"

"Me and some of the others, you know, if we didn't feel like climbing, we'd just crash in the house or in the cabins."

Right. The cabins. Those cabins, the main house, and even the treehouse all belonged to Sam. Well, technically, it all belonged to Edie, but what's the difference? They were married, and it was share and share alike. To Sam, this whole property represented a fresh start with easy income. People would pay good money to stay. Not hippies, of course, but fishermen and families with inflatable beach balls and picnic baskets. And money. They all would have pockets full of money.

"You seem like a nice kid," Sam started, his head still full of dollar signs. "But I don't think it's going to work out for you to stay here, treehouse or not. It's probably best if you two love birds mosey on to a new nest."

"The thing is…"

"Yes?"

"It's just that Garvey is too scared to come down. He's paranoid that someone is out to get him."

"Is that right?" Sam had heard that chronic drug users were prone to paranoia and what the kids called *freakouts*. "Well, no one is out to get him, are they? Like the law. Or maybe a drug dealer?"

"No, nothing like that."

"So, you guys are just going to have to pack it up." Sam continued. "I'll even give your truck a once-over, make sure it's roadworthy. I can't help much with that smashed windshield, though."

"I'm telling you, Garvey won't leave."

"Yes, he will." Sam became very uncool. "One way or another."

Avi shrugged, indifferent to the implicit threat. "You can tell him that yourself."

He watched in disbelief as she pulled herself up the barn-board ladder.

"Come on," she called behind her. From below, Sam watched the dirty soles of her bare feet going higher and higher, climbing like she was a kid. She was a kid, he realized. Just a kid.

A child of God.

"Shut up, Andy," Sam growled and started climbing.

Garvey was older than Sam expected. Older than twelve. Older than Sam, even. He must have been about fifty. At that age, he was probably afraid of breaking a hip from falling down the ladder. No wonder he wanted to stay up here.

His hair was frizzy, long. It hung on either side of his pale, ashen face, and he kept shaking his head from side to side to keep his hair from creeping into his eyes.

Sam didn't bother trying to shake hands with Garvey when Avi introduced them. He knew enough about hippie culture to understand they would consider a greeting like that as *square*.

The treehouse was big, as far as treehouses went. Eight feet by eight feet, an opening through the floor to admit climbers, and an actual glass-paned hinged window, which was mercifully open, allowing in a pleasant breeze to air out the smell of urine and cigarette smoke. A few crumpled packs of Winstons lay scattered around where Garvey sat.

Sam hated cigarettes, but he really hated Winstons. They'd killed his father. Sure, it was all fun and games when you tapped out a single cigarette from the pack. They were feather-light, full of crushed, dried tobacco, and wrapped in a paper-thin sleeve. Who's going to get hurt by that? No one. If one Winston cigarette landed on your head, you'd shrug it off. But put thousands of them together in a crate and stack that crate on a wobbly cart, hit an uneven spot on the pavement so that crate of Winston cigarettes tips over and flattens your father, then see if you're still a fan of cigarettes.

Sam now felt even better about asking them to leave the property. Avi, he didn't mind so much, but this Garvey, with his smoking and his red hair: that had to go.

"So, Garvey. Avi tells me you're not in too big a hurry to come down out of the treehouse. Sounds like someone's after you or something?"

Garvey's face twitched.

"Where'd you hear that?" He bolted upright, hugging his sitar to his body. "Do they know I'm here?"

"Whoa, whoa, whoa." Sam said. The man had clearly flipped his lid. Avi tried to calm him, stroking his face, which was pressed against the sitar's neck. "It's just what Avi was telling me, that you thought people were out to get you."

Garvey peered through narrowed slits at Sam and looked to Avi for reassurance.

"He's okay," Avi told him. "He's not one of them."

After taking three deep breaths, Garvey held the last one before closing his eyes and releasing a deep sonorous *ohmmmmm* that reverberated through the floor of the treehouse. When the first ohm lapsed into silence, he did it again.

"Is this what you kids call a freakout?" Sam asked.

"He's meditating. Opening his mind to the universal consciousness."

"Okay, but I really gotta get back. Whatever he's got to tell me is going to have to wait. I'm supposed to be looking for my kid, and my wife's wandering around in the woods. She is going to be in a huff if she catches me up here lallygagging."

"Before you go, help yourself to some brownies." Avi offered Sam a square baking pan of brownies with a knife lying across them. They looked delicious, and he was starving. Thick ridges of flaky, chocolaty goodness, just like you see in television commercials for those box mixes.

"Don't mind if I do." He cut himself a square and chewed it down in just a few bites.

"You can have more if you like," Avi suggested.

"Thanks, I'm starving." He scooped out a larger square and gobbled that down too, while Avi held on to the pan for dear life. Garvey and Avi looked at him with curiosity, as if they'd never seen a normal person eating normal brownies.

"Wow," Avi exclaimed as he cut yet another brownie with the finesse of a badger with an ice auger. "It's like you've got a serious case of the munchies."

It occurred to Sam that these might not be normal brownies. They might be "magic" brownies. He'd seen a special report about hippies on *60 Minutes.* Hippies sprinkled drugs on everything. They even wanted to put the LSD in the water supply. With horror, Sam realized these were the brownies that made you see strange colors and talk to people who weren't there. All things drug-laden, he knew, were the mainstays of the hippie diet: magic brownies, magic mushrooms, and brown rice, which may or may not be magic too.

Sam dropped the brownie like it was on fire. "I need to leave." He scrambled down the ladder back to ground level before the drugs really kicked in and rendered him a helpless victim of a hippie treehouse death cult.

Avi and Garvey looked at each other in disbelief.

"That dude was having a total freakout," Garvey said.

"But he really seemed to dig those brownies that Mrs. Svensson baked for us," Avi said, salvaging what was left of the brownies. "She said the secret was the sour cream."

"Far out, man," Garvey nodded. "That dude loves sour cream."

Garvey shifted the sitar into playing position and released a few slow chords that filled the treehouse with a sound not unlike wind chimes. He sang as the familiar Simon and Garfunkel tune formed on his sonorous silky sitar strains.

And here's to you, Missus Svensson. Heaven holds a place for those who bake. Brownie cake.

"You are *so* talented, Garv," Avi said as she clapped along.

◆◆◆◆◆◆

His heart was racing: what was in those brownies, and why did he want more of them? He was hooked. He would need to go to one of those methadone clinics to kick the habit.

Arne whizzed by, pulled behind a boat. "Look at me, Dad!" The boy did a spin and returned to face the boat. Maybe it was just a hallucination—it *must* be a hallucination. Arne didn't know how to waterski anymore than Sam knew how to macramé a plant holder. The hallucination kept on skiing and hollering just like the real Arne would. Sam rubbed his eyes. The big ears on that kid were unmistakable. It was Arne, and he really was waterskiing as if he'd been waterskiing his entire life.

"Hey, wait! Come back!" Sam shouted at the lake. If that waterskiing boy was real, that meant the shiny red Mercury 1250 Super BP outboard motor that was pulling was real too. It looked familiar, but his attention shifted to a young woman lounging full length at the back of the boat. She wore an itsy-bitsy two-piece bikini, only it wasn't yellow polka dots; it was light pink, making her look entirely nude from this distance.

Child of God, Voodoo Andy's voice cajoled.

"Oh, come on, Andy. She wants to be looked at!"

If Voodoo Andy were there, he'd be looking, too. You could appreciate a woman's look while still respecting her. Heck, Sam was the first to admit that women could be whatever they wanted to be: models, actresses, housewives, and waitresses. It was 1975, for cripe's sake!

The woman on the boat sat up, and Sam got a better look at her face. She sure looked familiar. Come to think of it, the guy driving the boat looked familiar too.

"Jeez-a-loo!" It clicked. That man was Russell Randall, the man whose beautiful Mercury outboard motor Sam had sabotaged with sugar.

He called up to Avi and Garvey, "Hey, can I stay up there with you for a while until this brownie trip is over?" As he gripped the first barn-board rung, a hand gripped his forearm and set him back on the ground.

"Where do you think you're going, mister?"

It was Edie, clearly not pleased to see him trying to climb a tree while their son did loop-de-loops on a lake.

"I was just chatting with Avi and Garvey, you know, having a snack." He wondered if she could tell he was out of his mind on baked goods. He didn't know what to do with his hands. Was he gesturing with them too much? Should he keep them by his side? What was an appropriate amount of hand movement in the normal world? No one had ever taught him this stuff. This is what kids should be learning in school: appropriate hand gestures and how to bake delicious, chocolaty brownies.

No! He chided himself. *You've got to stop thinking about those brownies.* The fudge chocolate monkey on his back wouldn't let go. Next thing you know, he'd be pawning Arne's Tonka Trucks for his next fix.

"Who's up there? Is it that hippie girl?"

"Yeah. And her husband. Or her spiritual husband, or something."

"Well, that's great. Our son is half-drowned out on the lake, being dragged around by some stranger and a half-naked bimbo…"

"She's more than half-naked, Edie," Sam corrected, squinting out to the lake to reconfirm that the bikini was still itsy-bitsy.

"…and here you are climbing trees like an infant."

Sam giggled. "I'd like to see that." The thought of a baby climbing a tree seemed wildly amusing to him at that moment.

The boat came to a stop and circled around to pick up Arne out of the water. Russell Randall collected the skis and the rope and turned toward shore. The more-than-half-naked young woman draped a towel around Arne and kissed his cheek.

"Let's get our boy and get out of here. We'll deal with all this..." She waved her hand dismissively, "once we're back in Minneapolis."

"We don't have enough money for gas," Sam reminded her.

Edie sighed. "I didn't want to do this. I mean, I *really* didn't want to do this, but I'll call my mom and ask her to wire money to us in Alexandria. Maybe we can find a real estate agent there too, who can sell this place and ask your new hippie friends to leave, or else."

"I sort of promised them they could stay here, just until they get on their feet." Sam winced as he spoke. His plan was clear. Maybe revealing it to Edie in small doses would get her used to it better. "They're good people. They can help out for a while with cleaning up and painting and stuff."

"Why would you promise that?"

"Because!" Sam said, too loudly, but then calmed himself. "Because I don't think we should sell it." He avoided direct eye contact with her, looking instead at the big main house, wishing he was inside it tucked under the covers so he could sleep off the effect of the brownies.

"What did you say?"

"I said, I think we should keep it. Make a go of it here. Run it as a resort."

Edie laughed as if a dam had burst within her.

"Run it? You just said we don't have enough money to fill the gas tank to get back to Minneapolis. We certainly don't have the money to put into fixing this place up. No, I'm just going to sell it as-is and be done with it. Then I'm going to split the money with cousin Jeffy and Lana because I just wouldn't feel right..."

"Screw cousin Jeffy! What about Edie? And little Arne? And your ever-loving Sam, huh? Don't they deserve the good life?"

They watched the boat approach. Arne waved wildly at them, lake water dripping from his ears.

"You earn the good life, Sam. You work hard for it. We're making our own good life in Nordeast. You've got your job. Rent is reasonable. Let's not mess that up. I'm selling this place, and we're going to have a normal life. Back in the city."

"Edie, there's something else I've got to tell you."

Edie breathed deep as if bracing herself.

"I got fired," Sam admitted. "We've got nothing to go back to. No job. We've got no money. We're going to get evicted from the apartment, which, I mean, let's be honest, is a crap hole, anyway."

"You're lying. You're just saying that so you can get your way."

"I'm not lying. I got fired."

"It's true," a gravelly voice sounded from the shore. It was Russell Randall, Teddy's fancy, rich client, walking up from the shore with Arne. "He got fired for *fercockting* my baby."

The bellowing voice came from the man Edie had seen in the boat pulling Arne around on skis. He was swarthy, stocky, and his gold chain was lost in a tangle of exposed chest hair on his bare torso. He jumped Sam and wrestled him to the ground, trying to choke him. Edie didn't know what this surprise hostility was about, but she was tempted—just for a second, mind you—tempted to let the man get in a few hits before she intervened.

She struggled to pull the man off her husband, but he was determined.

"Now, you I recognize. You're the *schmuck* who poured sugar in my gas tank."

Clearly, the man was crazy or on drugs. It occurred to her that the entire property could have just been one big front for drug running, what with the hippies and all. Her uncle may have been the Godfather of Little Paw Lake.

Sam was able to roll the man over and get to his feet.

"Whoa, whoa, whoa. Easy." He put out an open hand, which the other man smacked away.

"How'd you like it if I poured a pound of sugar down your throat?"

Sam seemed confused. Edie knew he was actually pondering the offer, wondering if he could consume a pound of sugar before choking to death. She answered for him.

"I think we all need to calm down," she said calmly. "You're probably just having a bad trip."

"Bad trip? This was a great trip until I saw this bozo. His handiwork at Teddy's shop cost me an extra two hundred bucks."

Teddy's shop was where Sam worked. Or maybe where he *used to* work.

"You mean, you actually know this man, Sam?"

"Yeah, I did some work on his boat motor."

"Some work? Some work, my keister. You deliberately killed my baby. My beautiful Mercury. Two hundred bucks. Stealing money right out of the mouths of my children."

"Ha!" A brief, contemptuous laugh erupted from overhead. Edie turned to find Avi Starshine hanging from the tree ladder, glaring at the swarthy man.

"Your children? You never cared one bit for your children."

"Avi? Baby?" The anger melted from the man's entire countenance as his eyes widened. "Where have you been? We've got missing fliers up all over the city. The police are dredging rivers. Come to your papa, baby."

"Don't you 'baby' me," Avi yelled. "You've had golf clubs you love more than me."

"That's not true."

"What about that five iron?"

"That five iron Bob Hope gave to me himself."

He rushed toward Avi, but she stepped back, and Sam stepped between them.

"Do you know Miss Starshine?" Avi asked as calmly as she could without a Dignity cigarette dangling from her lips.

"Starshine? You're not even using your own father's name?" He gripped his heart as if it pained him.

Avi laughed, but her face was angry.

"That's rich, coming from you, Benny Gerzberg."

"A year we've been looking for this one," the man pleaded with Edie. "One day, poof, she just vanishes without a note. Her mother was destroyed."

Arne padded up the stairs leading from the lake. He still dripped water.

"Mom! Did you see me?"

"Yes, Arne." She hugged him to her hip. "That was nice, sweetie. We'll talk about it later." And they certainly *would* talk about it later: how it wasn't safe to go waterskiing or get into boats with strange men. This was another last straw.

"That boy has a gift," the man told Edie. "Like my little Avi, who also has a gift. She has a brain from God for studying law."

"I'm not participating in the corrupt legal system, jerk."

"Jerk? This is how you speak to your father? The father who sweated blood to pay for your school with that nice Billy Mitchell."

"It's called William Mitchell Law School, Dad."

"Oh." Russell Randall threw up his hands, feigning astonishment. "Excuse me, now it's Dad again."

"You're no father of mine, jerk."

"And we're back to the jerk." Russell shook his head.

"What about her?" Avi pointed at the half-naked blonde who watched the scene, perplexed. "Is she your daughter? She's definitely young enough. Do you *love* her too?"

"Hi, everyone." The young woman waved. "I'm Candace."

Sam waved back to Candace and smiled, but Edie smacked him.

"Avi, baby, let's go have some nice pie and talk things out."

"I'm done talking to you. I've got a spiritual husband, and he's everything you're not. He's kind and giving and, and…"

"And hiding out in a treehouse," Sam added, trying to be helpful, but Avi's father interrupted him.

"If you married a *goyim,* you just killed your mother. You know that? You killed her."

Avi turned to scramble up the treehouse ladder while her father shouted for her to come down. Sam looked at Edie and shrugged, then he climbed after her.

"Cool!" Arne launched himself out of her grasp and was about to follow his father up the tree, but Edie hoisted him down by hooking an arm around his waist as he wriggled to get free.

"Not you too, mister. We've got enough to talk about without you getting involved with dirty hippies." She realized she'd said it loud enough for Avi's father to hear, so she tried Vicki Svensson's favorite response, quickly adding, "No offense."

<hr />

Even taking the barn-wood rungs as fast as he could, Sam had a tough time keeping up with Avi. He worried she would put up a barrier across the treehouse entrance, leaving him thirty feet in the air, half out of his mind on brownies, and forced to climb down to face some pretty harsh vibes from his wife. There was no barrier, thankfully, and he pulled himself back into the treehouse where Avi, sobbing, was being comforted by Garvey.

"Hey," Sam panted. "I know you're in the middle of something with your physical father, but can I just ask: how long does this crazy magic brownie trip last?"

Avi looked up at him like he was foaming at the mouth.

"They're just regular brownies, man." Garvey answered for her. "They were totally a gift from one of the neighbors. They're not laced or anything, except with delicious sour cream."

Avi sniffled, adding, "What kind of people do you think we are? That's so uncool."

Great. Now even the hippies were mad at him. Sam realized that there was a big difference between a basic sugar rush fueling an overactive imagination and a psychedelic experience from hippie drugs.

He climbed back down—very slowly—taking extra care with each rung, in no particular hurry to face Edie or Russell Randall. Then Sam remembered what Russell Randall said about Arne: *that boy has a gift.*

Arne Fisker was a natural at waterskiing.

What a relief: Arne was good at something.

The boy didn't have much else going for him besides big ears and an aggressive attitude. He wasn't doing particularly well in school. Couldn't throw a spiral when they tossed the football. Showed no interest in small engine repair. He was funny-looking, and he gave poor Edie headache after headache, and now there was a raft of angry parents in Nordeast who were out to get him.

He had an actual God-given gift, and a gifted person was supposed to share that gift with the world. If they made a little money from it, who was going to complain?

His son, that little big-eared troublemaking tike, was a gold mine that Sam could tally as a win in the column for *Reasons to Keep the Resort.* Reason number seven: the boy needs to practice his talent on an actual lake. Waterskiing wasn't like swimming lessons where you could just toss a kid into a decent-sized trough and teach him to doggy paddle. No, sir! For waterskiing, you needed a stretch of open water and supportive parents cheering you on.

Yup, this was all about Arne. Edie would be sure to see that. And if she didn't; well, he had one other card tucked up his sleeve.

Russell Randall and his "niece" returned to their boat and shoved off the shattered dock. Edie and Arne were on the way back to the driveway when Sam caught up with them.

"There's my superstar." He rubbed Arne's head, which caused his earlobes to wobble. "I caught your show on skis earlier. Wow, you are really good! How'd you learn to do all that?"

"I just did what my body told me to," Arne said, picking up steam. "Did you see the time I jumped in the air off the waves with my skis sideways? I thought I was flying!"

"That's amazing, kiddo." Sam leaned down. "Hey, can you do me a quick favor? Can you wait by the car for a couple minutes while I talk to your mother? You can play the radio." He handed Arne the car keys.

Arne ran off like a shot.

"Do not start the car," Edie yelled at him. "We need to conserve all the gas we can, okay?" When she faced Sam, her expression was a combination of complete exhaustion and outright disappointment. He recognized that look. It was the same one Edie's mother gave him whenever she visited.

Chapter 18

Helmets On!

TUESDAY NIGHTS WERE SONS of Gunnar meetings. John Kvalstad put on his most formal Hawaiian shirt, which featured an ancient Kalaupapa tribal pattern, part vine, part water waves. It would baffle the other Norwegians. That and his flip-flops. He wore those so often that he had a pale, white 'M' on each foot where the skin hadn't tanned under the toe straps.

His cabin on Long Ear Lake was small, just one bedroom and a small kitchen, but big enough for him. For him, the cabin was just a place to sleep when he wasn't working or on the boat. Long Ear was pretty quiet, as it was one of the "dead-end" lakes on the Rabbit Chain of Lakes. He could fish in peace when he wanted or have his neighbor pull him around when he felt like he needed to get up on waterskis. There wasn't much to John's cabin: the couch he'd scrounged from a thrift store in Brainerd that didn't smell too bad after he sprayed it down with Lysol; an old Zenith console record player and radio because sometimes he might entertain a lady guest with something classy, like *The Mantovani Scene*, while they drank Budweiser from the can; an electric fan. Not much to it, but enough.

To get to the Sons of Gunnar lodge, he could drive his work truck along the serpentine curves that wrapped around the lakes and downtown, or he could take his boat. It was a beautiful warm evening with low wind, so boat it was. Then he had another choice: the fastest route eastward across Stoker and Frost Lakes, or he could cruise to the south, through Big Jack Pine, for the best view of downtown, and then cross over to Big Paw at the inlet by the Viking longship. The scenic route had more open water to cross, so if he was in a hurry, he could take the shorter route. Except John wasn't in a hurry to get to the meeting.

Scenic route won that one. He grabbed the three remaining beers from the pack, and soon he was easing through the narrow inlet that led to Big Jack Pine Lake under the Back Cut Road bridge. He slowed the throttle to admire downtown Fornborg glowing in the early evening sun. Glints of silver sparked from the tips of waves from the lake, making the town shimmer like a gold-dipped mirage.

He was sorely tempted to drop a line in the water and set the anchor, a beautiful night like that. He had his fishing gear on board, but he was pretty sure his nightcrawlers had baked in the Styrofoam container over the past couple of days in what was fast becoming one of the warmest Mays on record. The only thing keeping him from blowing off the meeting was the announcement Bud Langskip was sure to make about promoting John to *forkvinne*. If he didn't turn up, Bud would get pretty miffed and find some way to take it out on John, so he throttled up, and the boat surged forward again towards the inlet to Big Paw. John saluted the longship memorial as he glided by, imagining a crew of Vikings on the deck shaking their oars at him.

<hr>

The Sons of Gunnar held their meetings in the old stave lodge building nestled between Big Paw and Frost lakes. It was an old building, stacked rectangles, each layer a little narrower than the one below it, but triangular roof peaks angled sharply to shed snow loads and hid the boxy shape of the lower level. You'd see something like it in Norway, in those old stave churches, but there was no spire on top of the Sons of Gunnar lodge: only four snarling dragon heads carved on beams extending into the big sky. Hand-cut cedar shakes for roofing, and bur oak timber gave the lodge both a natural softness, but also an enduring unbreakability.

A mix of fishing boats, pontoons, and muscle boats already crowded the other spots along the six docks owned by the Sons of Gunnar. John picked his way very carefully to the only open mooring, not wanting to scuff his paint job against the shoddy old skiff that bobbed like a drunken prizefighter. That skiff belonged to Lonnie "the Loon" Lonning, by far the Sons of Gunnar's oldest member at age ninety-eight. He was still sprightly enough to motor himself to meetings from his shack across Big Paw, but he couldn't tie up his boat for crap. John secured his own boat before finagling the lines on old Lonnie's skiff so it wouldn't swivel out and bang against the *Hanu Hauʻoli*, which is what John called his boat. It was

Hawaiian for "happy turtle," but the other Norwegians just called it the *Nude Ole*.

Luther Storhode, the sergeant-at-arms, handed him an iron helmet at the front door.

"Almost on time, Wahoo," Luther jibed. "You missed a button on your shirt."

John waved him off, tucked the helmet under his arm, and entered the lodge. His eyes drank in the interior of thick, tall beams, curved heartwood planking, and iron fixtures that held torches for special ceremonies. Standing inside the Sons of Gunnar lodge was like being transported across time in the hold of a longship.

John joined the other men as they chanted, *Norsk, Norsk, Norsk,* louder and louder, the volume building in intensity as Bud Langskip, chieftain of the Sons of Gunnar, walked down the aisle, an ancient broadsword trailing behind, brushing against his fur leggings. He wore a helmet chased with gold and a bear-fur mantle over his shoulders that must have been uncomfortably warm. He ascended the dais and lifted his arms; the chanting became a chatter of *skuh skuh skuh*. He dropped his arms, and all sound ceased.

"*God kveld*, gentlemen."

God kveld, came the unison response like a chorus of sad frogs in a shrinking pond.

Bud nodded to Luther Storhode, who lifted the long-handled mallet and struck a brass gong.

"*Hyal-mar,*" Bud announced with force. "That means helmets on, gents."

The room erupted in the sounds of folding chairs scraping the wooden floor, the rustle of cloth as elbows bent, the grunts of old men leaning forward to reach under their chairs. Then, one by one, the men all donned their helmets, iron and gray, some with flattened guards that covered the bridge of the nose, others that flared at the base to rest on broad shoulders.

"Glad you could all make it out tonight. First order of business is public relations." Bud stepped to the edge of the dais, his foot hanging partway off. "I'm sure you all know how excited we are about Fornborg's centennial coming up next year," Bud grinned, a hint of mischief sparkling in his eye. The men chuckled, filling the lodge with a low, warm reverberation.

"Some folks are even more excited about the town centennial than they are about the bicentennial of the United States."

This thought was so ridiculous to everyone that they burst out laughing.

"In fact, our very own mayor is quoted as saying that people can stay home and watch the bicentennial on television, but they better come out in person to celebrate Fornborg at a hundred years old. Heck, Lonnie Lonning is nearly a hundred himself. I'd ask him to stand up, but we don't have that much time."

This amused the men, and they chuckled.

"Neither does Lonnie," another member called out. The men laughed louder, all except Lonnie, who didn't hear so good anymore.

"But in all seriousness, Fornborg's civil leaders have forgotten what makes this city great." Bud raised his hand in a fist. "It's the Sons of Gunnar!"

"Yah! Yah!" The members stamped their feet.

"With that in mind, I asked our club historian to write up a little something for the *Daily Hawk*. Just to remind folks around here that long before there was a Fornborg—long before there was an America, even—there were the Sons of Gunnar."

The members erupted into hollers and clapping as Dave Fernriker, the club historian, stood, cleared his throat, and began warbling what he'd written.

"The State of Minnesota chartered Fornborg as a city in 1876," he began, gathering steam as he proceeded. "While most people of good sense will be as excited about this as they would be about federal Tax Day, the Fornburg City Council is planning to elevate this trivial event to the status of a holy day at the expense of taxpayers. While they lift up the memory of petty bureaucrats in St. Paul who signed little squiggles on scraps of paper a hundred years ago, they do so on the backs of the hardworking people of Fornborg. This comes at a time when the City Council, their power unchecked, ordered two hundred sets of stars-and-stripes bunting to adorn the stores along Gull Drive. Are they supporting cultural events? No! Are they supporting heritage classes? No! Beyond being proud Americans and proud Minnesotans, we must remain proud of the generations of farmers, warriors, fishermen, and craftsmen who made it possible for Fornborg and America to exist in the first place. To the people of Fornborg, the Sons of Gunnar say *Skol*!"

Bud grinned at the wild shouts of *skol* filling the hall. "Well, the Sons of Gunnar certainly isn't one of those rosy-cheeked, johnny-come-lately groups like the Rotary or the Lions Club, are we?" More applause. "Next order of business: *klager*. Who would like to start with a complaint?" Bud waited a few beats and moved on. No one ever complained, but the club was fair: you could complain if you wanted to be a non-conforming outcast and troublemaker.

"Next, *forkvinne* reports. Lester." Bud nodded to the sergeant-at-arms, and he dipped another torch head into the fire and brought it to Lester, who stood gripping the torch.

"The regular monthly intake went smooth," Lester reported. "Except over at the lumberyard. They were short fifty bucks."

Bud's eyebrows raised. "Fifty? What's the story there?"

"Some shipment of materials for a new cabin over on Stump Lake got delayed in transit, and they didn't get the money from the builder they expected."

Removing the torch from the stand behind him, Bud stepped down from the dais and into the aisle. He scanned the crowd until he found Tom Mergard, who worked at the lumberyard and was supposed to be an inside man for the club. Bud brought his fist down on Tom's helmet.

"Is this going to be a problem, Tom?"

"I'm not the boss there; I just…"

More pounding, this time with the butt of the torch, causing flaming debris to land on Tom's lap.

"That's right. You're not the boss there. I am the boss there." Bud stretched his arms wide and turned to face the larger group. "I am the boss everywhere. Understood?"

The men chanted again. *Norsk! Norsk! Norsk!*

"Now that you've had time to consider," Bud said, "I'm sure you've realized that you could easily make up that fifty-dollar shortfall incurred by your employer by, say, selling some old dusty two-by-fours to Vernon off the books. Vernon?" Bud called over his shoulder. "Are you still planning to build that boat shed this summer?"

"I am," Vernon Botskur answered.

"Have you purchased all your materials yet?"

"None of them, Chief," Vernon admitted. "Kind of been putting it off until I could scrape together all the money."

"Do you have fifty dollars?"

"Yeah, I can do fifty," Vernon answered. "Might have to break into Lolly's coffee can, but I can do fifty."

"And Tom, do you think you can manage to deliver the supplies to Vernon's place before, let's say, next week's meeting?"

"Well, it's just that…"

"Yes?"

"Well, you know, it's just that I have to be a little careful…"

Bud's hand holding the torch shot back over Tom's helmet.

"I agree," Bud growled. "You need to be very careful."

"No, it won't be a problem," Tom relented, clenching his teeth. "I'll need a list."

Bud strode triumphantly to the dais, the tension in the hall broken as if a storm had passed.

"Vernon, you get a list of everything you need to Tom along with fifty dollars. Lester, you mark the lumberyard's account as paid for now, but I want you to check in with them every few days. If they need extra support, we'll figure out next steps. Agreed?"

"Agreed," the men responded in unison.

Sheesh, John thought. *All that stress over fifty bucks.*

"Now, let's hear from our newest *forkvinne*, John Kvalstad."

John, startled to hear his own name, reflexively looked up. He noted Lester Langskip considering him with a furrowed brow. The announcement had come as a surprise to him. Judging by his dark expression, Lester didn't like it.

Bud nodded to Luther, who dipped an unlit torch in Bud's flame, walked it from the dais, and handed it to John.

"Congrats, Wahoo," Vernon called out, and other men, saluting him with *sköl*, turned to look at him as he rose. He was nervous. He was more of a behind-the-scenes guy or, more realistically, an under-the-sink kind of guy. He was more accustomed to holding a wrench than a torch.

"I put John in charge of the Lachmann property," Bud continued. "The one on Little Paw Lake. As you know, we've been trying to acquire that parcel to advance our long-term plans, but Nat Lachmann's untimely death and ill-conceived estate distribution…" Here, Bud glared at Phillip Logner, the town attorney who had overseen Nat Lachmann's will. "…has caused some unexpected clogs in our plan. And who better to fix clogs than our brother John?"

The men in the hall, except for Lester, chuckled appreciatively.

"John, give us an update on that family, who now owns the property."

John cleared his throat and adjusted his helmet by the nose bridge so he could see better. He knew many of the men would think he looked ridiculous standing in Heritage Hall (also known as *Valhalla*) holding a torch and wearing a warrior helmet while also donning his Hawaiian shirt, baggy shorts, and flip-flops.

"So, technically, it's the wife who is the owner." John nodded toward the attorney, causing his helmet to shift over his eyes once again. "Thanks to brother Phillip for setting me straight on that."

John explained what he knew about the Fisker family, how they were from Minneapolis, lived in a little upstairs apartment, and how the husband had recently been fired from his job as a small-engine mechanic.

"The husband doesn't have any prospects for fresh employment," John continued. "So he's pretty set on taking on the property and getting it operational as a resort again. The good news is the wife, Edie, doesn't want anything to do with the place. She just wants to sell it and wash her hands of it."

Bud nodded, his face relieved.

"Good. John, I want you to go in closer. Get involved one to one. Help them get that property on the market at the lowest price possible. Who's our real estate contact?"

Dwayne Fellgrad rose in the back.

"Rita Fellgrad, right here in Fornborg," Dwayne answered. Rita was his wife. "She got her license last year, and we'd sure appreciate the business."

Bud shook his head. "Sorry, Dwayne. I just can't go there, even in this crazy modern age. Nothing personal. Now, we all know Rita is a good woman and a fine mother, but we can't take risks with this. I mean, even if Gloria Steinham herself had a real estate license, I wouldn't let her at this deal. Who else?"

The red-headed Arthur Brevindal waved his gangly arms. "There's still me."

An audible groan arose. Everyone knew that Arthur Brevindal was one of the worst real estate agents in the area: terrible negotiator, no attention to detail, and brimming with an enthusiasm that was considered pushy by nearly all his dissatisfied clients. But he was a man, and because of that, Bud nodded again to Luther, who lit a torch and handed it to Arthur, who stood holding the torch like a child would hold a balloon at the zoo, looking up at it in admiration and letting his mouth hang open.

"Arthur, I want you to work with John on this, and for cripe's sake, don't mess this up."

"No way." Arthur beamed.

The meeting pressed on with plans for Flag Day in June when they planned to burn several Swedish flags, and Midsommar, where they also planned to burn Swedish flags and do other stuff too. By the end of the meeting, John's legs were tired. He, Lester, Andrew Brevindahl, and three other men remained standing with their torches in hand even after their portions of the meeting had concluded.

"Those of you who remain seated without torches must light your way with these men's glory."

Bud Langskip, torch in hand, stepped off the dais and strode down the aisle. Lester crab-walked past his bench mates into the aisle and followed his father to the back of the Hall with John, Arthur, and the other torchbearers close behind. Then the other members rose and followed the procession, removing their helmets as they walked, so they once again looked like grocers, machinists, farmers, and husbands of lady real estate agents.

Chapter 19

There Is No Good News

THE FISKER FAMILY WAS in a pinch. Where would they spend the night? They'd been banned from local lodging just because their room at the Lakeview Lodge was a smoldering wreck, and that was fine. Honest. Because they didn't have enough money for another night's stay, anyway. They'd been chased out of a state park by the DNR and had been labeled as Lake Lutherans by locals.

It was too late in the afternoon to begin the trek back to Minneapolis, which also was fine, seeing as they also didn't have enough money for gas—especially at fifty cents a gallon. Those bastards at OPEC had screwed over middle-class Americans like them, according to Sam. Edie had no idea who OPEC was, but if they were responsible for gas prices being so high, then she had to agree: they were bastards.

With no money for rooms, gas, or food, Edie resorted to desperate measures. She decided to sacrifice her dignity (her abstract sense of dignity, not her secret emergency stash of Dignity cigarettes). She called her mother collect in Arizona from the phone in the main house while Arne and Sam explored.

After her mother told the operator that she would accept the charges, it sounded as if she was in the middle of a shootout.

"Can you turn down the television, Mom?"

"What's wrong? Kojak is on."

"Glad to talk to you, too, Mom. I'm calling you from your dead brother's home."

That seemed to get her attention.

"Just a minute," she said sullenly. The sounds of gunfire and revving car engines disappeared magically. "Okay, I'm back. How did everything go?"

Edie snorted as all the images of the past day washed over her at once.

"I don't know where to start." She chuckled. Careful to omit certain details that might cast Sam and Arne in a less favorable light, Edie recounted their near-death experience with the rattlesnake on the trip up and concluded with Sam's suspicion that Uncle Nat's death had been anything but accidental.

"Murder?"

"Could be, based on what Sam said."

"Who would want to kill poor Nat?"

It occurred to Edie that more than one person might have a motive. Murder and motive went together naturally, as any television detective show worth its salt would point out. As she explained to her mother, there was more than one potential suspect: the mysterious men's club who wanted the property; unstable, drug-addled hippies crawling all over the place; cousins Jeffy and Lana; and even Nat's ex-wife, who still lived in the area.

"And those are just the people we know about so far," Edie concluded.

"Well, if we're making a complete list," Edie's mom added, "we need to include you and that husband of yours. You, after all, stood to get the property."

"But we didn't know anything about it," Edie said defensively. That was so like her mother, ready to fingerprint her and put her in a criminal lineup. Guilty until proven innocent.

"If anything, it's probably that men's club. Sounds like they really wanted that property. I might try to have a chat with some of them just to see what they have to say."

"Edie, I don't want you messing around with that men's club."

This was the second warning she'd received about that group in one day, Vicki Svensson having told her they were bad news too.

"How would you know anything about this men's club, Mom? You haven't been back for decades."

"Your uncle may have mentioned them once or twice over the years, that's all. Why aren't you back in Minneapolis? Did that husband of yours leave you?"

"You wish," Edie said bitterly. "No, we're kind of stuck here, what with the price of gas and everything. You'd mentioned that you might be willing to give us some money."

Even though they were seventeen hundred miles apart, talking on a really long wire, Edie could tell that her mother was smiling even before she responded.

"Certainly. I can wire money to you first thing tomorrow. But I will need you to do something for me."

Correction: seventeen hundred miles apart, talking on a really long string. Her mother loved strings.

"I need you to gather any documents from Nat's house."

"You mean, like, legal documents?"

"Yeah, sure. But any other papers too. Oh, like correspondence. Just get them all together, and mail them to me in a bundle."

"You want me to collect his electricity bill, things like that?"

"Just, um, the personal items. Letters and such."

Edie agreed she would do it, but her mother placed another condition.

"I need you to promise me something, Edie. Promise me you will not read any of the, uh, documents you find. Will you promise?"

She promised, but, dang! That only made her wonder what exactly she was going to get a hold of.

By the time she got off the phone, Arne had picked out which room he wanted to make his bedroom, and Sam had made a list of things that needed fixing up, removal, or that could be sold for cash.

"We're not moving here, people," Edie concluded, exasperated with them.

❧ · ◆ · ☙

Edie was able to scrape together enough ingredients for breakfast the next morning from the meager supplies remaining in the kitchen. The box of Bisquick looked like it had been pawed by a gang of raccoons, but it was probably those hippies, two of which still lurked on the property. A carton of milk was definitely past the point of freshness, but it gave the batter a nice buttermilk flavor. She skimmed a few flecks of mold from the surface of the maple syrup. Penicillin was from mold, so how bad could it be?

Sam reviewed his list aloud as Edie cooked. She only half-listened as he explained what needed fixing or cleaning or throwing out. In her mind, they were already at the bank in Alexandria, where she would receive her mother's wire transfer. Also, in her mind, Sam would go back to Teddy Irwin's repair shop and beg for his job. And in her mind, Arne would really get the hang of fifth grade this time around.

Everything would return to normal.

"There's the dock, of course," Sam said. "That's just got to go. The understructure is pretty corroded, and the wood that didn't blow off is rotting in places, anyway. Then there's the first cabin. Some kind of mildew on the ceiling in the bedroom. Might need to tear that out because that can spread. But the other cabins look pretty decent. Some paint. Maybe some Lysol."

Edie let him rattle on until it was time to plate up the stack of cakes from the warming oven.

"I'm selling it as-is, so you don't have to worry about anything," she declared flatly. "Arne, get your little heinie down here for breakfast."

Whereas she'd imagined Arne still lolling around in bed, half groggy and ready to fight any effort to rouse him, the boy came zipping into the kitchen fully dressed and hugged his mother's waist.

"I love it here. I saw a deer this morning. It looked at me through the window."

"Well, don't name it or anything," Edie warned. She guided him into a chair and set a plate of pancakes in front of him.

"Don't I need a fork?"

Edie checked the silverware drawer. Not a fork to be found. There were spoons, but most of them were filthy with bits of crust. She found a clean set of steak knives still in the box, so she set those out.

"Just use one of those."

Arne snatched up a knife, and in no time, had his stack looking like it went through a wood chipper. Syrup splattered all over the table, but Edie didn't care. As-is meant as-is.

"Can I go waterskiing with Mr. Russell again today?"

"Gee, Arne, I don't think that's going to work out," Sam answered.

"Is it because you ruined his outboard motor, Dad?"

"Yeah, something like that. But there are other boats out there and other motors. We'll figure out something to get you back on skis, a talent like yours."

Edie smacked the stovetop with her spatula.

"Now, wait a minute, you two. No one's going waterskiing or spraying Lysol or climbing into treehouses or anything else today. We are going to get some money, and then we're going home."

Arne and Sam looked at each other, a secret communication flowing psychically between their brains (or wherever psychic messages flowed between male members of the species).

She needed to do a search before they left Fornborg as part of the agreement with her mother. Somewhere in the house was a cache of papers, and Edie was to gather all the documents she could find: legal, correspondence, diaries—anything on paper that looked personal—and ship it off to her mother. Oh, and to not read any of it.

She told Arne to go run around outside for a while and burn off some of his excess energy before they got in the car. Then, to Sam, she said, "I want you to go tell those hippies to leave today. I'm pretty sure as-is can't legally include actual people as part of the real estate deal."

"I won't do it, Edie," Sam replied as he set down his steak knife. "This is where we're supposed to be. This is life just shoving an opportunity right under your nose, and all you gotta do is breathe it in."

Edie poured the rest of the sour milk over Sam's head.

"I breathed it. It smells like dirty hippies and rotting fish."

Sam slid the car keys off the table into his other hand and stood to leave.

"Where are you going?"

"I'm going to find your cousin and get the seat back for the car."

"But we need to get to Alexandria for the money."

"Wouldn't be there today. Your mom has to get to the bank today and arrange it all. Heck, that money might not be there for two, three days."

She wondered if marriage vows just boiled down to: *Do you take this man as-is?*

<hr>

The funny man in the tropical clothes and flip-flop sandals called to Arne from the driver's side of the white truck.

"Aloha, kid. Your parents around?"

Aloha. Maybe the guy was a big Elvis fan. Elvis had done a big concert on television in Hawaii, and his mom had watched it.

"Yeah, my mom's inside, and my dad's going to vik some hippies," Arne said.

"Vik? What's that mean?"

"Kick them out."

"Oh." The man laughed. "Evict. I see. So it sounds like you're moving in then?"

"I don't know," Arne replied, and he didn't know. His parents weren't exactly clear about what was happening except that they both agreed that storing snakes in the car was not a good idea. "I think my dad wants to stay, but my mom wants to sell asses."

"Did you say *asses*?"

"Yeah, she doesn't want to fix anything up. Just wants to sell it."

He laughed again, nodding. "As is. Okay, got it. Well, I just might be able to help. Better let me talk to your mommy."

"You got a boat?"

"Yeah, I bet most people around here have one. Why?"

"Does your boat go fast? Like fast enough to pull a waterskier?"

"You want to go waterskiing?"

Arne nodded.

"I'll tell you what. Let me talk to your mommy first, and then I'll see if your parents would be okay with me swinging by with my boat. I can probably rustle up some skis that would fit you."

"Okay!" Arne ran off toward the house, not even allowing the man enough time to slide out of the driver's side of the Aloha Plumbing truck.

Arne burst through the front door in search of his mom. She wasn't in the kitchen or the bedroom, so he just yelled as loud as he could right where he stood, which was pretty loud. The singing teacher at school once said Arne might have a future as a bank alarm.

"Mom, there's a guy here to talk to you. Mom! Mom!"

He heard the floorboards overhead creak, and then he heard his mother announce that she would be right down and to stop yelling. The man in the tropical clothes walked through the front door, which Arne had left wide open. He walked right into the living room and felt around under the sofa cushions. He clutched an item that looked like a bottle opener.

"I knew I left it somewhere," the man explained.

"What is it?"

"Uh, it's a plumbing tool. It's called a, um, longneck wrench."

"Oh, okay. Make yourself at home," Arne said, trying to sound hospitable like the normal families on television did. He almost offered the man a cocktail, but Arne didn't know if there were any cocktails around. "My name's Arne. What's yours?"

He wanted to be especially nice because he may just get another chance to go waterskiing, and there was nothing better than that. It was even better than pulling wax lips from the Perkins wishing well.

"Arne sounds like a Norwegian name. Are you Norwegian?"

"Seventy-five percent." Arne held up seven fingers and crooked his thumb to illustrate the point.

"My name's John Kvalstad. I'm a hundred percent. So, which of your parents let you down?"

His mother padded down the stairs, carrying a cardboard box with papers and junk in it. She froze on the staircase, pressing the box between her chest and the banister. "No one let him down," she insisted without context for the conversation.

"Aloha, Mrs. Fisker. I was just telling Arne that I'm full Norwegian, and he mentioned he was only three-quarters. Now, if my math's correct, most likely, that means that either you or Mr. Fisker is only half."

"I don't see how that's any of your business, Mister..."

"Kvalstad." He slid off his sunglasses and slipped them in a pocket in his baggy pants. "You can call me John, but a lot of people around here call me Wahoo."

"Why is that?" Edie asked. "Are you a thrill seeker?"

John laughed and explained the Hawaiian connection.

"John's going to take me waterskiing again today, Mom."

"Oh, no, he's not. You can't just go out on boats with strange men, Arne."

"Yeah," John agreed. "You should enlist in the navy if that's the sort of thing you like."

She laughed, and Arne figured that something about the navy must be funny, so he laughed too.

"I understand you and your husband might be a little unsure about how to proceed with the property." John put up a hand when she was about to tell him to mind his own business again. "I know, I should keep my nose on my side of the fence. But I think I can help you. Or, at least, give you a couple options to consider."

His mother seemed to take an interest in what John Kvalstad had to say. Arne was going to keep his swim trunks on because he might just get back on the water yet.

"Why don't you come into the kitchen, and I'll see if there's any coffee around here."

What did Edie know about John Kvalstad? According to Vicki Svensson, he was a member of the Norwegian Pontoon Mafia—a group that Edie's mother had already warned her against. Judging from his truck, he also was a plumber who liked Hawaii. He seemed nice enough. Laid back, even. He may even have been handsome under the beard and shaggy hair, but she didn't think very long about that. It looked like he had a tattoo barely peeking out from the sleeve of his shirt. He caught her looking and pushed it up.

"We do stupid things when we're young." He smiled. A curved red stripe bore the word SAPPER, the letters knocked out, so it was his tan skin that colored them.

"Lots of men get tattoos, I guess, and they're no worse for wear." Edie tried to sound diplomatic.

"The stupid thing wasn't the tattoo," he corrected. "The stupid thing was me for volunteering for the Marines." He let the sleeve drop back over his arm. "You ever see those t-shirts that say *I Went to Las Vegas and All I Got was this Stupid T-shirt*? Well, my tattoo is like that, only it was Vietnam, not Las Vegas."

"Well, thank God that war is over." She wasn't sure what else to say about it. Seemed like half the young men had gone over and died or gotten all turned around, and the other half stayed home and pretended to go to college or, like Sam, fix small engines.

"It's over for some people. Won't ever end for others." John shrugged indifferently. "Anyway, I didn't come over to bore you with my life history. What's past is past. Let's talk about this property."

"If you had any advice, I'd sure appreciate it."

John nodded. "Yeah, of course. I like to be straight with people, let them know what they're up against. Did you know the septic tank on this property was installed when Eisenhower was still a buck private? Probably leaking every which way to Sunday right into that lake."

"And that's bad?"

"You wouldn't want Arne to catch Pontiac fever or swimmer's ear, would you? You wouldn't want people to point out your boy and say, 'Hey, there's typhoid Arne,' would you?"

"Well, no, of course not."

"It's bad enough the kid has to go through life with those ears," John continued. "I'm sure you don't want him to spend his life crapping out his guts on top of that. So, the bad news is, if you keep this place, you're going to need to install a septic mound system."

"And the good news?"

John shrugged. "That's it. There is no good news. It's going to cost at least eight hundred bucks to tear out the old system to get all the cabins on the new system."

Edie rose, flipped open first one cabinet door and then another. They creaked as if they were big castle doors. She didn't know why she opened them. She already knew from her breakfast adventure that there was very little in Uncle Nat's kitchen that resembled anything of use. A cracked tennis racket. A wax bag full of twigs. A rusted roller skate key.

"I'm not seeing any coffee."

"That's okay. You should probably be careful what you eat or drink around here, anyway. Those, uh, *guests* your uncle had around here didn't have what you'd call a regular appetite."

Edie found a can with familiar contents.

"I can offer you some fruit cocktail," she mused, holding the can to show him.

His face contorted in instant disgust.

"Can't stand the stuff," he said. "It looks the same going down as it does coming up. Pretty good clue when even hippies wouldn't touch it."

Edie tried to hide her initial hurt reaction. After all, it wasn't as if this stranger even knew she had single-handedly challenged modern society's prevailing thinking on Glorified Rice with a similar can of fruit cocktail. Her secret shame remained protected. Besides, who was he to judge fruit cocktail so harshly? He was a grown man wearing flip-flops.

"I've to get going, anyway." He jotted down his phone number for her. "You can call that number anytime and not just to talk about septic mounds. If you have any drain clogs or if you need a toilet re-seated, just give me a call."

"I'll talk to my husband about what you said. Thanks for the information."

Arne ran into the kitchen wearing only his swim trunks.

"Can we go waterskiing now, John?"

The plumber looked sheepishly at Edie. "Sorry, I kinda mentioned to the kid that I have a boat and skis."

"That would do it," she lamented. "We just found out that he's got a natural talent for waterskiing. Couldn't have been talented at math or reading, huh, squirt?"

"That stuff's boring. Can we go, huh? Can we?"

"I'm sure Mr. Kvalstad was just offering to be polite, Arne."

"No, I meant it. No worries. I'd be happy to swing over with my boat and take him around the lake. In fact, you and your husband are welcome to tag along."

"He's off running an errand," she answered, wondering if cousin Jeffy would relinquish the car seat after thinking they were stealing his inheritance from him. "I guess I could come along to keep an eye on things."

Chapter 20

And There's No Pudding

SAM WAS OFF TO downtown Fornborg hoping to find the car seat to make the family wagon whole once more. The only problem was he didn't know for sure where the seat was nor where cousin Jeffy might be holed up, or even if he was still in town at all.

Checking the fuel gauge, he saw he still had half a tank. That was hopefully enough gas to find Jeffy and get to the bank in Alexandria when the time came.

"Well, no point suffering in silence," Sam determined, and he switched on the radio only to be greeted with static on the AM dial. He turned the knob in fits until he heard the static clear and form into speech. He found a voice he recognized. It was the Reverend E. Horseldoff, the local minister who had officiated at Uncle Nat's funeral and who had served as referee in the struggle between Sam, Jeffy, and the snake. He delivered his sermon about Jesus being a country boy for the benefit of those who'd been unable to attend the service owing to physical infirmity.

"Yeah, right," Sam said to the radio. "Since when did boredom become a physical infirmity?"

He switched to FM, a (mostly) clear channel for sounds from far-flung locations like Fargo and Winnipeg. Unfortunately, the only sounds being flung at Fornborg came from Roger Whittaker singing about some guy who was ditching his tropical girlfriend to take a boat ride back to England. He clicked it off, hearing Voodoo Andy's voice saying, *That is beautiful music, my friend.*

"Shut up, Andy."

Sam pressed down on the accelerator. If there was time later, he wanted to meet the local tradesmen and see what his fix-it list might cost to get the resort up and running.

Maybe he'd taken the bend around the lake a little too fast, and maybe his tires had dipped off the pavement, and, yes, maybe he'd overcorrected the steering, veering into the other lane, but it was only for a second. Unfortunately, the car he'd almost front-ended was the sheriff who whipped a U-turn, coming up on Sam's tail fast, with all the lights blazing.

"Crap!" Sam did not want to tack on a fine to his mounting money problems. Either he could gun it and try to outrun a Plymouth Fury in his station wagon, or he could turn on the Norwegian charm. There wasn't much a Norwegian couldn't talk his way out of. Or into.

He rolled down his window and watched as the sheriff strode up, adjusting his wide-brimmed hat. With his horn-rimmed glasses, if you slapped a curly wig on him, he'd look just like grandma. Dang it! He was old, like half-blind-and-time-for-a-nap old. Sam should have gunned it when he had the chance. No way this codger would want to get involved in a high-speed chase when he'd rather be sipping soup, nestled in a nice quilt.

"Mornin', officer."

The old man stuck a bent finger at the badge on his chest.

"Sheriff," he corrected. His voice was thin, an echo of a younger man, who probably rode up San Juan Hill with Teddy Roosevelt. The only thing riding up now was this old guy's support socks.

"You always drive like you're drunk?"

"No, Sheriff," Sam replied. "Only when I'm drunk." He chuckled. The sheriff did not. "I was, uh, just looking at my map…" Realizing there was no map visible as a supporting prop, Sam reached for the glove box where the official Minnesota highway map lay folded, but he froze when Sam felt the cold barrel of a .45 pistol pressed against his neck.

"I wouldn't do that if I was you," the old sheriff said. "Why don't you toss out your keys and then step out of your car nice and slow?"

Sam did just that. So far, the Norwegian charm hadn't kicked in, and it really didn't have time to shine through as he had to pose spread eagle against the car while the sheriff patted him down with one twitchy hand. Then he explored the contents of Sam's wallet with the same attention Edie used to sort through her coupons for a deal on canned tuna.

Holding Sam's license first at the tip of his nose, then at arm's length, the sheriff said, "Says here you aren't from here."

"That's true. We're up from the Cities for Nat Lachmann's funeral. My wife was his niece."

"You the fella who set fire to the motel?"

Sam chuckled. "Oh, that was just my boy. Got to fiddling with some gadgets, and things got a little out of control. You know what they say about idle hands and all that."

"And you were the one brawling at the funeral over a venomous snake? Sounds like your hands might be a little idle too. Just what do you do for a living, Mister…" The sheriff squinted again at Sam's driver's license. "Fisker?"

"I'm a mechanic," Sam said, craning his neck to answer the man behind him. "Small engines, boat motors, that sort of thing."

"Fisker. Is that German?"

"Nope, it's Norwegian. One hundred percent."

The sheriff nodded and told him to stand up. He handed back Sam's license and wallet, which Sam was relieved to see still had five one-dollar bills: all the money the Fiskers had left in the world.

"My name's Olmdahl," the sheriff said. "Norwegian."

"Well, Sheriff Olmdahl, you seem like a fella with a good sense of humor," Sam said brightly. "Seems there was a hockey tournament, and Ole and Lena were there selling hot dogs…"

"Don't finish that joke," the sheriff's hand returned to his holster. "The last man to tell an Ole and Lena joke ended up at the bottom of a well over in Ottertail County."

Anyone who has ever started a joke that's been interrupted knows it feels like when you start peeing and then stop halfway through. You want to keep going, and Sam tried.

"But it's…"

"It was a deep well, too," the sheriff said.

"I'm just…"

"I put him there myself," he warned, and Sam knew he was serious about the jokes. He tried to hold it in. Meanwhile, the sheriff's attention began snooping inside the station wagon.

"What happened to your back seat?"

"Oh, it's a long story, but that's why I was on my way to town. Looking for Nat's son, Jeffy, who might still have it."

"Not planning on smuggling a load of dynamite into Canada?"

"Uh, no," Sam answered. "Is that something a lot of people do?"

"A guy did just last week. Found a carload of dynamite. Completely deranged. He thought he was Snidely Whiplash and wanted to blow up Dudley Do-Right once and for all."

"No," Sam assured the sheriff. "I'd be much more likely to smuggle some of that whiskey out of Canada." He laughed hoarsely, but this didn't seem to amuse the lawman, who probably still stung from enforcing Prohibition. He changed subjects. "You wouldn't know where Jeffy Lachmann is, would you?"

The sheriff's brow furrowed as he scanned his memory. "Jeff Lachmann. Nasty troublemaker, he was. Had a sister who was pretty easy on the eyes."

"She's not easy on anything anymore at her size," Sam said.

The sheriff's face warmed.

"Put on a little weight, did she?"

"More like muscle. If she were wrestling a bear, I'd go ten-to-one on her."

The sheriff laughed out loud at that one. The Norwegian charm finally worked. It just took a while to crank it up like an old Model T.

"Last I heard," the sheriff recalled, "their mother married some quarry owner in Granite Rapids. So I don't know where these relatives of yours might be, but I do know where your car seat is." He handed Sam the keys to the station wagon. "Follow me. And Mr. Fisker," the sheriff peered at Sam over the top of his glasses, "when we get to town, don't you go driving erratically in my town again. Norwegian or not, I like to keep the citizens safe."

Driving slower than the speed limit was one thing, but jerking to a stop every time someone appeared on a sidewalk or whenever another car nosed up to a stop sign was downright annoying, but that's how the old sheriff liked to drive *in his town*. So Sam hit the brakes hard whenever the cruiser did. If he got the car seat back, it was worth it. At least that was one less thing to worry about. Might earn him some brownie points with Edie, soften her up a little on the whole resort discussion.

The two cars drove so slowly and jerked to panicked stops often enough that people stood and watched like it was a nightmare parade. Finally, they pulled in front of the county building, a boxy three-story affair that housed the courts, tax office, sheriff's office, and detention cells.

"We found it abandoned at the deer petting park," the sheriff explained. "Well, not quite abandoned. We found your wife's cousin passed out on it. Said he was waiting for the park to open so he could pet the deer. Seems like he's taking his father's death pretty hard. He waved over the same deputy who had responded to the Magic

Fingers incident at the motor lodge. Baxter, help Mr. Fisker get his seat out of the clink."

The deputy led him down a row of cells to the last one, where Sam saw the seat from the station wagon.

"This is where we cool the drunks." Deputy Baxter unlocked the door and swung it open. "Didn't realize that the bench belonged to anyone, so we decided to put it to good use here."

Sam nearly wretched.

"Looks like someone threw up fruit cocktail on it."

"How could you tell the difference?" the deputy replied. He pointed to a rag and a bucket of old gray mop water. "Looks the same going down as it does coming up."

The man had a point. Fruit cocktail defied the known conventions of gastric digestion, which was just one of the reasons why Sam didn't want anything to do with it: not in his car and not in his glorified rice. He wiped the bench down vigorously, wringing out the rag in a corner sink, and leaving bright red mushy cherries and soggy green grapes in the basin.

Together, Sam and the deputy lugged out the car seat, returning it to its rightful place in the station wagon. Sam readied his toolbox. All he really needed was a wrench to tighten the bolts, but he liked to have all his tools at hand. He set the bench in place, found the bolts he needed tucked safely in the glove compartment, and gripped his wrench, ready to get the station wagon back to normal.

The deputy tapped him on the shoulder, out of breath from running back from the county building. He handed Sam a piece of paper.

"The sheriff asked me to give this to you."

It was a twenty-dollar ticket for driving erratically.

"Cripes!" Sam shoved the ticket in his pocket next to the balled-up DNR ticket issued by Toby Svensson. "What is it with this town and all the fines?"

"Fornborg is a fine town." The deputy chuckled. "That's the city motto."

⇔⇒ • ◆ • ⇐⇔

After John drove off in the Aloha Plumbing truck to get his boat, Edie rushed to the bedroom to scavenge through her suitcase. Edie hadn't packed a swimsuit on principle. They were attending a family funeral, not going on vacation. She now regretted that decision as she stared at her very few options for lake wear. Fortunately, she had packed a summery print dress with a white collar and the hem cut above the knee. It was orange with little white and yellow daisies all over it. Not quite right for a casual boat ride, but it would have to do. She tied her hair back with a white scarf and hoped she didn't look too...too...what was the word?

Slutty?

That was her mother's voice.

No, not slutty. Too available. She didn't want to give the wrong impression, but what did the plumber expect? She hadn't packed her bikini and cover-up because they just buried her uncle, and now wasn't the time to judge her outfits, anyway. Who did he think he was?

Still, she looked cute, if she did say so herself. The effect was complete when she slipped on her big square sunglasses. Looking out the dining room window, she saw Arne scampering up the tree leading to the treehouse. The treehouse that she and Sam both had forbidden him from visiting. She slipped on her leather sandals and went out after him, feeling very old and very *square* as she shouted up a tree for her son to come down. She was careful not to use the word hippie in case they found the term as offensive as a Sven and Ole joke.

"Arne, get down here now, and leave those nice *people* alone."

A man's raspy voice called back, "He's cool. No bother at all."

My God, it sounded like Charlie Manson up in that treehouse. Probably going to make her son do drugs and shave his head before going on a wild crime spree.

"Do you want some pudding?" She knew Arne loved pudding. It might just lure him down, even though in reality she didn't have pudding.

"We'd love some pudding," the man called back. Sam said his name was Garvey, and he was the paranoid one who had seen people lurking around the night her uncle was killed.

"I was talking to Arne. My son. I'd like him to come down, please. Now."

She heard the indistinct murmur of the man's voice before the soles of Arne's bare feet appeared overhead, coming down the rickety ladder. She told Arne to be careful, not to get tetanus from rusty nails.

"Is there pudding?"

She grabbed him by the ear. "Didn't we tell you not to go up there?"

He yanked away from her, holding his ear with one hand.

"That's a little harsh, don't ya think?"

"No, I don't think so. When you don't mind your parents, there are consequences."

"Says you." Three minutes with Charles Manson, and the boy was already turning on her. "What kind of pudding is it?"

"There's no pudding, Arne. You just leave those…" she dropped her voice to a whispered hiss, "*hippies*...alone. Understand?"

"No pudding? Man, that bites the big one."

Her repertoire of corrective parenting techniques gleaned from the magazine had to wait because the plumber's speedboat, sleek with a sparkly blue metal flake finish, came into view. It was powered by two outboard motors that grumbled low as John Kvalstad pulled in as close to shore as he could, since Uncle Nat's dock was out of service. Edie walked gingerly into the water, yelping at the cold. The water was almost to her waist, so she lifted her skirt to avoid it getting drenched and stinking like lake water for the rest of the trip. She carried her sandals in one hand, too. Once she was near enough to the boat, John helped her over the side. Arne laughed at her for being so prissy. He splashed impatiently in the water and shouted for John to get the waterskis.

"You'll have to forgive him," Edie said as she steadied herself against John's solid frame. "He got his manners from his father."

"No worries." John replied as he slid a pair of children's waterskis to Arne. "Boy's got every right to be excited about life and not missing a minute of it." He then tossed Arne a life jacket, but Arne said he didn't want to wear a life jacket and tried tossing it back. Edie said if he didn't wear one, he could just run his little butt back into the house.

She reclined on a long bench with metallic red cushions. The interior seats were bright red and leather. John himself smelled like coconuts. He still wore his red-and-white Hawaiian shirt, but it was unbuttoned and flapping in a light breeze. He tossed Arne a tow rope, and they talked about hand signals that meant *stop, veer left, veer right, go around again*, and *I need a beer*.

"That's one hand signal you're not using, mister."

Arne glared at her from the water.

"How come *you're* not wearing a life jacket, Mom?"

Her smile tightened, looking at John, hoping that he didn't think they were one of those quarreling families that ruined funerals and ran with Lake Lutherans.

"Because I'm an adult," she quipped.

"Yes, you are." John gunned the engine, and Arne was up on the first try. "A full-grown woman."

The lake was stroking her body with its mist, and the sun kissed her cheeks. The hum of the boat was hypnotic. Edie had to admit it was lovely. She slowly relaxed, stretching her legs straight out in front of her (but not so relaxed as to let the hem of her skirt creep too high in the breeze). She admired Vicki and Toby Svensson's lake home. Everything was well-ordered, the landscape manicured, and red snapdragons and purple delphinium dotted the sunny borders.

Arne whooped in delight. She couldn't remember ever seeing him this thrilled. He was in a state of joy, and that made her happy too—until the tricks started.

Her little boy started drifting off to one side, leaning on his skis, then he hit the wake from the boat, and he was in the air. Edie sat up straight, her relaxing affair with the lake over in a flash.

"Be careful," she yelled, but she wasn't sure he could hear her. Even if he could have heard her, he wouldn't have listened.

"Don't worry," John Kvalstad called back to her. His open shirt was flapping behind him like a flag. "He's doing good. Maybe you want to try next?"

"No way," she answered.

At that moment, Arne pulled himself straight behind the boat and shouted, "Watch this!" Then he spun around—all the way around—so that he faced the boat again.

"Pretty cool, huh?" He was smiling at them like he had just won the World Series single handedly. His skis slipped out from under him, and the boat dragged him face first through the wake.

"Let go of the rope," John shouted, but Arne didn't let go. John cut the motor, and Arne's face appeared heaving in a deep breath, water dripping from his ears and hair.

"Are you okay?" Edie had moved to the very back of the boat, ready to dive in and pull him out of the lake herself if she needed to.

Arne spit out water. "Did you see me?"

"Yeah, we saw you," John stated flatly. "You've still got lots to learn. Number one: when you fall, let go of the rope."

"No way. That's like giving up." Arne pulled himself along the rope toward John's outstretched hand.

"Listen, kid. If you're not falling, you're failing."

"You listen to John," Edie agreed. She didn't know what John was talking about: falling didn't sound like a good thing. He was only the town plumber, but she sensed he was a very wise person; if not the wisest in the entire chain of lakes, then at least on the boat.

"I'm thirsty," Arne complained.

John nodded to the cooler. "Help yourself, kid."

"Wow! Grape soda. That's my favorite."

"It is," Edie added. "That's about as close as we can get to him eating fruits. Now, if only they made a broccoli soda."

"Ew!" Arne winced. "You almost made me spit out grape soda through my nose."

"There's a beer in there too." John flashed a smile at Edie. "You know, for full-grown women."

"Can I go again?"

"Sure, kid," John turned the boat toward a channel. "Why don't you take it easy for a few minutes, and then we'll get you back on the water." To Edie, he added, "Seriously, that kid is good."

"God, don't tell him that. His head will get so big, he'd just float away."

John's mouth tightened. He held back a smile.

"You were going to say something about his ears, weren't you?"

"Who, me? No way."

He revved the engine, and they headed through the mouth of the channel and under a bridge that spanned the inlet between Little Paw Lake and Big Jack Pine. John slowed the boat as they passed through, observing the NO WAKE signs. Then he gunned it again once the other lake opened in front of them. There were more boats on Big Jack Pine, some of them pulling waterskiers, and Arne watched them closely, anxious to get back on skis himself. John, however, maintained the boat's speed at full throttle, bouncing across the choppy wake of other boats. The wind was stronger, probably because this lake was maybe three or four times bigger than Little Paw.

They headed for another bridge leading to another inlet, and they passed into another lake.

"Where are we going?" Edie asked, wondering why they were so far from Uncle Nat's property.

John answered something, but his low voice was lost in the growl of the engines and the wind. He pointed to the eastern shore as they nosed toward a sprawling lake home at least twice as large as the Svensson's place. It wasn't quite what you'd call a mansion, but it certainly would hold a lot of sock drawers. Oddly enough, that seemed to be exactly where they were headed.

John throttled back as he guided them to a dock that bent like the letter L, a shape which people that far north called a *hockey stick*. Two serious-looking men waited there, standing next to the biggest pontoon that Edie had ever seen. It had two levels, the lower one had seating and the steering wheel, but the upper level had even more seating and tables.

John directed the boat towards the dock, having to compensate for the breeze. John told Arne to jump out and help the two men guide the boat in.

"Don't let them scratch my paint job, kid."

The motors were quieter now, so Edie asked again where they were going.

"I need you to talk to someone," John replied. "I'll take Arne out for another round of skiing, and we'll swing back in a little while to get you."

"You're going to leave me with these two men?"

"Rollo and Petie?" John pshawed. "They're barely one man between the both of them. You'll be fine."

They led Edie toward the house. Her first thought was to run away, but woods surrounded by woods them. She might as well wear a sign that said *Free Bear Food*. The two men blocked her retreat to the lake, so it was off to the unknown for Edie Fisker.

On their way to the house, they wended their way along walkways made with bricks laid in a herringbone pattern. The slope was tiered by landscaping block with several seating areas, the umbrellas on the patio tables flapping lightly in the breeze. This was no ordinary lake cabin. She couldn't get over how big it was and how expensive. To put it in Nordeast terms, that sucker was almost a block long and a bank loaned. Or maybe she was exaggerating the size: maybe everything else in her life had been small, living stacked on top of Mr. Jaworski in a crackerjack apartment.

They paused at the front door.

"Lift your arms," one of the men said. He was the ugly one.

"Why?"

The other man didn't wait for her to answer, and he lifted her arms and held them while the ugly one patted her down over her very vocal protests. "She's clean," he grunted.

"Did you think I was carrying a pistol or something?"

"Can never be too careful with Lake Lutherans," the ugly one said, holding the door open for her.

Edie scowled at him. "We are not Lake Lutherans, for cripes sake!" One of them tugged on her elbow to draw her forward into the house. To her they were just more male chauvinist pigs bossing her around—prodding her like cattle. Well, you know what? She was sick of it. She wouldn't move. She would just dig in her heels and look for the right moment to get away. If she went inside, there was no telling what would happen.

An insistent shove from behind sent her tripping over the threshold. Her escape plans would have to wait.

Chapter 21

Gonna Make It After All

EDIE RIGHTED HERSELF WITH one hand on a coat rack in the entryway as she stole a glance at herself in a tall mirror. The lady in the cute summer dress sure looked angry.

"What am I doing here?" Edie demanded, but neither Rollo nor Petie responded, and that silence unnerved her. They led her through an open living room that looked as big as Uncle Nat's entire house. The windows facing the lake afforded a breathtaking view of vivid blue water and the lush trees on the opposite shore. If there was divine judgment after you died, this would be the sort of beautiful thing you'd see to help soften the bad news. As far as the afterlife was concerned, there was plenty of judgement right here on Earth. No need to drag it out after you died. That was just adding insult to injury.

But the decor: definitely a man's touch. Whoever owned the place obviously was rich and liked dead animals and old weapons because the walls were clogged with them. Dead deer, dead fish, tarnished swords, a display case of spearheads, and a stuffed bear. The place was part museum and part carnival sideshow.

Just as Rollo the henchman grunted at her to keep moving, Edie saw John Kvalstad's metallic-blue speed boat whizz across the water. Arne spun around on skis behind it in a plume of white spray. The image burned in her brain: her son in the middle of a lake being dragged around my a Norwegian in a Hawaiian shirt. If something bad happened to her, she would come back as a ghost and haunt that man.

They led her to a door and knocked. "Come in," came the response, and Edie entered what old movies might call a 'study.' More man decor in this room: dead fish, fishing lures, fishing rods, and a big, dark desk behind which sat a man in his late fifties silver hair cropped close but bushy salt-and-pepper sideburns. It was kind of like a reverse face mullet.

"Good afternoon, Mrs. Fisker." The man rose when she entered, and he waved her to a chair across from him. He smiled more warmly than one would expect from a kidnapper. "I'm so glad you could make it. First of all, let me say how sorry to hear about your uncle's unfortunate accident."

"Excuse me," Edie interjected. "But who are you?"

The man slapped his forehead. "My apologies. I'm Bud Langskip." He did not offer to shake her hand the way some younger men might. He was from that generation that believed women were made from porcelain and chewing gum, liable to fall apart at the least interference.

"You're probably wondering," he continued, "why I invited you here."

"I didn't receive an invitation," Edie answered pointedly. "I was brought here by a man wearing a Hawaiian shirt who is now dragging my son around by a rope."

"Just the same, you'll want to talk to me. You and I have shared interests. You want to unburden yourself of that lake property, and I want to help you."

"So far, all you've helped is a kidnapping complaint."

"Oh, now, let's keep things in perspective. I'm very much on your side. I want to help you make a smooth transition. It's going to be good for everyone." He smiled again, and his eyes fixed on her. His mouth opened and closed again, like the fish on his wall used to do. Behind Bud Langskip, three old wooden crates were stacked on the floor, the letters 'TNT' stenciled on each side.

"Do you often keep explosives in your office?" she asked.

He looked confused until Edie pointed to the crates. "Ah, no." He swiveled around in his chair and hoisted a crate onto his desk, dropping it unceremoniously, making Edie wince in anticipation of an imminent explosion, but he just laughed softly at her, as he rifled through the crate. He withdrew a long, red cylindrical object with a glittery tail and hooks dangling from its body.

"This is our newest topwater fishing lure, the TNT. Guaranteed dynamite for largemouth bass. You like that? I thought of that tagline myself." Noticing her absent look, he added, "Maybe you didn't realize I am *the* Bud Langskip. Of Langskip Lures?" She shook her head, and he coughed, clearly disappointed his name meant nothing to her. "Well, I hope that our mutual friend, John, at least told you about some of the septic problems at your late uncle's property?"

"Yes, he mentioned the septic, and he told me about some other things that need fixing. And my husband has made a list too. All in all, it seems like a big mess."

"Oh, yes. It's definitely a money pit."

"Oh, and there are people still there from my uncle's..." She wanted to say *commune*, but that couldn't be the right word. "Guests," she concluded instead.

"I can help you with that too," Bud declared. For a kidnapper, he was being awfully friendly. She almost forgot she was a victim of a crime—almost. She knew all about Patty Hearst and how that poor woman turned from being a kidnap victim into becoming a willing political puppet. Edie would never rob a bank for anyone, no matter how nice they were. "You want some coffee?" Bud asked. "Or some smoked lake carp? Speared it myself."

What coffee and carp had to do with one another, she didn't know.

"Yuck. No."

"Good deal, but just say the word," Bud continued. "We can have those hippies scattered to the four winds by the end of the day."

"Well, there's only two of them, and they apparently live in a treehouse, so I don't think we need to get the wind involved."

Bud shrugged.

"Mrs. Fisker, Edie—can I call you Edie?"

"I don't care," she said, and that was the truth. She didn't plan on ever interacting socially again with Bud Langskip. Using first names now was just frosting a turd, as Sam liked to say.

"Look around. Everything you see came from foresight and planning. You can't leave things to chance. That's my lesson for the day."

He chuckled, clearly amusing himself.

Oh, boy, are we in trouble, Edie thought. Absolutely everything in her life had been left to chance: no money, Sam losing his job, an 'energetic' child, and no end of family drama.

"Well," she concluded. "I can't argue with you there, Mr. Langskip."

"Call me Bud, please."

"No. But I can talk to Avi myself, you know, like human beings do. Let her know things need to change, that she and her boyfriend need to leave."

"That is a very feminine approach," Bud said. "Soft, discrete. I can respect that. You have a kind heart. Perhaps you got that from your mother?" His voice pitched higher when he asked, and he sounded uncertain. The question dangled in front of her like the hook on a topwater lure.

"Do you know my mother?"

Bud frowned and looked to the ceiling in thought. "Hmmm, let's see, your mother was Dolores Schmidt, wasn't she?" He used her married name, which struck Edie as odd. "Yes, the name sounds familiar. Oh, Nat's sister, of course. She was active in the Shield Maidens, if I recall. You know, before she left Fornborg. But that was years ago."

"I don't know what a Shield Maiden is," Edie admitted. "But if there was any chance for her to show off to other people, then that sounds about right."

"Well, if you'd been raised in Fornborg, you'd certainly know. It's a women's auxiliary group for the Sons of Gunnar. All the good little Norwegian girls join when they're young. Your mother was a beautiful singer, as I recall. Did you inherit your mother's talent?"

Edie didn't answer and tried to steer the conversation back on track so she could save her son from drowning or breaking a leg or whatever trouble he was getting into just then.

"I will talk to the hippies myself," she stated.

"Fine. But if that doesn't work, you just let me know, and we will kick some hippie heinie."

Edie recalled Vicki Svensson's warning about the men's heritage club, but she hadn't called them the Sons of Gunnar. What had Vicki called them? Ah, yes. The Norwegian Pontoon Mafia. Vicki said they were crooked. Bud was their leader. He probably was the Norwegian Al Capone of Minnesota.

"Out of curiosity, what are you going to do with my uncle's property?"

"It's not what *I* would do with it. It's what *we* would do with it. The Sons of Gunnar. We have a vision for our little slice of heaven on this chain of lakes. That property will help us achieve that vision, another dot connected on the map." Bud's chest puffed out. He was clearly proud of himself. "We're in what you might call a growth phase, thanks to solid planning."

"I see," she said. He hadn't answered her question clearly, and she supposed that was intentional. Why would he tell a silly little woman anything of importance? Typical macho bull pucky. Still, it seemed like an ideal solution. She could just agree to sell the place with as little fuss as possible.

"What would you be willing to pay, Mr. Langskip?"

The question startled him.

"Well, I have a figure in mind, but I don't think you have to trouble yourself about that. Perhaps we can discuss it with your husband and a local land agent I know, Arthur Brevindal. I've got his business card right here." He slid the card to her, and she took it in hand without bothering to read it.

"Actually, my uncle left the property to me, not my husband."

"Of course, but if we get the law involved, they're not going to see it like that. As a man, your husband can exert his ownership rights."

"Sam doesn't own me!" Edie raged. "He gets confused putting on pillow cases."

"That's why you and I are having this initial conversation. It's why I invited you…"

Edie waggled a finger. "No. Again, I wasn't invited, unless kidnapping counts as some new passive-aggressive way of inviting people to your house. You know what bothers me about this, Mr. Langskip? I don't think you're being straight with me. And I think you'd run circles around my husband with your business smarts. You know, he's pretty set on keeping the property and running it as a resort."

"That would be a boondoggle. No two ways about it. Even the established resorts around here barely make ends meet, year to year. And a couple from the Twin Cities with no experience in running resorts or a successful business, with no cash reserves, why, you'd have to fold up in two years, at the latest."

"That's what I've been trying to tell my Sam. Those very same words." She hated to agree with this man on anything, but his words confirmed what she suspected.

"Well, by all accounts, your husband doesn't have much sense in his head. No offense. I've heard from one of my business associates that your Sam is more likely to torpedo an operation rather than run a smooth ship."

"Oh, so you know Russell Randall?"

Bud nodded. "Of course. He's the catalog king, and 60 percent of our revenue here at Langskip Lures comes from catalog sales. Russell is a big part of that success. Oh, which reminds me, are you still at…" Bud shuffled items on his desk and brought out a manilla folder that he flipped open. "Apartment two on Quincy Street in northeast Minneapolis?"

She stared at his hands holding the folder. She wondered what other information was in there about her family. He seemed to know an awful lot about them, and they'd only been in Fornborg for two days.

"You sound like one of those guys who got convicted for Watergate," she said, trying to sound confident, but it troubled her that he knew anything about her family.

"You mean Bob Haldeman, Nixon's Chief of Staff?" Bud laughed. "No. I'm Nixon, darling. Now, no offense to you, but I've found over the years that issues of money and property are best left decided by the menfolk."

"And does Mrs. Langskip settle for that nonsense?"

Bud stared at her for a moment. The light faded from his eyes, and his facial expression drooped.

"My wife is...she passed." He tightened his lips while his gaze fell on his hands. He regained his composure and stared her directly in the face. "Life is short. Too short to go around taking risks that you can't possibly manage. Look, Edie. I'm just looking out for you. A place like that, well, you'd be over your head, and then when you want to sell out of desperation, you'll never get the price you want."

Besides recipes, the women's magazine Edie read also included useful articles about how a person could be limited by negative conditioning. She recognized it all the time in phone calls to her mother, and she recognized it here at the desk of Bud Langskip. *You can't. You won't. You'll never.*

"I see I've hurt your feelings." Bud leaned back in his chair, making it squeak. "I meant no offense. Far from it. In fact, I'm here to help you out of this mess."

The mess to which he was referring just happened to be her life.

Edie put on a smile that she didn't feel. "Everything you say makes complete sense, Mr. Langskip. But when I hear you say all those things out loud, like a male chauvinist pig, I think maybe it's worth a shot. Just maybe Sam is right. We should take a chance."

With that, she arose even as Bud Langskip sputtered, "Now, don't get hysterical. Let's talk this through."

Edie marched out of the office and brushed past Opie and Dopie, or whatever their names were (she was too riled up to remember).

"Bring her back in here," Bud yelled, but his two lackeys hung back, watching her tromp down the hall.

"She's pretty mad," one of them said.

"I'm mad, alright!" Edie called over her shoulder. "I can see myself out." She marched out the front door and down to the dock, waiting until John Kvalstad's boat passed close enough for her to signal to him. He arced the boat toward the dock, slowing until Arne sank into the water.

"Have a good chat?" John called as he pulled Arne aboard and collected the skis. Before he could even get a hand on the dock, she leaped aboard and socked him in the kisser.

"Take us back," she demanded. "Now!"

Sam finished tightening the bolts on the seat. Now Arne wouldn't have to roll around like a little sausage when they rounded curves.

"There," Sam admired his handiwork. "Everything is back to normal, just like Edie likes it."

He heard a boat approaching. Sounded like two motors, so not Russell Randall's boat. He rounded the corner of the main house and saw his wife at the wheel of a speedboat and the Hawaiian shirt guy rubbing his jaw, sitting on a bench. She was coming in way too fast, nosing right for the remnants of the dock. The Hawaiian shirt guy jumped up and tried to grab the throttle, but she slapped his hand away, cut the engines just in time, and turned the wheel. The boat slid sideways, coming dangerously close to banging into a metal support post.

Edie looked furious. In their dozen years of marriage, he'd seen that look more than once.

There was no point trying to reach the boat from the shattered dock, so Sam ran down the slope and right into the water. He was already in water up to his waist when he remembered that his wallet and both tickets were getting soaked in his pockets. He wondered if an act of God, like lake water drenching your pants, was a legal justification for not paying government fines.

"Edie, what's going on?" he bellowed, splashing around next to the boat like a walrus trapped in a fishing net.

"Dad!" Arne shouted from the boat. "Did you see me?"

"Not now, Arne. I need to talk to your mom."

In the meantime, Edie moved like she was on fire. She practically pushed Arne overboard before jumping in the water herself. Her dress wicked water and clung snugly to her body. Despite his aching jaw, the Hawaiian shirt guy perked up to see her shape.

"What's going on here, hunny bunny?" Sam pleaded as he tried to shield her from the man's view.

"You tell that boss of yours," Edie yelled over Sam's shoulder, "we're going to make it after all, just like Mary Tyler-Moore." She turned her head to shoot Sam a burning look. "Do you still have that fix-it list?"

"Yeah." Sam tapped the breast pocket of his shirt. That, at least, wasn't wet.

"Might as well add creaky kitchen cupboard hinges to it."

It took him a minute to figure out what she meant, but then it dawned on him. They could stay. He scooped her in his arms and spun her around with glee. Arne splashed them and laughed, not understanding what all the excitement was about.

"Don't get too excited," Edie warned Sam. "We've got a lot of work to do."

Edie was still steamed: angry, yes, but also frightened that her world was crumbling. And there was something else. Excitement?

Maybe a fresh start was exactly what the Fisker family needed. Heck, if they didn't do it now when they were still young, then when would they?

She changed into the only other dry thing she had: the Sears catalog dress she'd packed special for the funeral. Edie needed to vent her many emotions. She needed to lay them all out and think through them with another reasonable adult, so she hiked to Vicki Svensson's house, moving swiftly through the woods with only the slightest worry about rabid squirrels.

She knocked on the front door but got no response, even though she could hear music playing—classical, the kind with the entire orchestra who dress up like headwaiters in French restaurants. The Fiskers never listened to classical music. A pang of envy pricked Edie. Vicki was so smart, beautiful, and classy. Maybe some of that class would rub off on her. Knowing that someone was home, Edie made her way around the side of the house and up the deck stairs. The double doors were wide open, with the music flowing outside along with a peculiar odor.

Not exactly a classy odor, either.

Edie stepped inside and announced herself. Her eyes adjusted, and when they did, she saw beautiful/smart/classy Vicki wielding a meat cleaver and covered in blood and gore. The cleaver hammered the cutting board, sending up more guts onto the lemon-yellow rubber apron Vicki wore. It was like watching a ballerina paint a living room with a mop.

"Oh, hello. Come on in!"

With her wardrobe options limited by poor packing decisions, Edie hung back from the action. She remained at the very edge of the counter opposite Vicki, a pile of fish in varying states of decapitation, and a bucket full of what looked like slimy water .

"What have we got going here?" Edie asked, trying not to allow her disgust to show through.

"I'm working on a batch of *surströmming*."

"I'm not familiar with...stir strummer?"

"*Surströmming*. It's a Swedish thing, of course."

"Of course."

"It means 'sour herring.' It's fermented in brine, and then I can it. It smells so bad when it's ready. I mean, truly awful. But Toby loves it because it reminds him of his grandfather." Vicki laughed, adding, "I mean, the terrible smell doesn't remind Toby of his grandfather, but the whole process does."

"You can the fish?"

"Oh, yeah. Do you think Charlie Tuna just gets in those little tin cans all by himself?"

"I suppose not."

"And *surströmming* is very versatile. You can add it to so many things. Sauces and what-not. I have to get a little creative since we don't have fresh herring here. 'Use what's around you,' that's what I say. And, well, to be honest, Toby has access to the DNR hatcheries, so he brought me buckets full of yellow perch. But you didn't hear that from me."

"Mum's the word," Edie agreed, watching the cleaver send another round of splatter into the air. "Is Toby out spinning turtles again today?"

"No, today he's exploding beaver dams, poor little fellas."

"You mean he's actually blowing up beavers?"

"Just their dams. If there are beavers inside, that's not really Toby's fault. Those dams are a real nuisance. They block up the channels between lakes and inflow points from the creeks. It's a real mess."

"Aren't you worried about him using explosives?"

"I worried about him every day for two years when he was in Vietnam," Vicki confided. "If he can make it through that, he can make it through a little beaver blasting."

Over coffee and cigarettes, Edie and Vicki chatted about a hundred little things: recipes, the price of steak, their favorite movies. It felt comfortable. It felt *normal.* That was what Edie wanted. She didn't even mention being kidnapped by the Norwegian Pontoon Mafia or her decision to run the resort.

Chapter 22

Americana 10¢

THE NEXT MORNING, EDIE stood in the kitchen (Her uncle's kitchen? Her kitchen?) wondering what to do about breakfast for herself. She had eked out enough dust from a cereal box to fill bowls for Sam and Arne before they left for the bank in Alexandria. She wrapped a kerchief around her head to keep her hair from falling in her face. One of Sam's shirts—much too big for her—hung from her like a tent, making her look like she'd been liberated from a prisoner-of-war camp, but it was the absolute final piece of adult clothing that didn't smell like lake water or pickled perch. If she had known that her uncle's funeral would turn into such an ordeal, she would have made different packing choices.

She caught herself daydreaming, staring out of the kitchen window, which was one of those big picture window affairs. A large sheet of solid glass faced the lake, occasionally brushed by the lowest branches of a basswood tree in the breeze. Only a few small fishing boats bobbed in the waves, working on their limit. In the last couple days, she'd already learned: people mostly fished for 'pannies' and walleyes this time of year; that a couple could spring for a shared fishing license (called a "combination angling license") for six bucks; and the daily limit for crappies was fifteen.

She dawdled all morning, plagued by a lack of motivation. No get-up-and-go, thanks in part to an absence of coffee, but also because of a dream she couldn't shake. It had lingered as she stayed under the covers, trying to recall the specifics. Something about hairy chests and Hawaiian print shirts. Her mother's voice rang in her head like an alarm clock: *I asked you to do one little thing for me.*

When a baby is born, the doctor cuts the umbilical cord, but he ignores a different cord that forever connects mother to child: guilt.

Well, Edie had a belly full of feeling bad recently, so she decided to quit dawdling and look for those letters. Maybe that would quiet her mother's voice. For the time being, anyway.

Besides, Edie really needed to sort through Uncle Nat's stuff, even if changed her mind about taking over the property—which she wouldn't. What other options did they have? Especially since she probably burned her bridges with the most likely buyer, Bud Langskip and his Norwegian Pontoon Mafia, or Sons of Guns, or whatever they were called.

Clearing out the place might give her a clearer picture of how the Fisker family might fit in there. For such a big house, there really wasn't much to go through. Probably the former guests had made off with whatever they wanted for selling or smoking out of. Mostly, all that remained were the meager artifacts of a lonely person. Some clothes. Some books. The furniture was all second-hand, mismatched stuff that he probably scrounged from garage sales. That gave Edie an idea: they would have a garage sale.

She armed herself with half a roll of masking tape and a blue ink pen. She priced every item as she went through them. Fifty cents for a pair of bowling shoes, men's size nine. Half-empty bottle of Wild Turkey whiskey, one dollar. Scuffed bedside table with knob missing on drawer, two dollars. Table lamp made from a genuine empty pickle jar, a dollar.

Yes, a garage sale. People loved garage sales as much as they loved saving ten cents on a can of tuna with a coupon. Sure, it was essentially just heaps of crap sold by weird-smelling strangers at low prices, but it was the adventure of the garage sale that was alluring. Edie operated on the premise that one man's junk is another man's treasure. Hopefully, they would make enough cash to cover whatever they needed for living expenses before her mother's money ran out.

Room by room, Edie grouped all the smaller items, leaving the bulkier things for Sam to move. It wasn't until she opened a built-in cabinet that she found more personal items, the kind that no one would buy: a cache of family photos, letters, and handmade cards. It was the cards that caught her eye first. They were the kind that would tear your heart out, just not in the conventional Hallmark Cards sort of way. For instance, a card from cousin Jeffy to his dad, made from lavender construction paper. He'd drawn an orange house and a peach-colored, frowning stick-figure man next to it. An adult clearly had written the message, not little Jeffy, scrawled by Uncle Nat's angry ex-wife, Gloria.

I hope you like celebrating Father's Day alone, you bastard.

Uncle Nat *had* died alone, at least in the sense that he was estranged from his children. Although Edie found it difficult to believe that being surrounded by hippies when you died could be very reassuring. But Uncle Nat had surrounded himself with seekers, like Avi Starshine and the other hippies in his lake commune. He was their "papa," which filled what must have been a missing piece in his life.

She flipped through black-and-white photos from a time before Uncle Nat's family fell apart. There were cousin Jeffy and little Lana, each riding a pony, Jeffy wearing a straw cowboy hat, his face scrunched in a goofy smile. Uncle Nat held the tether of both ponies. He had been a handsome man, Edie realized. Dark hair and dark eyes looking into the camera with one of those come-hither looks you saw on the front of movie magazines. Gloria, the ex-wife, must have taken the photo.

Edie tore off a small square of masking tape and wrote 'ten cents' on it and the word *Americana*. She stuck the price tag on the pony photo. At garage sales, you never knew what was going to sell, but the one thing that definitely would not sell is that which is not priced.

Edie noticed several envelopes kept together with a red rubber band. The return address was familiar, from Arizona, written in her mother's distinctive, neat handwriting. Dolores Schmidt née Lachmann had always prided herself on her penmanship. That her mother wrote to Uncle Nat came as no surprise, but the dates on the postmarks were. Some were very recent, only a month previous, but her mother had told her she hadn't spoken to Uncle Nat in years. Her mother wasn't one to lie, choosing instead to evade hard truths. So how could she claim that she hadn't been in contact with Uncle Nat?

Spoken: that was the key word, the little loophole that let her mother off the hook for lying. She hadn't *spoken* to him for years, but she had been *writing* to him until recently.

Her mother's voice haunted her as she removed the rubber band and slipped it around her wrist. *Warning! Warning! Not supposed to read! Just box them up and ship them off. They're personal things. You've got plenty of other things to do. No time to sit around getting lost in reading things you've got no right to.*

Edie found seven letters to Uncle Nat from her mother, totaling almost thirty pages of immaculate revelation. Her heart raced, and she felt faint after reading only the first few pages of rigid, straight-backed letters written on imaginary straight lines and with no flourishes. Maybe Edie had fallen asleep? Was this some sort of dream? Even after she shook her head, she still held the letters and was wide awake, despite not having coffee.

She reread two of the letters more slowly than the first time and reread the most recent one, dated March 15, 1975, a third time. She folded each of them and returned them to their respective envelopes before heading to the kitchen to unscrew the sticky bottle of Wild Turkey. Taking a swig, she realized too late she might catch some hippie disease of the mouth from the bottle. Maybe cigarette smoke would cure her. She dug around in her purse for her last emergency cigarette—her actual, last cigarette. If this wasn't an emergency, she didn't know what was.

Once Edie was good and dribbled on Wild Turkey, she called her mother, collect, and on day rates. She didn't care what it was going to cost that woman. She didn't care how much of a fuss her mother made. Edie had learned her mother's secret, and it wasn't pretty.

Sam and Arne had the windows rolled down for some of that double-nickel air conditioning—double nickel standing for fifty-five, the new national speed limit set the previous year to get people to conserve gas. The wind made it hard to hear the radio station, but occasionally, Sam could make out the strains of "The Hustle."

Arne had his head out the window, letting his mouth hang open, so his cheeks wobbled in the wind. His ears flapped too, and Sam swore he could hear them like the sound of someone knocking on a screen door. Sam hung his head out the window too, and when Arne started howling like a wolf, Sam joined him. The two Fisker men, howling at passing cars. Sam hadn't felt this good for a very long time.

They hit Alexandria around eleven and found the bank by driving up and down the main drag. Remembering the Magic Fingers incident, Sam wouldn't let Arne stay in the car while he went inside to collect the money.

"Come on in with me, kiddo. Let's get our dough and rustle up some lunch. Whaddya say?"

"Do they have a Big Boy burger here?"

"We'll figure that out later. Why? Are you hungry?"

"Dad, I'm *starving*," Arne whined.

Once they opened the glass doors and walked inside, the air temperature cooled. The bank had all the money, so of course they could afford an actual air conditioning system. In Sam's opinion, it seemed a little early in the season to run that far north, but if you've got it, flaunt it.

"Boy, can't you just smell that money?" Sam joked.

Arne sniffed the air. "I think I smell quarters."

The teller, a woman with tight curly, gray hair and a bright purple blazer, smiled at them as she looked up from counting a stack of ten-dollar bills.

"What can I do for you?"

Before Sam could answer, Arne stuck his finger at her and yelled, "Stick 'em up!"

The half-dozen employees inside the bank did not find this amusing, and Sam hastened to chastise Arne and apologize to the teller. She explained someone had robbed them rather recently, so the nerve was still a little raw.

"So, we're not here to rob the bank. Obviously," Sam said with a nervous chuckle. It was obvious to him anyway. The teller seemed less certain. "We are here to pick up a wire transfer for Fisker."

The teller asked him to spell the last name.

"It's just like it sounds," Sam assured her.

"F-I-T-Z-G-E-R," she spelled.

"Uh, no. Fisker."

"F-I-Z-Z-C-U-R?"

Growing impatient, Sam grabbed one of the empty deposit forms. He lifted the pen, chained to the counter like a circus elephant, and wrote out FISKER.

"Oh, I never would have gotten that." She tittered. "Is that German?"

"Norwegian. One hundred percent."

"Me too," Arne added as he tore off the leaf of a potted rubber plant that stood near the counter.

"No, sorry, you're only half." Sam chuckled as he tried to put the torn leaf back in place. It fell to the polished floor.

"I'll go check on your request." The teller reluctantly excused herself to see if the branch had received any transfer authorizations, but before fully turning away, she cast a dubious eye on Arne, who now waved the pen along the counter, causing its chain to undulate like a snake.

"Don't worry," Sam told her. "I'll keep an eye on him."

It took a couple of long minutes for her to return, during which Sam had to keep snapping at Arne to stand still and behave, but it was like the boy couldn't keep still. He ran over to a coffee table and started flipping through a magazine, holding up an ad with a woman wearing a filmy peach evening gown and holding a frying pan. He yelled, "How come Mom doesn't dress up to cook? Do you think that's why her food is so lousy, Dad?"

"Get. Over. Here. NOW!" Sam hissed through clenched teeth. The teller came back with the authorization form and asked to see Sam's identification.

"I'm sorry, Mr. Fisker, but this is made out to Edith Fisker."

"Yeah, that's my wife. Edie Fisker."

"Yes," the teller replied hesitantly. "The trouble is, first of all, I have no way of verifying that she's your wife based on your driver's license, and secondly, even if Mrs. Fisker is your wife, I have no way of verifying that she would approve this transaction."

"You could ask her."

"Oh, good." The teller seemed relieved. "Just ask her to step in and show us her identification."

"No, I mean you could ask her. If she was here. But she ain't here. She's on Little Paw Lake waiting for us to come home with the money so we can afford to buy groceries and gas money."

"I'm starving, Dad!" Arne whined again when he heard mention of food.

"There's nothing I can do about it. It's clearly made out to Edith Fisker, and I can't just give it to anyone who claims to be her husband. Why, we'd have a hundred Mr. Fiskers in here every day, like a parade. I'm so sorry."

"Well, if anyone else comes in claiming to be her husband, give me a call, will ya?"

As a sort of consolation prize, the teller offered Arne a sucker from a bowl. Arne took a handful of them.

"It's one per child, dear," the teller told him, extending the bowl toward him so he could return the extras. Instead, he grabbed another handful.

"So long, suckers!" Arne chittered as he ran out of the bank.

"Sorry about that," Sam said. He took a handful too and left in a hurry.

It was just like Dolores Schmidt to put the transfer in Edie's name out of sheer spite. That woman had as much heart as a caramel apple. Maybe it was because of the time he'd told her to mind her own business when she started huffing at him about holding down a "real" job. Like selling encyclopedias wasn't a real job. He'd like to see her lug around all twenty-two volumes of the 1972 World Encyclopedia in the middle of August while wearing a necktie.

Or maybe it had been because of the time she'd visited them for Easter and made Edie cry because she nitpicked that the glaze on the ham wasn't caramelized enough, and Sam had called her a hag, or a nag, or maybe something stronger. If anyone was going to make Edie cry, it should be her husband.

Back in the car, Sam looked over at Arne, who had a sucker in his mouth and looked pretty pleased with himself.

"We should really talk about how you behaved back there."

"Nah, pass. Dad, I'm still hungry."

"Hey, I know we talked about lunch, but…"

"But what?"

Sam handed Arne the suckers he'd taken from the teller. "Those suckers are going to have to hold you over. Don't tell your mom."

Checking the gas gauge, Sam wasn't excited about the math. They might make it back to Fornborg—if it were mostly downhill and there was a wind at their backs. Sam noticed a service station across the road, one of those three-bay places where they changed oil and sold tires. They'd have what he needed.

"Arne, if I ask you to stay here and, uh, guard the car, could you do it?"

"Maybe. Can I start a fire with the lighter?"

Sam wished Arne hadn't said that. The boy probably wouldn't burn the car down like he did with the motel room, but now Sam wasn't willing to take the chance. Eleven-year-old boys and space-age car technology didn't go well together.

"No, you won't need a fire." Sam pulled the car lighter from the socket and shoved it in his pocket. Boys Arne's age loved starting fires, which really was the only good reason to join the Boy Scouts. "Just keep your eyes open. I saw some scary-looking criminal types wandering around. I don't want 'em busting in and trying to steal the car. Can you hold down the fort for about ten minutes?"

"Hey, Dad!" Arne pulled his hair back away from his forehead. "Who loves ya, baby?" He said with his best Telly Savalas impersonation.

"Spittin' image, kiddo. You stay put."

After a little sweet-talking, Sam convinced the mechanic over at the garage to let him take some radiator tubing that he promised to return. He even offered to leave his driver's license as collateral, but the mechanic told him to just return the tubing when he was through.

Sam returned to the car, relieved to discover that Arne had not ignited, cracked, or short-circuited anything. He drove to the back of the bank and pulled into the spot next to a new Cadillac parked in front of the BANK PRESIDENT sign. Sam unscrewed the station wagon's gas tank cap and the cap on the Cadillac. Then he inserted one end of the tube in the bank president's gas tank and sucked on the other end until gas began to flow through it. A little got gas in his mouth, and it burned, but that was a small price to pay to make sure they could make it back to Fornborg.

Arne leaned out the passenger side. He now had a bouquet of multi-colored suckers crammed in his mouth, making it hard to understand him, but it sounded like he said, "Fill 'er up, Dad!"

When Sam returned to the main house, he didn't recognize the inside. A sea of Nat's old junk surrounded Edie, and she was half-crocked.

"What happened? It looks like a tornado went through here."

"Oh, nothing," Edie drawled. "Just that I found out my dad wasn't my real dad, and my mom practically begged Uncle Nat to leave us the property in his will because we're ink, *hic*, ink, *hic*, incapable of taking care of ourselves."

"But you're so drunk. I don't remember you being this drunk when I left this morning."

"Bird must have flown in through the window. The beautiful window. I do love that window, Sam, and I love you too. I don't want to move to Hawaii."

"Okie dokie," Sam replied. "I love you too, I guess."

Arne came running in, took one look at the chaos and his mother sitting on the floor, and he froze.

"Why don't you go play in the woods or something," Sam suggested. Arne shrugged and ran off.

Sam assured her they would figure out everything just as soon as he could make sense of what she was talking about. Edie explained she had called her mother, and Dolores, the ol' mutton-in-law, admitted that her first husband was not, in fact, Edie's actual father.

"Did the letters say who *is* your father?"

"No."

"Did you ask your mother when you called her?"

Edie knocked over the empty bottle of Wild Turkey. "Why do you think I got dribbled first, dummy?"

"And did she tell you who it is?"

"No. That woman got mad at me for asking. Can you believe that? She said I drink too much and shouldn't smoke, and then she lectured me for reading her private letters."

"Sounds about right." Sam shook his head sympathetically. "You know what really chaps my hide, Edie? Why did that mother of yours pick a bank all the way over in Alexandria when there's a perfectly good bank right here in Fornborg?" He exhaled sharply in frustration. "It's like she tried to make everything twice as hard on purpose."

"I dunno," Edie slurred. "A for Alexandria. F for Fornborg. Maybe she let her fingers do the walking in the Yellow Pages. Wrap your little mind around this." She thrust a fist full of letters at him and drooped over sideways.

Sam read the letters. It's true they stopped short of revealing who Edie's real father was, but they certainly made clear that she didn't like Sam. Not a surprise, but there it was in that meticulous handwriting.

That man has as much sense as a doorframe.

The letters contained some interesting tidbits about cousins Jeffy and Lana. Apparently, Dolores had been keeping in contact with Nat's ex-wife, too, and fed Nat updates about his former family. Like how Jeffy's wife divorced him for "monkey business," whatever that meant. And how he'd been discharged early from the army for psychological issues. You didn't have to be a military psychologist to know putting a gun in Jeffy's hands and telling him to kill would be a bad idea. Sam knew that from watching him charge down the aisle at the funeral, waving around a snake, and hollering at his dead father.

According to the letters, Jeffy's sister, Lana, had shown little interest in men. Then again, knowing what she looked like, it might have been more like men just didn't show any interest in her. Sort of a chicken-and-egg thing. But, as the letters said, Lana liked her job at her stepfather's quarry. She was learning it top to bottom so she could take it over someday.

Sam took pleasure in the fact that Edie's family was so messed up. She was always on his case about trying harder and doing better and making ends meet and *blah blah blah.* At least *he* knew who his real dad was. Unless there were revealing letters from his mom lying around somewhere.

By this time, Edie was fussing like Arne used to when he was a baby. Overtired. Ready for a nap. He carried her to the bedroom, pulled off her shoes, and laid her under the covers. He removed a stray price tag from her forehead that said *Americana 10¢*. She lolled off to sleep.

⋘ ⋅ ⋅ ◆ ⋅ ⋅ ⋙

Edie was a little worse for wear by late afternoon. Sam tried to keep Arne from hounding her.

"Mommy's a little under the weather," Sam explained.

"What does that mean? Is she caught in a storm or something?"

"Pretty much, kiddo." *If it was raining Wild Turkey*, he thought.

He jumped when he heard knocking on the front door.

"I'll get it," Arne announced. He ran out of the kitchen and through the living room. He came running back into the kitchen a few moments later, breathing hard, his eyes wide.

"Dad! It's the fuzz!"

Sam rose as Sheriff Olmdahl stepped out of the living room behind Arne. He held a coil of black tubing.

"Do you recognize this hose, Mr. Fisker?"

Edie bleary-eyed, her face ashen, asked, "What did you do, Sam?"

"Nothing," Sam said through gritted teeth. "I didn't do anything."

The sheriff leaned in closer to Sam. "Have you been drinking gasoline today, Mr. Fisker?"

"No. Just some orange juice from concentrate, that's all. I didn't steal any gas if that's what you're implying."

"But you were in Alexandria today?"

Sam blinked, carefully choosing his words. "Sure, but just because someone goes to Alexandria, it doesn't mean they steal gas."

"Well, that's not what the bank president thinks. It's funny because he just filled his gas tank this morning, and next thing you know, *poof*! The tank is half-empty."

"I'm more of a tank-is-half-full person, myself," Sam replied. "But what does that have to do with me?"

"Oh, nothing I can run you in for. Yet. But the bank teller said the man's name was Fisker, that they took more than one lollipop from the bowl, and they were heading to Little Paw Lake. She saw this man—who matches your description, by the way, down to the clothes—walk across Broadway Street to a service station and return to the bank parking lot with this length of radiator hose in hand."

"Wasn't me." Sam shrugged.

The sheriff's eye twitched, but otherwise, his expression froze.

"I've been in the law since J. Edgar Hoover's mom was still wiping his nose for him. I know bull crap when I smell it."

Edie pushed between the men. "If my husband says he didn't do it, then he didn't do it, Sheriff. Now either arrest him or leave us alone. We have a lot going on around here."

"Alright." The sheriff nodded. "But I've got my eye on you." He sniffed Edie for good measure and crinkled his nose. She probably smelled like an old barroom mop. "Both of you."

Edie watched from the living room window as the sheriff lowered himself gingerly into his car and drove off. Sam came up behind her.

"Is he gone?"

She whirled around and threw her arms around him.

"Stealing gas, Sam? You've got to stop doing those things," she sobbed. "I can't lose you. Not now."

A glimmer of recognition lit Sam's eyes: recognition that she was right. She needed him. Arne needed him.

What the heck had he been doing?

"Baby," he whispered, pressing her against his chest. "Do you have a Certs in your purse? Your breath smells like the dumpster behind the Big Boy."

◆》 • ◆ • 《◆

They decided Edie should go to the bank in Alexandria the next day, and Sam and Arne would stay at the lake. The bank teller would call the cops if she saw Arne anywhere near the lollipops. Sam assured her that she had enough gas to make it there, but she would need to fill the tank in Alexandria before she headed back.

"You better call your mother, though, and have her double-check with the bank to make sure everything is still okay."

Edie sighed. The last time she'd spoken with her mother, she'd been very upset and very drunk. Things were said. Names were called.

"Do I have to?" she whined.

"Unless you like to get stranded in strange cities without a nickel to your name."

"I know; I just don't want to get into it with her all over again. I hate that we have to ask for help."

"Tell you what," Sam suggested. "Think of her money as a loan. We can pay her back as soon as we get this place up and running and tourists are spilling out of every nook and cranny."

Edie finished buttoning her blouse and leaned down to kiss his forehead.

"You're an idiot," she said. "But I'll call her anyway." She paused in the doorway. "And suppose I head to Alexandria tomorrow on my own, get the money, and don't come back?"

Sam stretched himself long on the bed, pushing back the sheet to expose his powder-blue boxers and knobby knees.

"And miss out on all this?" he asked. "You'd be kicking yourself the rest of your life."

She laughed. "What will you and Arne do tomorrow while I'm gone? I don't want to come home to any fires or hostage situations or anything."

"You really don't trust us, do you?"

"You mean *Butch Cassidy and the Sundance Kid*? No."

"Well, don't worry. Arne and me can set things up for the garage sale. I found some paint and old plywood. We can make signs for it, and we'll pound those suckers in at the turnoff from the county road. Get some of that town traffic."

"That's great, but don't do that until I get back. We won't be ready just because you put up a sign."

"Sure," Sam shrugged.

Edie went to the kitchen before she finished getting ready. She placed a collect call—again, at the higher daytime rates—but her mother didn't answer the phone. And she didn't answer two hours later, or the hour after that, or even the next morning. Edie drove off to Alexandria anyway, hoping she could collect the wire transfer without incident and that her mother hadn't died before she could apologize for saying some pretty nasty things the last time they spoke.

Wouldn't her mother love that? Something else to hold over Edie's head. Well, Edie Fisker was going to have the last word.

Chapter 23

Water-Oriented Activities

AFTER SWALLOWING A COUPLE handfuls of decidedly stale corn flakes without milk, the Fisker men, Arne and Sam, set to work. They moved crap outside so the local suckers would pay them to haul it off. It was a brilliant plan. You could literally stick a price tag on a bag of smelly garbage, and some idiot would buy it.

They set out their first piles on sheets of plywood that Sam had set on cinder blocks and sawhorses. He pulled Arne to his side and walked him into the yard.

"Let's take a moment, son." He stretched his arms and took a deep breath; Arne copied him.

"Smell that air, Arne?"

"Yeah! Smells lakey. Is that from fish poop?"

"That's your air now. And your lake."

"This is ours? All of it?"

"Well, not the whole lake," Sam amended. He had to be careful because Arne might take something literally, and soon, he'd be chasing down fishermen for trespassing on 'his' lake.

"From there," Sam pointed, "to about there. A few hundred feet of shoreline, those four cabins, and the main house."

"What about the trees?" Arne pointed to the woods surrounding the resort lot.

"Sure. Lots and lots of trees." Sam hoisted Arne, who wriggled into the air. "We'll find you a grimy old tire for a rope swing. Or you can just dive right off your own dock."

"After you fix it, you mean?"

"Yeah." Sam's voice trailed off. He wasn't exactly sure how to fix docks. Maybe it was just as easy to get a whole new dock rather than monkey around with a crummy old blown-up one.

"And I bet we'll fish a lot too, won't we, Dad?"

"Heck, yeah. We'll go fishing every day. Didn't I ever tell you our name means fishing?"

"Does it really?"

"Sure! I never told you that? It's Norwegian, just like us."

"How do you say waterski in Norwegian?"

Sam didn't know any other Norwegian words besides *uffda* and *lutefisk*, which often were uttered in the same breath. He just smiled and nodded, pretending not to hear Arne's question.

"And waterskiing too, Dad? We'll go waterskiing every day?"

"You betcha. Now let's get back to work so we can unload some of this junk."

Between the two of them, Arne and Sam lugged out all the items to the garage and driveway, tossing what they could on dusted off folding tables. The presentation of the clothes, knick-knacks, mysterious gadgets, and pockmarked antique furniture needed a woman's touch, but it was all out of the house. Sam and Arne walked together with the signs they'd painted, and Arne held the post while Sam hammered it in. They did the same a quarter-mile up at the intersection with the county road.

"Now, we're ready for business," Sam announced as they turned to tromp back to the property. But they really weren't ready for business, as they soon discovered. They had just begun their hike back to the house when they heard tires screeching and brakes squealing. Passing cars on the county road took sharp, veering turns at the sign, beelining for the Fisker's garage sale. A veritable parade of cars and trucks passed them by, but Sam realized just how unready they were when an Amish wagon passed them by.

By the time Arne and Sam reached the end of their driveway, vehicles filled the yard and crushed hedges. A white Wonder Bread box van with little red, yellow, and blue balloons on the front and the slogan *Helps Build Strong Bodies 12 Ways* on the side had shattered a terracotta planter of marigolds. Sam and Arne arrived just as an altercation began between a teenaged boy and the Wonder Bread delivery driver, all in white, just like the bread he delivered. As punches flew, Sam rushed to break it up, pulling away the gangly youth who gripped a rolled-up magazine like a cudgel.

"What's the hubbub here?"

"This little snot grabbed the issue I was looking for right out of my hands."

"You set it down," the teenager warbled. "Didn't have your name on it!"

The contested magazine had come from a stack of other *Art Photo Forum* magazines from the 1960s. It was the kind of magazine that purported to help photographers with useful articles about focal points, composition, and camera gear, but it really was just an excuse to put a bunch of photos of half-naked models in a magazine without being too smutty.

"There are plenty of other issues to choose from," Sam pointed out. Sam was no fool. He had held back two issues of the *Art Photo Forum* for himself, August 1966 and June 1967, because someday he just might take up photography himself.

"I've got all those other ones." The driver pointed to the magazine still in the boy's hand. "I want *that* one."

"You must be a very good photographer," Sam said, trying to smooth the situation.

The driver shook his head. "I'm just, uh, learning right now. I need to get the right equipment."

The teenager flashed the cover of the magazine at them, a buxom brunette in a leopard-print halter kneeling at the edge of the sea.

"You'll never have the equipment for this, mister," the kid said.

"And I suppose," Sam said as he pulled the magazine from the kid's grasp, "you're interested in art photography too?"

"Heck, no. But I'm sure interested in chicks."

Sam handed the magazine to the driver.

"Ten cents."

"Take a nickel for it?"

"Ha!" The boy showed Sam a dime. "I would have paid full price, sucker."

Sam sighed but took the nickel. At least they were now officially in the black by five cents.

The next paying customer, a man in brand-spanking-new quick-dry clothes and a fly-fishing vest, revealed a distinct flaw in Sam's business launch. He dragged a rickety old piece of garbage to Sam.

"I'll take it," he said. Just judging from the man's clothes, Sam bet this guy was one of those Lake Lutherans that the locals scorned. His wrinkle-free fishing shirt probably came right off the rack at some fancy store in the Twin Cities, like Dayton's. It must be new, because it didn't even smell like fish. He probably was rich and only came up to Fornborg on weekends, with pockets full of cash, when the weather was nice.

"Good choice. That's a lovely end table."

"It's for our weekend cabin over on Little Jack Pine lake. We just had it built. My wife, she's just crazy for rustic décor."

"We're swimming in rustic here," Sam assured him. His palm itched with the anticipation of selling this guy everything that wasn't nailed down.

"Are these stains authentic?"

"Yup, they are. But if your wife doesn't like the color, you bring it back here and I'll have my son spill something different on it," Sam said. "And some putty will do the trick for those deep gouges. Why, nail a broomstick handle right on that wobbly leg, and this baby's as good as new. That's three dollars."

The man opened his wallet, and Sam saw only a solitary bill unfold within it.

"Do you have change for a hundred?"

"No, sorry." Sam had no change. Zero. Maybe that was one of the things Edie was going to take care of after she got back. Sam hadn't even thought about making change. He'd thought only of collecting cash from these junk scavengers. "Do you have anything smaller?"

The man frowned and dug around in his front pants pocket, his hand coming out in a balled fist. He opened his fingers to reveal one shiny coin.

"Would you take a nickel for it?"

"That's all you got?"

The man showed him the hundred-dollar bill again.

"Tell you what," Sam offered. "Why not take everything here for the hundred?"

"Don't want anything else." The man shook his head. "Just this."

"Fine, I'll take the nickel, but could you swing by sometime and drop off a couple bucks? This isn't a charity."

The man said that sounded fine, and Sam took the nickel. Even Lake Lutherans should respect the honor system, right? Meanwhile, more vehicles came pouring in, and more customers asked if he would take a nickel for this or a dime for that.

"Heck, the masking tape for the price tag is worth that alone," he'd countered, but it was no use. He was being swallowed by a sea of cheapskatery.

"Arne!" Sam yelled, feeling overwhelmed by all the nickel-and-diming. "Pray for rain!"

Sam heard the whine of a boat motor. A double-decker custom pontoon nosed full-bore toward the resort with a half-dozen people, all men, standing like statues on the forward deck.

"Geez, they're on a mission," Sam muttered. "Now I know how the Germans felt on D-Day."

"Who are they, Dad?"

"Beats me, but they're heading this way. Maybe they're here for the garage sale."

The pontoon's motor cut out, and it glided alongside the remnant of the dock where Nat Lachmann had met his tragic end. Two men jumped into the water and moored the boat in quick looping movements.

"Sam Fisker?" An older man called, his hands cupped around his mouth.

"Yeah?"

He waved for Sam to come down to the shore like a football coach waving a struggling quarterback in to the sidelines.

"Dad, what do they want?"

"I'll go find out."

"Can I come with?"

Sam scanned the faces of the strangers.

"No, I better check them out first, Arne. They might be more of those Lake Lutherans," Sam quipped. "You stay here and take money. You know how to do math, right?"

"Sort of," Arne hesitated.

"Just...figure it out." Sam knew Arne wasn't the sharpest cheese in the lunchpail, but he probably could add and subtract by now. "And don't take anything less than what it says on the price tag."

"Got it."

"And don't start any fires." Sam thought it best to mention fire specifically to Arne. The boy hadn't quite grasped the idea of learning from your mistakes. Maybe it ran in the family, Sam mused, his attention returning to the men on the biggest pontoon Sam had ever seen. The upper deck, bordered by aluminum railing, had a diving board sticking off the back. They maneuvered it to the remaining section of dock. "You fellas here for the sale?" Sam called.

The men conferred, too quietly for Sam to hear.

"Uh, yeah," the older man said. He jerked his chin to one side, and two men jumped off the pontoon and headed up the slope to the garage sale. "And don't pay asking price," he called after them. "They always jack the prices at these things. No offense," he said to Sam.

"None taken," Sam replied. "Are they interested in photography at all? I can give them a good price on some how-to guides."

The other men just stared at him, unsmilingly, until the older man spoke.

"Why don't you come on board?" It was a command rather than a suggestion. Sam couldn't think of any reason why it might not be a good idea to get on a giant party pontoon with a group of burly looking strangers. After all, the one who was driving was the guy with the Hawaiian shirt, and if his guess was correct, the cooler was full of beer.

The leader urged Sam to sit on the bench. Air farted out of the cushion along with tiny flecks of Styrofoam, and the swirled for a moment as the pontoon revved to life. A cool, fine mist coated his bare arms, giving him a little chill. He sat back like a lord, his arms stretched out behind him on the railing as he admired the property from a new perspective. Those four cabins were the golden goose just waiting to be plucked. The place would clean up nice, he knew it would. They'd get some good photos of it and make fliers, and pretty soon they'd be crawling with fishermen.

The older man with the bushy gray sideburns leaned in close. "You comfortable with boats, Sam?" He had to talk loud so Sam could hear over the wind and the motor.

"Well, I work on boat motors a lot," Sam shouted to be heard. "But I haven't had much chance to be on them. But it turns out my boy, Arne, is quite the waterskier. Like a real natural athlete, so I guess I might try to pull him around a little."

"I see," the man responded, clearly disappointed in Sam's response. "I'm more of a fisherman myself," he yelled. "I enjoy the tranquility of fishing. It's very meditative, don't you think?"

"Oh, sure. Real peaceful," Sam agreed in his loudest voice.

"Best performed in the stillness and quietude of nature without a lot of shouting and carrying on and making a lot of waves, don't you think?"

"Uh, yes, I guess that makes for the best fishing."

"And are you a fisherman also, Mr. Fisker?"

"Please, just call me Sam. I've dabbled."

"You've what?"

"I've dabbled," Sam hollered. "I've taken Arne—that's my son—out now and again. But now that we're reopening the resort, I bet I'll dip a line in the water." The man's tight smile revealed he didn't believe Sam. "I bet you're that Bud Langskip, aren't you?" Sam said in dawning awareness. "You kidnapped my wife yesterday."

"Kidnapping is a strong word for it." Bud pursed his lips in disdain. "An opening negotiation was all it was. You're a man of the world who understands how business works."

The compliment pleased Sam. That's something he didn't hear too often, but still these guys shouldn't go around snatching people's wives. After reaching the middle of Little Paw Lake, the pontoon veered toward the southern edge past a bay dotted with lily pads. The engines quieted as they slowed to trawling speed.

"You didn't make a new friend with Edie," Sam said bluntly. "She was mad as spit. We've had a rough start here these past few days, so when you add getting kidnapped to the list, I could see why she was annoyed."

"Let's just say it was a mutual misunderstanding. Static on the line. The important thing now is the men are talking."

"Yes, we are," Sam eyed the cooler in hopes it might trigger the offer of a cold beer. "Man-o a man-o." The clue didn't register, and Sam remained beerless and thirsty.

"I'm actually here to help you and Edie."

Sam nodded. "She said you want to buy the resort, but, to tell you the truth, Mr. Langskip, I'm pretty excited about running the place ourselves."

"And have you and Edie run a resort before?"

"No, this will be our first time."

"It's quite an undertaking."

"I know."

"It will change your life."

"I suppose it will."

"Since we're speaking of the resort, I should let you know that Ned Lachmann—he was your wife's uncle, I believe?" Sam nodded. "Well, Ned often needed our help," Bud Langskip continued. "It seems the resort wasn't doing as well as everyone had hoped. He needed a little, hmmm, *support* from time to time. Fortunately, he belonged to our mutual aid society, the Sons of Gunnar. One that I hope you'll consider joining, although I should caution you that membership is not guaranteed."

"What did you say it was? A mutual aid society?"

"Yes, sort of a men's heritage club. For Norwegians. I am the president of that club. We look out for one another and our families."

He pointed to a man about Sam's age who was watching them with a tight, grim expression. "In fact, that's my son, Lester."

Sam nodded and smiled at Lester, but he received no sign of recognition from Lester, no hint of a greeting.

"You know, Edie has been saying how we need to get involved in the community and all," Sam added. "Probably makes sense to rub elbows with some of my fellow Norwegians. Be good for business. Where do I sign up?"

"We have several requirements, Sam. First, are you at least half Norwegian?"

"Heck, I'm all Norwegian."

Bud nodded, satisfied. "I thought so. You have an innate intelligence."

At least that's what Sam assumed Bud said. His voice kind of trailed off at the end. He also could have said, *You have absolutely no sense.* The other men chuckled.

Bud explained there were certain stages—rites of passage, he called them—that Sam would have to undergo before he would be admitted into the Sons of Gunnar.

"Sounds interesting. I really want us to fit in around here, you know. Give us the best possible start. When can I begin?"

"I suppose now's as good a time as any."

Bud put out his hand, and they shook on it.

"Oh, and Sam, because a lot of our activities are water-oriented, I should ask, can you swim?"

"Like a fish."

Bud signaled with a sharp nod. His son, Lester Langskip, sprang forward from his seat. With the force of a lion on a gazelle, he easily shoved Sam into the cold, deep water. The pontoon roared to life and sped off toward the channel exiting Little Paw Lake.

<hr />

Sam alternated between breaststroke and floating on his back as he made slow but steady progress toward the property. *Concentrate on your breathing. Don't panic.* These were the helpful little voices to which Sam clung.

He saw Arne pointing to him from shore and Edie standing at his side. She was back from the bank, but she didn't look happy. Hopefully she got the money and her consternation was only because he was struggling in the middle of the lake. If she got the money and he drowned, at least she'd have enough to buy him a nice snake-proof casket.

Edie waited with a dun-colored towel, pounding him with questions as he finally made it to the shallows. His toes found the sandy bottom, and he could wade the rest of the way. His teeth chattered in the cold air.

"Why are you out taking a swim while your son is getting bamboozled by the local Lake Lutherans? He took a dime for a silver quarter," she fumed. "And you're out there pretending to be Mark Spitz."

"Edie, I'm not out here for my health, I swear." His torso was out of the water, and he rubbed his arms vigorously. "I met your new friend, Bud Langskip, and they pushed me out of the boat in the middle of the lake."

Arne galloped sideways down the slope and stopped at his mother's side.

"You sure can swim, Dad!"

"Thanks, kiddo."

"I didn't think you were going to make it. A couple times, you were like…" Arne made gurgling sounds and waved his arms wildly over his head.

"Yeah, well, thanks for the moral support."

Edie told Arne to get back to the garage sale, so all the big-ticket items didn't get stolen.

"And look at the price on the sticker," she called to him as he dashed back up the slope. "That's what things cost." Returning her attention to Sam, Edie asked, "It was those Norwegian Pontoon Mafia people who pushed you in?"

"Yeah." He tipped his head to one side, trying to get the water out of his ears.

Edie shook her head. "You'd expect something like this in a big city. My mom and Vicki both said those men are bad news."

"It's okay." Sam reached for the towel and wrapped himself in it. "They want me to join. I guess you say I took the plunge."

"You're not joining those crooks," Edie stated flatly.

"But you said you wanted us to get involved in the community."

"But not the Norwegian Manson family. I meant we could join a church. The PTA. Bake sales and Advent family affairs, not committing extortion and wearing funny hats."

"I'm not joining any church," Sam countered. "Next time I'm in church, it'll be for my funeral."

"I can make that happen," Edie warned.

He took her in his arms and pressed against her so that her clothes got damp. Then in his sexiest voice, he said, "Why don't you..."

"Yes?"

"Take me somewhere private..." He nuzzled her cheek, breathing in her ear.

"Yes?"

"And check me for leeches."

◆◆◆ — ◆ ◆ ◆ — ◆◆◆

His mom and dad eventually took over the garage sale from Arne. Apparently, they didn't trust his negotiating skills—plus they'd discovered the items he'd squirreled away for himself, the kind of stuff every boy needed: a hunting knife, a photography magazine, a pair of binoculars with one shattered lens, and a roadmap of South Dakota.

They didn't think to check his pockets, though. He had three old keys, a naked lady bottle opener, and nearly three dollars in coins—his cut of the take, he'd decided. Fair was fair.

He wandered the yard, taking it all in as his dad had framed it: His! His yard, his house, his lake, his woods! His, his, his! Arne didn't care about ever going back to that crummy old Minneapolis now. They were going to buy a speedboat and waterskis, and Arne was going to ski all the time. Probably drop out of school, too. He doubted fifth grade would be any better the second time around anyway.

Arne heard a branch crack in the woods (his woods!), and he darted toward the sound. Maybe it was a bear or a bigfoot or something cool. He looked through the branches but couldn't see any animals, just underbrush and fallen, moldering logs, and something white and speckled with green mold, like a rock, but smoother. Was it a gravestone?

"Kid."

A voice behind him nearly sent him through his own skin. Arne got a little scared and was about to run away, but the man in the Hawaiian shirt appeared, putting up both hands to calm him. Arne noticed that one of the pinky fingers looked shorter than the others.

It was John Kvalstad, who'd taken him waterskiing and who his mother called a bad name afterward.

"No worries, little man. I'm not going to hurt you."

"Hi, John," Arne replied in his usual exuberant manner. "What are you doing in there?"

John hushed him and told him to be mellow, whatever that meant.

"It's *vannski*, by the way."

"What's a van ski?" Arne asked. His imagination reeled. He could see himself being pulled on skis behind the Scooby-Doo Mystery Machine.

"I heard you ask your dad earlier about the Norwegian word for waterski. It's *vannski*. See, I'm Norwegian myself," John explained.

Arne wondered how John had heard them talking earlier. Had he been in the woods all this time?

"Do you live near here?" Arne asked.

"Oh, not too far. I have a place over on Long Ear."

"Long Ear?"

"Yeah, that's another lake. Part of the Rabbit Chain." John folded his hands together as if to cast a complicated shadow puppet, a tangle of fingers and knuckles, that vaguely resembled a rabbit. He waggled one thumb. "You're here on Little Paw." He wriggled his pointer. "And I'm on Long Ear." Arne wondered what the stump of a pinky was supposed to be.

"People tell me, 'Wahoo, you need to sell your place once and for all and just move to Hawaii for good.' But I tell 'em…"

"They call you Wahoo? Why?"

"Because they're idiots who are too lazy to call me Oahu John. See, I winter in Hawaii. On the Big Island. It's called Oahu. It's paradise. So, when they say I should just move there for good, I tell 'em, 'If no one's around here to bring the aloha spirit, then you'll all be miserable in Minnesota without me.' You see, I try to bring the Hawaiian spirit—the aloha—with me wherever I go."

"Like Elvis?" Arne remembered watching the live Elvis special, *Aloha from Hawaii*, a couple years back. Apparently, old people liked that sort of thing.

"Sure, just like Elvis." John chuckled, which told Arne that it had nothing to do with Elvis at all. "So, enough about me. Tell me about your dad. What did he do before?"

"This and that," Arne replied, mimicking how his dad would respond to that question. "Mostly that, but he takes this when he can't get that."

"So, he's sort of a jack of all trades?"

"I guess."

"Does he drink too much sometimes? Maybe hit you and your mom?"

"No!" Arne noticed John's arm tattoo peeking out from under his shirt sleeve. "What's that?"

John pushed up his sleeve to reveal the SAPPER tattoo.

"Got that done in a little shack in Saigon."

"What does 'sapper' mean? Like tree sap?"

"No, more like blowing things up. Sapping their strength. Like sapping a bridge's structural integrity, for example, so it collapses, or figuring out how to bring down a building. Back in the old days, sappers figured out how to knock walls over so the knights could get in the castle and rescue the princess."

"And steal the gold?"

"Yeah." John laughed. "And steal the gold."

"You spelled it wrong. It's supposed to have a Z for zapping stuff."

"Okay, you win. Was your dad in the military? Did he serve in Vietnam?"

"No."

"I sure wish I could have dodged 'Nam too." He held up his pinky stump. "See this?"

Arne nodded.

"You know how I lost the tip of my pinky?"

Arne shook his head fast. He really wanted to know.

"My finger got stuck in a hand grenade, and I threw it so hard the tip just went flying with it. Blasted into a million pieces."

"Whoa!" Arne's eyes widened. Then Arne recalled all the other times he'd believed whatever an adult had told him, like how a perfectly good bookshelf was only worth a dime. He shouldn't just believe everything adults say, even if they had a cool boat.

"Is that true?" he added incredulously.

"You caught me." John raised both hands in the air like he was getting stuck up in a stagecoach robbery. "Actually, a rat chewed it off when I was a prisoner of war."

"A rat!" Arne laughed again. He made his front teeth stick out like a rodent as he nibbled his lower lip in jest. The stern look that Wahoo John gave him told him that, this time, the man wasn't joking.

❧❧ • ❦ • ❧❧

The first day of the garage sale, they'd made seventeen dollars and sixty-five cents. With the wire transfer from Dolores of five hundred dollars, the Fiskers were now flush with cash, so Edie went grocery shopping at the Sack N' Save, which hadn't changed much over the years. She and her cousins each got a shiny quarter to spend from Uncle Nat, and Edie had spent hers on a book with cut-out dolls with paper outfits—a decision she later regretted after enduring hours of Lana and Jeffy stuffing their mouths with candy and taunting her.

Probably the biggest changes since 1956 were the products on the shelves. Maybe. Some of the canned goods were dusty enough that they could have been there when she was still in her favorite pink romper. The handful of people she passed, a clerk and some other last shoppers, each said hello to her, which confused her. Did they know her? Had they been at Uncle Nat's funeral and recognized her? Then she realized it was more common for people in small towns like Fornborg to be friendlier than in Minneapolis. She vowed to respond in a more relaxed manner the next time a stranger greeted her instead of wincing.

Her grocery cart was essentially a wire basket welded to squeaky wheels with a split personality. One of the wheels refused to budge at all, which forced Edie to push the cart with the same level of force you might use to mow your lawn or to shove your husband off a pontoon. Of course, the cart didn't get any easier to maneuver the more items she added to it. She got the staples: coffee, bread, milk, eggs, fruit cocktail, peanut butter, jelly, Oscar Mayer hot dogs—God, wouldn't Arne enjoy a weenie roast in the great outdoors?

She splurged a little, too: a pound of various Brach's candies from the Pick-A-Mix display and three sirloin steaks. Oh, and a carton of Dignity cigarettes for emergencies.

A nice young man in a light blue smock carried her groceries to the station wagon for her, and she tipped him with a fistful of nickels and dimes fresh from the tackle box they'd used at the garage sale for a cash register.

She lit a Dignity right there in the driver's seat. There was probably an emergency somewhere.

Chapter 24

Zucchini Face

EDIE HONKED THE CAR horn when she returned to the property—their property. She turned off the car just as Linda Ronstadt's voice faded out on "You're No Good."

Arne appeared first, jamming his head through the open driver's side window. Sometimes she swore he was more dog than boy.

"Did you get potato chips?"

Crap. She'd forgotten potato chips. They had been on the list even, but maybe she'd subconsciously sabotaged the potato chips because of latent hostility? She had read something about that in an article from *Today's Sophisticated Woman* about "Hidden Hostility in the Household."

"No, but I got you some Count Chocula."

"Oh, yay!" He literally jumped up and down at the news. "Can we have cereal for supper?"

"No."

Sam wandered out wearing his boxer shorts and a t-shirt that folded over his paunchy belly.

"You made it." He gave her a kiss.

"Gentlemen," Edie announced. "Unload the groceries."

"Sure, sure," Sam dismissed her, pulling Arne to his side. "Give us a minute. We're just going to take another gander at our new kingdom. Care to join us, my queen?" She rolled her eyes. "Oh, come on over here, Edie," Sam insisted. He and Arne walked up the drive, and Edie followed, but only reluctantly. She hoped no one drove by and saw her husband wandering around in his underwear. Scratch that: *in her dead uncle's underwear*. Sam didn't normally wear boxer shorts.

"There's probably mail in the mailbox, anyway," she admitted, but Sam wasn't heading to the mailbox. He veered to the raised flower bed where the resort's entrance sign stood. Its faded and flaked lettering read *The Sleep Tight Resort*, which is what Uncle Nat's parents had named it.

"We've got to make this place our own," Sam announced brightly. "What should we call it?"

"Wouldn't we just keep the same name?" Arne asked. "It's already on the sign."

Without warning, Sam punched the sign so hard it shattered in half.

"Nope, I don't think so."

"Coo-ewl!" Arne exclaimed. "You're like Hong Kong Phooey!"

Sam covered his punching hand, but not before Edie noticed his scratched knuckles. *Idiot*, she thought.

"Number one super guy?" Sam smiled. "You betcha."

"That was a foolish thing to do," Edie interrupted. "It was kind of a cute name."

"Yeah, exactly," Sam countered. "Too cute. We don't want cute old ladies coming here to darn stockings. We're trying to lure he-men for fishing and hunting, not their grandmothers. Besides, your uncle didn't exactly have a stellar reputation around here. Time for a fresh start and a new name. That way, everyone will know the resort is under new management."

"How about Ski Town USA?" Arne interjected.

"Hmm..." Sam pretended to consider Arne's suggestion. "You know what, kiddo? That might scare off the fishermen." He snapped his fingers as if a brilliant idea had just occurred to him. "Hey, I've got it. How about Fisker's Resort? Simple, elegant."

"But no one knows us," Edie pointed out. "So, our name doesn't mean anything around here."

"I get that," Sam agreed. "But people will get to know us. I mean, we're getting involved, remember?"

"Like church?" Edie arched her eyebrows. She hadn't been able to drag Sam into a church more than a handful of times, and usually only for big events like funerals and christenings. Come to think of it, they had been acting like a bunch of Lake Lutherans, just without the lake, until now.

"Well, let's not get crazy."

She pressed forward. "In the scheme of things, we're only passing through here, just like Uncle Nat and all the other people before him."

"Wow, that's some fancy hippie talk. Have you been hanging around Avi and Garvey in the treehouse?"

She glowered at him. "What I mean is the lake is always here, no matter who lives on it."

Sam nodded. "That's true. You think we can ask Toby to get the DNR to rename it to Fisker's Lake?"

Edie sighed. She could almost taste that next emergency cigarette.

"Just kidding. Okay, so the lake's called Little Paw."

"Little Paw!" Arne repeated, chuckling. "That cracks me up!"

Sam studied the lake. "And there are nice sandy beaches, three bays, and a public landing. Does any of that inspire you? I mean, it's probably got some really nice fishing holes."

Her eyes widened. "That's a start. Fishing holes. That's what we've got here, right?"

"Sure," Sam agreed. "The entire county is lousy with 'em."

"Okay," Edie continued. "Then how about *The Hole on Little Paw Lake*?"

"Little Paw," Arne chuckled again.

"Every time, huh?" Sam roughed Arne's hair.

"Yeah," Arne giggled. "It's funny."

Returning his attention to Edie, Sam agreed.

"Yeah. Yeah, I really like that, baby. Congratulations. You just won the naming contest. A name like that is sure to bring in the fishing crowd, or my name isn't Uffda Lutefisk."

Arne and Sam laughed, but Edie was saving her laughs for a special occasion.

A blue Volvo pulled into their driveway from the dirt road.

"Who is it, Mom?"

"It's our neighbors. Remember Mr. Svensson? The one who works for the DNR?"

"Is he the fuzz who gave us the ticket?"

"Yes, sweetie, but it's not polite to call people 'the fuzz.' "

"Maybe we can sell them the rest of this junk." Sam clapped his hands together and rubbed them together like a cartoon miser.

"Well, we can't just stand around gabbing," Edie cautioned. "Today's the day you evict those treehouse hippies."

"Yeah, Dad. Don't get to gabbing."

Toby Svensson, at the wheel of the Swedish box, was indeed the DNR officer who ticketed them for unauthorized camping, but he wore a a maroon jersey instead of his DNR get-up. He drove cautiously, peering over the hood as if looking for land mines.

Vicki Svensson waved to Edie from the passenger seat. Edie stopped short of rolling her eyes because her perfect neighbor never seemed to have a bad day whereas Edie felt grimy in old jeans and one of Sam's old raggedy button-up shirts. She hadn't planned on receiving company, not until everything was in order, including herself. Edie's desire to crawl under the nearest rock only grew when she saw how Vicki's strawberry-blonde hair was done-up so that her bangs cascaded in curls around her perfect face, giving an air of a carefree hairstyle. But Edie knew the truth: that woman had spent plenty of time in rollers and pointing a hairdryer at her head to achieve the carefree look.

As discreetly as possible, Edie adjusted the kerchief that barely held her own unstyled hair from drooping over her face like the mustache on a walrus. That's probably how it was when people died and got judged in heaven: just seeing God with His perfect hair and His perfect teeth made people's faults and blemishes burn like they were in Hell.

Vicki emerged from the passenger side, long and sleek. She wore high-waisted maroon slacks that flared over her black wedgies. A snug-fitting maroon v-neck top revealed wide lapels of a white silk undershirt. Toby wore tartan-patterned pants with maroon-and-gold stripes. His maroon jersey clung to his trim frame. They'd coordinated their outfits for cripes sake, while Edie looked like something you swept from under the stove. And Sam—well, he was wearing boxer shorts and a tattered red t-shirt with oil splatter. God! It was like the Vanderbilts visiting a hobo camp.

Edie put on one of those false smiles known as 'zucchini face.' It's the polite look you give someone after receiving an unwanted, oversized, and seedy vegetable gift from someone else's garden.

"Hi," she said, trying to sound friendly.

"Hello, hello!" Toby waved.

Vicki hugged Edie, even though Edie felt disgusting, and the men shook hands. Arne offered his hand to Toby, too.

"You got any kids?" Arne asked. Toby shot a concerned glance at Vicki.

"Arne, that's personal," Edie scolded.

"That's okay," Vicki said. "No, Arne, we don't have children. Yet."

"But it's not for lack of trying, is it, sweetie?" Toby hugged his wife to his side. "Almost a full-time job in and of itself, but when the good Lord wills it…"

"So, Toby, how are things at the DNR?" Sam interrupted. "You know, when you're not…" He lifted his eyebrows: code for *sexual relations*. If Edie had a stick in her hand, she would have poked him.

"Pretty busy. Wildlife never sleeps. Well, I mean it does, but there's enough of the wildlife around that it's always getting into trouble."

Edie automatically looked at Arne who was chewing on a stick. Maybe the DNR would babysit for them sometime.

"I've been at it right out of college." Toby smiled, clearly proud of his work. "Met this little gal at the U. I was studying forestry. We got hitched before I joined up for the service. Were you in?"

Sam shook his head. "Too busy minding my own business back here. Say, what does that DNR pay you nowadays?"

"Ignore him," Edie chuckled as she tried to sound nonplussed. "He's overstimulated."

"Speaking of the DNR," Toby said, "while I have your ear, there are a few things I should mention about the resort that need attention."

"Don't forget the groceries, Sam." Edie pointed to the station wagon. "Maybe he could take a rain check?"

"Edie says I'm not supposed to get to gabbing."

Edie rolled her eyes, but only as a signal to Vicki, sending the wifely code for *Men—We'll never completely fix them, but maybe we can shore them up a little.*

Vicki leaned into the car and brought out a foil-covered baking pan that she passed to Edie.

"We won't keep you, but we were just on our way to town and wanted to welcome you. You know, officially."

Like a bear, Sam pawed open the foil to reveal a thick, brown cake. He sniffed it noisily, rustling the foil with his nose. Edie wanted to crawl under a rock.

"Ooh, that smells spicy."

"Oh, I hope I didn't overdo the pumpkin pie spice."

"I'm sure it's delicious," Edie assured her, returning the foil. "Is it a pumpkin cake, then?"

"No, it's a sausage cake."

Something tried to slither up Edie's throat, but Toby rubbed his belly, an ecstatic look washing over his face.

"Vicki is working her way through her Betty Crocker recipe cards, and I am getting fat!"

He laughed, and the Fiskers laughed too, but clearly, Toby Svensson was *not* getting fat. He was lean and long and good-looking. And he was wearing pants, unlike certain husbands.

"Are you Gopher fans?" Vicki asked.

"Are you gonna shoot gophers today at the DNR?" Arne blurted.

"No." Toby chuckled and patted Arne's head like the boy was an unruly golden retriever. "That was last week. We're talking about the U of M baseball team."

"Yes, Toby and I are big fans of the Golden Gophers. We actually met at a game."

Edie and Sam searched one another's faces for a clue as to what they were hearing.

Seeing their confusion, Vicki Svensson added, very slowly, "The U of M is a *college*." She drew out the last word like 'cowl edge.' "We're going to listen to the game on the radio later. They're playing the boys from Western Michigan."

"And there might be beer involved," Toby added, directing the comment at Sam with a wink.

"That doesn't sound too bad," Sam responded.

"We would love to, but—" she elbowed Sam in the ribs, "we have a lot to do."

"Of course you do," Toby agreed. "And here we are discussing higher education while you have lawn mowing and tree trimming. And there's that dock, of course. Why, it'll take you weeks to get all this figured out."

If not months, Edie muttered to herself.

"Well, it was nice to see you, officially," Edie stated. "And thank you for the…" She almost wretched from the thought of what she was holding, a sausage cake. "…thoughtful gift." She put on her zucchini face again.

"Of course."

The Svenssons returned to their shiny little box of a Volvo and zipped off to town. Once they were out of sight, Edie shoved the baking pan at Sam.

"Take this and bury it in the woods before I throw up."

With the baking pan tucked under his arm like a football, Sam headed to the treehouse. He definitely wouldn't bury a perfectly good sausage cake. Instead he would kill two birds with one stone, the stone being the sausage cake, and the birds being hippies. Offering it as a gesture of goodwill to Avi and Garvey might soften the blow of evicting them. If it worked, he might just gain a few points with Edie, the Fiskers get the property to themselves, and the hippies start a new adventure someplace else. Everybody wins.

Sitar music drifted dreamily toward Sam, a piece of Americana folk music he recognized instantly from his childhood. How did it go? Oh, yeah. *I've been working on the railroad.*

Hearing that brought back memories. His favorite red yo-yo with the knot in the middle of the string.

All the live-long day!

Mr. Chitters (the loving family mutt) loping after an old rubber ball.

Just to pass the time away.

Sitting around a campfire with his neighborhood pals in the backyard late one autumn afternoon.

Can't you hear the whistle blowing?

Yes, that was the song they'd been singing when Sam's mom pulled him away from his friends to tell him that his dad had been killed by cigarettes.

Dinah, blow your horn!

Sam pushed aside this terrible memory and willed himself up the rickety tree ladder with one hand balancing the baking pan. As he neared the floor hole, he heard Garvey's voice singing, except the lyrics were much different from the version Sam remembered. Something about licking all the wet toads? Sam shouted to announce his arrival, and the music stopped. Avi's fresh face appeared at the entrance.

"Hey, it's Mr. Brownie Lover. Don't you just dig Garvey's songs? He's so talented."

He handed her the pan and lifted himself through.

"Yeah, that one brings back memories," Sam said, but Avi looked puzzled. Garvey stopped playing and glared at Sam.

"No, man. I just wrote this one."

"It's called 'Nixon Licked a Toad'," Avi explained.

"Yeah," Garvey thumped his heart with his fist and closed his eyes, perhaps about ready to slip into meditation. "It's political."

"It's catchy, too," Avi added. "Oh, did you bring more brownies for us?"

"Not quite. It's a spicy sausage cake that Mrs. Svensson baked."

Garvey's eyes shot open and focused on Sam.

"Sausage sounds like meat."

"Can't argue with that, Garvey." Sam rubbed his hands together. "Let's dig in."

Avi set the pan down on the floor and nudged it through the hole so that it clattered against the branches below and thumped against the ground.

"Meat is murder," she explained. "We don't eat meat."

"Don't eat meat?" Sam couldn't believe it. He read about those vegetarians, but he thought they were just weirdos out in California. Now California weirdness had leaked into Minnesota. "What about all the vitamins, that kind of crap?" Sam was no nutrition expert, but he'd been led to believe meat was a crucial part of the human diet, thanks to research provided by the American Beef Council.

"There are plenty of ways to get the nutrition you need without assassinating Bambi," Avi said. "Sprouts. Mushrooms. Even deep breathing gives your body sustenance, doesn't it, Garv?" Garvey took a deep breath and held it.

Sam's stomach rumbled, already primed to digest some sausage cake,. Now it was angry. He looked around for brownies or anything else edible. No luck. Was it any wonder that hippies were so skinny? Not only did they avoid meat, but they seemed to skip eating altogether. Too busy making love, probably, or eating mold and twigs.

Sam tried to arrange his legs in the pretzel shape that Garvey and Avi's legs made. Failing that, he stretched his legs out straight. "Well, I've got some bad news for you."

Garvey blew out the breath he'd been holding. "Aw, man. You're gonna hassle us, aren't you? Just like the fascists."

Sam wasn't entirely clear who the fascists were, but he didn't want people to think he was one of them. He was a man of the people. He was the velvet glove. Now Edie: she was the iron fist.

"Now, this comes straight from the boss lady, not from me. I really tried to work something out," Sam said. "I personally like the idea of having you both up here, keeping the treehouse safe and all, but the wife, she's just not into it, you know?"

Avi prodded Garvey. "You've got to tell him." Garvey tucked his head behind the neck of the sitar as if he were suddenly shy, and she prodded him again. "Tell him, Garvey."

"No, man. I don't want any hassles."

"What if we told you something really important?" Avi asked Sam. "Would you consider letting us stay?"

Sam could hear Edie's voice, how she had warned him about hippies infesting the place.

"I guess that depends on what it is."

Garvey contemplated for a moment, looking out the window into the tree foliage that surrounded them.

"Go ahead, Garv," Avi urged. "The truth will set us free, baby."

Garv looked in danger of slipping into a meditative coma, but then he blurted, "I saw them, man. They don't know I saw them, but I saw them."

Sam looked at Avi for a translation.

"He's talking about the Sons of Gunnar, that men's club," she explained. "You know how they really wanted this property? Well, they're trouble with a capital 'T.'"

"Yeah, man," Garvey added. "They run everything around here. It's like, if you're not one of them, then you're nobody to them."

"Garvey thinks they killed Papa Lock."

"Whoa, whoa, whoa." Sam's mind reeled. These deep-breathing weirdos must be eating the wrong kind of mushrooms. "I think you might be a little off base here, Garvey. Maybe you misunderstood what you saw..." *Or hallucinated*, he added mentally.

"No, man. I saw them. It was definitely the Sons of Gunnar goons."

"So this men's club," Sam asked Garvey, "you're saying you saw them here the night Nat died? And you think they were responsible for his death."

"Do the math. Supposed to be an accident, right? Supposed to have been killed by an exploding boat motor, right? Well, dig this. There was only one boat motor here before the explosion, and that same boat motor is still here."

That was true. The Evinrude Lark outboard was on a stand in the garage, waiting for him to give it a tune-up. It came with the property, just like the lawyer said at the reading of the will, and it definitely hadn't exploded.

"I only know what I saw. A pontoon pulled up. A bunch of those hairy Norwegians barged their way onto the dock, and Papa Lock went over to talk to them." Garvey closed his eyes and spoke more dreamily, transported to the night of Nat Lachmann's death. "They were arguing, and then they finally left, but Papa Lock was sad. Later, around sunset, I was serenading the lake when I heard splashing. *Splash*! *Splash*! Someone was swimming with a breathing tube offshore. They swam straight up to the dock and set a bag, like a rubber bag, on the dock, and they started tinkering. I couldn't tell who it was, but I saw him go under the dock and pull wires through, and then he swam away. The only thing I could see after he left was this crazy banana peel on the dock."

"Ah," Sam said knowingly. This reinforced the hallucination theory. "A banana peel. Okay."

"No, man. It was definitely a banana peel."

"Why would Garvey lie about fruit skins?" Avi defended.

"Okay, but why didn't you say something to the police or someone?"

"Yeah, we've got a lot of confidence that Johnny Law is gonna listen to us." Garvey's voice dripped sarcasm. "We live in a treehouse."

"Besides," Avi added, "they're all in on it. The whole town is rigged just like that banana peel."

"Garvey, were you, you know, clear-headed when you saw all this?"

"You mean was I stoned out of my gourd? Not any more than I am right now, and I still know that you're Mr. Brownie man, and you brought dead animal food up here. That's all real, ain't it?"

He was pretty riled up. He took a deep breath and held it until his face turned red.

"Breathe it out, Garvey," Avi urged him. He shook his head like a disobedient child. "Come on, Garv, you'll feel better if you keep breathing."

His face beginning to turn purple, he finally exhaled loudly and panted to regain his breath. "Sorry, man," he panted, "I still got a short fuse from the old days, but I'm working on it, you know?"

"It's okay," Sam offered. "I guess nobody's perfect."

"You're right, though," Garvey nodded, his beard dipping against the strings on the sitar. "I mean, even I wondered at the time if I was seeing things, you know? Like a flashback or something. But now, I know. Someone rigged that banana to blow up Papa Lock, and I saw it happen."

"That is really something." What was Sam supposed to do with that information? And who would want to kill Nat Lachmann? And with a banana peel? Well, that just sounded like a little much. Garvey was right: no one would believe a sitar-strumming treehouse hippie.

On the other hand...

Was it possible that a gang of Norwegians had assassinated Edie's uncle? And if they wanted the property that bad, would Bud Langskip and the Sons of Gunnar be willing to kill strangers from Minneapolis if they got in the way?

"I'll get back to you," Sam set his feet on the ladder and made his way carefully down. Toward the bottom, Arne's chipper voice startled him, especially as it was underscored by the snarling of a wild animal.

"Dad! Can we keep 'em?"

The boy was feeding chunks of sausage cake to two fat raccoons. They growled at Sam as they stood on their back legs at crotch level. He slowly backed as he wondered how bad it would hurt to get rabies shots in the private parts.

<hr>

After driving off the scavengers, Sam lectured Arne about the dangers of wildlife.

"Why do you think Mr. Svensson at the DNR is always having to shoot animals and blow them up?"

"Because it's fun?"

"No, because wildlife is dangerous and needs to be managed with force. Otherwise, nature wins. Besides, those raccoons could have given you rabies. Now go play in the lake for a while or something. I need to talk to your mother."

Edie was still futzing with the garage sale items when he found her. He gathered her by the arm, forcing her to release a roll of player piano music she marked down to a dime. He sat her on a nearby bench constructed of rough-hewn timber and held together by a thin tissue of moss.

"I need to tell you something," he said. She fidgeted, about to complain. "No, it's nothing I did this time. This is about your uncle. There's something going on around here."

Arne wandered up to them with his hands outstretched. He showed them a big yellow-and-black spider and asked if it was poisonous.

"Maybe." Sam smacked it out of his hand. "What did I just tell you about wildlife? Just sit down here next to us for a minute."

Arne, dejected, mumbled something about being bored, but he plopped down next to them on the bench. Sam told Edie what Garvey had said about seeing the local men, how they had a dispute with Nat Lachmann about the property, and the mysterious swimmer who may have planted an explosive device on the dock. He left off the part about the banana peel.

"Bud Langskip never mentioned having an argument with Uncle Nat," Edie told him. "He wants the property, sure. But would someone really commit murder for this place?"

"I would!" Arne raised his hand.

"I appreciate the enthusiasm, Arne. Now, just sit on your hands for a minute, please? The thing is, your uncle's death was ruled an accident because of an exploding boat motor. But the only boat motor around here is in that garage and marked at ten dollars. So, it wasn't an accident. Besides, boat motors don't just explode."

"Especially if they're full of sugar?" she retorted sharply.

"Come on." He frowned. "That was two weeks ago."

She closed her eyes. "So, we know it wasn't an accident. There was an explosion but no boat motor. That means there was some type of dynamite or something, right?"

"Something," Sam agreed. "I mean, probably not a lit stick of dynamite. That's not something a person would walk up to. Probably some other kind of explosive set in a booby trap."

"Booby!" Arne laughed, and Sam ruffled his hair.

"You know, when I got picked up that first time by the sheriff, he asked me if I was smuggling explosives because they'd just caught someone with a carful of explosives heading to Canada."

"You think Canadians blew up my uncle?"

"I wouldn't put it past 'em. But what I meant was when they caught those smugglers, the sheriff's office confiscated the explosives."

"But why would the sheriff want to blow up Uncle Nat?"

"Sheriff Olmdahl is a member of that men's club too. Hundred percent Norwegian. It sure seems like he's part of the group covering up the murder by calling it an accident, so they're definitely in on something."

"But can just anybody blow someone else up?" Edie asked. "Or does it take some kind of training?"

"Good point," Sam agreed. "It's like having a hammer and some wood. Just because you have the tools and materials, it doesn't mean you can build a house."

"Army guys blow stuff up!" Arne announced.

"That's right. Lots of men around here were in the military." Edie looked at the lake, thinking. "Like Vicki's husband, Toby. He was in

Vietnam. Oh, and he uses explosives all the time to blow up beavers."

"Okay, let's add the sheriff and Toby Svensson to the list."

"What about John Kvalstad?" Edie asked.

"You mean the plumber with the Hawaiian get-up? What about him?"

"He was in the military," Edie explained. "I saw his tattoo."

"What kind of tattoo?"

"It was a red stripe, like a patch on a soldier's uniform, and it said SAPPER."

"Sapper? What is that?"

"I saw it too, Mom," Arne said. "And I asked him about it. He said a sapper blows things up. And he was in a prisoner of war camp and a rat ate off his finger."

Edie and Sam looked at each other.

"Add him to the list," Edie said. "Sam, you know what would be fun?" Edie had a twinkle in her eye.

"Geez. Right now? In front of the kid?"

"Not that," she snapped, a smile curling the corners of her mouth. "I meant solving Uncle Nat's murder. Maybe we could get all the suspects together in one place and figure this thing out, just like they do on television."

"That's your idea of fun now? You've been watching too much *Barnaby Jones*," Sam chided.

"Or *Kojak*," Arne added, pulling back his hair for his Telly Savalas impression.

"Who loves ya, baby?" The Fiskers said in unison.

"Well, if we're going to get everyone who's a suspect together in one place, then you'd better include Garvey," Sam suggested. "He was the only witness. Maybe he could identify the man who set that explosive."

"Or woman," Edie added.

"Yeah, good point," Sam said. "What about your cousin Lana? Sounds like she pretty much runs her stepfather's quarry."

"So?"

"Well, they do blasting at quarries to break loose new rock. With dynamite."

"Add her to the list," Edie shook her head in disbelief. "It seems like everyone in America is blowing things up, except for us."

"Mom?" Arne began tentatively.

"No!" Both Sam and Edie answered. They knew he was about to ask if they could blow things up too.

After talking through potential suspects, their list included everyone at the reading of the will (themselves excluded) and Bud Langskip, leader of the Sons of Gunnar. After all, he had the clout to make things happen. Bad things, like kidnapping Edie and eating carp.

Chapter 25

Illicit Norwegian Union

EDIE REMINDED SAM THEY could attract more flies with honey. Her idea was to disguise their crime-solving event as a social event, something people would want to attend.

"We'll be like detectives only wearing party hats," Edie said, but Sam wasn't too sure.

"How about we just invite them to the garage sale and make some money out of the deal?"

"No, it's got to be bigger than that. More fun. But something that wouldn't let the murderer—"

"Or murderers," Sam amended.

"Or murderers," she agreed. "Somewhere they can't just get away. We need a captive audience."

"You know what would be perfect?" Sam snapped his fingers. "Get them all on a big boat, and go to the middle of the lake."

"Oh, like a sunset dinner cruise?"

"Sure, but maybe not so fancy. I know of a boat that would hold thirty people, and you happen to know the man who owns it."

"I don't like what you're thinking," Edie glowered at him. He was talking about Bud Langskip's double-decker custom pontoon. "That man kidnapped me."

"Hey, at least he didn't push you overboard in the middle of a lake and make you swim for your life."

"So the man kidnaps me and tries to drown you," Edie reasoned. "So what makes you think he would help solve a murder that he very well might be responsible for?"

"Even if Bud Langskip *was* guilty of your uncle's death, his motive would have been to get the resort, right?" Sam waited until Edie nodded. "Well, if he thinks this party helps him get any closer to taking the property, he'll do it. He's got to show up anyway because he's number two on our suspect list."

She had to admit, anchoring the pontoon in the middle of the lake would definitely create a captive audience while weaving the illusion of a strictly recreational outing. Edie had never mastered the ability to snap her fingers, so she clapped her hands instead. "We can make it a potluck. Each person can bring something to eat."

"I like that. Put me down for hotdog buns."

"Before we get too far ahead of ourselves, we better pin down the boat. We need to tell our 'guests' where to show up."

"Good deal," Sam said. "We better start with Bud Langskip, then. Get him on board, so to speak."

On the drive to the Langskip home on Big Paw Lake, Sam coached Edie on how to talk tough.

"We're gonna make you an offer you can't refuse," he said in his Don Corleone *Godfather* voice. "Now you say it."

"We're gonna make you—" She clacked her tongue. "Oh, really. As if talking tough to the most powerful man in town is going to sway him. He's Norwegian, not Sicilian."

"And I suppose you just want to be nice to him? Say 'please' and 'thank you?' *Please, Mr. Langskip, can we borrow your boat for a little tea party?*"

"More flies with honey, remember? Do you even know where you're going?"

"Sure, I'm *going* to ask these people for directions." He pulled the car to the side of the road where an older couple futzed around in their garden bed. Their cabin was tiny, but their lot was about the size of a football field, and it faced a very large lake. Edie watched Sam get to gabbing with the couple, who had more than happily stopped hoeing the garden to talk to him about the weather and what-not. Edie made no move to get out of the car. She just waved and smiled (zucchini face) from the passenger seat. She wasn't prepared to meet new people. In her mood, they might just end up on her list of suspects.

Sam finally returned to the car. "We're on the right lake. This is Big Paw. Good name for it, because it sure is big." They waved goodbye to the couple and set off, following the directions the old man had given Sam: go past three fire signs, veer left at the tee, even though you'll think to go right, then turn right after you pass the old Granberg place.

"How will we know if it's the Granberg place?" Edie asked.

"I don't know, but he said we couldn't miss it."

Finding the Granberg place turned out not to be a problem. All the Granbergs since about 1870 were buried under headstones, clearly marked with their last name, in front of an abandoned house. Sam and Edie eventually found a long driveway with an open wrought-iron gate, but a long iron chain blocked their passage. The sign hung from the chain at headlight level read, VELKOMMEN. NO TRESPASSERS.

"Talk about passive-aggressive. This has got to be Bud Langskip's place," Edie said. "That sign is just his style."

Sam got out and unfastened the chain so they could pass. The driveway took them through a parklike setting: lots of trees with squirrels and chipmunks scrambling from tree to tree.

"Boy, I bet Toby would have a field day managing wildlife over here," Sam said as he rounded the final curve.

"You mean blowing them up?" Edie laughed in spite of herself, but her laughter died when Bud Langskip's house appeared in front of them. "Holy crap!"

"Edie, did you just say 'crap'?" Sam did a double-take as he parked alongside three other cars.

"I just can't believe how big this place is." Edie had only seen the house from the back when she'd seen it as she left John's boat at the dock. She'd been in such a huff about being kidnapped that she hadn't appreciated how beautiful the house was, crafted with big stones and thick timber and lots and lots of windows. They probably weren't even nailed shut like the ones in the Minneapolis apartment.

"This place is a mansion," Sam said. "Pretty good money in fishing lures, I guess."

"And whatever else he has his hands in," Edie said in a lowered voice.

Sam rang the doorbell, and they waited. Neatly trimmed shrubs dotted the exterior of the house, edged with bricks and topped with wood mulch.

"No one's home," Sam shrugged. "We could try calling later."

"There are three vehicles in the drive, and that big pontoon is at the dock," Edie said. "Someone's home." Edie knew that Lieutenant Colombo wouldn't stop now, so neither would she.

They walked around to the lakeside of the house, Edie telling Sam about all the weird old junk Bud Langskip collected. Sam cupped his hands to peer in each window they passed.

"Wow. This guy is rich."

"I'm telling you, Sam. Someone's home, and they're going to see you snooping."

"Nah, I don't see anyone in there."

Edie caught a flash of movement overhead. She looked up to see a very shocked woman looking back at her—a very shocked and very familiar woman. Edie grabbed Sam's hand and dragged him back to the front door.

"Come on," she grunted to Sam. She did not press the bell, but turned the handle and shouldered her way in.

"What are you doing? You were the one who was saying how dangerous this guy is."

"Just keep up," she said dismissively, marching through the living room. "I know the way."

"The way to what? Getting us whacked?" Sam's voice trailed off as he caught sight of the enormous living room and all the furnishings.

"Wow." He turned this way and that, taking in all the old stuff and the blatant displays of taxidermy. "The hippies sure wouldn't dig all these dead animals," Sam mused, running his hand along the belly of a long, striped fish.

"You're worse than Arne," Edie declared, dragging him by the hand. "Stay focused."

"What's your hurry?"

"I want to say hi to my mother."

"What?" Sam's mouth dropped as Edie continued her frantic march down the corridor. When they reached Bud Langskip's office, Edie didn't bother to knock. She threw open the door and there stood Edie's mother, Dolores Schmidt née Lachmann, cowering like she wanted to disappear into the woodwork. She looked tan and fit. No doubt she'd been playing golf through the winter while the rest of the world (well, the part of the world in Minnesota) holed up until the snow melted.

"You can't just barge in here like that," Bud sputtered and stood from behind his desk in a hurry.

"What in the heck is going on here?" Edie demanded. "Did you kidnap my mother, too?"

Sam rounded the doorway and entered the office. He did a double-take when he saw his mother-in-law in the flesh.

"Ope!" He said and took a step back into the corridor.

"Get in here, Sam," Edie told him. "Don't let those two goons of his in here if they try to get in."

"I sure can try," Sam said meekly. "But maybe I'll just shut the door quietly, and we can just keep our voices down so as not to attract their attention."

"Leave that door open," Edie declared, her eyes burning on her mother. "I may need something to slam shut."

"Hi, sweetie." Dolores approached Edie to embrace her, but Edie crossed her arms and took a step back. "Don't you 'hi, sweetie' me. What's going on?"

Dolores looked at Bud, her eyebrows raised expectantly. "Should I tell her?"

Bud nodded once. "She's going to find out, eventually."

"It's time you knew," her mother told her, still holding Edie at arm's length. "I know you weren't happy to learn that Robert Schmidt wasn't your real father."

"Uh, yeah!" Edie shot back. "Especially having to find out about it by reading a letter."

"Which is why I asked you not to go snooping." Dolores took a deep breath. "I want you to hear the whole truth. Bud is your real father."

It was a good thing her mother was standing nearby because Edie got very lightheaded, and her knees gave out. She collapsed into her mother's arms, and Sam rushed over to them to cradle Edie's head so it wouldn't thwack the corner of Bud's desk on the way down.

"Rollo," Bud called, and, within moments, the burly henchman appeared.

"Yeah, Chief?"

"Get us the whiskey. Quick."

While Sam patted Edie's cheeks to bring her around, she saw the dead fish mounted on Bud's wall and a bronze statue of Leif Erikson, the Viking explorer. Her muddled mind formed a little movie in which Leif Erikson, singing "The Happy Wanderer", poked his sword in the shelf below him and pulled out a big fish with each stroke.

Val deri!

He flung the fish on the wall and then...

Val dera!

Impaled another and another.

Ha-ha-ha-ha-ha

The vision faded as Sam hoisted her into a sitting position against the desk.

"Edie, are you okay?"

"With a knapsack on my back," she murmured. Sam took the tumbler of whiskey and poured some into her mouth. She wheezed and sputtered like a Briggs and Stratton lawnmower engine with a clogged carburetor, but she came-to quickly.

Sam guided her to the nearest chair.

"Why don't we all take a seat," Bud offered. "Just in case."

Sam pulled a chair close to Edie and, tumblers of whiskey in hand, the two Fiskers faced off against Dolores Schmidt née Lachmann, now perched on Bud's knee.

"Mom," Edie said slowly and as calmly as she could, "could you please explain what's going on?"

Edie's mom took one deep breath to fill the bellows, and then she unburdened herself of long-held secrets.

"When I was young, I was active in the Shield Maidens here in Fornborg."

"What's that?" Sam asked.

"It's the women's auxiliary group for the Sons of Gunnar," Bud explained, giving Dolores a little bounce so that she chirped in surprise. "She was the prettiest Shield in the bunch."

She gave Bud a smooch on the cheek, and Edie felt lightheaded again, but she tried to stay alert.

"Well, put simply, Bud and I fell in love, only things were a little complicated."

Edie snorted. "You mean like the fact that he was married, and you were only sixteen?"

"Is your life so perfect?" Dolores shot back, with a sharp look directed at Sam.

"Hey," Sam said. "What did I ever do to you?"

Edie's mother was about to answer that, but Bud's hand smoothed the fabric on her shoulder.

"So anyway, because of those unsettled circumstances, when I found out you were coming along, I needed to make some tough choices. One of them was marrying Robert. He'd just gotten discharged from the Navy and was looking to settle down."

"And fortunately," Bud quipped, "he wasn't very good at math because you, little Edie, came along five months later."

"You mean you tricked the poor man."

"He loved you as his own," Dolores stated. "You know that. Do you think he would have changed anything if he'd known everything?"

"You didn't give him that choice, though, did you?"

"Times were different then..." her mother began.

"That's what you've said for years. *Times were different.* That's just to cover your own mistakes. Well, the time is now, Mom. Now! And now you're hanging on this old man like a...a..." Edie struggled to find the right word. "Hussy."

"If you think there's something wrong with two people who love each other reconnecting after years, I don't want to live in your world."

"Okay, Mom, but why now? Why did you wait so long to tell me the truth?"

"Because this isn't just something you publish in the newspaper. I knew you'd be upset, but then you went snooping anyway." She looked affectionately at Bud. "This man has been very good to us over the years, even if you didn't know it. Remember that Mary Hartline TV Circus Princess doll you wanted so bad? Well, Bud was Santa Claus that Christmas. And he's supported me over the years, here and there, but I wanted to help you get settled once and for all."

"I want that too, Mom. But they don't make white picket fences out of family skeletons, do they?"

Dolores pursed her lips. "That's why I wanted Nat to give you the resort, to give you something that would get you settled. But then, with you nosing around like a little piggy in my letters, well, I knew I had to come back to Fornborg and take care of things myself."

"I'm so glad you did," Bud purred as he hugged Dolores and jostled her on his knee. "I've really missed you. Why don't you give us a nice Norwegian song like old times?"

Dolores touched his face.

"Not now, darling, but maybe later I'll give you a private concert."

Sam shifted uncomfortably in his chair and winced.

"Edie," he pleaded, "could you make this stop, please?"

Ignoring her husband, Edie rested her elbows on Bud's desk. She was going to talk tough, just like Sam taught her. "You won't be so glad when this gets out, will you?"

Bud's eyes narrowed on her.

"What do you mean by that?"

"Well, you've got a son, which means I have a half-brother who has no idea about all this monkey business."

Dolores looked back at Bud. "Are you going to tell Lester about us?" she asked.

Bud's eyebrows twitched a little, but he didn't seem to be in any hurry to answer. Dolores pulled herself upright and sat on the corner of the desk to face him.

"I just flew all the way up here, putting the relationship with my only child at risk, and you're not going to tell your son about us?"

"It's complicated," Bud began. "There are a lot of considerations."

"Such as?"

"Such as the business. The men's club. And, yes, Lester. This could hit him pretty hard, and I don't want to damage my relationship with him or my granddaughter."

"Well, there's a brave Viking warrior," Dolores disparaged him. It was refreshing to see someone else on the receiving end of her jibes. "And speaking of grandchildren, I wish you'd brought my grandson to see me. Where is Arne?"

Sam shot upright. "Holy crap! I just realized that means Bud is Arne's grandfather."

"Is Arne the kid with the big ears?" Bud shook his head. "He didn't get those ears from the Langskip side of the family, I can tell you that."

"How are we supposed to move forward here?" Edie asked. "Here we are, sitting on a potentially explosive, potentially damaging secret, and there you are, being rich and stubborn."

"Couldn't we just keep it under our hats?" Bud's expression melted into one of boyish helplessness. "At least for a little while." Everyone in Bud's office except Bud Langskip snorted derisively.

"Like Nixon tried?" Edie sniped, hearkening back to her conversation with Bud about the Watergate scandal. "The cat's already out of the bag."

"Bud, I know it's been a long time since I was in the Shield Maidens, but I do remember the oath you men take to the Sons of Gunnar. Do you remember it?"

Bud titled his head and frowned.

"Of course."

"What is it?"

"I don't want to say it."

Dolores leaned in and pinched Bud's perfectly normal-sized ear. "Say it."

"*Ære, tapperhet og verdighet er grunnlaget for vår kultur. Vi vil ikke gjøre denne sannheten mer komplisert enn den trenger å være.*"

"And what does it mean?"

Bud pulled his head free from Dolores's pinching fingers.

"It means honor, bravery, and dignity are the foundations of our culture. We will not make this truth more complicated than it needs to be."

"And do you think you can live up to that oath by continuing to hide the truth?"

"Maybe?" Bud answered tentatively. "If we all agree. Possibly work out some mutually beneficial arrangement?" He looked at Edie and Sam hopefully.

"Edie." Sam nudged her. "Go ahead. Ask about the pontoon. Now's the time to strike when the iron is hot. The man is your dad, after all."

She glared at him and whispered through gritted teeth, "It doesn't mean he didn't kill Uncle Nat, dummy."

"Ask me what?"

Edie forced a smile. "We'd like to borrow your boat for a little party, *Father*. Sort of a 'hello, neighbor' thing. Day after tomorrow."

"My boat? You mean the pontoon?" Bud frowned. "That pontoon is custom from bow to stern. Cost me almost ten thousand dollars."

Sam whistled, impressed by the amount. Edie cut him off before he could start asking questions about engine sizes. "Oh, that's just a start. Secrets cost. The longer something remains a secret, the more expensive it gets."

Bud sighed deeply. "It's not easy for me, you know. You don't know me, Edie, but I know you. I've kept track over the years."

"I had no idea you existed," Edie replied. "And to learn you're my father, well, that was just three minutes ago. So this is all pretty fresh."

"Another thing about this boat party," Sam added. "We want you to be there."

"Oh, I don't have time for..." Bud began to answer, but Dolores pinched him again, and he relented. "But I guess I could drop by."

"Actually, we were hoping you might do more than drop by," Sam explained. "We want you to play host."

Bud eyed them suspiciously. "Just what is this party?"

"Oh, it's just a potluck on your pontoon," Edie answered.

"A pontoon potluck, huh?" Bud said. "Well, if that's what it's going to take, then a pontoon potluck it is."

"Great. Saturday, then," Edie confirmed.

"You're not going to cook anything, are you dear?" Dolores looked innocently at her daughter.

"Don't worry," Sam said. "We're just bringing hot dog buns." He laughed, and Edie's mom laughed too. Turns out those two shared something in common: a mutual dislike of Edie's cooking. Edie thwacked Sam's shoulder with the back of her hand.

"Oh," Edie added. "And if certain guests on our invitation list seem reluctant to attend, we need your men from your little club to help them clear their schedules."

Bud's eyebrows raised. "I don't know how they do it down in Minneapolis, but people around Fornborg turn up to potlucks on their own. They typically don't have to be manhandled."

"Do you only kidnap family members?" Edie said bitterly, but Sam rushed to smooth over the tension.

"It'll just make things easier if you can help with the invitations, Mr. Langskip."

"Okay, okay. Sheesh, you're a spitfire, just like your mother. I can get a couple guys to round up your guests, no problem."

Edie and Sam ran through the guest list, pointing out they needed help with Jeffy and Lana. Dolores volunteered to track them down, which left only the hippies (Avi Starshine and Garvey) and the Svenssons, and Sam and Edie could handle that on their own.

"I'll make my glorified rice," Dolores whispered to Bud, nibbling on his earlobe.

"You always did make the best glorified rice." Bud's lips landed on hers, but she broke away and stood up straight.

She pulled away. "I want to make sure Edie hears this. Listen up, Edie. Bud, did my glorified rice have any fruit cocktail in it?"

Bud's nose wrinkled in disgust. "God, no."

She returned to Bud's arm, and Sam and Edie decided they'd better leave the two alone before they lost their lunches.

<hr />

When they returned to the main house, they were relieved to find nothing amiss: no fires, police, or angry strangers. Arne had settled in front of the television to watch a Frankenstein movie, and he looked pretty drowsy. All the activity of the past few days must have finally started to catch up with the poor kid.

Sam peeked around the living room. "Everything seems fine."

"Thank God for small miracles."

"I'll go to talk to Avi and Garvey about the potluck, but I'm not sure Garvey will want to come down from the treehouse. He's pretty spooked about what he saw."

"Just tell them there's free food, and some of it isn't even meat. Oh, and Sam?" Edie called after him. "Be sure to tell them that the 'pot' part of 'potluck' is just a figure of speech."

She just couldn't shake the shock that came from learning she was the product of an illicit union between the leader of a Norwegian gang and an underaged girl (out of wedlock, she hastened to remind herself). The very thought of her mother and Bud Langskip canoodling made her shudder. Her world was upside-down and definitely not normal. In fact, everything around her seemed just wrong: the kitchen counters sticky with God-knows-what kind of preserves, desiccated pill bugs curled up in every corner, cobwebs in the wood beam rafters, enough to make an Einstein wig. It was altogether too much to deal with, and she was in no mood to clean just then; although, she would have to face it at some point.

Left to their own devices, Sam and Arne would be quite content to scavenge through empty cans of those miniature Vienna sausages and Tang containers like a pack of raccoons. No point waiting for them to pitch in, but Edie needed just a little time away to process things. Someplace clean. Somewhere she could smoke a calming Dignity cigarette without being accused of killing Sam's father.

Yes, a Dignity would be nice. After all, if all these recent, earth-shattering revelations weren't an emergency, she didn't know what was.

First things first. She needed to finish rounding up the suspects for the pontoon potluck. She found what was left of a local phone book jammed in a drawer. Some pages had been ripped out. No doubt to be used as rolling papers by the dirty hippies. Fortunately, the page of S's remained, and she dialed the Svenssons.

"Hi, neighbor," Vicki exclaimed. "Isn't this nice? Two neighbors just having a friendly chat on the phone."

"I hope you still feel that way after I ask for a big favor. Well, two big favors, actually."

"We're neighbors. Of course. What do you need?"

"First off, what are you and Toby doing Saturday?"

"Oh, it's Toby's weekend off, so I was going to cook a nice dinner. Why?"

"I've got a better offer for you. Do you think you could spare a couple hours in the afternoon? We're throwing a potluck on the lake."

"I can check with Toby to make sure he's okay with that, but a potluck with neighbors sounds nice. Is it at Nat's place?"

"No. Bud Langskip is letting us use his big pontoon."

"Oh, I don't know about that," Vicki's voice quavered. "We don't want to get mixed up with the pontoon mafia."

"Pretty please?" Edie begged. She'd learned it from Arne's way of badgering her to get what he wanted. "Just to be neighborly?"

Of course, it was more than just neighborly hospitality that Edie had in mind. The Svenssons were definitely suspects in the death of Nat Lachmann, neighbors or not. Edie imagined Vicki Svensson, perfect hair, perfect smile, perfect life, being found guilty by a judge and sentenced to life in a perfect penitentiary.

"Well, okay, we can be there. What's the second thing you needed?"

"I wondered if maybe I could use your kitchen to whip up a little something for the potluck."

The silence lasted for five, six seconds. Edie wondered if the line had gone dead.

"Are you still there, Vicki?"

"Yes…" Vicki replied hesitantly. "You want to do what?"

"Just to use your kitchen for an hour, seeing as ours is such a mess right now."

"Well, uh, it's just that…" Vicki had that twitchy nervousness that comes when Minnesotans want to say no but cannot form the words. Edie could relate. She once bought two vacuum cleaners from a door-to-door salesman because he mentioned his wife was ill, and Sam had to go to their main office and demand the money back in person.

"If it's a problem, don't worry." Edie smiled to herself. It was the Offering of the False Way Out. It was the polite way of saying, *You could say no, but then you'll look like a real jerk, and everyone will know you're a bad person.*

As expected, Vicki gave in, trying to sound as gracious as possible after being put on the spot.

"Sure, that'll be fine," Vicki said.

"I'll be right over," Edie announced before hanging up the phone. From her latest grocery run, she gathered the supplies she needed for glorified rice.

Yes, she would make her version and put it head-to-head with her mother's boring, old, unglamorous glorified rice.

Her mother was always saying how times were different back then; well, now it was time for a fresh take on everything, even boring, old, glorified rice. They put a man on the moon, for cripes sake: why not throw some fruit cocktail in there?

"Into the bag, Uncle Ben," she said, dropping the orange box of rice in. "You too, fruit cocktail." Likewise, she dropped in a bag of marshmallows and a tub of Cool Whip. She'd forgotten to buy vanilla. Either she would beg some from Vicki's supply, or she would just go without. She wasn't about to go back to the store and spend another fifty cents.

Outside, she walked up to an old beat-up milk can that rusted away next to the tool shed. She looked around to make sure no one was looking, and then she unscrewed the lid. Reaching in her hand, she pulled out a pack of Dignities from the carton. Once on the path in the woods, she lit one and inhaled deeply. Fresh lake air, birds singing, and a surge of calming low-tar nicotine coursing through her body.

One foot in front of the other, Edie Fisker, Uncle Ben, Libby's, and Dignity made their way to the Svensson's house.

⋘ • ♦ • ⋙

After stubbing out her cigarette in the peonies, Edie knocked on the door. Vicki opened it and hesitated, warily eyeing the grocery bag Edie held.

You're not saying 'no' to me, Edie thought. *Not with all I've got going on.*

Before Vicki even said a word, Edie walked through the doorway, forcing Vicki to step back and open the door wider.

"Come in," Vicki relented. "I'll make coffee."

"I really appreciate this. I just found out my mother is in town."

"You said it was a potluck, right?" Vicki interrupted. "What are you making?"

"Glorified rice."

"Oh, that's nice."

"Anyway, so my mom flew here from Arizona, and I found out that the man I thought was my dad wasn't my dad, but my real dad is Bud Langskip."

It seemed to Edie that Vicki only half-listened as she measured out scoops of freeze-dried coffee grounds from a metal oval tin. It was the fancy stuff, of course. Café Francais International Coffee. Edie and Sam were pretty happy to have a can of Maxwell House in the cupboard. She scooped it into the percolator basket and plugged it in.

"That's kind of big news," Edie said, expecting more of a dramatic response. "Don't you think?"

"Oh, uh, yes, very big news. Do you take milk?"

"I do," Edie answered as she opened the refrigerator door. "I can get it."

"Wait. Don't!" Vicki nearly tripped over her own feet as she tried to slam the refrigerator shut, which only made Edie more curious. She blocked the door open with her hip to get a good look. There, on the top shelf, a hotdish in a glass baking dish hulked under a layer of aluminum foil. A long piece of masking tape on the lid caught Edie's eye with writing that looked familiar.

"What's this?"

"Nothing," Vicki tried to sound pleasant even as she hip-checked Edie away from the refrigerator. "Now why not have a seat, and I'll cut us a slice of *vetebröd*. It's..."

"Swedish," Edie interrupted. "I get it. You're Swedish and beautiful and perfect."

Edie grabbed for the refrigerator door handle, but Vicki slapped away her hand.

"Let me see what it says."

"No. Stop it!" Vicki screeched. "Relax and have some coffee."

The two women slapped at one another's hands until Edie, putting on her most horrified expression, looked over Vicki's shoulder.

"Is that a juice stain?"

"Where?" Vicki couldn't help herself. She turned to look, and at that moment, Edie pried open the refrigerator and got a closer look at what was written on the casserole.

For my new neighbor, it read in Dolores Schmidt née Lachmann's handwriting.

Chapter 26

The Devil Dangles Strings

EDIE WASN'T THINKING STRAIGHT, but one thing she knew for sure was that she was tired of secrets, especially secrets kept from her. She grabbed the nearest implement she could find, a fork.

"I swear to God, Vicki, I will scratch the paint on this pretty yellow stove unless you tell me what's going on."

"Your mother told me I should give you some space. I should have listened to her."

Edie pounded the top of the counter. "No, you shouldn't listen to her." Edie tried to calm her voice. *More flies with honey*, she reminded herself. "Look, I've had a few difficult days recently, and you probably won't understand this because your life is, you know, perfect." Edie paused so Vicki could humbly reject that claim of perfection and volunteer some nugget about how her life was *not*, in fact, perfect. But Vicki said nothing. She continued. "My relationship with the man I thought was my father was a lie, and my mother, my sweet, kind mother, was at the center of it. I just want to get the truth. Please."

"She said not to tell you just yet," Vicki's voice strained. She had backed away, putting the length of the breakfast bar between her and Edie.

"Tell me what?" Edie gripped the fork, menacing the glossy butter-yellow stove.

"You have every right to be upset, but none of this is my business, and it's certainly not the fault of my stove,"

Edie snorted. "When you opened the door to that woman, you invited in the devil."

"No offense," Vicki said as she smiled a zucchini-face smile, "but you're the crazy one, threatening me with a dessert fork. Your mother actually seemed very nice."

"That's her trick." Edie pounded the counter again. "Next thing you know, you're burdened with impossible casserole recipes and advice about your wardrobe. Then she'll have you doubting your husband. Her voice will get in your head, and you'll never be a professional singer. Oh, no! The downstairs neighbor will see to that."

Breaking into sharp sobs, Edie didn't resist when Vicki worked the fork free of her grasp. Vicki guided her to a chair at the table set with coordinated placemats and yellow-and-white checkered napkins. You know, perfect.

"Edie," Her voice was gentle and smooth, like a Dignity cigarette. "I have a mother too, ya know. And we have some doozie spats. Every family has problems. Not as bad as yours, of course, no offense."

"None taken." Having calmed herself to the sniffling stage, Edie lifted the waiting slice of sweetbread (*vetebröd* or whatever the heck Vicki called it) by hand, seeing as Vicki had moved all the silverware from Edie's reach. The rich, dark coffee swirled in the dainty cup when Vicki poured it.

"You just have a nice cup of coffee, and let your problems wait for you outside, okay?"

"Okay," Edie whimpered. "Can I have a tissue? And a cigarette?"

"Of course. Just don't get them mixed up. Wouldn't that look silly, you with a cigarette hanging out of your nose?" She spoke to Edie like a mother speaking to a young child, and just at that moment, Edie didn't mind so much. Well, assuming it was acceptable for a mother to give a young child a cigarette, that is.

"Please, tell me what my mother said."

"Okay," Vicki relented. "But I want you to talk to her yourself right after this. Promise?"

Edie nodded.

"Here goes. Your mom told me... that..."

"Just say it."

"Well, she's moving in with you."

Edie slammed the palms of her hands on the polished oak table, making various platters and candlesticks rattle.

"No, she is not."

"Like I said, you two really need to talk."

"I know what she's doing." Edie stood, fuming once more. "She's going around like Henry Kissinger, making backroom deals, and then she'll show up on my front door with the Marines."

"I don't know about that, Edie. She might show up with a hotdish, but probably not the Marines."

"Strings," Edie snarled. "I knew there were strings attached to that money."

"That reminds me of an old Swedish saying, *Djävulen dinglar strängar.*"

"What does that mean?"

"The devil dangles strings."

"Yes," Edie said in relief. "Exactly." Then she ranted for several minutes, finishing two emergency cigarettes, three cups of coffee, and another slice of sweetbread. Vicki let her get it all out. She probably read that article in *Sophistication for Women* about being a good ear when you're surrounded by mouths.

Finally, Edie was spent. She thanked Vicki for being so understanding and apologized for her outburst.

"I hope I didn't spoil anything between us, Vicki."

"Oh, of course not." Vicki placed her hand on Edie's and patted it. "This is how we'll become the best of friends. Now, can I ask you an odd question?"

Happy to have a change of topics, Edie answered, "Of course."

"Okay, what's the absolute weirdest thing you've ever done as a birthday present for your husband?"

Edie blushed. It was the kind of question Bob Eubanks would ask on *The Newlywed Game*. "Why do you ask?"

"Oh, no real reason. It's nothing."

The conversation moved to lighter topics: the weather, the husbands, lake gossip, and then Vicki mentioned the potluck.

"The potluck!" Edie panted. "I got so caught up with my mother's head games, I nearly forgot the reason why I came over to begin with." She rose and went to the counter, where she began unpacking the ingredients for her glorified rice.

Sizing up the ingredients lined up next to Edie, Vicki's eyes narrowed in on the can of fruit cocktail.

"I hope you're not going to do what I think you're going to do."

Instead of responding to Vicki's loaded comment, Edie simply asked where she kept the can opener, wondering what the old Swedish saying was for *Mind your own business.*

Edie didn't bother boasting to Sam about the glorified rice dish she'd prepared at the Svenssons. He wouldn't appreciate it with that unrefined palate of his. She told him how her mother planned to weasel her way into their home.

"Oh, no," Sam declared. "I'm putting my foot down on that turd right now!"

For once, they both agreed: there was absolutely no way in heck that Dolores Schmidt née Lachmann could weasel her way into their happy home, especially at the very beginning of their new life on Little Paw Lake.

"She's up to something, Sam," Edie warned. "We've got to stay strong. No matter what tricks she tries."

Sam guffawed. "It's not like she's the Godfather."

"Maybe not, but she was sitting on the Godfather's lap yesterday. I'm going to call her now. You'll never guess where she's staying."

"Not the Lakeview Lodge?" Sam guessed, and Edie nodded. "With the Magic Fingers and the smoke damage? Geez, if they knew she was related to us, they'd probably toss her out on her ear."

"Then she definitely would have to stay with us," Edie lamented.

"Let's make sure they never find out we're related."

"Where's Arne?"

Sam waved his hand absently toward a window. "I don't know. He's outside running around somewhere."

As long as he wasn't up in the treehouse with hippies or swimming in the middle of the lake or lighting himself on fire, Edie wasn't too worried.

<hr />

Forewarned is forearmed, and Edie knew Dale at the Lakeview Lodge was not the Fisker's biggest fan, thanks to the Magic Fingers Fire of '75. But she needed to call the lodge to find out her mother's room number. She could rule out room 105. That room was probably still smoldering from their stay.

So as not to alert Dale to her identity and trigger an uncomfortable conversation about money owed for damages, Edie would disguise her voice when she called. Her vocal repertoire was limited, so she settled on what she hoped would pass for a Southern accent. To be on the safe side, she also developed a cover story in case the clerk pressed her. She was Mrs. Beatrice Dudley from Framingham, Georgia, wife of Franklin Donovan Dudley, the noted agriculturalist.

Mrs. Dudley and Mrs. Schmidt were longtime pen pals, and she had urgent news for Mrs. Schmidt regarding this year's peach crop.

The news, which, if the cover story needed to go that far, was that a late frost had damaged the peach blossoms. *That crop is sure to be sorely affected,* she added to her mental script. This was a true story. Edie had heard it on the radio, and it meant that the price of canned fruit cocktail was sure to skyrocket.

Not wanting to be tripped up during the call, Edie made notes: *Beatrice Dudley, pen pal, Framingham GA, peach frost.* She rehearsed her introduction several times, remembering to speak slowly: Mrs. Dudley was genteel, after all. Mrs. Dudley took her time when she spoke to others. Mrs. Dudley was polite, even to irate motel clerks in the north. When Edie felt ready, she called the motor lodge and pinched her nose for added voice-disguising properties.

"Good afternoon," she drawled. "I was hopeful ya'll might connect little ol me to Mrs. Doh Lorris Shuh-miiit."

She heard sniggering on the other end of the call.

"Lady, that accent's as phony as a three-dollar bill," the manager responded sharply. "I'll connect you, but you still owe us three hundred and seventy-two dollars for that room damage."

"Dang it!" Edie cursed as the phone rang in her mother's room.

Edie asked her mother to go out for a cup of coffee because what they needed to discuss was too important to do over the phone. Her mother insisted that buying coffee from a stranger was a frivolous expense, and why couldn't Edie make her own pot of coffee? Was her stove broken?

"You don't have to order coffee, Mom. You can have a milkshake or pickle juice for all I care. I'll pick you up in fifteen minutes."

She hung up, and the question that haunted women worldwide buzzed in her head: *What am I going to wear?*

Her choices were few, and she relied on her Sears special, the jacquard weave double-knit with a beet-red-and-white pattern that had seen her through the funeral debacle, the reading of Uncle Nat's will, and now coffee with her mother. It was a little worse for wear, what with the warm weather, so she spritzed it with Lysol.

The label inside the dress said *Machine Wash. Warm Water.* But Edie knew that was a lie.

❖❥⋯❖⋯❦❖

Edie pulled the station wagon off on a side street and parked in front of a live bait store just south of the motor lodge. The men inside were talking loudly about how expensive the new Langskip fishing lure was.

"They call it dynamite," the dubious customer stated. "But the only thing it's going to blow is a buck-seventy-five."

The men inside laughed.

"Yeah, they forget the common man. Trying to pick-pocket rich guys," another lamented.

"Well, you can't talk sense into Bud when he's got an idea in mind," the first man replied. "I tried to tell him after the last club meeting…"

The man's wheedling voice tapered off as the three men noticed Edie walking past. She grew instantly self-conscious, aware they were looking. She had to remind herself how to walk like a normal person, one foot in front of the other, right? Did it look natural?

"Hey, lady. Whatcha got under the hood?"

She turned to face them, three older men at the entrance of the store.

"I beg your pardon?" She was about to unleash her inner Betty Friedan on those male chauvinist pigs.

"The station wagon. What size engine?"

"I…" She blinked. That wasn't what she expected to hear. "I don't know."

"It's probably a three-fifty-one," one man ventured.

"I don't know. Could be a four-oh-two."

The third man hissed. "I doubt it."

Edie let them figure out the engine specs without her as she walked toward the lodge's motor court—the kind where you parked your vehicle directly in front of the room you stayed in. She noted that the parking space in front of the Fiskers' old room was empty. There was an out-of-order sign hanging on the door.

Edie hugged the wall, hoping she wasn't visible from the front office. She edged down the line of rooms until she reached number 113 and knocked. Her mother cracked open the door, only enough to reveal a tight smile.

"Yes?"

"Are you ready, Mom?"

"Come back in another hour, will you?"

Edie used her knee to pry open the door. "I'm not coming back here in an hour. I barely made it this time."

Her mother, half-shielded by the door, wore only a pink lace nightgown. Her mussed hair, the sheets tangled around the pillows, and the bedspread sprawled on the floor suggested a brawl.

"Who is it, Dolo?"

Bud Langskip appeared from the bathroom. He wore dusty yellow boxers, but nothing else.

"Edie, you remember Bud, your father, don't you?"

"Mom!" Oh, Edie was beyond furious. The more she tried to find a sense of normalcy, the more weirdness crept out to bite her. Now her mother was acting like a teenager, which is exactly how things went wrong the first time.

"Meet me in front of the bait shop in ten minutes." Edie stormed out of the room, slamming the door behind her. Ten minutes would give Edie enough time to smoke an emergency cigarette. If this wasn't an emergency, she didn't know what was. The image of a pile of quarters next to the Magic Fingers coin box still burned her brain.

They found a quiet booth at Lulu's Cafe. 'Lulu' turned out to be Louis Vangen. A burly, bald man with a cigar dangling from his mouth poured coffee for them. Dolores looked disparaging at the filthy dishcloth draped over the man's shoulder.

Edie cut in before her mother could complain.

"I talked to Vicki Svensson, Mom. I know all about your big plan."

Her mother shook her head. "The rat!" But to her credit, she didn't deny her intention to move in with them. "I've thought this through, and I've decided I want to help you and that husband of yours."

"Haven't you helped enough, Mother?"

"Life's too short. And Arne is growing up so fast."

"Don't bring Arne into it. What changed from the time of the funeral until now? You couldn't make it to your brother's funeral, but you could make it from Arizona to play doctor with Bud Langskip?"

"Now that you and Sam know the whole story and Bud's wife is gone…"

"Let me ask, was she, by any chance, killed in a mysterious explosion?"

"No," Dolores said solemnly. "It was…cancer. From smoking. Or a boat accident. Bud wasn't clear, but he did say she was smoking at the time." She dug out folded sheets of paper from her purse and spread them flat in front of her on the table, still damp from Lulu's rag. "Now, I've been talking with Bud about the property. He's been so keen to offer his advice."

"Is that what you call it?" Edie shot back.

"Based on these estimates for repairs and operating costs, you're going to need an awful lot of money to get the resort up and running. I know you might not feel comfortable taking money from me…"

"You're darn tootin'."

"There is another option. Bud is willing to invest—not loan, invest," she emphasized, "to get the resort ship-shape. The septic, roof repairs, painting, signs, everything."

Everything. That sounded tempting, and wherever temptation appeared, Edie knew the devil was dangling a string.

"What's the catch?" she asked.

"No catch," her mother exclaimed. "Well, except that I will need to live with you. In one of the cabins is fine, for a start. After it's renovated, of course."

"Why don't you just move in with Bud?"

She shook her head and looked down. "You have to understand, Bud is a very important man around here. He can't just shack up with an old flame. We have to ease into it."

"And what's in it for him? Besides free rides on Magic Fingers Mountain?"

"Edie, he's your father. Of course, he wants to help you."

"And?"

"And once the resort opens, he wants twenty percent."

"I knew it. 'Father' my hind end."

"You're going to have to decide sooner than later, I'm afraid. Nat let things sort of pile up, and the County is clamoring for back taxes."

"How much?" Edie wanted all the facts. No more smokescreens, no more lies.

Sorting through her purse again, Dolores pulled out a facsimile copy of a letter with the Donnelly County seal and showed it to Edie.

"Eight hundred dollars." Edie stared at the number. That was two months' wages if Sam was still earning wages. Bud's tempting offer looked even more tempting when viewed from a corner.

"I'll talk to Sam about it."

"Good. And just do the opposite of whatever he says," Dolores snarked.

"Did you find cousins Jeffy and Lana? Are they going to be at the pontoon potluck?"

"They'll be there with bells on." Dolores lowered her voice and leaned nearer to Edie. "They think it's got something to do with the will."

"Why would they think that?"

"I may have suggested it."
"Oh, Mother."

Chapter 27

Pontoon Potluck

THE MORNING OF THE potluck, Edie and Sam reviewed their list of suspects over coffee. Sam wanted to bet. He was sure that cousin Lana was the culprit, but Edie didn't think it was likely.

"If not Lana, who do you think it was?" he asked.

"I don't want to say."

"Chicken!" Sam scoffed, and Arne laughed.

"Yeah, Mom! Chicken!"

"Just eat your cereal, and then we're going to get you cleaned up."

The boy hadn't had a proper cleaning in weeks, and he probably had leeches, ticks, and muck in just about every orifice, and he had the faint odor of a trash can on the last day of the State Fair.

But Edie had a suspect in mind, and it wasn't pleasant. Maybe she had been watching too many television shows. Her brain was rotting with implausible suspicions. But what if...What if Uncle Nat, a lonely, divorced man, who was kind and funny, had gotten together with a married woman? A married *neighbor* woman. And what if that neighbor woman's husband had found out? And what if that neighbor's husband was used to blowing things up in the great outdoors?

"I still think it's Lana," Sam said. "She is one tough piece of jerky."

Edie sighed. Even when women were strong and brave, they were just various types of meat to these male chauvinist pigs.

"Arne, let's get you in the tub." She grabbed him before he wriggled away. Yes, he could bathe on his own if he had a mind to do it. Today, she just needed him clean. Not eleven-year-old-boy clean, either, but actually clean. She muscled him in the bathroom. Was he getting strong! His protests came in laughs at first. She alternately threatened and cajoled him as she gripped him by the arm to make him hold still in the tub. Promises were made that she had no intention of fulfilling—anything to make the boy presentable. He liked to put up a big show of being a little tough guy, but at heart, he was still Edie's little big-eared boy. Still, that didn't take her mind from the end goal, and she scrubbed him until he was red and glistening. Oh, and did he fight her the whole time! But Edie wasn't taking no for an answer.

By the end, they were both traumatized and soaking wet, but the job was done. She told him in no uncertain terms that he shouldn't even think about getting dirty.

"Can we go to town and buy a rabbit?" Arne asked as she rubbed him with a blanket.

"If you don't get dirty before the potluck, sure." Throw the bunny on the list of promises that weren't worth the Mr. Bubble they were written on.

Then it was her turn. Edie showered and shampooed her hair, and it felt glorious. She let the water run over her, washing away her troubles. She even caught herself singing but clamped her mouth shut. It was too soon for singing after the incident with the Minneapolis police. She dried herself in the center of the bathroom floor and wiped away the steam from the mirror. Her reflection stared back in disbelief. Where her straight, chestnut hair used to be now exploded an orange tangle of frizz. It wasn't exactly Bozo the Clown, but it was in the same circus.

Yelling for Sam only made her reflection look like an insane Oompa Loompa. Sam opened the door in a panic and—quite unhelpfully—broke out laughing.

She smacked him, of course, but that didn't slow him down.

"Must be the iron in the water. What do you want me to do about it? I'm not a hairdresser. Now, if your hair needs new spark plugs or the cylinders need boring, I'm your man."

"Just get out." She pushed him out of the bathroom.

"Are you sure you don't want to fool around? I've always wanted a redhead."

"Touch me again, and they'll find both your hands in different counties."

She pushed him out and shut the door as he hungrily fought to wedge it open.

"So, what they say about redheads being more fiery is true, then?"

Oh, Sam. What an idiot. Still, an unwilling smile formed at his attention. Maybe rust-colored hair wasn't as bad as she thought.

"It's different," her mirror image mouthed. But the frizz had to go. Smoothing it as best she could with a dab of Wella Balsam shampoo, she got everything to lay down at least. It looked a little...greasy.

Thank God for scarves. A scarf covered a multitude of sins, including wild hair. Now it was on to wardrobe. She just couldn't bring herself to suffer in the jacquard dress one more time, especially on a boat. She sniffed the orange summer dress with the little daisies. A little Lysol, and it was fine.

"Oh, good," she said sarcastically when she noticed the orange fabric matched her new hair color.

She readied the Tupperware container with her glorified rice as her mind leaped to some pretty dark scenarios. Everyone would hate it. They would get violently sick from eating it. They would ostracize her and only let her attend church on Christmas and Easter like a Lake Lutheran.

Well, up theirs. That's what she decided. She was tired of the weight of imagined social scorn bearing down on her, mostly in her mother's voice. It was time she stood up for herself. She tucked a spare can of fruit cocktail in her purse right next to the Dignity cigarettes she had crammed into a hollowed-out compact, sabotage in mind.

If worse came to worst, she would secretly spike her mother's glorified rice. It was a lowdown, dirty trick, she knew, but her mother wasn't above dirty tricks.

All's fair in love and potlucks.

Edie watched as John Kvalstad navigated Bud Langskip's double-decker custom pontoon toward their new home, the Hole on Little Paw Lake. With the help of Rollo and Petie, John maneuvered parallel to the shore in the shallows and dropped anchor. The three men shifted a long section of dock that extended the remaining distance between the boat and the most solid section of the exploded dock. John, in his Hawaiian shirt, moved gracefully. While the other two grumped about the work, he guided them firmly, but in a gentle voice.

She'd been watching John work as if hypnotized. He noticed her watching from shore, and he smiled, rubbing his jaw where she'd punched him for kidnapping her and Arne.

"Aloha, Mrs. Fisker," he called as he finished lashing the gangplank. She felt her face warm. She waved back but hurried off to tell Sam the boat was here and to track down Arne. That boy better not be in a mud puddle somewhere. Oh, and she needed her purse. And maybe one more quick look at her hair to make sure the scarf was staying in place. She headed to the house—their house, she reminded herself—the Hole on Little Paw Lake. She really liked that name.

Armed with her purse and the confidence that her scarf would hold (thanks to four cleverly placed bobby pins), she returned to the driveway as other "guests" trickled in. Cousin Jeffy and Lana first. They pulled up in Jeffy's car, which jerked along, sending Jeffy and Lana bouncing off the front seat.

"What's wrong with your car?" Edie asked when they got out, gray smoke still seeping from under the hood.

"No idea. I was hoping Sam could look at it since he's so good with engines." He handed Edie two six-packs of beer and put his hands on his hips to survey the property. "I'll probably have another look around in the house to see if anything else belongs to me."

Edie diverted him to the bay door of the garage where the old crap on folding tables still waited for buyers.

"Just help yourself to any of that stuff," she told him. "Especially the big stuff."

"I kind of hope he doesn't get his car fixed," Lana told Edie. "That was kind of a fun ride." Lana stuck a finger at Edie's forehead and squinted. "What's going on with your hair?"

Edie patted the scarf with one hand to make sure it was still in place.

"I love that color," Lana said. "Just like mine."

Lana held a cake carrier, which seemed like an odd accessory for such a non-dainty person. It was like seeing John Wayne holding baby booties.

"Hey! My two favorite redheads." Sam appeared from the garage, carrying folding chairs that still had prices marked on them.

"Did Jeffy ask you about his car?" Edie wanted to change topics from hair color to anything else, including cars. "It was jerking around and making some awful smoke."

"Yeah." Sam nodded. "I said I'd look at it, but I have a pretty good idea what's wrong with it."

"Wow!" Lana enthused. "Without even looking, huh? You're good."

"What did you bring?" Edie pointed to the cake carrier, and Lana lifted the lid to reveal an elaborate, three-tiered Jell-O tower with a sun design pressed on the top layer. It really was a work of art. She never would have expected Lana to be...what? A dab hand in the kitchen?

"The middle layer has grapes," Lana explained.

"Lana, this is gorgeous."

"Wasn't sure it was going to make it in one piece, what with dingbat Jeffy's car running so rough. But that's the miracle of Jell-O."

Edie wondered if she could make anything so attractive. Even her fancy glorified rice just kind of laid there in a colorful clump. "Seriously, Lana. This could be in a magazine like *Today's Sophisticated Woman.*"

"I don't know about all that," Lana shrugged off the compliment. "But I do like building things."

Sam shot Edie a knowing look. He still wanted to bet her that Lana did it.

After scampering down the ladder from the treehouse, Avi waved to them. "I talked him into it. He's coming down."

"That's great!" Sam waved back. To Edie he said, "Our only witness lives in a treehouse, but at least he's going to make the potluck."

Avi called up to Garvey. "Okay, Garv. Send it down." Garvey lowered a bucket by rope to her. The neck of a stringed musical instrument stuck out the top—presumably the sitar. Avi set that aside and then retrieved a round plastic container. She approached the Fiskers and handed Edie the container.

"That nice Mrs. Svensson let me use her beautiful kitchen to make a raisin pudding pie."

"You could have used our kitchen such as it is." Edie fretted, but she was only trying to sound polite. She didn't want strangers and hippies wandering around her house.

"Oh, that's okay. I really like Vicki's kitchen better. She had all the ingredients, too; the raisins, the instant pudding, the vanilla..."

The thought of raisins floating in crusted pudding nearly made Edie lose it right there. She shoved the container into Sam's midsection.

"Speak of the devil." Avi waved to Vicki and Toby Svensson as they appeared from the path through the woods. Toby fell into conversation with Sam about lake life while Garvey wandered off on his own. He slid against the trunk of the tree and rested the sitar across his lap. He gave it a few strums, filling the air with that weird, exotic resonance you sometimes heard in movies about faraway places.

Avi looked at him admiringly. "That's his gift, man. Music! He was nervous about coming down, but, you know, music calms him."

Soon Garvey's sitar found a tune that Edie recognized from the radio, "Another Somebody Done Somebody Wrong Song." She risked it and sang along. Avi looked at her like she was crazy.

"Those aren't the words."

Edie was startled. She'd heard the song dozens of times and was fairly sure she knew it by heart. "I think they are?" She answered with uncertainty.

"No, he just wrote that song for me this week." Avi shook her long, loose hair (which wasn't frizzy and orange), so it flowed freely in the breeze. "It's called 'Avi, Baby, You're So Outta Sight.'"

Edie frowned but decided not to break the news about B. J. Thomas and the pop singles charts while Avi sang along with the "correct" chorus:

Avi, sweet like taffy, oh baby, you're so outta sight, right!
And like a mellow song.
On a yellow gong.
While we smoke a bong.

"I didn't know you could sing, Avi. And so well," Vicki gushed. No compliment was forthcoming for Edie's singing, however. "Will you and Garvey be serenading us on the pontoon?"

"Oh, no," Edie answered for Avi. There was a murder to solve after the potluck, after all. "It gets pretty wet on the lake, I imagine. You wouldn't want that beautiful instrument to get ruined. Let's just leave it on shore, shall we?"

A low purring engine sounded on the dirt road, and Edie saw a convertible stop on the road near the mailbox, where it turned into the resort's driveway. The passenger door opened, and Edie's mom got out. She blew a kiss to the driver, and the car continued into the driveway, honking at Edie as he passed. It was Bud Langskip, her "real" father. He was still not ready to go public with Dolores, who had to make the walk of shame on her own, past the shattered resort sign, toward Edie.

Far from looking ashamed, Edie's mom looked happy, presumably having spent the night on Magic Fingers Mountain again. In fact, she looked happier than Edie had ever seen her before. Edie didn't like it.

Before Edie could point out how toxic secrets were, Dolores held up a finger and kept walking on by.

"Not now, Edie. I'm in too good of a mood for small-mindedness." She joined Toby, Vicki, and the cousins in conversation—until the men (and Lana) noticed Bud's convertible.

"Holy crap, that's one of them Cadillac Eldorados!" Jeffy said.

Bud (or more likely one of his henchmen) had waxed its mustard-yellow finish. Even the white sidewalls glistened. Well, any hope of getting the men (or Lana) to board the pontoon was ruined. They formed a horseshoe around the hood, hoping that Bud might pop the top for them to have a peek. Bud eased back in his seat, arm stretched across, his arm on the passenger-side headrest. He clearly relished the attention, answering all of their questions about the car's specifications, its performance, its price tag. When he told the car's admirers that his Eldorado had a *five hundred* engine with four hundred horses, well, they practically went into fits. He might as well have told them the car could fly or that it came with a trunk full of gold bars.

Of course, none of that meant anything to Edie.

"It's a nice-looking car," Edie told Vicki and Avi.

"I like the color," Vicki admitted. "It goes with my kitchen."

"My father," Avi said softly, referring to Russell Randall, "he always drives the most expensive cars too, and wears the best clothes and chases the prettiest girls. It's all so materialistic."

Materialistic wasn't a word Edie was familiar with, but she liked the sound of it.

Vicki chimed in, "I think they do it because they're afraid of death, the men. They try to insulate themselves against it with all their shiny objects."

"I love that," Avi agreed. She embraced Vicki without warning. "That's exactly what it is."

Edie didn't know why Avi was so excited about it. She was pretty sure Vicki was just quoting from an article in *Woman's Day*.

Vicki pulled away, clearly not comfortable with spontaneous physical affection.

"But I do like the color," Vicki said, her cheeks flush with embarrassment.

Sheriff Olmdahl was the last on the list to arrive. He pulled in with the county cruiser and was in full uniform. Edie wondered if he was on duty and being paid to potluck. He hoisted plastic buckets of store-bought potato salad and chicken whip spread, which was disappointing. But maybe the sheriff's wife was dead. Sometimes you had to give people the benefit of the doubt.

Edie handed Sam the six-packs of beer and retrieved her purse from under a lawn chair.

"Looks like we're all here," she announced, trying to get everyone's attention. It didn't work. Everyone was chattering away, sneaking peeks at covered dishes, pointing out various features of Bud's Eldorado. Sam was completely useless, having cracked open one of Jeffy's beers. He flitted from dish to dish, sampling. Finally, he made his move on Vicki and her meatballs.

"Mmm!" Sam said as he lifted the lid while she gripped the container for dear life. "What's that? Is that jelly on there?"

Vicki pressed the cover down and sealed it. "They're *Swedish* meatballs. That's lingonberry sauce."

"Well, anything you make is bound to be delicious," Sam crooned. Edie rolled her eyes but caught herself.

"That's wonderful, Vicki!" Edie said. "You and Toby just scoot on board, and we'll be right out." To Sam, she added in a low, meaningful voice, "We've got a murder to solve, remember?"

"Oh, yeah." Sam cupped his hands and shouted, "Hey, everybody. Get on the boat!"

And they did, crossing the gangplank like meek little sheep prodded in the butt with the shepherd staff. Bud held Dolores's arm as she crossed, but they pretended not to know each other well to disguise their rekindled romance.

"Thank you, Mr. Langskip," Edie's mother said in her most formal tone.

"Dee-lighted, Mrs. Schmidt."

"Oh, please," she answered, loud enough for everyone to hear. "Please call me Dolores. After all, you and I have known each other for many years."

Now Edie knew where she got her acting skills, or lack of them. She guided Arne on the temporary dock, reassured when no one else had fallen off and hit their heads when they'd crossed it. Those pontoon mafia guys really knew their stuff.

"Look, Mom!" About halfway across, Arne swiveled his hips, which shook the platform, making Edie feel like she might fall in the lake. She clutched her purse tightly, afraid of losing her hidden Dignities to Little Paw Lake.

"Stop it, Arne."

"Aww, I'm just being Elvis."

Edie noted lingonberry jelly stains on Arne's lips. God forbid he should get a taste for Swedish cooking.

"Hey, you with the cute ears," Dolores called to Arne. "Come here. I want you to meet somebody."

"Grandma!" Arne took off running onto the boat, leaving Edie fall toward the pontoon's railing to steady herself. She kept one eye on her mother as Arne was introduced to Bud, his secret grandfather.

Oh, Lord, Edie prayed. *Please don't let Arne find out too soon.* If Arne realized that his real grandfather was rich and controlled a Norwegian lake gang, there's no telling how big that boy's head might get.

After absently shaking Bud's hand, Arne announced he was hungry.

"You know, I am too, Arne." Bud clapped his hands. "Some of us are getting pretty hungry, so if you haven't yet, please bring your dishes and yourselves to the top deck to get this potluck started. He led the way, climbing the angle-bar ladder leading from the main deck to his top deck, and for a man in his late fifties, Bud seemed to be in good shape. Arne scrambled behind him, followed by Dolores.

Edie gathered Sam by the arm as he veered toward Vicki. "Hiya, Vicki." He waved at her.

"Stop moving your arms around or they might get broken off," Edie warned him. "We've got a murder to solve." He helped her up the ladder until she stood on the top deck. She'd never known pontoons could have two stories, but there it was, with a wrap-around railing system and a diving board—so much more spacious than the lower level. The view of the lake was gorgeous. It looked like the ocean, if you sort of blocked out the shore with your hand. A table stood in the center, already laden with plates, utensils, baking dishes, and crockpots.

"Mom! It's got a diving board!" Arne dashed past her, intent on leaping into the lake, but she grabbed him by the neck.

"Nope. That's not a diving board, mister. That's a You Better Behave board, understand? And if you don't behave, I will rip it off and spank you with it."

Once everyone was settled, the boat shoved off. Arne scrambled back down the ladder with a mouthful of chewy Scotcheroo bars.

"I want to drive the boat!" he yelled, and John Kvalstad let him throttle the pontoon forward toward the center of Little Paw Lake. The sun was warm, but the breeze and the mist from the waves felt wonderful. They cruised to a quiet bay where, at Bud's signal, Arne pressed the button that dropped the anchor.

"Looks like we're here," Edie said to Sam.

"Yup. Your cousin Lana can't escape now."

"She didn't do it, Sam."

"Oh, yeah?" Sam stuck his hand out. "If you're so sure, why won't you bet on it?"

"Okay, okay. I'll bet. You want to bet money we don't have?"

"Nah." Sam shook his head. "I already have all the money I need."

Edie laughed. "Yeah, right."

"I was thinking of something more...special." He winked at her.

"What'd you have in mind?"

"If you lose..."

"Yes?"

"If you lose, then on Monday nights—and, Edie, I mean *every* Monday night..."

"Yes?"

"I want you to..."

"You want me to what?" Edie's imagination went into overdrive.

"Let Arne and me watch *S.W.A.T.* instead of that dopey *Rhoda* show."

"That's what you want? You could have had anything, and you want *S.W.A.T.?* Well, it won't matter because you're wrong."

They shook on it and then fell into conversations with the other guests (*suspects*, she reminded herself) as they filled their plates with dollops of potato salad and pickled beets. The hiss of air escaping cans of beer punctuated sentences. The pontoon potluck had warmed up. The guests were having a good time except for Garvey. He seemed agitated. He'd settled into a cushy bench next to Avi but was eyeing the other passengers suspiciously.

Edie nudged Sam.

"Look at how weird Garvey is acting," she told him. "Maybe he recognizes Uncle Nat's murderer after all. He could be the key to busting this case wide open."

"Okay, Colombo, settle down." Sam popped a grape in his mouth. "He's probably just freaked out from being out of the treehouse. Besides, we all know Lana did it."

"Lana did what?" Lana asked, and Edie had to think quick.

"...made the prettiest dish here. Isn't that right, Sam? Sam was just saying how lovely the Jell-O tower turned out."

"Yeah, almost a shame to eat it," he said.

Edie noticed her mother urging the others in discreet whispers to put a little dab of Edie's version of glorified rice on their plates. She clearly saw her lips form the words, *You don't have to eat it if you don't want to.*

And that's how Dolores Schmidt née Lachmann supported her daughter.

It was humiliating, and Edie had enough. She grumbled to Sam about it, but he was unsympathetic, pointing out that adding fruit cocktail to glorified rice was disgusting and that they were there to solve a murder, not to earn approval.

"I can do both, stupid." But she was on her own.

"Oh, Edie. This is really good!" Avi was effusive in her praise.

"Do you really think so?" Maybe she was on drugs? Maybe she just had no taste? After all, everyone else was avoiding her glorified rice like it was a container full of napalm. Probably, she was just being polite. Everyone was supposed to be polite, even when it was sarcasm. That was Minnesota Nice.

"Oh, yeah. It's just so unexpected. I mean, not that the other one isn't fine, but it's, like, so predictable, you know?"

The other one, as Avi called it, was her mother's classic recipe: nameless and predictable.

"Garvey, what do you think?"

Garvey's eyes flitted from side to side as he nodded, chewing absently.

"That's different," he said after swallowing.

"He means that in a good way, not the Minnesotan way." Avi laughed. "Your glorified rice is like Hollywood, you know?"

"Yeah," Edie agreed. "Hollywood." Her glorified rice was action and adventure, bright lights and big names, bigger than life, and filled with happy endings. Some people were just too small to see the stars shining right in front of them. Look out spotlight, Edie Fisker's Hollywood Style Glorified Rice is stepping in!

Edie regretted all the negative things she'd said about the treehouse hippies. They still weren't welcome to stay, but they were all right in her book.

"Would you mind if I tuck my purse here behind the cooler?" Edie asked Avi. "Don't want it to get wet."

"Got your stash in it?" Avi asked jokingly, not knowing that she was correct.

Sheriff Olmdahl approached her, holding a plate with one hand.

"I'm told you made this." He jabbed at Edie's glorified rice with his fork. "It's not bad," he said, which was just about the highest praise you could expect from a Minnesotan. She was feeling so good just then that maybe she wouldn't spike her mother's version with fruit cocktail, after all.

Arne scampered up the ladder for another round of food, followed by John Kvalstad.

"No more soda pop today, Arne," she instructed. "You've got enough vim the way it is."

The pontoon swayed gently in the bay, and the sounds of conversation and the communal sharing of food in the sunshine made for such a pleasant scene that Edie nearly forgot about the day's darker edge. Now it was time for them to concentrate on what they'd come to do. Her pulse quickened as she realized they really were going to do it: they were going to confront suspects about Uncle Nat's murder. But how to begin? Broaching the subject of murder wasn't easy, especially when the line-up of suspects was just warming to your Hollywood-style glorified rice. She looked to Sam, busy chatting with Toby and Vicki—mostly with Vicki—but she caught his attention.

"Are we ready?" he asked her. She nodded.

"Thanks, everyone!" Sam rose to address the passengers gathered on the top deck. "For coming out today. It's a great chance for us to get to know you better."

Polite clapping ensued. Vicki Svensson touched Edie's arm in support.

"But there's another reason why we're all here. It's got to do with Nat Lachmann's death."

A murmur of confusion erupted among them. Edie quickly scanned their reactions: a look of shock passed over Vicki Svensson; Jeffy sat up straight and looked at his sister in alarm; Bud Langskip frowned, realizing he'd loaned them his pontoon under false pretenses; and Avi gasped and looked as if she were about to cry. And Garvey, next to her, looked down at the can of fruit cocktail in his hands. Had that hippie rummaged through her purse? Her Dignity cigarettes better still be in there.

"I'd like to have Sheriff Olmdahl tell us about the investigation into Nat's death. As an elected servant of the people, I'm sure he'll set us straight."

The sheriff's mouth hung open, about to receive another spoonful of Hollywood-style glorified rice, some of which had found its way to his chin.

"I'm not at liberty to divulge certain facts of the case," he said, clearing his throat. "But I can tell you what we all know. The coroner ruled it an accident involving a boat motor that exploded, and Mr. Lachmann became deceased. End of story."

"Is it, though?" Sam stepped over to Garvey and placed his hand on his shoulders. "This man is what they call a material witness on *Rockford Files*. He saw members of the Sons of Gunnar have a heated conversation with Nat on the dock—the same dock that later exploded without an outboard motor anywhere near it. Now, I might only be a simple mechanic, but something doesn't add up."

Edie blinked. Her husband was running the show better than she could have imagined, but she also knew him well enough to know he wouldn't be able to sustain it. And, then, sure enough...

"You!" Sam spun around and pointed at Lana. "Isn't it true you and your father had problems?"

Edie shook her head, disappointed that she was right. He only wanted to cast blame on Lana to win control of Monday night television.

"Well, yeah," Lana sputtered. "Same as any family where the deadbeat ditches his family, but why would I want him dead?"

"Because you were angry, and you wanted payback. After you killed him, you'd get the resort, or so you thought. Until that woman..." Sam spun and pointed at his mother-in-law, "interfered and ruined your plans."

"Edie, you tell that man to put his filthy finger down," Dolores said.

"I don't want the resort, for cripes sake," Lana continued. "I got all the money I need and I like my job."

Sam spun back to face Lana. "At the quarry, you mean!"

"Yeah, at the quarry."

"Where you work with explosives, right?"

"Well, yeah." Lana shrugged her muscled shoulders and looked to the other passengers. "But I mean, show of hands, who else here blows stuff up?"

Hands went up: John, Toby, Jeffy, Sheriff Olmdahl, and...Dolores Lachmann neé Schmidt.

"Mother?" Edie rose. "When have you ever blown up anything?"

"Remember when that coyote ate my poodle, Luxor, last year? Well, I bought some M-80 firecrackers, and I tracked that monster to a barranca and blew up its den. So fulfilling."

"Isn't it?" Toby Svensson agreed. "Wildlife management separates us from the apes."

"I made an exploding volcano for school," Arne announced, waving his hand.

"And did your volcano kill my Uncle Nat?" Edie asked. Arne shook his head. "Then put your hand down and let the grown-ups solve the murder."

Bud stood up and waved off Sam. "Listen, before this thing gets out of hand, I think we can clear some things up. Sheriff, just go ahead and tell them."

The sheriff adjusted his holster and brushing off crumbs from his badge. He looked sheepishly at Bud.

"Are you sure about this, Bud?"

Bud nodded.

"Go ahead. You can tell them."

"Well, it's like this. Like you said, Mr. Fisker, Nat Lachmann didn't die in a boat motor accident. Truth is, it wasn't an accident at all. It *was* murder."

This sent the passengers into an outburst of chattering and unanswered questions. The sheriff lifted his hands to calm them. A raisin, adhered by white pudding, slid down one hand and dropped to the floor of the pontoon.

"We knew from the coroner that it wasn't an accident, but, well, this is going to sound funny to some of you, but I kind of thought that maybe John had a hand in it."

John laughed.

"Me? Why would I have killed Nat? He was a cool guy."

"Again," the sheriff explained, "this is going to sound funny, but I thought maybe Bud might have told you to kill Nat. You know, on account he wanted the property for the Sons of Gunnar."

Cousin Jeffy stepped toward the sheriff, going chest to chest with him.

"So you covered up my father's murder to protect a...a tropical plumber?"

"We covered it up to protect *us*." The sheriff shooed Jeffy back to his seat. "We rise and fall together, right Chief?"

Bud nodded. "Couldn't have said it better myself."

"And now," the sheriff said and nodded to Garvey, "I'd like to hear from that man about what he saw."

Garvey rose to address them, his ponytail flapped in the breeze. "So, like, I looked out the window and saw this crazy cat set the bomb, man."

"To be clear, you're saying you actually saw the person who set the explosives?"

"Yeah, man, and it was..." Garvey's head swiveled as he considered each passenger. "It was her!" He pointed at Vicki Svensson. "Yeah, I saw her from the treehouse as clear as day."

Vicki bowed her head at the accusation.

"Wait a minute." Sam jumped up, spilling whipped tuna spread on the pontoon deck. "That's a lie!"

"Aw, man, don't give me a hassle." Garvey grumbled.

"I've been in that treehouse, and I remember trying to look out the window, because there's only one, you can't see the dock from up there. It's blocked by the tree itself."

"That's true," Vicki agreed.

Sam and Edie looked at Vicki like she'd sprouted another head. How would Vicki know how the treehouse looked inside?

"No, man. You're just uptight because I'm not square like you. Blame the peace-loving hippies, right? That's what fascists do."

"Facts are facts, Garv," Sam said.

"Well, maybe I was on the ladder when I saw it."

"Nope," Sam shook his head. "Same deal. You couldn't have seen it from there unless you were swinging on a branch."

"Were you swinging on a branch, son?" The sheriff asked.

"Yeah, man." Garvey's grip tightened on the can of fruit cocktail. If his hands were stronger like Sam's, maybe he would crush the can in his grasp like Popeye. "I was swinging like a monkey."

"Garvey, I know you're lying," Avi said. Tears flowed down her cheek. "We can't see the dock from the window. And you can't swing like a monkey or anything else because of your war injury."

"War injury?" Sam did a double take. "What war was that? The War on Poverty?"

"Shut your mouth, Mr. Brownies. I was in 'Nam, man, which is more than you ever did. But when Papa Lock got blown up, I was up in the treehouse."

"Too bad you can't prove it," Bud Langskip replied.

"I got an alibi."

"It's true." Vicki Svensson stood. "I was up in the treehouse with Garvey when it happened."

"Wait, what?" It was Toby's turn to be shocked, just before trying Edie's Hollywood-style glorified rice.

"It's true," she said. "I was up there, and we heard the explosion."

"What were you doing with that man?" Toby asked. He looked hurt, but he still looked good.

"Oh, nothing like that, Toby. Trust me. There's not enough Jergens to scrub that off a person. I wanted to surprise you for your birthday by playing the 'Minnesota Rouser' on the sitar, so I took lessons from Garvey."

"There," Garvey announced. "That proves it wasn't me."

"Except it doesn't prove that," Wahoo John interjected. "You could have set the charge earlier."

"That's crazy. I just play the sitar and eat delicious brownies. How would I know how to booby trap somebody with explosives?"

"I don't know." John puffed out his chest and leaned toward Garvey. "Maybe the sitar isn't the only thing you used to blow people's minds."

Garvey snarled. He pushed up his sleeves and was about to start throwing punches in a very un-hippie manner, but Sam grabbed him and held his arms back.

"His arm. Look at his arm."

Edie, confused at first, followed Sam's lead and while Garvey struggled, Edie and John pulled up his sleeve to reveal a red stripe tattoo with the word SAPPER running across it, just like John's tattoo.

"Son of a gun!" Sam declared. "This hippie blows up stuff too!"

"I remember hearing about this guy," John said as he tightened his grip on Garvey. "He got kicked out of the Marines for being too dangerous."

The sheriff read Garvey his rights and cuffed him.

"But why'd you do it, Garvey?" Avi pleaded, holding his face in her hands, but he wouldn't look at her.

"I saw Nat talking to those Norwegian bastards," Garvey said. "He was making some kind of deal to sell the property to them. That's our home, Avi. He was going to kick us to the curb, and I didn't want to leave. It was safe there, you and me, up in the treehouse. No one could touch us. I thought he would leave us the place, you know, like in his will? Because he really dug you, like a father would."

"So, you killed him?" Avi sobbed and let him go. "That's not cool, Garvey." Edie stepped up and embraced Avi.

"Anyone else take music lessons from this man?" Bud asked. "How about you, John?"

"Ukulele is more my speed." John laughed.

Chapter 28

The Versatility of Fruit Cocktail

TOBY SVENSSON HELD HIS wife. "That man could have killed you in a treehouse and I wouldn't have known until I saw the turkey vultures circling."

"I just wanted to do something different for your birthday, you know?"

"That's different alright." He kissed her perfect nose.

They pulled up anchor and headed back to the resort so the sheriff could take Garvey in for processing. A fancy boat with a shiny red outboard motor rooster tailed lake water like a fire hose. The man driving it was the same guy Sam had fought—the one who claimed to be Avi's father.

"Is that your dad?" Edie asked Avi, who still cried in Edie's arms.

Avi looked up, and her expression darkened. She pulled away from Edie and folded her arms. "As if things couldn't get any worse, there *he* is."

Russell Randall glided his boat alongside the pontoon. The men's heads swiveled as if they watched a slow-motion tennis game, not because of Russell Randall or his clearly expensive gear. They watched his bikini-clad companion. In fact, the men all shifted to that side of the upper deck for a better view. The uneven weight distribution tilted the pontoon.

"Not everyone at once," Bud yelled. "Some of you guys, back off. Sheriff, your gun handle is poking me somewhere special."

Edie marched over and pulled Sam to the other side. "You'll tip us over."

"What?" He said as if startled from a deep sleep. "She's not wearing a life jacket. We're concerned for her safety."

"I'm not wearing a life jacket," Edie pointed out.

"Yeah, but she's *really* not wearing a life jacket."

The speedboat's engine cut and Russell Randall called to his daughter. Avi ducked behind Sam and Edie.

"Have I got news, *bubeleh*. You're going to love this."

"Love, he says," Avi harrumphed.

"Listen, sweetie. In Shakopee, there's this *meshugenah* thing called the Renaissance Festival. I know some people. It's got the costumes, the theatre people, the carousing...all those things you love."

"What are you talking about?"

"A job, my *maideleh*. A job that suits you. They need help getting things together. Dealing with artistic types, tying lots of loose ends. It's like those madrigal dinner things you did in school except with booze."

"I thought you wanted me to go to law school." Avi's voice dripped with sarcasm.

Russell Randall shrugged. "Better you should be *a nishtikeit* near your mother than *a nishtikeit* in the middle of nowhere with these bumpkins. No offense."

"None taken," the passengers on the pontoon replied in unison.

Avi looked over at Garvey. He sat precariously on a bait bucket, his hands cuffed behind him. To Edie, she whispered, "What should I do?"

Avi was at a crossroads, to be sure. There was no turning back. The treehouse was closed for business, and Garvey was headed to prison. She and Edie had something in common: an abrupt change in circumstances forcing a major life choice.

"Normally, I'd say follow your heart," Edie began. "But your heart makes bad choices. No offense, Garvey."

"None taken," he replied.

"So, I'd say take a chance on this new thing. Opportunities don't come out of nowhere very often, trust me." Edie very well could have given herself the same talk. It was time to take chances and try new things, to let go of normal and see what life offered.

The men talked amongst themselves so as not to appear nosy, but their eyes remained riveted on the young woman on the boat, and she knew it. She lay on her stomach and kicked her feet slowly.

"How about it, sweetie?" Russell Randall called to Avi. She stepped to the railing and looked down at her father.

"And what about me?" His young bikini-clad companion bolted upright. "I'm not a nothing, ya know."

"You want to work at the Renaissance Festival, too?" Russell Randall wiped his hands together. "No problem. I can get you in."

"That's not what I mean, and you know it." The young woman, hands on hips, went nose-to-nose with him. Clearly she was venting something that had been building up a long time. "When we first got together, you told me no kids, no boyfriends, no baggage. Now you're picking up baggage? Are you just going to run off with her?"

"She's my daughter, baby. What are you talking about? My daughter is coming home with me."

The young woman rose, incensed. She seemed ready to dive into the lake and swim off as part of a tantrum, but the men on the pontoon chattered at once, warning her how dangerous that would be, especially since she wasn't wearing a life jacket, or much of anything else.

"It'll just be better if you hop over here on the pontoon," Sam insisted.

"Yeah, I'll help you across." John Kvalstad headed toward the ladder to climb down to the lower deck.

Edie took Avi's hand. "He loves you. He obviously isn't perfect, I can see that. But can I ask you to do something?"

"What?" Confusion clouded Avi's expression.

"Just for a moment, imagine that man on that boat, with all his imperfections, dead. Just gone."

Avi took a deep breath and closed her eyes. "Okay." Then she opened her eyes. Russell Randall was looking right at her with a dopey smile. He waved for her to get on board.

"I guess it's worth a shot," Avi said. "But Edie, if it doesn't work out, can I come back?"

"Sure, sweetie," Edie purred. "We'll give you a good deal on a cabin. Half off your first night."

After helping the catalog model cross to the main deck of the pontoon, John Kvalstad helped Avi cross over to her father. If Avi still held resentment towards her dad, Edie couldn't tell: she was lost in her father's embrace. They both cried and told one another how much they loved each other. Russell laid his big hand on the back of her head and pressed her to his chest while he thanked God for returning his daughter.

Without warning, Garvey wriggled out of the handcuffs. He dived frantically from the upper deck, his arms and legs outstretched like a hippie pterodactyl. Landing hard in the powerboat, Garvey sprang into a fighting position before shoving Russell aside. He started the engine. As the boat roared off, the force pinned Avi and her father to the floor with the momentum of takeoff.

"He seemed pretty eager to get out of here," John observed.

"Well, he won't get too far." The sheriff slid a walkie-talkie from his belt and alerted his deputies.

"Oh, I hope he doesn't hurt Avi or her father," Edie said. "He seems crazy."

"Ooh, what is this?" The catalog model had discovered Edie's Hollywood-style glorified rice on the potluck table. Edie watched as the young woman lifted a spoon to her mouth. It was then that Arne pointed to the can of fruit cocktail sitting on the bait bucket.

"Why is this ticking?" Arne asked.

As Arne reached for the can, the thought occurred to Edie that a murderer with nothing to lose might just be willing to blow up a pontoon full of potluckers if it meant he could get away.

"There's a bomb!" She scooped up Arne before he could grasp the fruit cocktail.

Bud Langskip rushed to the bucket, but John stopped his hand. "Don't touch it, Chief. We gotta go. That fruit cocktail is wired to blow!"

"Go?" Bud asked. John shoved him overboard using his shoulder. Bud hollered as he flailing into the lake.

"Everyone overboard. Now!" John grabbed Toby and Vicki, leading them to the side. "This pontoon is about to self-destruct."

Sam swung Arne over and tossed him as far as he could before shoving Dolores in. Edie dived in on her own, her body arcing under the cold water before surfacing. Everyone else made it over on their own. The last one in was the sheriff, whose holster got caught on the rail. His face turned red in panic as precious seconds ticked by. He unbuckled holster and let it drop to the upper deck as he pushed himself off the side.

"Arne!" She called. "Sam!" They were bobbing with the others, and Edie swam over to them. For a few moments, they watched the double-decker custom pontoon splashing happily, bobbing up and down, until it exploded. The floats ruptured and sucked in great gasps of water. The pontoon sank aft first, leaving only an assortment of cushions and empty beer bottles floating on the lake.

"Cripes," Bud cursed. "I better get that insured."

Chapter 29

Marriage Isn't A Democracy

THE EXPLOSION WAS LOUD enough to be heard as far as Utgard Lake, and a plume of black smoke shot into the sky. Fortunately for the potluck survivors, plenty of lake residents noticed the explosion. Boats raced to the bay to pluck them from the water, first Arne and the women, then the men. Soon the Svenssons, the Fiskers, and the others arrived at the Hole on Little Paw Lake.

The sheriff, dripping wet in his uniform, plodded up to his car. His boots squeaked when he walked. He radioed his deputies. Edie handed him the last towel when he returned to the group.

Only two hours earlier, the men had been admiring Bud's car and chatting about the weather. Now they were panting from excitement and looked like drowned rats as they recounted their near-death encounters.

"And the fruit cocktail just blew up? Was it past the expiration date or something?" Jeffy asked, incredulous.

"No, the bait bucket had the explosives," John explained. "He must have suspected something was going down at the potluck."

"Well, they got him," the sheriff interrupted. "That Russell Randall fella bopped Garvey over the head with an oar and regained control of the boat. They're heading over now."

A few minutes later, Russell Randall's boat glided to the temporary dock. Avi held a rope that coiled around Garvey while Russell prodded him with the business end of an oar. Garvey was angry, definitely not in a meditative state of bliss. On shore, Randall shoved Garvey to the ground.

"Don't let him move a muscle," the sheriff told them. "Backup is on the way."

Being nearly killed at a potluck pontoon really drew people together: Dolores placed a hand on Bud's back; Toby and Vicki held one another, talking affectionately about college fight songs; Cousin Jeffy sweet-talked the catalog model into riding with him into town; Avi and her father smiled at each other after she gave Garvey a kick in the shin; and Sam took Edie in his arms and kissed her neck.

"We're off to a rough start, aren't we?"

"Could be worse," Edie said.

"Oh? How's that?"

"We could all catch food poisoning from that disgusting raisin pudding pie."

Vicki Svensson pulled away from her husband and clapped. "Ladies, let's head over to my place in case something else explodes. I've got coffee and dry things." Under her breath, she added to Edie, "And cigarettes."

"Arne, you stay here with your father," Edie yelled. "And don't touch the hippie."

⟡⟡⟡

Vicki Svensson led Edie and Lana along the trail to her house with the promise of fluffy towels and spare dry clothes. The air was warm as they walked, and Edie breathed in the earthy smell of the woods, just happy to be alive.

"Do you smell that?" she asked the other women.

"Smells like a meatloaf," Lana replied, and by God it did. "Is that Avi coming over?"

"She said to go ahead without her," Vicki explained. "She'll be over just as soon as the deputies take over."

"She probably wants to get some more body shots in on that Garvey," Lana said. "Lord knows I'd like a swing at him myself. Trying to kill us like that."

"What was it that Gandhi said?" Vicki began. "In the face of violence…"

"Smack it one on the nose," Lana finished.

"Not quite." Vicki smiled politely, but she dropped the topic of nonviolence. When they reached her house, she pointed them to the bathroom and the bedroom. Lana remained on the threshold, looking in.

"I don't want to break anything," she said.

"Then don't," Vicki chirped encouragingly. "While you two change, I'll make us some coffee."

"I'll take something stronger if you have it," Lana said as she disappeared into the bathroom.

"You don't have to make anything for me, Vicki," Edie answered. "I want to get back over there, so I won't stay long."

"Not even long enough for a cup of coffee?" Vicki pouted. Then she lifted a pack of Virginia Slims. "...and a cigarette?"

"Okay, maybe one," she agreed. "Just to be social."

Lana had changed into one of Vicki's floral-print summer dresses. She brushed back her hair, which was still wet and looked straight and sleek. After pulling the chair out, she joined the others at the table, leaning back so the chair was on two legs, much to Vicki's consternation. She sat like a man: her knees spread wider than the length of a football. Apparently, her mother had never taught her the rules for women. And maybe, Edie wondered, maybe that was okay.

"I feel like a priss in a dress," she chortled. "No offense."

"None taken," the other two women replied automatically.

Vicki passed around the pack of Virginia Slims. They drank coffee, smoked, and talked about having to swim for their lives. Edie recounted how she'd been kidnapped only a few days before.

"Fornburg is in the midst of a crime spree," Vicki lamented.

Avi appeared on the back deck. She carried a long, black leather case with plenty of wear and tear. Vicki waved her in, and Avi handed Vicki the case.

"It's Garvey's sitar, the one you were learning on. I want you to have it. That bastard Garvey won't need it where he's going."

"But why don't you keep it?" Vicki tried to give it back. "You must play it beautifully."

Avi shook her head. "I never really learned. I was more of a lute girl."

Vicki opened the case, and tears welled in her eyes.

"You know, I haven't played since the night Nat died."

"What the hell kind of banjo is that?" Lana wanted to know.

"It's a sitar," Vicki explained. "I was learning to play, you know, before Nat died."

"You play the sitar too?" Edie shook her head in admiration. "Is there anything you can't do?"

"Papa Lock wanted you to have your own sitar," Avi added. "That's why he left you the savings bond."

"I thought so too," Vicki agreed.

"But now that Garvey is going to jail, this would go to waste."

As if nipping in the bud any salacious thoughts the other women might have had about her time with Garvey, Vicki was quick to add, "And, ladies, it was only sitar lessons. Trust me. As a surprise for Toby. I wanted to learn his favorite song."

"And you took lessons in the treehouse?" Edie asked, bewildered. "Were you there when he...he..."

"Went kablooey?" Lana finished.

"I was, but I didn't see anything, and I didn't want to confuse things, you know, being alone with another man."

"A very strange man, by the way," Lana added. "No offense," she said to Avi.

"None taken, I guess?" Avi replied.

Edie could imagine how that would complicate things between a couple. For example, if she'd told Sam about the boat ride with John Kvalstad and their flirting, Sam might have gotten more jealous. Or if she told Sam how John smiled at her and how his arm muscles flexed when he tied a rope around docks, Sam might have gotten jealous at that, too. But it was hard to imagine Toby Svensson being too passionate about anything other than counting endangered gray wolves before executing them, or whatever else the DNR got up to.

"But honestly, nothing ever happened," Vicki assured them.

"It's true," Avi said. "Garvey didn't swing that way."

"You mean he's gay?" Lana asked.

Avi broke out laughing. "No, man. He didn't groove on blondes."

This set all the women rolling with laughter, and tears streamed from all their eyes in an ecstatic release. It felt good to laugh.

"Why don't you play the song for us?" Edie encouraged her.

"Oh, I couldn't play in front of people."

"We'll be your dry run for when you play for Toby."

"Okay, but don't expect much."

Vicki rested her cigarette in a yellow ashtray in the shape of a flower. She lifted the sitar from the battered case and lowered herself onto a shag throw rug, her legs crossed Indian style. Fingers on the neck, she shifted the instrument and then filled the yellow kitchen with droning hypnotic strains of the "Minnesota Rouser."

⋘ ─ ◆ ─ ⋙

Edie returned to the resort just in time to see Sam being dragged off by Bud and those two beefy men who worked for him.

Your father, she corrected herself.

"Where are you taking him?"

"We're just borrowing him for a private chat over at my office," Bud Langskip answered. "We'll bring him back in one piece."

"One living piece, please," she called out to them. She had almost told them to bring him back as good as new, but she was realistic. Alive was a good start.

<hr />

Sam was getting to be such a local now that he could tell Bud's two goons apart: Rollo was the stupid one, and Petie was the ugly one. Little memory tricks like that really help a fella get through awkward social events. He'd have to clue Arne in on those types of life lessons now that Arne was going to be making something of himself as a waterskiing star.

He didn't get time to admire all the décor in Bud's living room like last time. They hustled him down the corridor to the office. Bud took a seat behind his desk, and the henchman stood at the door behind Sam.

"Have a seat," Bud said, but Sam didn't sit. He was too antsy. Plus, there were so many things to look at on the shelves and the walls, and even though he'd seen most of it previously, there was even more he'd missed.

"You sure have a lot of interesting stuff in here."

"Please," Bud pointed to the chair. "Sit down. Seriously." Sam sat. The smile Bud gave him meant, *I'm supposed to like you, but I don't think I do.*

"I heard you're giving the resort a go."

"Yup, definitely going to give it the old college try," Sam answered. "Of course, I just barely finished high school."

"Well, the trick is promotion," Bud leaned back in his chair. "You're going to need a good name for the business. Something that lets people know they've found the right place."

"Yeah, we figured it out. The Hole on Little Paw. It's a name the wife dreamed up. She's kind of artsy, I guess. Personally, I just wanted to call it Fisker's Resort because our name means fishing."

"Hmm, your name means fishing. I kinda like that."

"Yeah, well, I got outvoted, one to one." Sam chuckled. "Marriage isn't a democracy."

"Sam, speaking of the Sons of Gunnar..." They hadn't been speaking of the Sons of Gunnar, but that didn't stop Bud. He got what he wanted. "I'm going to make a formal announcement to the club about your mother and Edie. Just to clear things up. I know rumors are already flying around town. I might as well make sure the rumors are true."

"Okay," Sam nodded thoughtfully. "Thanks for telling me."

"I'd like you to be there. Next Tuesday. I want to introduce you around. Maybe you can get a good feel for the club and…"

"Thank you, Bud, but I gotta stop you there. I don't think Edie would be too thrilled about me getting mixed up in the Norwegian Pontoon Mafia. She's thinking more about church softball and Boy Scouts."

Bud's face clouded.

"Norwegian what?"

"Pontoon mafia," Sam laughed nervously. "It's what some people call you behind your back."

For a moment, it looked like Bud might call for one of his henchmen to rough some sense into Sam, but then—just maybe—the recollection that this man was his son-in-law may have changed his mind. He cleared his throat.

"Sam, as a businessman, I've calculated the value of a man's life and even adjusted it for inflation. You want to know how much your life, my life, his life is worth?"

"A buck a gallon?" Sam laughed.

"One bar of gold. That's it."

"Okay, where do I collect?"

"You're collecting every day, Sam. Every day the sun rises, you get another little piece of gold. And that bar of gold I was talking about? That's what you leave when you die. A big bar, a little bar, but a bar of gold. The value of your life comes from the living of it. Understand?"

"Sure," Sam nodded. "But it'd be nice to cash in a little of it before then."

Bud shook his head. "Not much for delayed gratification, are you?"

"Some people say there is only *now*."

"Some people are dirty hippies!" Bud pounded the desk but then calmed himself with a deep breath. "And if you could cash in on your bar of gold, what would you use it for? Chip away little flecks of gold to trade for sandwiches? Maybe make coins and start your own country? Or maybe you'd just trade it all in for dollar bills?"

"I'd make a nice ring for Edie," Sam cut in. "She's pure gold."

Bud leaned back in his chair. It creaked but didn't collapse.

"I'm glad to hear you say that, Sam. A man needs to understand the value of his family." He jotted something down on a legal pad. "And the value of advertising."

Chapter 30

Aloha, Fornborg

EDIE SLEPT SOUNDLY THAT night. In fact, she hadn't slept so well for months. She tried not to wake Sam when she made her way into the kitchen, admiring the view: so different from their view in Minneapolis. Here, there was a lake and trees and space and birds. Minneapolis had those things too, but here they were all put together in one vista, not scattered between industrial sites.

And that morning air! The wild plums were in flower and fragrant. She clicked on the radio and heard the strains of Karen Carpenter's beautiful voice singing "We've Only Just Begun," and Edie clicked it off. It was too tempting to sing along. She didn't want to get hauled off to county lockup by the sheriff for disturbing the peace. She set to work making a proper hot breakfast for the first time since the Fiskers had arrived in Fornborg. The meal would consist entirely of their own groceries: toast, eggs, bacon, and coffee—heck, yes, coffee! The smell of bacon must have roused the sleeping bears. Soon enough, Arne came padding in, rubbing his eyes. He sipped his glass of Tang while he played with the Lincoln Logs they'd discovered in the crawlspace.

"Those probably belonged to your second cousins when they were kids," Edie pointed out, but he was too busy building something they would trip over later. At least Lincoln Logs were quiet. Arne wasn't making them yell like did with his other toys, which seemed angry and screamed when they suffered deaths imagined by Arne. Once they moved all their stuff from the Minneapolis apartment, he'd have more toy options, like his Playmobil cowboys and his Godzilla doll. *Excuse me: his Godzilla action figure,* she corrected. Until then, he would just have to play with miniature slotted wood logs or use his imagination in the great outdoors, which he didn't seem to mind too much.

Sam appeared, already dressed for the day. That was a good sign. Maybe it meant he was ready to tackle some projects on the list. He went outside for a moment to grab the newspaper and settled in at the table, sipping coffee.

"You know," Sam lowered the Thursday edition of the *Fornborg Daily Hawk*. "This almost feels normal, know what I mean? Like a Norman Rockwell painting or something."

Edie supposed it was about as normal as she could expect. That's what she'd wanted, alright. A little normalcy. Of course, no sooner had she thought that when she saw her mother shuffle into the kitchen wearing a silk kimono and a pair of fuzzy blue shearling lamb slippers.

"Good morning, everyone," Dolores announced as she pulled two coffee mugs from the rack.

How could everything be so strange and so normal all at once?

"Mother! You can't run around here half-naked."

Edie's mom sneered at her as she opened her kimono to reveal a nightgown beneath.

"I'm wearing layers, dear. You've always got to wear layers in Minnesota. I haven't been gone that long." She reached down to fondle Arne's ear lobe. "My, those ears just seem to get bigger every day."

"Don't tease the boy, Dolo," a gruff voice sounded behind her. "You'll give him a complex."

Bud Langskip emerged from the hallway wearing only those dusty yellow boxer shorts and a white v-neck t-shirt. Edie had really been seeing a lot more of her father than she bargained for.

"Morning, Grandma! Morning, Grandpa!"

"Grandpa!" Bud chuckled and scooped Arne in the air. He was still in pretty good shape for a cradle-robbing dirty old man. "I like the sound of that. Good morning, my grandson."

"Oh crap!" Edie closed her eyes in despair.

"What's wrong?" Sam looked up from the paper, startled.

"I just realized, if Bud's my real dad, that means I'm full Norwegian."

"Ha!" Sam declared. "All those years, you said Norwegians were stubborn and stupid! Well, who's Norwegian now, baby?"

"*Gratulerer!*" Bud laughed. "That means congratulations in Stubborn and Stupid."

"Can we go waterskiing today, Grandpa? I mean *vannski*."

Bud looked impressed. "Smart little fella, isn't he?"

Sam and Edie looked at each other. That wasn't something they heard very often.

"Well, you can waterski today, if it's okay with your parents, that is."

"What do you think, Sam?" Edie hoped Sam would say he had other plans for the boy.

"Of course," Sam blurted. "Arne needs to get more practice on the water if he's going to get better."

Arne wiggled out of Bud's arms and jumped around, flapping his arms like a drunk chicken.

"I'll get my shorts on!"

"I'll have John Kvalstad take him out on the speedboat. He's one of my top men," Bud assured them. "You can trust him."

"I'd like to go with," Sam added. "How about you, hunny bunny?"

Edie shook her head. She had lots to do. Sam did too, but that was a conversation for later. She also felt funny about spending too much time with John on the boat. There was definitely a...tension? Connection? Something. And it troubled her.

Arne came tearing back in the dining room wearing his swim trunks and his favorite shirt, a red-and-white striped tank top. "Okay, Grandpa, I'm ready."

"Well, let the rest of the world catch up with you, tiger."

"Will you pretty please pull me really, really fast?"

"You'll have to ask Captain John about that. I'll leave all the pleasure boating to the younger generation." Bud scratched his cheek where a silver-white stubble cropped up. "Besides, I personally don't like driving a boat around in circles all day. Not when there are better things to do." He made clawing motions at Dolores, who yelped and scampered away.

"Not in front of our grandson," she giggled.

"You're really turning me on, Dolo. Close your eyes, boy." Bud lunged at Dolores, chasing her around the table like she had the last nickel at closing time while the jukebox played a sad song.

"What did we do?" Edie lamented. Granted, her mother staying with them was only temporary, right? After Bud revealed the truth about his illicit affair and illegitimate child, his little men's club might not be too happy with him. And there was his son, Lester, to think about. How would he react to the news that he had a half-sister and a new mommy being chased around the kitchen? Until the truth came out, Bud and Dolores seemed content to frolic at the Hole on Little Paw Lake.

Bud sipped a cup of coffee but nearly spit it out when he looked at the clock on the wall.

"Is that the time?" He hurriedly took another sip, pecked Dolores on the cheek, and set down his mug. "I've got to get to the warehouse. Big photo shoot today for our new Dynamite lures."

Arne clapped his hands sharply and yelled, "Die-no-mite!"

Edie and Sam laughed. They knew he was doing his Jimmie Walker impression from *Good Times*, but *Good Times* wasn't the kind of show Bud Langskip watched.

"What's with him?" Bud asked.

"Let's just say with a name like Dynamite, you just might end up with some unexpected customers for your new lure," Edie answered.

Bud and Dolores disappeared back into the guest room, presumably to get Bud ready for his big day, but they were gone long enough for Edie to wonder what they were *really* up to.

You try to raise your parents the best you can, she lamented.

"Edie, I've been thinking," Sam said.

"Uh oh," Edie replied.

"You know how there are tons of resorts around here. Lots of competition. Why would a fisherman choose our resort over another resort?"

"I don't know. Price?"

"No, we need a gimmick."

"But do we, though?"

"What does a lonely fisherman want more than anything when he's away from hearth and home?"

"More beer?"

"No, a vibrating bed. Edie, I'm telling you, if we install those Magic Fingers in the cabins, we'll make a killing."

"That's what I'm afraid of," Edie laughed. "Or don't you remember the fire our son started with his 'magic fingers'?"

"Well, it's worth considering." He gave her puppy dog eyes.

"I'll consider it," she nodded, knowing that she would *consider it* a really dumb idea, but she wanted to be as diplomatic about it as possible. Coffee in hand, Edie finally sat down to attack her own breakfast. It had been more than twelve hours since she'd had an emergency, and her stash of Dignity cigarettes was safe for now, although she would longingly think of them throughout her day. Sam swore and flattened the newspaper on the table, right over his plate that was gooey with egg yolk and toast crumbs.

"Edie, look at this."

Sam jabbed a finger at an ad for Langskip Lures. It showed a line drawing of a lunker northern about to chomp down on a minnow lure. The copy read *Langskip Lures. Our Name Means Fishing.*

"Can you believe that crap?" Sam blurted.

"Samuel! Language."

"Well?" He looked at her as if whatever upset him should be obvious to her. It wasn't.

"I see a cartoon fish about to bite a cartoon fishing lure thingie."

"I know it's a cartoon, but look at the words. That's my line. I told Bud our name means fishing, and he turned right around and used it in this ad."

"Well, maybe you should march right into the guest room and give that man a piece of your mind." She knew he wouldn't do it.

"Yeah, maybe I should," Sam fumed. "His name means 'big boat' or something, not fishing. This ad doesn't even make sense."

"It's not right, the rich profiting from a regular Joe's ingenuity like that."

"No, it is not. Of course..."

"Why, telling that man off would be a step forward for all the little guys out there. You'd be a national hero."

"You're absolutely right. Still..." Sam's expression troubled. "He is family, after all."

"But right is right. Right?"

"Yeah, I guess."

Ha, Edie thought. *I knew it.* He was afraid of Bud Langskip. Correction: *her father*. That'll keep him on his toes. She heard a knock on the front door.

"I'll get it." She rose, dabbing her lips with a napkin. "I hope it's not the sheriff again or those two meatheads who work for Bud."

She opened the door to find...no one. Whoever knocked had left in a hurry or was hiding nearby, but she saw no trace of them. Resting on the grimy welcome mat at her feet was a cardboard box. She gave it a nudge. It was heavy. Her thoughts immediately went to bombs.

"Who would put a bomb in a cardboard box?" She laughed at herself.

Well, anyone might, came the response in her mind, delivered in her mother's voice. *Like the hippie who would put a bomb in a bait bucket.*

"Okay, but what are the odds?" Garvey was safely behind bars in county lockup, waiting for his first hearing, and it was too soon to have any enemies. Probably. What's the worst that could happen? Well, the worst thing is she could die, but she really wanted to know what was in the box.

No sounds of ticking. Carefully, slowly, Edie lifted one flap and then another until she could see inside. Three dozen shiny cans of fruit cocktail awaited her, stacked in six rows of six.

She scanned the gravel road again, half expecting to see someone there, someone who believed in her glorified rice.

END OF BOOK 1

About the Author

Chaunce Stanton is writer, reader, forager, gnome guardian, and Rugged Individualist—in a good way.

Raised in the lake town of Annandale, Minnesota, Chaunce Stanton's imagination ran wild. It hasn't stopped running, and he is trying to keep up with it. Warped at an early age by his father's offbeat humor and by Monty Python, Chaunce was always a little different. He put on his best Chuck Taylor hi top shoes to nab his degree in English, Creative Writing from Saint Cloud State University. His favorite courses included British Romantic Writers and American Transcendentalist Literature.

Now he and his wife, Naomi, guard Minnesota's southern border from invading Iowegians from their hobby farm. They plant a huge organic garden and practice permaculture.

Chaunce is the author of *Rough Start* (2021), *Grave of Songs* (2020), *Blank Slate Boarding House for Creatives* (2013), and *Luano's Luckiest Day* (2012).

While he doesn't have the dance moves for Tik-Tok, he is active on Facebook at **@ChaunceStantonAuthor**.

Visit chaunce.biz for even more info. IF YOU DARE!

CHAUNCE ANSWERS YOUR MOST PRESSING QUESTIONS

Here are the answers to the top ten most frequently asked questions Chaunce Stanton receives:

1. Thirteen, if you count the one we didn't spill on.

2. Because it was there.

3. Fiction: *Jonathan Strange & Mr. Norrell* by Susanna Clarke

4. Nonfiction: *Devil in the White City* by Erik Larson

5. *The Shining, Philadelphia Story, The Mothman Prophecies, Casablanca, Ghost World, Treasure of the Sierra Madre, Office Space*

6. None that I know of, but it does itch sometimes.

7. Sloppy toms, which are like sloppy joes, only made with ground turkey.

8. Yes, on a dare. But I had to get it surgically removed.

9. Paper.

10. What do you mean? An African or European swallow?

Also By the Author

Need some interesting reading to tide you over before Book 2 of the **Resort of Last Resort** series hits the shelves? Try this book smorgasbord from Chaunce Stanton.

Grave of Songs

[HISTORICAL FICTION]

What other secrets lie buried on the Nelson family farm—besides the bones of ancient giants?

Every family has secrets. A father dies protecting his son, and the boy's life is turned upside-down. He struggles to be the man his father was to build a future on the family farm, but his strict aunt and uncle seem bent on tearing everything down.

Set in Annandale, Minnesota in 1888, this is the story of a family confronted by a changing world. The *Grave of Songs* is a powerful confluence of historical family drama, folklore, imagination, and coming-of-age storytelling.

Grave of Songs

The Blank Slate Boarding House for Creatives
[DARK HISTORICAL FANTASY]

The magician's greatest trick is to use our own imaginations against us.

In this intelligent tale of supernatural suspense set in the Jazz Age, the world's greatest mind magician accepts a challenge from his nemesis, Harry Houdini. Who will be the world's greatest magician? Perjos or Houdini? Only a very public showdown can settle it once and for all.

Perjos returns to America to answer Houdini's challenge, stopping over at an unusual boarding house that caters to artists and other creative types—and he has bizarre scores to settle there. The house's newest servant, Emily, must resist the magician's powers alone after her only friend disappears, leaving her vulnerable to his domineering and sinister control. The Blank Slate Boarding House for Creatives welcomes believers and skeptics alike in its dark and historical setting. Ultimately, readers will wonder, "What is magic?" Or, perhaps, "What is reality?"

The story will appeal to readers of *Jonathan Strange and Mr Norrell* and Laurie R. King as it twists history with magic and flights of fancy in rich layers.

Blank Slate Boarding House for Creatives

Luano's Luckiest Day
[MAGICAL REALISM]

A dreamlike coming-of-age story.

Luano is a normal nine-year-old boy who lives in an isolated desert town. He wants nothing more than to be reunited with the woman who abandoned him soon after he was born. When two deadly spiders appear in his bedroom, the boy makes a dangerous decision to believe their promise—the promise of his mother's return.

Beautifully written, this story will touch your heart, but beware the spiders!

Luano's Luckiest Day

Made in the USA
Middletown, DE
06 February 2023